CAPT

Hearts

Three heroines captured by love!

CAPTIVE *Hearts*

CRIME OF PASSION
by
Lynne Graham

DYING FOR YOU
by
Charlotte Lamb

PRINCE OF LIES
by
Robyn Donald

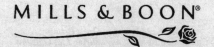
MILLS & BOON®

*MILLS & BOON and MILLS & BOON with the Rose Device
are registered trademarks of the publisher.*
*Harlequin Mills & Boon Limited,
Eton House, 18-24 Paradise Road, Richmond, Surrey, TW9 1SR*

CAPTIVE HEARTS
© by Harlequin Enterprises II B.V., 1998

*Crime of Passion, Dying for You and Prince of Lies were first published
in separate, single volumes by Mills & Boon Limited.
Crime of Passion in 1995, Dying for You in 1994
and Prince of Lies in 1995.*

*Crime of Passion © Lynne Graham 1995
Dying for You © Charlotte Lamb 1994
Prince of Lies © Robyn Donald 1995*

ISBN 0 263 81134 4

05-9811

*Printed and bound in Great Britain
by Caledonian Book Manufacturing Ltd, Glasgow*

Lynne Graham was born in Northern Ireland and has been a keen Mills & Boon® reader since her teens. She is very happily married with an understanding husband, who has learned to cook since she started to write! Her five children keep her on her toes. She has a very large old English sheepdog, which knocks everything over, and two cats. When time allows, she is a keen gardener. Lynne has been writing for Mills & Boon since 1987 and has now written 25 books, which are loved by readers worldwide— there have been over 10 million copies of her books in print.

CRIME OF PASSION
by
LYNNE GRAHAM

CHAPTER ONE

THE Bolivian policeman growled across the table. '*Es usted inglesa? Donde se aloja usted?*'

The small room was unbelievably hot and airless. Georgie shot her interrogator a glittering glance from furious violet eyes and threw back her head, a torrent of tousled multi-coloured curls every shade from gold to copper to Titian red dancing round her pale triangular face. 'I do not speak Spanish!' she said for the twentieth time.

He thumped the table with a clenched fist. '*Como?*' he demanded in frustration.

Her teeth gritted, the naturally sultry line of her mouth flattening. Suddenly something just exploded inside her. 'I've been robbed and I've been attacked and I'm not going to just sit here while you shout at me!' she burst out, her strained voice threatening to crack right down the middle.

Plunging upright, the man strode over to the door and threw it wide. Georgie gaped in disbelief as her attacker was ushered in. All the fear she had striven to hide behind her defiant front flooded back, images of rape and violence taking over. She flew up out of her chair and stumbled backwards into the corner, one trembling hand attempting to hitch up the torn T-shirt which threatened to expose the bare slope of her breasts.

Her assailant, a heavily built young man, glowered accusingly and self-righteously across the room at her and burst into vituperative Spanish.

5

Georgie blinked bemusedly. Her own blank sense of incomprehension was the most terrifying aspect of all. Why did the creep who had mauled her in his truck behave as though he was the one entitled to make a complaint to the police? In fact, the lunatic, apparently ignorant of the fact that the attempted sexual assault was a crime, had actually dragged *her* into the tiny, dilapidated police station!

In exaggerated dumb-show, the policeman indicated the bloody tracks of Georgie's nails down one side of the younger man's unshaven face.

Dear heaven, was a woman not allowed to defend herself when she was assaulted in Bolivia? Without warning, the artificial strength of outrage began to fail Georgie. Her independent spirit quailed and, for the first time in her life, she longed for family back-up.

But her father and stepmother were enjoying a three-week cruise of the Greek islands in celebration of their twentieth wedding-anniversary and her stepbrother, Steve, was in central Africa reporting on some civil war that had recently blown up. Her family didn't even know where she was. Georgie had impulsively splurged her late grandmother's legacy on her flight to Bolivia. A once in a lifetime holiday, she had promised herself.

Just thirty-six hours ago she had landed at La Paz, cheerfully anticipating her coming reunion with her friend, María Cristina Reveron. How many times had María Cristina pleaded with her to come and stay? It had undoubtedly never occurred to her friend, an heiress from the day of her birth, that simple lack of money might lie behind Georgie's well-worn excuses. In the same way, it had not occurred to Georgie that María Cristina and her husband, Antonio, might not be in residence when she finally arrived!

The Reveron villa had been closed up, guarded by a security man with two vicious dogs. He had not had a word of English. Refusing to surrender to panic, Georgie had checked into the cheapest hotel she could find and had decided to do a little exploring on her own while she waited for the Reverons to return to La Paz. Since María Cristina was eight months pregnant, Georgie was convinced that her friend could only be away for the weekend at most.

'A little exploring,' she reflected now, on the edge of hysteria as she studied the two angrily gesticulating men several feet away. Panic was threatening her. She was more than out of her depth, she was drowning. Intelligence told her that it was time to play the one card she had refused to play when she found the Reveron villa inconveniently and dismayingly empty of welcoming hosts. The wild card, the one move that she had never dreamt she would ever be forced to make.

She could have phoned Rafael to ask him where his sister was... but her every skin-cell had cringed from the idea of contacting *him*, asking *him* for his assistance. Stupid pride, she saw now, hardly the behaviour of a responsible adult. Four years was a long time. So he had dumped her. So he had hurt and misjudged her. So he had humiliated her. Well, join the real world, Georgie, she taunted herself, with the thickness of tears convulsing her throat, you are not the only woman ever to suffer that way!

Approaching the table, where a notepad and pen lay, Georgie drew in a deep sustaining breath. But suppose they had never heard of Rafael? Suppose he wasn't the big wheel her friend had always led her to believe? And, even if both those fears proved unfounded, just how likely was it that Rafael Cristóbal Rodriguez Berganza would flex a single aristocratic finger to come to her aid?

With an unsteady hand, Georgie carefully block-printed Rafael Rodriguez Berganza across the pad and then pressed it across the table. It hurt to do it—oh, yes, it hurt to write that name.

A furrow appeared between the policeman's brows. With an air of questioning confusion, he looked up and across at her. He repeated the name out loud with more than a touch of reverence. '*No entiendo*,' he said, frowning his lack of understanding.

'Friend! Good friend!' Georgie tapped the pad with feverish desperation and then crossed her arms defensively over her breasts. 'Very good friend,' she lied, forcing a bright and hopefully confident smile, while inside herself she curled up and died with mortification.

The policeman looked frankly incredulous, and then he vented a slightly nervous laugh. He pointed to her and then he tapped his own head and shook it. He cut right across the language barrier. You're nuts, the gesture said.

'I am telling the truth!' Georgie protested frantically. 'I've known Rafael for years. Rafael and I... we're like this!' She clutched her hands together, striving to look sincere and meaningful.

The policeman flushed and studied his shoes, as though she had embarrassed him. Then, abruptly, as the youthful truck-driver exploded back into speech again, the policeman thrust him unceremoniously out of the room and slammed the door on him.

'I want you to telephone Rafael!' Feeling idiotic, but now convinced that she was actually getting somewhere, Georgie mimicked dialling a number and lifting a phone while he watched her.

With a sigh, the policeman moved forward. He clamped a hand round her narrow wrist, prodded her out into the corridor and from there at speed down into the dirty barred cell at the foot. He had turned the key and pocketed it before Georgie even knew what was happening to her.

'Let me out of here!' she shrieked incredulously.

He disappeared out of view. A door closed, sealing her into silence. Georgie stood there, both hands gripping the rusting bars. She was shaking like a leaf. Well, so much for the influence of the Berganza name! A gush of hot burning tears suddenly stung her eyes. She stumbled down on to the edge of the narrow, creaking bed, with its threadbare blanket covering, and buried her aching head in her hands.

About an hour later an ancient woman clad in black appeared, to thrust a plate through a slot in the bars. Georgie hadn't eaten since breakfast but her stomach totally rebelled against the threat of food. The chipped cup of black coffee was more welcome. She hadn't realised how thirsty she was.

After a while she lay down, fighting back the tears. Sooner or later, they would get an interpreter. This whole stupid mess would be cleared up. She did not need Rafael to get her out of trouble. But she was a walking disaster, she decided furiously. Her first solo trip abroad, she had boobed with spectacular effect. Why? She was impulsive, always had been, probably always would be. This was not the first time impetuosity had landed Georgie in trouble... but it was absolutely going to be the last, she swore.

Male voices were talking in Spanish when Georgie wakened. Disorientated, she sat up, hair tumbling in wild disarray round her. The heat was back. The new day pierced a shard of sunlight through the tiny barred window high up the wall. Sleepy violet eyes focused on the two male figures beyond the bars.

One was the policeman, the other was... Her heartbeat went skidding into frantic acceleration. 'Rafael!' she gasped, positively sick with relief in that first flaring instant of recognition.

In the act of offering the policeman a cigar, Rafael flicked her a stabbing glance from deep-set dark eyes, treacherous as black ice, and murmured lazily in aside, 'Pull your skirt down and cover yourself... you look like a whore.'

Without missing a beat in his apparently chummy chat with the policeman, Rafael presented her with his hard-edged golden profile again. Georgie's mouth had dropped inelegantly wide, a tide of burning colour assailing her fair skin. With clumsy hands she scrabbled rather pointlessly to pull down her denim skirt, already no more than a modest two inches above the knee. She fumbled with the sagging T-shirt, angry violet eyes flashing.

'Don't you dare speak to me like that,' she hissed.

Both male heads spun back.

'If you don't shut up, I walk,' Rafael spelt out, without an ounce of compassion.

Georgie believed him. That was the terrifying truth. Just give him the excuse and he would leave her here to rot—it was etched in the icy impassivity of his slashing gaze, the unhidden distaste twisting his beautifully shaped mouth. He had worn that same look four years ago in London... and then it had almost killed her.

Her throat closed over. Suddenly it hurt to breathe. She fought back the memories and doggedly lifted her chin again, refusing with all the fire of her temperament to be cowed or embarrassed. But Georgie could still wake up in a cold sweat at night just reliving the humiliation of their final meeting. She hated Rafael like poison for the way he had treated her. It was a tribute to the strength of her fondness for his sister that their friendship had survived that devastating experience.

As the two men continued to talk, ignoring her with supreme indifference, Georgie studied Rafael. Against this shabby setting he looked incongruous, exotically alien in a fabulously well-cut grey suit, every fibre of which shrieked expense. The rich fabric draped powerful shoulders, accentuated narrow hips and lithe long legs. Her nails clenched convulsively into the hem of her far from revealing skirt. Maybe he thought she looked like a tart because he was so bitterly prejudiced against her.

His photograph had been splashed all over the cover of *Time* magazine the previous summer. Berganza, the Bolivian billionaire, enemy of the corrupt, defender of the weak. Berganza, the great philanthropist, directly descended in an unbroken line from a blue-blooded Castilian nobleman, who had arrived in Bolivia in the sixteenth century. The journalist had lovingly dwelt on his long line of illustrious ancestors.

Georgie had been curious enough to devour the photographs first. He was very tall, but he dominated not by size but by the sheer force of his physical presence. A staggeringly handsome male animal, he was possessed of a devastating and undeniable charisma. His magnificent bone-structure would still turn female heads thirty years from now.

She searched his golden features, helplessly marking the stunning symmetry of each, the wide forehead, the thin arrogant nose and the savagely high cheekbones. She wished she could exorcise him the way she had burned that magazine, in a ceremonial outpouring of self-loathing and hatred. Her voluptuous mouth thinned with the stress of her emotions.

A split-second later, it fell wide again as she watched the 'enemy of the corrupt' smoothly press a handful of notes extracted from his wallet into the grateful policeman's hands. He was bribing him. In spite of the fact that Georgie had always refused to believe in the reality of Rafael Rodriguez Berganza, the saint of the Latin-American media, she was absolutely shattered by the sight of those notes changing hands.

Her cell door swung open. Rafael stepped in. His nostrils flaring as he cast a fastidious glance round the cell, he swept the blanket off the makeshift bed and draped it round her stiff shoulders. 'I almost didn't come,' he admitted without remorse, his fluid, unbearably sexy accent nipping down her taut spinal cord, increasing her tension.

'Then I won't bother saying thanks for springing me,' Georgie stabbed back, infuriated by the concealing blanket he appeared to find necessary and provoked by the unhappy fact that she had to throw her head back just to see him, her height less than his by more than a foot. But beneath both superficial responses lurked a boiling pool of bitter resentment and remembered pain which she was determined to conceal.

'Were it not for my sister, I would have left you here,' Rafael imparted with harsh emphasis. 'It would have been a character-building experience from which you would have gained immense benefit.'

'You hateful bastard!' Georgie finally lost control. Having been subjected to the most frightening experience of her life, his inhuman lack of sympathy was the last straw. 'I've been robbed, assaulted and imprisoned!'

'And you are very close now to being beaten as well, *es verdad*?' Rafael slotted in, his low-pitched voice cracking like a whiplash. 'For if I will not tolerate a man offering me such disrespect, how do I tolerate it from a mere woman?'

Hot-cheeked and furious, Georgie literally stalked out of the cell. A mere woman? How could she ever have imagined herself in love with Rafael Rodriguez Berganza? Then, it hadn't been love, she told herself fiercely. It had been pure, unvarnished lust, masquerading as a bad teenage crush. But at nineteen she had been too mealy-mouthed to admit that reality.

He planted a hand to her narrow back and pushed her down the corridor, and she was momentarily too shaken by the raw depth of naked rage she had ignited in those dark eyes to object. What the blazes did he have to be so angry about? OK, so it had no doubt been inconvenient for him to come and fish her out of a cell at eight in the morning, but dire straits demanded desperate measures and surely even a self-centred swine like him could acknowledge that?

Outside, the sunlight was blinding, but she was disorientated by the crowd of heaving bodies surrounding the two Range Rovers awaiting them outside. With a slight hiss of irritation, Rafael suddenly planted two hands round her waist, swept her off the ground and thrust her into the passenger seat in the front one. Then he turned back to his ecstatic audience.

All the men had their hats off. Some of the women were crying. Kids were pressing round his knees, clutching at him. And then the crowd parted and the policeman reappeared, with an elderly priest by his side. The priest was grinning all over his face, reaching for Rafael's hands, clearly calling down blessings on his head.

What it was to be a hero! It made her stomach heave. Georgie looked away, only to stiffen in dismay as she noticed the squirming sack on the driver's seat. What the blue blazes was in the sack? She shrank up against the door.

Frozen into stillness, Georgie watched the sack wobble and shiver. There was something alive in it, unless she was very much mistaken ... With an ear-splitting shriek of alarm, Georgie catapulted herself head-first out of the car. She came down on the hard dusty ground with enough force to knock the breath from her lungs.

'Not happy unless you're the centre of male attention, are you?' Rafael breathed unpleasantly, bending over

her as she scrambled up on to her knees. Two of his
security men had climbed out of the vehicle behind to
see what was happening.

Red as a beetroot but outraged, Georgie gasped,
'There's a snake in that sack!'

'So?' Rafael enquired drily. 'It's a local delicacy.'

He dumped her back in the seat she had left in such
haste, the blanket firmly wrapped round her quivering
limbs. Perspiring with fright, impervious to the
amusement surrounding her, Georgie watched the
policeman smilingly tie the sack more securely shut and
deposit it back in the car.

'Please take it away, Rafael,' she mumbled sickly,
leaning out of the window. '*Please*!'

A lean brown hand reached for the offending article
and removed it, putting it in the back seat.

'Thank you,' she whispered as he swung into the
driver's seat. A stray shaft of sunlight gleamed over the
blue-black luxuriance of his silky hair. Like a reformed
kleptomaniac in an untended store of goodies, Georgie
clasped her hands, removed her eyes from temptation
and hated herself. Why did memory have to be so
physical? She shifted on the seat, bitterly ashamed that
she could still remember just how silky his hair felt.

'So tell me, how—in your view—did you land yourself
in a cell less than twenty-four hours after your arrival
in my country?' he invited curtly, making it clear that
whatever was on his mind, it was certainly not on a
similar plane to hers.

'Yesterday, I decided to go and see the Zongo Valley
ice-caves——'

'Dressed as you are now?' Rafael cut in incredulously.
'In a mini skirt and high heels?'

'I——' A mini skirt? He regarded a glimpse of her
knees as provocative?

'The climb to the caves takes almost two hours even for an experienced hill-walker!'

Georgie's teeth clenched. 'Look, I simply saw this poster in the hotel. I didn't know you had to be an athlete to get up there!'

'When did reality dawn?'

'When I got out of the taxi and saw a trio of brawny, booted, bearded types swarming up the hill,' she admitted in a frozen voice, empty of amusement. 'So I thought I'd walk back and see the lake instead, and I turned back to tell the taxi-driver that I wouldn't be long and he'd gone...with my handbag!'

'Jorge suspected something of that nature.'

'Who is Jorge?'

'The village policeman,' Rafael said drily.

'My bag was stolen. The driver just took off with it on the back seat!'

'It may have been an oversight on his part. Had you asked him to wait?'

Georgie stiffened. 'Well, I thought he under-stood——'

'Do you know the registration of the taxi?' Rafael surveyed her with an offensive lack of expectation.

Angrily she shook her head.

'Your bag may yet reappear,' Rafael asserted. 'If your bag is not handed in, then you may say that it has been stolen, not before. You were stupendously careless!'

'Lecture over yet?' she demanded shortly.

'When you found yourself stranded, what did you do?'

'By the time I realised he wasn't coming back, the place was deserted, so I started walking and then I...' She hesitated. 'Then I hitched a lift. You wouldn't believe how pleasant and unthreatening the driver was when I got into his truck——'

'I believe you. I should imagine he came to a wheel-screeching halt,' Rafael murmured with withering sarcasm. 'Then what?'

Georgie lifted her chin. 'He offered me money and while I was pushing it away he lunged at me. I thought I was going to be raped!'

'I understand you kneed him in the groin and drew blood. One may assume you are reasonably capable of self-defence. He thought you were a prostitute——'

'A what?' she exploded.

'Why do you think he offered you money? Female tourists do not travel alone in Bolivia, nor do they hitch alone.' Grim dark eyes flicked a glance at her outraged face before returning to the road.

'Have you any idea how scared I was when he drove off and wouldn't let me out of his truck?'

'He was determined to report you for what he saw as an attempt to rip him off. But he was happy to drop the charge once he realised that his neighbours would laugh heartily at him for being attacked by a woman half his size!'

Georgie was enraged by his attitude. The message was: you asked for it.

'You had a very narrow escape. He might have beaten you up to avenge the slur upon his manhood. This country has been dominated by the cult of *machismo* for four centuries,' Rafael drawled in a murderously polite tone. 'It will take more than a handful of tourists to change that but, happily, the great majority of travellers are infinitely more careful of their own safety than you have been.'

'So I asked for what I got . . . in *your* view!' she flared.

'An attempted kiss, a hand on your knee—he swore that was all. He said you went crazy and I believe him. It'll be weeks before he can show his face without his neighbours sniggering.' Rafael actually sounded sympathetic towards the truck-driver.

Silence stretched endlessly. He made no attempt to break it. The four-wheel-drive lurched and bounced over the appalling road surface with the vehicle behind following at a discreet distance. Briefly, Rafael stopped the car and sprang out. Incredulously she watched him open the sack to release the snake. Wow, environmentally friendly man, and sensitive enough not to offend the villagers by refusing the unwanted gift. It crossed her mind bitterly that the snake was getting more attention than she was.

Then, that was hardly a surprise. Four years ago, Rafael had made it brutally clear that she failed his standards in every way possible. Her morals, her behaviour—her sexually provocative behaviour, she recalled angrily—had all been comprehensively shredded by that cruel, whiplash tongue. But what still hurt the most, she was honest enough to admit, was that she hadn't had the wit to take it on the chin and walk away with dignity. Like a fool, she had attempted to prove her innocence.

'He's from a different world,' her stepbrother Steve had derided once. 'And he belongs to a culture you don't even begin to understand. Don't be fooled by the fact that he speaks English as well as we do. Rafael's a very traditional Latin-American male and the women in his life fall into two categories. Angels and whores. The females in his family—they're the angels. The females who share his bed—they're the whores. When he marries, he'll select an angel straight out of a convent and she'll be as well-born and rich as he is. So where are you planning to fit in?'

And ultimately Steve had been proved right, that dreadful evening when her short-lived relationship with Rafael had been blown apart at the seams. Rafael *had* treated her like a whore. Scorched by that memory,

Georgie sank back to the present and cast aside the sweltering blanket in a gesture of rebellion. She stretched out her lithe, wonderfully shapely legs and crossed them. She didn't give two hoots for *his* opinion, did she? She wasn't a stupid, besotted little teenager any more, was she?

'Where are you staying in La Paz?' he asked after a perceptible pause, firing the engine again.

She told him. That was the end of the conversation, but the atmosphere was so thick all of a sudden that she could taste it. It tasted like oil waiting for a flame—explosive. She tilted her head back, a helplessly feminine smile of satisfaction curving her lips as she noticed the tense grip of his lean hands on the wheel. So, in spite of all the insults, Rafael was still not impervious to her on the most basic level of all. A little voice in the back of her mind demanded to know what she was doing, why she was behaving in this utterly uncharacteristic way. She suppressed it.

She was surprised when he sprang out of the car and silently accompanied her into her shabby hotel, but she chose not to comment. Why lower herself to talk to him? She strolled ahead of him, every tiny swing of her hips an art-form. Presumably he was intending to take her straight to his sister. María Cristina was probably home again by now. But how on earth was Georgie to settle her hotel bill? Her missing handbag had contained not only her passport, but all her money as well.

Her room looked as though a bomb had hit it. Yesterday, she had gone out in a rush. Reddening, Georgie grabbed up her squashy travel-bag and snatched up discarded items of clothing and stuffed them out of sight. Rafael lounged back against the door, like a bloody great black storm-cloud, she found herself thinking, suddenly made nervous and grossly uncomfortable by his presence in the comparative isolation of the small room.

'You can wait outside while I get changed,' she muttered, because there was no *en suite* bathroom, just a washbasin.

'Don't be ridiculous,' Rafael murmured very drily.

'I am not being ridiculous,' Georgie returned tautly, her colour heightening even more. Dear heaven, surely he wasn't seriously expecting her to strip in front of him?

Intent black eyes collided with violet bemusement. *Whoosh*! It was like grasping a live wire, plunging a finger into a light-socket. Violent shock thundered through Georgie's suddenly taut body. She was electrified, wildly energised, before she strained mental bone and sinew to shut out the rich dark entrapment of his gaze, badly shaken by that terrifying burst of raw excitement.

No... no, it simply couldn't happen to her again. She was immune to all that smouldering Latin-American masculinity now. She had not felt like that, she told herself frantically. She had not felt that stabbing, shooting sensation of almost unbearable physical awareness which had reduced her to such mindless idiocy in the past. That was behind her now, a mortifying teenage crush in which hormones had briefly triumphed over all else.

Rafael bent down fluidly and lifted a silky white pair of very brief panties off the worn carpet and tossed them to her. Already sufficiently on edge, Georgie failed to catch them and ended up scrabbling foolishly on the floor, stuffing the wretched things into her bag with hands that were trembling so badly that they were all fingers and thumbs.

'You wouldn't have given me a knee in the groin,' Rafael murmured very softly.

Crouching over her bag, Georgie slewed wildly confused eyes in his direction, chose to focus safely on his Italian leather shoes.

He moved forward. She froze, the sound of her own breathing loud in her ears.

'You would have knocked me flat with enthusiasm,' Rafael completed thickly.

Bastard, she thought, absolutely shattered by his cruelty. She had believed she was in love, had held nothing back, had often told herself since that she was lucky he had dumped her before she ended up in his bed. But now shame drenched her and she hated him for that. He didn't have to make her sound so *cheap*, did he? In the most essential way of all, she had been innocent, and there had been nothing calculated about her response to him.

'Teenagers aren't very subtle when they have a crush on someone.' Determined not to show that his cracks had got to her, Georgie even managed a sharp little laugh.

'But it wasn't a crush,' Rafael breathed, subjecting her to the full onslaught of deep-set dark eyes that disturbingly lingered and somehow held her evasive gaze steady. 'You were violently in love with me.'

Georgie very nearly choked. The bag in her hand dropped unnoticed as her fingers lost their grip. Abruptly, she turned away, sick inside. What kind of sadist was he? Did it give him some sort of perverse kick to throw that in her teeth? It had not been love, it had *never* been love—she had told herself that ever since.

'And the vibrations are still there...I feel them,' Rafael delivered in a purring undertone that still sliced through the throbbing silence.

'I feel nothing...nothing!' Georgie threw back tremulously over her shoulder, wildy disconcerted by the direction of the dialogue, it having been the last subject she would have believed him likely to refer to. She had thought herself safe from any reference to the past, had been grimly aware of his aloof detachment. Now the tables were turned with a vengeance.

Rafael reached out a strong hand and spun her back to face him. 'Why pretend? We're both adults now, and I know that you take your pleasure where and when you find it... and with any man who attracts you.'

Oxygen rasped in her throat and she trembled under the onslaught of that character assassination, fighting off the memories threatening to assail her. 'How dare you?'

Insolent dark eyes mocked her ferocious tension and her sudden pronounced pallor. He lifted his other hand calmly and ran a forefinger along the full curve of her taut lower lip. 'Does it scare you that I know you for what you are? Why should that matter? We don't have to like each other, we don't even have to talk,' he murmured in a deep, dark voice. 'I just want you in that bed under me once... and I really don't care if it *is* sordid, I'll still be the best lover you've ever had.'

The fingertip grazing her lip was sending tiny little shivers through her. Georgie tried and failed to swallow. She couldn't believe what he was saying to her. She just couldn't get her mind round the shock of such a proposal. 'You have to be joking...'

He laughed softly. 'You were always so honest... in this, if nothing else,' he breathed, with a sudden edge of harshness roughening his intonation. 'You want me. I want you. Why should we not make love?'

Georgie shuddered with barely concealed fury, but beneath the fury was a pain she flatly refused to acknowledge. 'Because I *don't* want you! I'm not that desperate!' she spelt out hotly, and jerked free of him, ashamed that her breasts were swollen and full beneath her wispy bra, ashamed that it should actually have taken will-power to step back, and ashamed that for a split-second she had allowed herself to think of that intimacy she had once craved with the man she loved.

Yes, loved—why continue to pretend otherwise when even he knew just how deeply she had been involved? A small sop to pride? 'We're both adults now.' The ultimate humiliation and he just hadn't been able to resist the temptation. She was good enough for a sleazy roll in a grotty hotel room, not good enough for anything else, and even with all that smooth sophistication and experience at his fingertips he hadn't bothered to wrap up that reality.

'I'd like you to leave,' Georgie said with as much dignity as she could muster, and it was not a lot.

'I won't visit you in London. There will be no second chance. You see, I know where you live,' he spelt out with sizzling bite, his dark golden features rigidly cast.

Georgie lived in a tiny attic flat of a terraced house which belonged to her stepbrother, Steve. But the significance of Rafael's reference to that fact quite escaped her. What did where she lived have to do with anything? she wondered briefly, but she was in such turmoil that the oddity of the comment as quickly left her mind again.

She was enraged by the awareness that Rafael had not expected her to refuse that sordid proposition. Rafael had actually expected her to spread herself willingly on the bed. Her narrow shoulders rigid, she turned back to him. 'Just forget where I live——'

'I try to.' Rafael dealt her a chilling look of derision, his nostrils flaring. 'But why else did you come to Bolivia? You knew we would meet again...and that was what you wanted, *es verdad*?'

Georgie was stunned by his arrogance. 'Like hell it was! I want nothing to do with you...absolutely nothing!'

'Prove it,' he taunted, reaching out without warning to drag her up against him with an easy strength that shook her.

'Get your hands off me!' she gasped.

But his mouth crashed down on hers, hard, hungry, hot, forcing her lips apart. And, for Georgie, the world rocked right off its axis, dredging a shocked whimper of sound from deep in her throat. Every physical sense she possessed was violently jolted. His tongue expertly probed the sensitive interior of her mouth, blatantly imitating an infinitely more intimate penetration, and her bones turned to water and she quivered and moaned, electrified by the fierce excitement he awakened. He crushed her slender length to him with bruising hands and she gasped, her thighs trembling, an unbearable ache stirring low in her stomach.

Rafael lifted his dark head slowly. 'Do I take you on that bed or do I take you to the airport?' he prompted silkily, blatant masculine satisfaction in the narrowed gaze scanning her rapt face. 'The choice is yours.'

CHAPTER TWO

'THE *airport*?' Georgie repeated blankly, endeavouring to return to rational thought and finding it unbelievably difficult.

'For your flight home,' Rafael extended, with a slashing and sardonic smile.

'But I'm not going home.' Georgie broke slowly from the loosened circle of his arms, still reeling from the effects of his lovemaking and trying very hard not to show just how shattered she was by the response he had dredged from her. She was in shock. 'I'm going to stay with María Christina.'

'My sister is in California.'

'California?' Georgie parroted after a shattered pause. Incredulously she stared at him. 'What are you talking about?'

'Antonio's mother lives there and María Cristina and Rosa are very close,' Rafael explained smoothly. 'My sister is expecting her first child and, since her own mother is dead, it is natural that she should want Rosa's support at such a time.'

Georgie was in a daze. 'But I received a letter from her less than two weeks ago, inviting me over here. She hoped I'd still be here when she had her baby!'

'She only decided to go to San Francisco last week. She couldn't have been expecting you to come.' Rafael exhibited a magnificent disregard for her natural distress.

'It was a last-minute decision and I got cancellation tickets,' Georgie conceded tautly. 'I tried to phone her the night before the flight but she wasn't in——'

'But you came all the same,' Rafael drawled with an ironic lack of surprise.

'I wanted to surprise her!' Georgie slung back. 'Why didn't you tell me immediately? Obviously you knew I was here to stay with your sister——'

'I had hoped you were not that foolish. I told you to stay away from María Cristina four years ago,' he reminded her with grim emphasis. 'It is a most unsuitable friendship and I made my feelings clear then——'

'Stuff your bloody feelings!' Georgie gasped, suddenly swinging away from him, her voice embarrassingly choked. 'My friendship with María Cristina is none of your business.'

Her bruised eyes were filled with tears. So this was what it felt like to be at the end of her tether. She had really been looking forward to staying with her friend. This disappointment was the last straw. She also knew that, as a recently graduated student teacher, who had yet to find employment, it would be many years before she could hope to repeat such an expensive trip.

It was unlikely that María Cristina would come to London under her own steam. Rafael's sister was very much a home-bird, who had only tolerated her English boarding-school education because it had been her late mother's wish and who had freely admitted that she hadn't the faintest desire to ever leave Bolivia again once her education was completed. Her marriage to a doctor, no more fond of travelling than she was, had set the seal on that insularity.

'Anything which threatens my family is my business.'

'Threatens?' Georgie queried jerkily, fighting for composure. 'And how do I threaten your family?'

'I will not allow you to hurt my sister, and the day that she realises what kind of a woman you really are, she will be hurt.'

'God forgive you...I would never hurt María Cristina!' Georgie gasped painfully, swinging back to him in a rage. 'She'd be a whole lot more hurt if she knew that the brother she idolises is a slimy toe-rag!'

'What did you call me?' Dark eyes had turned incandescent gold, his savagely handsome features freezing into sudden incredulous stillness.

Georgie vented a shaky little laugh. All that bowing and scraping people did in his vicinity did not accustom him to derision. But she knew that she would never forget the depths to which he had sunk in his desire to humiliate her today. 'I think you heard me, and let me assure you that your seduction routine leaves a lot to be desired!' she spelt out, hot with anger and bitterness.

'Seduction was quite unnecessary,' Rafael asserted softly, his beautifully shaped mouth twisting with blatant contempt. 'If I'd kept quiet, I'd be inside you now, and the only sounds in this room would be your moans of pleasure. You'd share a bed with any man who attracted you! I don't pride myself on the idea that there is anything exclusive about your response to me.'

Georgie was trembling violently. Every scrap of colour had drained from her features, leaving her white as snow. Her hand flew up of its own volition but steel-hard fingers snapped round her wrist in mid-air.

'Don't you dare,' Rafael grated down at her in a snarling undertone.

And the violence in the atmosphere was explosive, catching her breath in her dry throat. Raw aggression had flared in his smouldering gaze and instinctively she backed away, massaging her bruised wrist as he freed her, her heartbeat thumping so loudly in her ears that she felt faint and sick, but still she wanted to kill him, still she wanted to punish him for saying those filthy things to her.

'I'm not like that,' she murmured tightly, turning away, despising the little shake that had somehow crept into her voice, betraying her distress. 'And even if I was, it would be a cold day in hell before I let you touch me.'

There was so much more she wanted to say but she didn't trust herself. Once before, she had attempted to reason with Rafael in her own defence. He hadn't listened. He had shot her every plea down in flames, immovably convinced that she had betrayed him in another man's bed. Afterwards she had felt even more soiled and humiliated by his derision. She would never put herself in that position again.

The silence went on forever, reverberating around her in soundless waves.

'Are you able to settle your bill here?'

Four centuries of ice in that chilling enquiry—well, what did she care? Numbly she shook her head.

'I'll take care of it.'

For five minutes, she simply stayed there in the empty room, struggling harder than she had ever had to struggle for control. When she had managed it, she walked down to Reception and found him just moving away from the desk. Without once glancing in his direction, she climbed back into the Range Rover. He would take her to the airport, put her on a flight back home. She really didn't care any more.

The silence smouldered, chipping away at nerves that were already raw and bleeding. 'I presume you can take care of the passport problem,' she muttered, half under her breath, thinking of the bribery he had apparently employed to get her out of her cell.

'What passport problem?' His accented drawl was dangerously quiet.

'Well, obviously it went with everything else in my bag,' she pointed out, surprised that he hadn't grasped that fact yet.

He uttered a raw imprecation in his own language.

'Oh, don't be shy...say it in English!' Georgie suddenly heard herself rake back with a sob in her voice. 'You think I'm a stupid bitch!'

'Georgie...' Fluent though his English was, he couldn't quite handle the two syllables of her name coming so close to each other. He slurred them slightly, his rich dark voice provoking painful memories. 'Don't start crying——'

'I am not crying!' She bit her tongue, tasted blood, blinked back the scorching tide dammed up behind her eyelids.

Soon after that, he stopped the car and got out, leaving her alone for about ten minutes. She waited, enveloped by a giant cloud of unfamiliar depression. It took Rafael to do this to her. He slammed a lid down on her usually bubbly personality. He made her seethingly, horribly angry. And he hurt her. Nothing had changed. She didn't even lift her head when he rejoined her.

'We're here.'

Rafael opened the door. One of his security men already had her bag in one beefy hand.

Rafael extended a black coat.

'What's this?' Georgie had yet to focus on any part of him above the level of his sky-blue silk tie.

'I bought it for you. You cannot walk through the airport with—with your top falling off,' Rafael shared flatly.

She wanted to laugh, because she had managed to forget that she was still wearing yesterday's torn and dirty clothes. But somehow she couldn't laugh. She stuck her arms in the sleeves of the expensive silk-lined raincoat. It was light as a feather but so long it had to look like a nun's habit. Numbly she watched Rafael's fingers do up the buttons. It took him a surprisingly long time, his hands less deft than she had expected.

His double standards were perhaps what she most loathed about Rafael Rodriguez Berganza. He had undoubtedly stripped more women than Casanova. María Cristina had been a gossip while they were at school. Rafael had a notorious reputation for loving and leaving beautiful women. But Georgie would have *known* anyway.

Many very good-looking men missed out on being sexy. But not Rafael. Rafael was a blatantly sexual male animal, flagrantly attuned to the physical. The air around him positively sizzled. So why the heck was this sophisticated, experienced Latin-American lover having so much difficulty buttoning up her coat? Unwarily she collided with glittering golden eyes, and it was like being struck by lightning.

He was so close she could smell a hint of citrusy aftershave, overlying clean, husky male. Her nostrils flared. Her nipples tightened into painful sensitivity, a spiralling ache twisting low in her stomach. Nearby, someone cleared their throat. She tore her gaze from Rafael's and met the looks of visible fascination emanating from his bodyguards, standing several feet away. She realised that she and Rafael had simply been standing there staring at each other. Devastated by her overpowering physical awareness of him, Georgie turned away, her throat closing over.

In silence they entered the airport. Her head felt incredibly light and her lower limbs weak and clumsy. Exhaustion, stress and lack of food, she registered, were finally catching up with her.

Officialdom leapt out of nowhere at them. The crowds parted. Uniformed guards paved every step through the airport, down an eerily empty concourse, their footsteps echoing. There was no sign of other passengers. Clearly she was being put on the flight home either first or last.

As they emerged into the fresh air and crossed the tarmac, she realised incredulously that Rafael intended to see her right on to the plane to be sure she went. It made her feel as though she was being deported in disgrace. And that was when it happened—something that had never happened to Georgie before. As she fought to focus on him and say something smart on parting, her head swam alarmingly. The blackness folded in and she fainted.

'Lie still.' As Rafael made the instruction for the second time and Georgie attempted to defy it, he lost patience and planted a powerful hand to her shoulder, to force her back into the comfortable seat in which she was securely strapped. 'I don't want you to swoon again.'

If he used that word again, she would surely hit him. 'I didn't swoon, I passed out!' she hissed, twisting away from his unwelcome ministrations. 'And will you take that wet flannel out of my face?'

Dense black lashes screened his clear gaze from her view, a curious stillness to his strong, dark face. 'I was trying to help,' he proffered very quietly.

'I don't want your help.' She turned her head away defensively.

You swooned with Rafael and you really hit the jackpot, though, she conceded. The entire aircrew seemed to be hovering with wet flannels, tablets, and glasses of water and brandy. Any minute now the pilot would appear and offer her some fresh air! Dear Lord, she hoped *not!* Her violet eyes widened in disbelief on the clouds swirling past the port-hole across the aisle...they were already airborne!

'What are you doing on this flight?' Georgie demanded, feverishly short of breath. 'We've already taken off!'

Rafael rose up off his knees, smoothed down the knife creases on his superbly tailored trousers and said something to the crew. Everybody went into retreat. He lowered his long, lithe frame fluidly into the seat opposite and fixed hooded dark eyes on her.

'This is my private jet.'

'Your what?' Georgie gaped at him.

'I am taking you home with me. Until your passport can be replaced, you are stuck in Bolivia.'

'But I don't have to be stuck with you!'

Unexpectedly, Rafael sent her a shimmering, sardonic smile. 'A lamb to the slaughter...I don't think.'

'I don't know what the heck you're getting at, but I do know you could have left me in my hotel...or thrown a few backhanders in the right direction the way you did to get me out of my prison cell!' Georgie derided, horrified at the prospect of being forced to accept his grudging hospitality.

He went white beneath his dark skin, his facial muscles freezing. 'How dare you accuse me of sinking to such a level?' he ground out incredulously. 'I have never stooped to bribery in my life!'

Georgie licked at her dry lips. 'I saw you give the policeman the money,' she whispered.

Rafael surveyed her with growing outrage, registering with an air of disbelief that his denial had not been accepted. 'I do not believe that I am hearing this. The policeman, Jorge, took the money straight to the village priest! The roof of the village church has fallen in and my donation will repair it, thereby enhancing Jorge's standing in the community but granting him no personal financial gain,' Rafael spelt out with biting emphasis. 'I wanted to reward him for his efforts on your behalf. Although he did not believe that you were entitled to claim my friendship, and he was afraid of being made to look foolish, he telephoned me. Were it not for his persistence and his conscientious scruples, you would still be in that cell!'

His explanation made greater sense of the villagers' response to him than her own hasty assumption that he had used cash to grease the wheels of justice. She reddened, but she did not apologise.

'The young truck-driver had lied about you but he withdrew his story,' Rafael continued icily. 'You were then free to leave without any further output from me. I did nothing but straighten out a misunderstanding.'

She bent her head, her empty stomach rumbling. 'Do you think you could feed me while you lecture me?'

'Feed you?'

'I haven't eaten since breakfast yesterday.'

'*Por Dios,*' Rafael grated with raw impatience. 'Why did you not say so?'

A microwaved meal arrived at speed. Georgie ate, grateful for any excuse not to have to speak while she attempted to put her thoughts in order. 'I am taking you home with me,' he had said, as if she was a stray dog or cat. 'Home' was the ancestral *estancia* on the vast savannah bounded by the Amazon. And the concept of Rafael taking her back there quite shattered Georgie. Even when she had been María Cristina's best friend at school, Rafael had blocked his sister's every request to bring Georgie out to stay on the *estancia* with them during the holidays.

Memory was taking her back, although she didn't want it to. Georgie had won a fee-assisted place at an exclusive girls' school to study for her A levels. She had met María Cristina in the lower sixth. At half-term, she had invited her friend home for the weekend but, in some embarrassment, the Bolivian girl had explained that her brother, Rafael, who was her guardian, would not allow that unless he had first met Georgie and her parents.

Georgie's father had been amused when he received a phone call from Rafael, requesting permission to take Georgie out for the afternoon in company with his sister.

'Charming but very formal for this day and age,' he had pronounced. 'You'd better mind your "p"s and "q"s there, my girl. I think you're about to be vetted.'

Georgie still remembered coming down the steps in front of the school as the limousine swept up. She had guessed just by the way María Cristina talked that her friend was from a wealthy background, but she had not been prepared for a stretch limousine complete with chauffeur and security men. Then Rafael appeared and Georgie had been so busy looking at him that she had missed the last step and almost fallen flat on her face.

He had reached out and caught her before she fell, laughing softly, dark eyes rich as golden honey sweeping her embarrassed face. 'My sister said you were accident-prone.'

As María Cristina introduced them, his hand had lingered on hers, his narrowed gaze oddly intent until rather abruptly he had stepped back, a slight flush accentuating his hard cheekbones.

He had taken them to the Ritz for afternoon tea. Georgie had been quieter than she had ever been in her life before and painfully shy, a condition equally new to her experience. Right from that first moment of meeting, Rafael had attracted her to a frighteningly strong degree. And Georgie hadn't known how to handle that attraction. It had come out of nowhere and swallowed her alive, draining her of self-will. She had sat there on the edge of her seat, barely able to take her eyes off him, terrified he would notice.

After the Ritz, he had taken them shopping in Harrods. María Cristina had casually spent an absolute fortune on trifles, and when Rafael had bought his sister a gold locket he had insisted on buying one identical for Georgie, smoothly dismissing her protests. Then he had ferried them back to her parents' home where he had been invited to stay to dinner.

Newly conscious of just how rich her friend and her brother were, Georgie had been uncomfortable at first, fearfully watching for any signs of snobbish discomfiture from either of them. Her father was a primary schoolteacher and her stepmother, Jenny, a post-office clerk. Their home was a small, neat semi-detached. Half the neighbourhood had come out to stare at the stretch limousine. But Rafael and María Cristina had made themselves perfectly at home with her family... Steve hadn't been there that first time, Georgie recalled absently.

'Do you want to know the only thing Rafael asked about you?' María Cristina had laughed after her brother had gone, shaking her head in wonderment. 'Is that hair natural?'

For the remainder of her time at school, Georgie had been included in all of her friend's term-time outings with her brother. Gradually she had lost her awe of Rafael, learning to judge her reception by the frequency of that rare and spontaneous smile of his that turned her heart inside out, but also learning to accept that he observed strict boundaries in his behaviour towards her and was prone to cool withdrawal when her impulsive tongue came anywhere near breaching that barrier.

'Rafael likes you,' María Cristina had said once—just one of many desperately gathered little titbits.

'You make him laugh...'

'He thinks you're very intelligent...'

'He wonders why you aren't studyng Spanish...' What an agony of hope that had put her in! But then, it hadn't all been good news.

'He thinks you flirt too much...'

'He said if you wore your skirts any shorter, you'd be arrested...'

'He believes that the two of us will only be adults when we stop telling each other absolutely everything!'

But Georgie had never told María Cristina whose photograph she kept in that locket which she wore constantly. She had been horribly embarrassed the day her friend chose to tease her about that secrecy in front of Rafael. He had silenced his sister. Dark eyes had intercepted Georgie's anxious gaze and he had smiled lazily, and she had known that he knew perfectly well that it was his photo, taken by her with immensely careful casualness the previous year.

She had met Danny Peters at a sports event a few months before she sat her final exams. They had run into each other several times, quickly forming an easy friendship. Danny had just been ditched by his steady girlfriend and Georgie had supplied a sympathetic ear. When he had asked Georgie to attend his school formal with him, she had agreed, well aware that he merely wanted to save face in front of his friends. It had been a fun night out, nothing more. But María Cristina had gone all giggly about it and had insisted on talking about Danny as Georgie's boyfriend. Had she mentioned Danny to Rafael?

For, one week later, Georgie had come home from visiting her grandmother one afternoon and a scarlet Ferrari had been parked in the driveway. She had raced into the house and frozen on the threshold of the lounge, seeing only Rafael, nothing else but Rafael impinging on her awareness. His very presence in her home without his sister in tow had told Georgie all she needed to know.

'Rafael thought you might like to go for a drive,' her stepmother had mumbled in a dazed voice. 'You should get changed.'

She remembered Steve catching her by the arm before she disappeared into her bedroom. 'He's going to make a bloody fool of you,' he had condemned in a furious undertone. 'But money talks, doesn't it? I can't believe my mother is encouraging him!'

Georgie sank back to the present. With a not quite steady hand, she massaged her stiff neck and strove not to lift her head and look at Rafael. But it was so difficult when she was remembering that glorious afternoon, the sheer joy that he had come, the overwhelming excitement of just being alone with him for the very first time. She had walked on air into that Ferrari.

Before he reversed the car, he had lifted a hand and quite calmly reached for her locket to open it. And then he had smiled lazily, pressed a teasing promise of a kiss against her readily parted lips and dropped a bunch of red roses on her lap. 'If it had been anyone else, I do believe I would have killed you,' he had laughed softly.

He had been outrageously confident of his reception, hadn't even tried to hide the fact. Georgie had had the bewildering feeling that she was being smoothly slotted into a pre-arranged plan, and in a sense that had offended her pride. She might have been head over heels in love with Rafael but she hadn't liked the idea that he knew it too.

He had been entirely complacent about the idea that she had spent eighteen months waiting for him to show an interest in her, that he was indeed her first real boyfriend...if a male of his sophistication could even qualify for such a label. But he had also been careful to tell her that the day she told her sister she was seeing him, their relationship would be at an end. At the time, not telling

María Cristina had really hurt. But later she had been grateful that she had kept quiet.

'She's asking you if you want coffee.'

Georgie's head jerked up, her cheeks warming as she found both the stewardess and Rafael regarding her enquiringly. 'I'd love some,' she mumbled, shaking her head as if to clear it and hurriedly fixing her attention elsewhere.

Rafael added that she liked her coffee with both milk and sugar.

Georgie tensed, childishly tempted to say she now took it black and unsweetened but biting her lip instead. Four years ago, Rafael had chosen her food for her, and had allowed her only the occasional glass of wine, refusing to allow her any other form of alcohol in his company.

'He's a flipping tyrant,' Steve had sneered that final evening, witnessing Rafael's unashamed domination in action. 'I can't believe the way you let him order you around. If you want a drink, I'll get it for you!'

And he had. He had got her several, just daring Rafael to interfere. Georgie did not want to recall where that foolishness had led. Her cup in an unsteady hand, she sipped at her coffee, badly shaken by the uncontrollable force of the memories washing over her.

It had upset Georgie then that her stepbrother and Rafael should barely be able to tolerate each other. Nor had she ever been able to decide who was most at fault— Steve for being a bossy, interfering big brother, who didn't like to see his kid sister being bossed about by anyone else, or Rafael for never once utilising an ounce of his smooth diplomacy in Steve's hot-headed direction.

In those days she had been very proud of Steve's success as a photo-journalist. He was four years her senior, her brother in all but blood ties, and she had relied heavily on Steve's opinions, Steve's advice ... And

then those ties had been almost completely severed the
same night that she had lost Rafael. Truly the worst night
of her life, she conceded painfully.

'This is Rurrenabaque,' Rafael informed her as the
jet came in to land.

Georgie concentrated on the fantastic views as the land
dropped dramatically away below them to spread out
into the thickly forested expanse of the Amazon basin.
Less than half an hour after landing they were airborne
again in a helicopter, from which she saw the very
physical evidence of the logging operations in the area.
Then the rough tracks forged by man-made machinery
petered to a halt, leaving them flying over untouched
wilderness, broken only by lonely mountain plateaus and
dark winding rivers until the rainforest finally gave way
to the vast savannah, cleared centuries earlier for cattle
ranching.

'You will want to rest.' Rafael sprang down from the
helicopter in her wake and something she caught in his
voice made her turn her head.

She met icy dark eyes, read the harsh line of his compressed mouth and the fierce tension in his strong features as he stared fulminatingly back at her. He doesn't
want me here. That reality hit her like a bucket of cold
water on too-hot skin. Defensively she looked away
again, wondering why on earth he had brought her to
his home if he felt that strongly and cursing her own
weakened, stressed condition earlier.

'At the airport, you let me think you were going to
put me on a flight home,' she reminded him accusingly.
'Why didn't you tell me the truth?'

'I was abducting you,' Rafael delivered smoothly.
'Why would I explain my intentions in advance?'

Her bright head spun back, violet eyes wide, her brow
furrowed. Then she laughed a little breathlessly. 'I never

could tell when you were joking and when you were serious!'

'You will learn.' Unreadable dark eyes glittered intently over her animated face. 'I'm looking forward to teaching you.'

CHAPTER THREE

SUDDENLY cold, even in the sunlight, Georgie stilled. Two dark-skinned men were attending to their luggage. Rafael spoke to them in a language that was definitely not Spanish and then strode forward to greet the older man who was approaching them.

He was Rafael's estate manager, Joaquín Paez. He shook hands with her. 'Señorita Morrison,' he murmured gravely, with an old-world courtesy much in keeping with their gracious surroundings.

The *estancia* was a beautiful white villa, built in the Spanish style. The rambling spacious contours hinted at the alterations made by different generations. Fabulous gardens, lushly planted with shrubs and mature trees, ringed the house, and beyond she could see a whole host of other buildings stretching into the distance. María Cristina had told her that the ranch was a self-contained world of its own, with homes for its workers and their families, a small school, a church and even accommodation for the business conferences which Rafael occasionally held here.

A small, plump woman in a black dress appeared as they reached the elegant veranda at the front of the house. As Rafael addressed her in Spanish, the little woman's smile faltered. She shot a shocked glance at Georgie and then quickly glanced away again to mutter something that just might have been a protest to Rafael.

Georgie hovered, feeling incredibly uncomfortable. Of course they weren't talking about her...why should they be? She was here at the Berganza home on sufferance until such time as her passport could be replaced. Rafael had come to her aid when she got herself locked up in prison purely because she was his sister's friend and María Cristina would have been deeply shocked had he done otherwise. In the same way, Rafael's sister would doubtless also expect her brother to offer hospitality to Georgie in her own unfortunate absence.

So, Rafael was grimly going through the civilised motions for the sake of appearances, Georgie told herself. María Cristina had no idea how her brother and her best friend felt about each other and, at this late stage, neither one of them could wish to be forced to make pointless explanations. Georgie's passport would be replaced within record time if Rafael had anything to do with it . . . she was convinced of that fact.

'My housekeeper, Teresa, will show you to your room,' Rafael drawled.

Teresa, whose wide smile had almost split her face on their arrival, now bore a closer resemblance to a little stone statue. With a bowed head, the housekeeper moved a hand, indicating that Georgie should follow her.

Georgie entered the impressive hall and stepped on to an exquisite Persian rug, spread over a highly polished wooden floor. Rafael swept off through one of the heavy, carved doors to the left. A wrought-iron staircase of fantastically ornate design wound up to the floors above. Georgie climbed it in Teresa's rigid-backed wake. The walls were covered with paintings, some of which were clearly very old. They crossed a huge landing, Georgie's heels clicking at every step. A door was flung wide with a faint suggestion of melodrama.

'What a heavenly room,' Georgie whispered helplessly, absorbing a level of opulence which quite took her breath away. And the décor was so wonderfully feminine, from the delicate contours of the gleaming antique furniture to the gloriously draped bed awash with lace. Lemon and blue and white—her favourite colours. Doors led out on to a balcony, adorned with tubs of riotously blooming flowers.

Unselfconscious in her enchantment, Georgie walked past the silent older woman and opened a door that revealed first a fully fitted dressing-room and then, beyond it, a positively sinfully sybaritic bathroom with a marble jacuzzi bath, gilded mirrors and gold fitments shaped like…mermaids. *Mermaids*? As a child Georgie had been fascinated by fantasy tales of mermaids and unicorns. A peculiar sense of *déjà vu* swept her, a funny little chill running down her taut spinal cord.

'Ees crazy bathroom,' Teresa said almost aggressively, and Georgie spun. 'You like crazy bathroom, *señorita*?'

Georgie moistened her suddenly dry lips with the tip of her tongue and simultaneously caught a glimpse of the wonderful painting on the wall opposite the bed. Unless she was very much mistaken—and closer examination told her she was not—the exquisitely detailed oil portrayed a unicorn in a forest…

Realising that Teresa was still awaiting a reply, Georgie mumbled weakly, 'I like the bathroom, the room…everything, but I feel a little—a little tired.'

'Dinner is served at nine. I send maids to unpack,' Teresa announced with a stiff little nod, and indicated a bell-pull on the wall. 'You wish anything, you call, *señorita*.'

On cottonwool legs, Georgie sank down on the edge of the bed. It was coincidence that the décor should mirror her own taste to such an extent. What else could it be *but* coincidence, for goodness' sake? Kicking off her shoes and dispensing with the coat, Georgie lay down, smothering a yawn. In a minute, she would get up and wash and change and explore. She intended to make the best of this unexpected stay at the *estancia*.

After all, she was on holiday and, had the concept of being grateful to Rafael not been utterly repellent to her, she would have thanked him for making it possible for her to spend at least a few more days abroad.

A lamp was burning by the bed when she woke and the curtains had been drawn. Checking the time, Georgie rose in a hurry. Her pitifully slender wardrobe had been hung in a capacious closet in the dressing-room while she slept and *every* crumpled garment had been ironed as well. A single drawer contained the rest of her clothing and she sighed. Her collection of neat skirts and jackets which she had worn on teaching practice had all been winter-weight and, when it had come to packing for a hot climate, Georgie had had to fall back largely on outfits last worn in Majorca two years earlier on a family holiday. Beachwear, strictly speaking, she conceded, fingering a pair of Lycra shorts with a frown.

She was desperate for a bath but there was only time for a quick shower. Then, donning her one smart outfit, the elegantly cut fine white dress which she had worn for her graduation ceremony, Georgie brushed her rippling mane of curls and dug through her few cosmetics to add some delicate colour to her cheeks and lips. A maid passing through the hall showed her into a formal drawing-room which she found rather oppressive. She was studying a portrait of a forbidding but very handsome man when the door opened behind her.

'You find your accommodation comfortable?'

She turned, her wide hesitant gaze falling on Rafael and, although she had told herself that she would be perfectly composed, her stomach cramped instantly with nerves. The sight of Rafael in a dinner-jacket, a white shirt accentuating the exotic gold of his skin and the darkness of his eyes, took her back in time and she tensed, tearing her attention from him and sliding down on to the nearest seat. 'Very,' she said stiffly.

'What would you like to drink?'

Georgie tensed even more and she was furious with herself for being so over-sensitive. 'Anything,' she muttered.

Taut as a bowstring, she watched him cross the room to a cabinet and listened to the clink of glass. How did he contrive to make her feel that every sentence he spoke to her was a put-down? A someone's-walking-over-my-grave sensation seemed to take over more strongly with every minute she remained in his radius. Angrily, she bent her head. She hated him. Naturally it was a severe strain to be forced to accept his hospitality and feel the need to be at least superficially polite.

Indeed, Georgie only had to think of the damage he had done when she had been at a very impressionable age, and her blood boiled. Rafael's deliberate attempt to reduce her to the level of a promiscuous slut back in her hotel room had simply provided fresh fodder for the bitterness of the past. But it had also brought alive again raw emotions which she had put behind her a long time ago, and she was finding that experience unexpectedly painful.

Right now, she was recalling the staggering response she had given him when he had kissed her, a response she had been too confused even to think about earlier in the day. Now that memory haunted her, shamed her. Four years ago, Rafael had taught her things about herself that, afterwards, she would have given anything to forget. She was a very physical person, or at least she had been with him. In his arms, she had never been in control. She had been entrapped by an uncontrollable passion which made mincemeat of every moral principle Jenny had dinned into her while she was growing up.

Had he so desired, Rafael could have gone to bed with her on the first date and, long after he had gone, Georgie had tortured herself with the fear that that wanton ability

to forget everything when he touched her had actually
laid the basis of Rafael's cruel misjudgement of her.
Angels and whores... Steve's reading of Rafael had often
returned to haunt her. And she had told herself that if
Rafael was that primitive, she had had a very lucky
escape indeed.

But what did she tell herself *now*? How could she have
stood there and allowed him to kiss her in that horribly
intimate way? She wasn't a besotted teenager any more.
Admittedly, she was still sexually inexperienced, she allowed grudgingly, but then, having been scorched as
badly by passion as she had been at nineteen, that was
not really surprising. So why hadn't she objected to being
manhandled this morning?

Because you liked it, a dry little voice put in to her
flood of inner turmoil. She froze, her pallor suddenly
washed by hot colour. Rafael chose that same moment
to slot a tall glass between her nerveless fingers.

'A Tequila Sunrise,' Rafael drawled softly. 'I have an
excellent memory and I can only hope that you have no
ambition to get seriously sloshed tonight.'

Georgie stared at the glass in stricken horror. The offer
of a cup of poison could not have made her feel more
threatened. One sip of that mixture and she was convinced she would throw up. His brutality absolutely devastated her. That evening, that ghastly final evening four
years ago... Her narrow shoulders clenched as though
he had laid a whip across them. The lousy sadist, she
thought wildly, burning tears of sheer humiliation lashing
her lowered eyelids. If there had been a gun within reach,
she would have shot him dead without remorse.

'I see you remember too,' Rafael murmured smoothly.

Georgie threw her head up, a blaze of raw hostility
leaping through her veins. She put that glass to her lips
and she drank like a sailor on shore-leave after six months

of sobriety. In her rage, she tasted nothing. 'Thanks,' she said tautly. 'I needed that!'

'Evidently, you did.' A hard smile curved Rafael's sensual mouth.

If he fondly imagined she was about to hang her head in shame because one time in her life she had got stupidly drunk, he was wrong!

'Do you think there would be time before dinner for another one?' Georgie murmured hopefully, taking up the challenge with a vengeance. If he chose to think that she was a drunk as well as a slut, he was quite free to do so. Anything was better than letting him see that he could still get to her. And displaying a total lack of concern for Rafael's prehistoric ideal of how a 'lady' ought to behave was surely the best way possible to demonstrate her complete indifference to him?

Recalling her own eagerness to please in the past could only make her cringe. All her life she had been extrovert, fiery and opinionated. But Rafael had put a clamp on such emotional excesses, making her feel that to be acceptable she had to tone herself down into a paler version of herself. Afraid that if she couldn't be what he wanted, she would lose him, Georgie had done a very fair imitation of a doormat until inevitably she had begun to resent his arrogant assumption of supremacy.

Another drink arrived. Georgie swallowed hard in a silence that was beginning to slice along her nerve-endings and made herself sip through clenched teeth.

'I have often wished that I had taken you up on your offer that night,' Rafael delivered, fixing brilliant golden eyes to her openly transfixed face. 'But it would have meant breaking every honourable instinct I possessed. I've never made love to a woman under the influence of alcohol before, but with you it would have paid dividends. I would have known then that I wasn't your first lover——'

'And I dare say I would have known that I wasn't yours either!' Georgie slung back at him in growing outrage. In throwing up her reckless behaviour that night, Rafael demonstrated a savage, unashamed desire to humiliate her.

'Naturally not . . . what would you expect?' Rafael demanded shortly, after a decidedly stunned pause that such an irrelevance as *his* sexual experience should be mentioned. Dark colour accentuated the fierce angles of his hard cheekbones, his handsome mouth a compressed line.

Georgie tossed back another swig of alcohol, well aware she had disconcerted him. 'Oops, to think I had one chance in my entire life to be ravished in a Ferrari and I blew it!' She fluttered her lashes in an attitude of deep regret, beginning to enjoy herself as much as she had thoroughly enjoyed herself in the amateur dramatic society at college. 'That one perfect spontaneous moment missed . . . But then, you're not a spontaneous kind of guy, are you?'

'Not in a public car park . . . no,' Rafael breathed in a driven undertone, with more than a suggestion of gritted white teeth to the reply as he studied her with lancing dark eyes. 'I find it hard to believe that you can refer to that night so casually.'

Georgie flicked him a glance, adrenalin fairly roaring through her. A determined smile tilted her mobile mouth as she regarded him from below her thick copper lashes. 'Why not? After all, you weren't the only one deceived four years ago . . . I was as well.'

'*You* were?' Rafael breathed, with an incredulous expression.

'You put out an impression which you don't deliver,' Georgie sighed. 'I hope you don't mind me being frank——'

Rafael shot her a glittering glance from the cabinet where he was pouring himself another drink that looked very much like a double. It was good to know she was penetrating that truly enormous ego and puncturing it just a little. 'Feel free...'

Georgie was really getting into her role now. 'Well, you say I was violently in love with you but, frankly, like most teenagers, I was more in love with love. I was also very easily impressed. Your limousine and your accent knocked me sideways and I don't mind admitting it,' she assured him cheerfully. 'But I'd have been just as impressed if you hadn't had a word of English or the ability to voice a single intelligent sentence. I fell in love with my own fanatasies——'

'No doubt you intend to share those with me as well,' Rafael countered with a blazing smile of challenge.

Georgie wrinkled her nose and strove to look coy. 'Only with my lovers... Some men do need a little push in the right direction.'

'I need no push.'

That was getting just a bit too close to the bone for Georgie and she blinked rapidly, her cheeks colouring. 'How fascinating,' she said, in a deliberately unfascinated voice.

'What is this impression which I put out and didn't deliver?' Rafael enquired silkily.

'I really don't think I should say. My big mouth,' Georgie groaned, as he settled yet another glass into her hand. 'It's such a long time ago——'

'But I insist.'

'Well...you see, I expected you to be...' Georgie licked at her taut lower lip and her eyes collided involuntarily with incandescent golden ones that were nailed to her with relentless force and, not surprisingly, that alarming collision silenced her.

'You expected me to be what?' Rafael demanded with flaring impatience.

'I expected you to live up to your bad reputation...but you didn't,' Georgie imparted with unhidden venom. 'I expected you to be incredibly passionate and sexy...and, frankly, you were a disappointment——'

'I was so much of a disappointment, you came to me and you begged me to take you back,' Rafael slotted in, hooded eyes showing a mere glimmer of gleaming gold below the inky black luxuriance of his lashes. 'You wept and you pleaded and you lied...'

Georgie turned white, stared down into her untouched glass, slaughtered utterly by the reminder of her lowest hour. 'And it was like taking the cure,' she whispered between clenched teeth. 'So much for love. It died there and then and I'm happy to tell you that I've never fancied myself in love since.'

'Love has nothing to do with what is between us.'

Her knuckles showed white as she tightened her grip on her glass. 'There is nothing between us.'

'Look at me and tell me that—show the courage of your conviction,' Rafael derided.

Georgie felt as though she was being torn apart. Just minutes earlier she had been playing games with him but that false bravado had now deserted her. She felt cornered, intimidated, suddenly knew that she had been very naïve indeed to allow him to bring her to the *estancia*, even more naïve to imagine that he would play the polite host to her role of guest.

'I said...look at me.'

The command, given by a male accustomed to absolute authority, sent her tension climbing to meteoric heights. A lean hand removed the glass from her convulsed grip. Powerful fingers closed round her forearm, literally forcing her upright, and instantly she attempted to pull away.

'Stop it,' Rafael commanded rawly, scanning her drawn face with scorchingly angry dark eyes. 'Do you think I enjoy wanting you? Do you think I am proud of the desire you arouse in me? But this time I will not walk away. Why should I? Why shouldn't I take what I want? You owe me...'

Georgie was trembling, shaken by the force of anger she had unleashed. 'I owe you nothing, not even the time of day!'

'But you'll still give me everything,' he assured her.

'Never!' Georgie vowed. 'And stop threatening me!'

'Do you feel threatened when I make love to you?' With a husky sound of very male amusement, Rafael drew her closer and ran an insolently expert hand down over the full curve of her breasts and she shuddered helplessly.

'Don't touch me!' On the edge of panic, Georgie sought to break free of his hold as a blunt forefinger circled the erect bud of a nipple, visibly thrusting through the thin fabric of her dress. A quivering, hateful excitement leapt into being inside her but she fought it to the last ditch.

'Do all your lovers turn you on this hard and this fast?' Rafael lowered his dark head and allowed the tip of his tongue to slide erotically between her lips, just once, in a darting foray that sent heat coursing through her in a debilitating wave.

'Every one of them!' she slammed back in a breathless rush.

'But I'll be the one you remember long after I'm gone,' Rafael completed with predatory assurance, quite untouched by her attempt to repel him, a strong hand splaying across her hips to jerk her into even closer contact, and she stopped breathing altogether as he moved fluidly against her, bringing her into unashamed contact with the hard thrust of his arousal.

Her treacherous body was on fire and she closed her eyes, struggling to think, struggling not to react. 'No,' she whispered shakily.

He lifted her with ease and one of her shoes fell off. She opened startled eyes a split-second before he brought his mouth crashing down on hers. She stopped thinking, she started simply feeling. The effect was that immediate. Her hands bit into his broad shoulders as she strained against the hard heat of his muscular length. Her fingers drifted into his hair and she was lost, controlled by an intolerable need that sent the blood pounding at an insane rate through her veins. Slowly, very slowly, he slid her down the length of his body on to her feet again and lifted his head.

'You go to pieces when I touch you. I like that... I love that,' Rafael muttered with a ragged groan of satisfaction. 'It gives me an incredible sexual high no other woman has ever matched. I saw you lying asleep in that cell and every decent thought, every piece of self-restraint fled instantaneously. I'd have killed to get you out of there and into my bed.'

Finding herself lop-sided, minus one shoe, Georgie crouched down in a dazed and trembling search to locate the missing item. That she couldn't think straight didn't help. But then, Rafael was proving a whole lot harder to handle than she could ever have imagined. She didn't know Rafael as a lover. In that field, she didn't know Rafael at all. And in this mood, Rafael was a revelation, a distinctly intimidating revelation. Nothing she had read, nothing she had ever heard, could save her from feeling gruesomely out of her own limited depth.

'What are you doing?' Rafael enquired huskily.

He pressed her back on a nearby sofa, produced her shoe and proceeded to slide it back on, but he didn't get back up again. He smoothed his lean hands slowly up over her slender calves to her knees, watching her intently from beneath indolently lowered black lashes that a woman would have killed to possess.

'Dinner,' Georgie said jerkily, every muscle tightening in stricken response.

'Dinner is served when I ring,' Rafael leant forward and brushed his mouth very softly across hers, his breath fanning her cheek as long fingers pushed her knees gently apart. '*Dios mío ...*' he murmured softly, letting his tongue probe smoothly between her lips and making her shake like leaf in a high wind, a tiny whisper of shaken protest escaping her throat. 'Food to die for, clothes to die for... your expression. This has to be sex to die for.'

'No,' she mumbled, but she opened her mouth for his exploration, shivering as the intrusion became less playful.

'Why are you so tense?' Caressing fingers slid below the hem of her dress, stroking along the tender skin of her inner thigh, forcing a stifled gasp to erupt from her.

'T-Tense?'

'Surely it has not been that long since a man made love to you?'

Her hands were in his hair, and she didn't honestly know how they had got there. One half of her was petrified, the other half of her was mesmerised by what he was doing to her. 'Forever.' Her voice was a thin thread of barely recognisable sound.

She clashed with devouring golden eyes, drowned as though time had stopped, leaving her in limbo. Never in the twenty-three years of her existence had she experienced anything even approaching what she was feeling now. He was barely touching her and her entire body was in meltdown. The intensity of her own arousal

devastated her every attempt to regain her hold on a
situation which had moved with incredible rapidity out
of her control.

'*Por Dios* . . . I want you so badly it hurts,' he muttered fiercely, raking a single fingertip across the tautly
stretched scrap of lace covering the very heart of her,
jolting every bone in her body with an intolerable rush
of erotic sensation.

Somebody banged on the door. In fact, somebody
banged on the door so loudly that Georgie very nearly
hit the ceiling in shock. Far less susceptible to the disturbance, Rafael dragged shimmering golden eyes from
her and sprang fluidly upright. Georgie swallowed hard
and rearranged her hemline with trembling hands.

'We will eat,' Rafael murmured flatly.

Hectically flushed, and barely able to stand on legs
that were wobbling with shock, Georgie espied Teresa
in the doorway and, if possible, felt her blush spread
down to encompass every other part of her exposed body.
A dark, deep hole to hide in would have been extraordinarily welcome. Saved in the very nick of time by
the housekeeper, she thought, on the quivering edge of
hysteria.

She made it into the palatial dining-room and down
onto a chair. Inside her head pounded a relentless refrain. How could you be so stupid . . . how could you be
so weak? What was she, some sort of brainless puppet?
Was she so over-sexed that she couldn't say no like any
other decent woman? What did it say about her that
after all the insults, all the cruelty, she had still allowed
Rafael to touch her?

Rafael said something sharp in Spanish, ice dripping
off every syllable. Teresa retreated at speed.

'You don't seem to get on very well with
your housekeeper.'

'She does not approve of your presence here. But what I do in my own home is entirely my affair.' Rafael shook out a white linen napkin with an air of magnificent unconcern. 'Teresa does not know whether to save you or condemn you. The taxing question of whether you are a virtuous woman being wickedly seduced, or a shameless hussy, will no doubt keep her awake all night. But by tomorrow the truth will out. She will decide that you are beyond saving and that I am no better and no worse than any other man in giving way to temptation. Then peace will be restored to my household!'

Frozen, with a spoon hovering indecisively over the very tempting fruit concoction set before her, Georgie cleared her throat. 'What truth will out?'

'That we are lovers.'

'I am not going to sleep with you!' Darkened violet eyes flared furiously down the table at him.

'I hope not. Sleep does not feature anywhere in my expectations of the night ahead,' Rafael delivered lazily, lifting his wine-glass and resting back in his chair to survey her with slumbrous dark eyes. He toasted her with a graceful movement of one brown hand. '*Salud* . . . to every fantasy being fulfilled. Sadly, the Ferrari is in London, but I don't lack imagination in the bedroom and I doubt very much that you will be disappointed.'

Georgie tossed aside her spoon, any idea of eating now abandoned. 'If you think for one moment that I intend to allow you to use me——' she returned in seething indignation.

'But I intend to reciprocate in being used,' Rafael interrupted mockingly, but there was a current of something distinctly more menacing in the assurance. 'Our hunger is mutual, but I have never had a purely sexual affair before. If I'm a little clumsy sometimes, remember that. I don't quite know how to treat you. Perhaps that is because the minute I take my hands off

you, I see your every flaw... then I wonder what the hell
I'm doing with you.'

Georgie flew upright, her facial muscles rigid, her
beautiful eyes aflame with fury. 'I want to return to my
hotel tomorrow!'

'No way,' Rafael said softly. 'You go when I say it is
time, not before.'

Georgie lifted her glass and stalked down the length
of the polished table. With a flick of her wrist, she tossed
the contents in his face. 'But *I* say it is time now, and I
expect you to listen.'

A hand snaked out and trapped her fingers, preventing her retreat. Calmly he dried himself with a
napkin while retaining that punishing grip on her. Only
then did he turn blazing dark eyes on her furiously
flushed profile. 'It really hasn't dawned on you yet, has
it?' he demanded, jerking her round so that she had to
face him. 'You bounce through life like an exuberant,
destructive child—undisciplined, wholly self-centred and
greedy, careless of the damage you cause, never counting
the cost. But today is the day you start paying for being
a shallow, opportunistic little bitch.'

Georgie stared back at him in stunned disbelief.
'You're—you're out of your mind...' she whispered.

'No,' Rafael murmured softly, silkily, 'I'm the kind
of unforgiving bastard you wouldn't find in your worst
nightmares. And you really don't know why, do you?'

'I think you're acting like someone unhinged,' she
muttered helplessly.

'I was very unhinged four years ago,' Rafael agreed,
his fingers tightening so savagely on hers that her smaller
hand was crushed. He threw his handsome dark head
back and studied her with unflinching intensity, his eloquent mouth hardening. 'Take a good long look at those
rooms upstairs. Take a note of the severe lack of good
taste in that Hollywood film-star bathroom. Ask yourself

who you know with a vulgar penchant for mermaid taps and marble. And then ask yourself why I would have wasted an obscene amount of money actually paying someone to make them.'

Transfixed by the savage onslaught of his biting dark eyes, Georgie's stomach cramped up. She couldn't feel her hand any more but she was beyond that awareness. She couldn't breathe, couldn't move, because she was paralysed by what he was telling her, unable to credit that her insanely confused thoughts could be heading in the right direction. 'I—I . . .' And for the life of her, she couldn't think of what to say.

'That suite was decorated for my bride—for my beautiful, *pure* bride.' Rafael drew her bruised fingers to his mouth and kissed them in a scathing demonstration of derision before dropping her hand again.

'You wanted to marry me?' Georgie demanded starkly, her voice cracking loudly in the charged silence.

'You really didn't know... I always wondered.' Rafael vented a grimly amused laugh as he read the sheer astonishment in her dazed eyes. 'But then, how *could* you know how to deal with a man who treated you with respect? Naturally, I did not want to make love to you before our wedding-night, but that restraint on my part was not appreciated. You got bored, didn't you?'

Every scrap of pink had drained from Georgie's vibrantly beautiful face. 'No...no!' she said again shakily.

'So you went to bed with someone else—someone wise enough to know that the very last thing you wanted was respect—another teenager.' All the raw savagery of Rafael's *conquistador* ancestry was stamped into the harsh lines of his golden features, his embittered fury starkly apparent in his blazing stare. 'I, Rafael Rodriguez Berganza, made to look a fool by a teenage boy!'

Trembling, Georgie whispered jerkily, 'Danny was a friend, nothing more——'

Rafael reached out and curved a cruelly strong hand round her elbow, forcing her closer. 'You think that makes a difference? That it meant nothing to you, that it was a drunken one-night stand which I was never intended to know about? I always knew that! But was it worth it? I ask you now, *querida mía* was it worth what you lost? Looking at you now, I would say not,' he derided, thrusting her back from him with contempt. 'Because you still want me. You still want me so much it terrifies you... and if you had had any intelligence at all, you would have known yourself safer in that prison cell than you are here with me!'

Georgie backed away. 'I don't like being threatened!' she spat back at him in a tempest of emotion too tangled for her even to comprehend. All she could recognise was the terrible rage which dominated her every other reaction. 'And I didn't want to marry you anyway! My idea of marriage is not being told what to do from dawn to dusk and getting the big freeze when you fail... and my ideal partner is not some international playboy, who sleeps with every woman he wants and then thinks he's got some God-given right to marry a virgin!'

Rafael plunged upright. 'I did not think it my right——'

'No, evidently you selected me at school and hoped to God you'd got me in time!' Georgie slung back in disgust. 'You know something? You are everything Steve ever said you were. Primitive, backward and bigoted.'

Rafael froze and shot her a seething look of such frightening anger that her voice simply died away. 'You say that name once more in my presence and I will surely kill you...'

Georgie spun on her heel and took off through the dining-room like a rocket. She flew up the stairs, raced across the landing and slammed breathlessly into her bedroom. Then she flung herself on the bed in the darkness and burst into helpless floods of tears.

CHAPTER FOUR

was hovering with a large laden tray when
walked back into the bedroom. She aimed an
smile at Georgie, but Georgie was so embar-
by her red, puffy face that she lowered her head.
have dinner, señorita?

Distress hadn't killed Georgie's appetite. But
food had been pretty thin on the ground over the
forty-eight hours.
eight hours, she reflected sickly. That swine had
wiped her out in little more than twelve hours!
years ago, Rafael had actually planned to marry

CHAPTER FOUR

A GOOD cry was supposed to be therapeutic. Georgie
peered at herself through swollen eyes half an hour later,
acknowledged the tumultuous state of her jangling nerves
and distraught emotions, and decided dully that the good
cry had utterly failed.

Teresa was hovering with a large laden tray when
Georgie walked back into the bedroom. She aimed an
uncertain smile at Georgie, but Georgie was so embarrassed by her red, puffy face that she lowered her head.

'You have dinner, *señorita*?'

'Thanks.' Distress hadn't killed Georgie's appetite. But
then, food had been pretty thin on the ground over the
past forty-eight hours.

Forty-eight hours, she reflected sickly. That swine had
all but wiped her out in little more than twelve hours!
Yet, four years ago, Rafael had actually planned to marry
her! Finding out that now shook her rigid. Pick a teenage
bride and mould her like unformed clay into the correct
image... She hadn't been rich or well-born but, heaven
knew, she had been malleable! And Rafael must have
wanted her; Rafael must very badly have wanted her,
she decided dazedly, to overlook all her other
deficiencies.

For a few minutes, Georgie hugged that new knowledge to her. It shed a different light on that long-ago
summer, briefly mollified her damaged pride. Then, with
protective parents hovering, not to mention her youth
and close friendship with his sister, he hadn't had that
many options, she conceded ruefully. How could he have

59

embarked on an affair with her? There would always have been the risk that she might tell María Cristina when it was over. And how did you have an affair with a girl who had to be home by midnight unless her stepbrother was in tow? A choky little laugh escaped Georgie. Was that why he had gone up in flames at the mere mention of Steve?

It would be foolish to deny that her parents had been worried by Rafael's interest in her, their concern exacerbated by Steve, who had slated the idea that Rafael could be trusted with their precious daughter. Throughout those weeks with Rafael, Georgie had been irritated by Steve's attitude, but she had grudgingly conceded his genuine concern that she was going to be badly hurt.

And when Steve's expectations had been fulfilled, Georgie had been grateful for his smooth and careless dismissal of their parents' astonishment that her relationship with Rafael had been so abruptly concluded. In fact, that understated kindness in shielding her from awkward questions had helped Georgie more than anything else to forget her stepbrother's disturbing behaviour on that final night.

She shivered, for she liked to recall that least of all. But, whether she liked it or not, the events of that catastrophic evening were flooding back to her. Did she blame everything on the amount of alcohol she had recklessly consumed? No, she could not allow that excuse. And, even without Steve's encouragement, she would have rebelled against Rafael's arrogance sooner or later.

She remembered Steve's girlfriend, a very pretty girl, only a couple of years her senior. It had been the first time she had met Janet. But that evening she had noticed how very careless Steve was of Janet's feelings. He hadn't paid her much attention. It had been a new view of Steve which she hadn't liked. It had made her wonder if all men were like that. Once a man knew you loved him, did you then become boring?

Georgie had been so much on edge that night, conscious that Rafael had been disturbingly distant on the last two occasions she had been with him. She had felt threatened and insecure and she had simultaneously despised herself for being so weak. She had told herself that if Rafael was getting bored with her, she could handle it. But she hadn't handled it. She had got childishly, stupidly drunk.

'I'm taking you home,' Rafael had told her grimly.

'If you take her home in that state, my stepfather will kill her!' Steve had protested.

'As opposed to me killing her?' Rafael had drawled with flat indifference. 'I'll take her home to her father and let him do it. Will that make you happy?'

Steve had become abusive. Rafael had ignored him and dragged Georgie out to his car. She hadn't wanted to go home. At that point, the evening had gone totally haywire. She had started to scream at Rafael in the Ferrari, and it was amazing how much she had said that later, she had to acknowledge, had truly come from the heart. Alcohol had filled her with the Dutch courage to list her every resentment.

'I thought you were more mature. Now I face reality—the inescapable gap between hope and self-delusion,' Rafael had commented very drily. 'Then, how do I blame you? One does not rob the schoolroom and expect to be rewarded with an adult. But, right now, I feel that I robbed the nursery department!'

Georgie had subsided like a pricked balloon but she had been wildly confused by the unfamilair strength of the emotions tearing her apart. One minute she loved him, the next she felt she hated him. And when he talked down to her like that, hatred rose uppermost.

But he had rewarded her sullen silence with a kiss, yet another in a long line of fleeting salutes, as if she was in very truth, the child he accused her of being. Still, there had not been an ounce of the passion she craved. And she had wanted so badly to prove that she was a woman, a *real* woman capable of satisfying his every adult desire.

And maybe she had also been trying to convince herself that she in turn had some power over him. So what had she done? Even four years after the event, Georgie cringed from recalling the fact that she had shamelessly thrown herself at Rafael in the car, employing every atom of wanton encouragement she had ever read about in racy female magazine articles of the 'How to hang on to your man' variety.

And it had worked... briefly. Rafael had uttered a ragged groan. With satisfying speed, all that infuriating restraint of his had vanished. She had ended up flat on the passenger seat, his mouth hotly sealed to hers, his body hard and demanding, crushing her yielding curves, all the red-hot passion she had for him finally matched. It hadn't even occurred to her that they were in a public car park. Georgie had been beyond such trivialities. But then Rafael had sworn viciously in Spanish and thrust himself back from her, an unholy glitter in his dark probing gaze.

'Who taught you how to arouse a man?' he had demanded, without hesitation ablaze with suspicion and distrust.

He hadn't been impressed by her stammered assurance that nobody had taught her anything. Georgie had been eaten alive by mortification. In the end she had been in such a state of sobbing incoherence that when she had seen Steve crossing the car park she had leapt out of the Ferrari and raced after him.

Steve had had a row with Janet, who had already gone home in a taxi. He had taken Georgie back to his house, sooner than subject her to the horror of facing her father in the condition she was in. And then her nightmare evening had taken its second very bad turn for the worse ... in many ways, at the time, the very worst turn of all.

Georgie paced the richly carpeted floor, recalling with a shudder how she had felt when Steve had, without any prior warning that she had noticed, switched from understanding big brother to would-be lover. He had had a comforting arm round her shoulders as they walked into the lounge and then he had suddenly grabbed her and begun kissing her! Georgie had been shattered and repelled. Steve might not be her real brother, but she had always regarded him in the asexual guise of one. His forceful embrace might only have lasted a short time but it had shocked and frightened Georgie as much as attempted rape.

'Hell, I'm *not* your brother ... don't look at me like that!' Steve had shouted at her before she escaped upstairs to lock herself in the bathroom and be horribly sick.

He had tried to talk to her through the door. He had had too much to drink. He was upset about Janet. Couldn't she understand? But that night Georgie hadn't been capable of understanding. She had shrunk from the challenge of opening that door and facing him again. And when Steve had told her that he was going out to check that he had locked his car, Georgie had fled through the back door.

She had gone to Danny's apartment, hadn't been able to think of any other place to run, would certainly not have turned to Rafael after the treatment he had meted out earlier. Danny had given her his bed and slept on the lounge sofa. Georgie had been so upset, he really

hadn't known what to do with her. In the end he had
just made her a cup of coffee and left her in peace.

The next morning, raised voices had wakened her. She
had sat up, naked in the tumbled bed, to find Rafael
standing in the bedroom doorway in a sort of seething
silent rage of incredulity. Without a word he had swung
on his heel and stridden back out of the flat. Danny had
appeared then, shivering wet and dripping from the
shower, still wrapped in a bath-towel. 'He just forced
his way in...' he had mumbled. 'And he's a lot bigger
than I am. Hope you didn't mind me making myself
scarce.'

Steve had been their second visitor, close on Rafael's
heels. Georgie hadn't been able to meet her stepbrother's eyes.

'How did Rafael know where I was?' she had
demanded.

'I guessed you had to be here and I told him.' Steve
had sighed. 'I thought you'd want to see him and smooth
over that stupid row you had with him.'

And, of course, had Rafael not completely misinterpreted what he had seen, she would indeed have been
glad to see him.

Steve had bent over backwards to make peace with
her, fervently apologising for upsetting her the night
before. He had papered over the cracks of her discomfiture, made it easier for her to try and pretend that
nothing had changed between them. But it had, she acknowledged sadly. A new distance had gradually eroded
their once close ties.

Later that day, when she had approached Rafael, it
had not initially occurred to Georgie that Rafael might
not listen to her. She had been incredibly naïve in her
assumption that Rafael would believe her when she explained that things might have *looked* suspicious at
Danny's but that in actuality everything had been en-

tirely innocent. But then, she had naturally assumed that
Rafael knew her well enough to have *some* degree of
trust in her...

She had put his ridiculous suspicions in the Ferrari
down to her own childish behaviour and mutually frayed
tempers. Indeed, travelling up in the lift to Rafael's
penthouse apartment, Georgie had been so far removed
from reality that she had been happily thinking that
Rafael must have been jealous and that jealousy had to
mean he *cared*. And, right now, remembering that piece
of inane stupidity made Georgie want to tear her hair
out and scream. That day she had been a lamb to the
slaughter.

But never again, she reminded herself doggedly and,
since sleep was the last thing on her over-active mind,
she stripped, filled the marble bath with hot water and
bubbles and climbed in to wash her hair and then lie
back and thoughtfully survey the mermaid taps. For her
benefit... Incredible. When, when had he done all this?
And how had everything contrived to go so badly wrong?
Her throat ached. Running a flannel under the cold tap,
she draped it irritably across her still reddened eyes.

Rafael had fallen off his pedestal with a resounding
crash. First love—nothing more painful, nothing more
intense. It was those memories which saddened her, not
any sense of loss or regret. The marriage would have
been a disaster. Like Desdemona but without the saint-
liness, she conceded ruefully, she might have ended up
murdered by her enraged and jealous husband. Rafael
hadn't trusted her one inch.

She could not have been the wife his intelligence would
have chosen. Perhaps it had been the awareness that they
were temperamentally unsuited which had made him seize
on the escape-clause supplied by her supposed fling with
Danny. Rafael had not had grounds to judge her that
harshly. He had known how much she loved him. How

could he have seriously believed that after one stupid row she would jump into bed with a boy almost a year younger than she was? What kind of sense did that make?

'I knew you wouldn't be able to resist the bath...'

Tearing the flannel from her eyes in shock, Georgie reeled up into a sitting position, water sloshing noisily everywhere. 'What the hell are you doing in here?' she gasped in outrage.

Rafael angled a splintering smile over her startled features and laughed with genuine amusement. 'You're such a curious mixture, Georgie. Puritan and sybarite.' His dinner-jacket hooked in one hand, his white silk dress-shirt undone at his brown throat, he sat down on the edge of the bath. 'You radiate conflicting signals which confuse. Looking at you now, I see why I was taken in four years ago. That look of shock and indignation is very impressive, but the way you're hugging your knees is decided overkill,' he murmured silkily, surveying her with glittering golden eyes. 'You have a very beautiful body... why hide it?'

'Get out of here!' Georgie sizzled back at him furiously.

He tugged a fleecy towel off the rail just out of her reach and extended it with a faintly derisive smile. 'Then you've already learnt that a little mystique is more stimulating than a floor-show?'

Georgie snatched at the towel and wrapped it clumsily round herself as she stood up, her cheeks burning hotly. 'I want you to leave,' she told him stiffly, striving for a note of command and dignity.

Rafael flung his ebony head back and laughed spontaneously.

Georgie stood there, violet eyes flashing with rage. 'Look, I have got the message that you consider yourself absolutely irresistible, but I've made it clear that I am not interested!'

'Where was I?' Rafael prompted.

'Where were you when?' Georgie snapped.

Rafael slid fluidly upright. 'Where was I when you were making it very clear that you were not interested?' he enquired lethally.

Georgie's teeth clenched. 'Look, I just want to go back to La Paz and sort out my passport!'

'You are really running scared.' Sensual dark eyes scanned her shrewdly. 'Why is that? Pride?'

'I don't know what you're talking about.' Georgie stepped out of the bath.

He reached for her without warning, curving two powerful arms round her and sweeping her off her feet. 'I won't let you run.'

'Put me down, for heaven's sake!' Georgie shrieked.

'No.'

He stared down at her, golden eyes meshing with violet. Her own heartbeat thundered slowly, heavily through her body, stretching every tiny nerve taut. 'Rafael...'

'You burn for me...you can't hide that,' he told her. 'I see it in your eyes, in the way you move, in the very voice you use when you speak to me.'

'So you attract me...so what?' Georgie dared in desperation. 'We don't all follow our most basic instincts!'

'But you do...all the time. However, here you will follow your most basic instincts for my benefit alone,' Rafael asserted, settling her down on the bed and dropping down beside her in one powerful movement. 'No strings on either side, no lies, no misunderstandings. We share a bed, nothing more.'

The hectic pink in her cheeks had receded, leaving her pale. He was peeling off his silk shirt to reveal the bronzed breadth of his shoulders and the curling black triangle of hair hazing his pectoral muscles. As though impelled by a force outside her control, Georgie's unwittingly fascinated gaze lingered and she swallowed hard. On one level she couldn't believe that she was actually in a bedroom on a bed with Rafael. It felt so *unreal*.

'If you touch me, I'll scream blue murder!'

'What a novel promise,' Rafael breathed huskily, winding long brown fingers into her tangled damp hair as she attempted to sit up and preventing the movement.

'Now just back off before this gets embarrassing for both of us!' Georgie hissed up at him. 'If I scream, your servants will come running!'

'We are alone in the house.'

As he lowered his weight down on to hers, Georgie froze, and stared up at him with darkened violet eyes. 'We can't be...'

'We are.' He bent over her and nipped playfully at her lower lip with the kind of sensual expertise she was defenceless against, the tip of his tongue following gently in the wake of the tiny pain to further inflame. 'I have waited so long to see you on this bed in this room,' he confessed. 'And when it's over, when you're gone, everything will be ripped out and these rooms will be renovated. It will be as though you never existed——'

The assurance dug sudden fear into her bones, banishing her momentary loss of concentration. Georgie put up her hands and hit out at him with raw hostility. With a stifled imprecation, he anchored both her hands to the sheet and gazed down at her with incandescent golden eyes, his strong jawline clenching as he absorbed the apprehension in her upturned gaze.

'*Por Dios*...why should you fear me?' he demanded abruptly, releasing her wrists.

Trembling, Georgie thrust him away from her and sat up, clutching with desperate hands at the bath-towel's

dipping edge across her full breasts. It was a kind of fear
he could never have understood, for he would not have
believed its source. She was afraid of herself *and* him.
'I just want you to l-leave me alone!' she muttered
shakily.

He murmured something soft in his own language and
pulled her close. Stiffening, she shivered violently as the
towel lurched dangerously downward. 'No!' she gasped,
panicking.

'*Sí...*' Rafael countered, choosing to gather her even
closer and cover her lips hungrily with his. The towel
slipped; she didn't notice, but a tiny gasp was torn from
her as her taut nipples were abraided by his hair-
roughened chest.

She was electrified by the way he was making love to
her mouth. He searched out every sensitive spot and explored it, making the breath rasp in her throat. It felt
so good, indeed, it felt so incredibly exciting that she
clutched him with her hands, seduced by her own helpless
response. As he settled her smoothly back against the
crisp white sheet, she was overwhelmed by the sheer
welter of sensation that attacked her when he sealed every
virile inch of his lean, powerful body to hers.

He stared down at her with a raw, sexual hunger that
burned through clear to her bones. Heat flooded her in
a blinding surge. A hard thigh sank between hers and
she quivered violently, the fevered pulse-point of desire
thrumming ever higher inside her.

'You see...' Rafael muttered thickly. 'And I haven't
even begun yet.'

As he buried his mouth in a tiny hollow below her
fragile collarbone, he let his thumbs rub expertly across
her thrusting pink nipples. She jerked, an involuntary
moan torn from her, and he lowered his head to employ
his mouth and that wickedly knowing tongue on those
unbearaby sensitive buds. He drove her crazy. Sensation

like white-hot lightning licked at every nerve-ending and she twisted and gasped in helpless excitement. She was in thrall to a dark enchantment of the senses and the most extraordinary pleasure.

Her fingers dug into the thick silky depths of his hair and tightened as he sucked a swollen nipple into his mouth. 'Rafael ... oh, God, Rafael ...' she moaned, out of control and burning up.

Through passion-glazed eyes she focused on him, the darkness of his head against her pale skin, the gold of his hands shaping her treacherously responsive flesh. Her palms moved restively over the satin-smooth muscles in his shoulders and then her fingertips drove into his hair again as her heavy eyelids slid down. There was an ache between her thighs, an absolutely unbearable ache. Her teeth clenched. She wanted, needed ...

He slid up and twisted a hand painfully into her hair as he devoured her mouth again, bruising her lips but answering her every unspoken need. She kissed him back with wild passion, trembling all over, lost in the depths of her own excruciating excitement. He moaned something raggedly in Spanish, cupping her cheekbones, meeting that passion with a savagery that dominated, drove, demanded ...

'*Tentadora ... bruja,*' Rafael groaned, and then he tensed ever so slightly.

At first Georgie didn't hear the faint buzzing somewhere in the background. Rafael's fingertips were roaming through the damp tangle of curls at the apex of her thighs and she was on a knife-edge of tormented pleasure, quivering skittishly, unable to stay still as he suddenly crushed her mouth beneath his again. And then, with quite paralysing abruptness, he released her and sprang off the bed.

'Rafael?' she mumbled.

'The phone,' he grated.

'What phone?' And then she heard it, buzzing away somewhere like an angry bee.

'My private line—it must be an emergency. *Dios*,' Rafael swore, shooting her a torn-in-two glance of dark smouldering hunger and incredulous frustration.

Georgie only managed to focus on him as he strode back out of the bathroom, retrieving a mobile phone from his dinner-jacket. And then she got the full effect of Rafael, stark naked. Her lower lip dropped as she stared, for she had no recollection of him removing the rest of his clothes. Sheer shock grabbed her by the throat. Gulping, Georgie took in his uninhibited stance several feet away, not a centimetre of his magnificent golden physique concealed from her. Her gaze wandered on a compulsive journey of its own and absorbed with frank alarm her first sight of a rampantly aroused male. She reddened to the roots of her hair.

'One minute... I promise you, *querida*,' Rafael murmured with erotic emphasis as he surveyed her with blatant male anticipation.

Georgie hauled the sheet over her shamelessly exposed flesh. She started to shake. Aftershock. I am wanton, she thought in a sudden agony of self-reproach. Desire still ached inside her and she was too honest to deny the fact. Rafael had told her that they didn't even need to like each other and she had refused to believe that. But Rafael, veteran of many more such encounters than she, had known better.

From below her lashes, she watched him turn away from her, sounding oddly taut and then breaking into an apparently animated flood of Spanish. You are everything he called you, a nasty little inner voice insisted. She buried her burning face in the pillow. No, she wasn't. Who had ever heard of a promiscuous virgin? But with Rafael her blood ran hot enough to burn her alive. Although right now that same blood was freezing

in her veins, because she realised how very close she had
come to surrendering her body to a male who despised
her.

Yet she wanted him just the way he said she did. Helplessly, instinctively, as though on some frightening sub-
conscious level he had stamped her as his four years ago
and her body alone knew it and accepted that reality.
Sex, she decided wretchedly, was a primal hunger that
respected no boundaries. Rafael Rodriguez Berganza
should be the very last male alive capable of awakening
her most basic urges. And yet he did, he *did*. On every
primitive, physical level, Rafael drew her slavishly to her
own destruction. Evidently sexual desire required nothing
more intellectual.

'Georgie...'

For a split-second she couldn't face him, and she had
to force herself to roll back, push her hair out of her
eyes and look at him. She was intensely relieved to see
that he was already half dressed. Brilliant dark eyes rested
on her with paint-stripping intensity. He reached for his
shirt, a wolfish smile hardening his sensual mouth.

'*Perdone*...but we must postpone our pleasure,' he
imparted with slumbrous mockery. 'That was Antonio
on the phone. María Cristina has given birth to a son
and the task of spreading the good news among our many
relatives falls on me.'

Astonishment filled Georgie's eyes. 'María Cristina
has had her baby? But surely she wasn't due for another
couple——'

'He came a little early, but both mother and baby are
well. There were no complications,' Rafael assured her,
and slowly expelled his breath, a softer light than she
had ever seen briefly gentling his strong dark features.
'But I understand they barely made it to the hospital in
time! A little boy...' His chiselled jawline clenched and
he cast her a sardonic glance. 'He is to be called George.'

His pronounced relief that María Cristina had come through childbirth safely, and the open emotion with which he contemplated his nephew's arrival in the world, twisted something painfully inside Georgie, reminding her just how close were the ties between brother and sister. Then she caught his final statement and her eyes widened. 'She remembered ... She called him after me?' she gasped, tickled pink by the announcement. 'Gosh, I can't wait to see him——'

'But you won't unless my sister chooses to travel to London,' Rafael cut in harshly, his change of mood brutally swift. 'By the time she flies home next week, you will be long gone.'

Losing her short-lived animation, Georgie stilled. Reality had never been less welcome. She collided with his cold dark scrutiny, and her stomach clenched painfully under the onslaught of that unashamed snub. She felt sick with shame, remembering their intimacy brief minutes earlier.

'Is that clear?' Rafael persisted, with what she felt to be quite unnecessary cruelty.

Two years earlier, she had missed out on her best friend's wedding. María Cristina had asked her to be one of her bridesmaids and it had almost broken Georgie's heart to refuse, for her parents had been willing to dig into their savings to make the trip possible for her. She had been afraid of running into Rafael again, although at the time she had not admitted that fear to herself. Her end-of-term exams had been just around the corner and she had used them as an excuse. But this time—*this time*, she told herself with sudden ferocity— she would not play the coward.

'I'll do what I want,' she said tightly, and studied him, a tempestuous gleam in her bitter stare. 'You can't make me leave Bolivia.'

'But you cannot stay here.'

'I'll have money sent out from home,' she threw back.
'I don't care if I have to sleep on the street but I am not
leaving without seeing María Cristina and George.'

'I will not allow it,' Rafael drawled in a tone of forbidding finality.

Hunched below her sheet, rawly conscious of her lack
of clothing, Georgie sent him a look of naked loathing.
'I want transport out of here tomorrow... do you hear
me?'

Rafael dealt her a glittering glance of hard amusement.
'No transport available. You don't leave until I want you
to leave, and that won't be until I am finished with you.'

'I'm finished now... I've had enough,' Georgie
launched at him with a sob of rage in her shaking voice.
'If you don't get me back to La Paz fast, I'll make you
very sorry!'

Rafael lifted his dinner-jacket and viewed her with an
insulting lack of concern. 'And how do you plan to do
that?'

'Wouldn't you just love to know?'

'I would, indeed. Are you always this childish when
you are thwarted?'

'I am not childish!' Georgie spat back, raising her
burnished head so that her hair tumbled like tongues of
flame in the lamplight. 'If you keep me here against my
will, that is an offence... you're breaking the law!'

'But here I *am* the law,' Rafael told her gently.

'I'll be six feet under the day I accept that!' Georgie
slung back truthfully.

'No... you'll very probably be under me,' he murmured silkily.

'How dare you?' Georgie's hot temper simply boiled
over. 'There's a whole lot of ways I can get even, so
don't push me! I can tell tales to María Cristina! I can
go home and scream rape and kidnapping!'

'And what proof will you have? These are empty threats. If you had any real affection for my sister, you would not wish to upset her but, even if you did,' Rafael countered very drily, 'she would not believe me capable of such behaviour. As for rape, there has never been any question of force. Kidnapping? You came here willingly as my guest.'

The door thudded shut in his wake and she shuddered with frustration, inflamed by her inability to pierce his tough hide. It was slowly sinking in on her that Rafael hadn't been joking when he had said that she stayed until he chose to let her go. But she still found that incredibly hard to accept. Rafael was an outstandingly well-educated man with a brilliant intellect, outwardly the very epitome of cultured sophistication.

He spoke half a dozen languages fluently, oversaw a vast and flourishing business empire spread across the globe, and still found time to lend considerable support to several international charities, not to mention his environmental interests and the numerous philanthropic projects which made the Berganza name revered on the world stage... and this was the man now telling her that she was a prisoner in his home until such time as she satisfied his desire for revenge?

Little wonder that she was feeling confused. But revenge was Rafael's aim. He had brought her here to the *estancia* and put her in the bedroom she would have occupied as his wife. Her stomach lurched sickly as she recalled his assurance that when she was gone these rooms would be stripped, every reminder of her eradicated forever. But, before he reached that dramatic and gothic conclusion, Rafael intended to possess her body in the very same bed in which she would have lain as his bride. Her skin literally chilled as she saw the savage parody he desired to enact to slake his macho pride of the slur she had cast on it four years ago by her apparent betrayal.

As his bride, she would have been treated with respect and tenderness. But now Rafael saw her as a sort of any time, any place and with any available man kind of girl. He despised her and he wanted to humiliate her and he had chosen the most machiavellian method possible. The dark, primal depths of Rafael's essentially savage inner self stood revealed, unleashed by anger and unquenchable arrogance. Why shouldn't he have what he firmly believed she had given every other man she had ever been with? She was the available space on his sexual score-card, she reflected in disgust.

Four years ago, she had believed she knew Rafael... but she hadn't known him at all. For a start, she had accused him of being a sanctimonious stuffed shirt that final night! Then, she hadn't known she was being subjected to courtship Bolivian style, where you received flowers, occasionally held hands, barely kissed and generally conducted yourself with immense restraint and maturity. But at just turned nineteen... I wanted to dance all night in stuffy clubs, break speed limits in the Ferrari, neck in the Ferrari, be seduced in the Ferrari, drink pink champagne, wear outrageous attention-grabbing clothes—his attention—be seen by all my friends in a stretch limousine...

Glory be... She had been far less grown-up then than she had fondly imagined. She only saw that now, looking back, and frankly marvelled that Rafael could ever have thought of marrying her. Had the wedding taken place, there would probably be a gravestone out there somewhere by now, she thought, an almost hysterical giggle lodged in her throat. She would have driven him crazy by the end of the first six months!

The giggle died, her facial muscles tautening. But she had loved him in the wild, head over heels, obsessive style of her strong emotions. And, had he married her, she would no doubt have tried very hard to live up to his high standards...and with every failure she would have lost a little more courage. Rafael had a very powerful personality and a naturally domineering temperament. That came from being filthy rich and a lot brighter than ninety-nine per cent of the people around him. He would have swallowed her alive as a husband—only think of the traits he was freely demonstrating now...

Crazy... Yes, she had to be crazy, but she just couldn't help the thought that Rafael was a whole lot more exciting a prospect as a vengeful lover than he had ever been as an unnaturally courteous and yet despotic potential husband, striving to contain and control a naturally exuberant and rebellious teenager. They met as equals now, she told herself squarely—well, almost equals, she adjusted. He couldn't humiliate her unless she allowed him to do so. And he couldn't keep her here unless she chose to stay.

It was a kind of a compliment, she decided sleepily, that she should have left that strong an impression on a male of his experience. It was good to know that she hadn't been the only one burned that summer...but it was time he appreciated that, these days, Georgie was positively fireproof. A flame-thrower couldn't scorch her.

Only love could hurt—*love*. Her sultry mouth down-curved expressively. That prison of the mind which had made such a fool of her in the past? When she fell in love again, some day in the future, it would be with someone blond and blue-eyed and frightfully British, someone who fully appreciated her brains, her guts and her passion, and who thought he was one hell of a lucky guy to catch her. As she slid into sleep, at peace with herself at last, she smiled at that consoling image.

CHAPTER FIVE

GEORGIE made her plans while she was getting dressed the next morning. One way or another she needed to get off the *estancia* and persuading Rafael to do it for her would be the very easiest way to accomplish her escape. Deliciously sneaky, wonderfully simple. She strolled into the dining-room, vibrantly eye-catching in clinging pink Lycra shorts and an off-the-shoulder emerald lace-edged top. 'It's kind of quiet around here, isn't it?' she complained.

Rafael's brilliant dark eyes slowly swept over her. He lowered his newspaper, his expressive mouth twisting.

'Oh, no,' Georgie sighed mockingly. 'You don't like what I am wearing?'

'You are not on the beach,' Rafael responded drily.

'I have a thought for the day.' Georgie angled a brilliant smile at him. It wobbled slightly as she collided with piercing dark eyes, screened by lush ebony lashes, and her intended act slipped momentarily. He really was gorgeous—devastatingly, dangerously gorgeous. Had she married him and been able to tape his nasty mouth shut, she could probably have passed her time just looking at him and thinking utterly brainless thoughts of the 'he's mine' variety.

'Don't keep me in suspense,' he said with a distinctly cutting lack of interest.

Georgie tore a croissant to pieces with her restive hands, angry and dismayed by the sudden lurch of lost concentration evoked by her response to all that virile masculinity lounging at the other side of the polished table. 'Thank God, we *didn't* get married,' she said with helpless sincerity.

'You expect me to credit that you feel that way?' Rafael derided, arrogantly unimpressed.

'You'd have felt that way within two weeks if you had married me, and I bet there's never been a divorce in the family.' Georgie cast a speaking glance at the humourless dark faces of the portraits on the wall. 'Your ancestors were a pretty miserable bunch, weren't they? The men probably got rid of undesirable wives with childbirth. In those days, pregnancy was as dangerous as sky-diving. Poison was quite a common method too, or a fall down the stairs. In the Dark Ages, being a woman was being a victim. You could be beaten to death by your husband and nobody did a thing.'

Rafael murmured in a slightly strained tone, '*Desde luego*...of course, you were always fascinated by history. But to my knowledge none of my ancestors ever became that desperate.' He spread fluid hands and, without warning, his spontaneous laughter rang out, banishing the austerity from his dark features. 'Then, no doubt they took such dark secrets to their graves with them and, sadly, no one had the good sense to leave a diary of confession behind!'

Georgie was furious with herself for straying off stupidly into actual conversation with him and, worst of all, making him laugh. For a split-second, she absorbed his blatant amusement, and never before had she been more disturbingly aware of the intense charisma he possessed. Her face tightened. Hurriedly, she dived into the first move of her plan.

'Do we have to stay here?' she pressed abruptly.

His laughter died away, his eyes narrowing. 'I don't think I understand.'

She leant forward confidingly. 'I would be a whole lot more amenable—if you know what I mean—somewhere where I could have a little fun,' she told him softly, damning the tide of pink rising below her skin, terrified it would betray her. 'Twelve more hours out here in the boonies and I will drop dead with boredom. There is nothing but grass, cows and peasants out there.'

Inwardly, Georgie winced at the ignorant role she had chosen to play.

'My people are not peasants,' Rafael retorted with a flash of even white teeth, faint red darkening his hard cheekbones.

Georgie shrugged and thrust her chin back up again with determination, ready to play out her plan to the bitter end. 'Let's just put our cards on the table. You want me, you can have me, but there are certain—er—terms.'

'I want you, I can have you?' Intense golden eyes whipped over her beautiful face, resting on her hot cheeks. '*Now*, then . . . let us go upstairs,' he challenged smoothly.

Georgie's sip of coffee went down the wrong way. She coughed painfully, struggling to appear cool. 'Terms,' she reminded him chokily.

'Am I to understand this is a form of negotiation?' Rafael enquired with immense calm, lounging back in his carved chair to study her, very much as though she was the hired entertainment. 'Would you mind telling me what I am to receive in return?'

'You know damned fine what I'm offering you!' Georgie snapped back.

A beautifully shaped ebony brow elevated. 'What I could have had for nothing last night,' he prompted very softly.

Her teeth gnashed together, violence shimmering in her outraged violet eyes.

But, as she parted her lips, Rafael moved a silencing hand. He watched her with intense stillness. 'How amenable is amenable?' he encouraged lazily.

Hooked, she thought in triumph. 'Anything you want...whenever you want,' she whispered throatily, but she had to study the table to say it.

'And my side of the deal? Taking you somewhere without cattle and peasants?'

'I just want to have a good time and I'm not going to have it here, am I?' she pointed out tautly.

'Anything I want, whenever I want,' Rafael mused smoothly. 'But I have everything that I want right here. No deal.'

She stole a glance at his starkly handsome features, the cool dispassionate expression which revealed nothing. 'No deal?' she queried.

'Next time you try to bargain with me, be sure to arm yourself with the promise of something which isn't already mine for the taking.' Diamond-bright dark eyes raked over her furious face. 'For you are mine. And next time—and I hope there is a next time, for this has been the most entertaining breakfast I have had in years,' he confessed lethally, 'struggle not to look as if you're overdosing on cyanide when you're offering to be my sex-slave!'

'I am not yours and I never will be!' Georgie asserted fiercely. 'And I haven't got the temperament to be any-body's sex-slave!'

'But mine—and that awareness is killing you, isn't it?' Rafael traded lazily. 'You can screw around with all the men you like, but why not with me? What makes me different? Shall I tell you why you fight me to the best of your limited ability?'

A chill was enclosing her flesh. Another game had come to an end. She wanted to cover her ears and run but she sat there, looking blankly back at him, forcing herself not to reveal how sick she felt inside.

'You remember what it was like between us four years ago, before it started coming apart... and, deep down inside, you would very much like to have that romantic illusion back.'

She tasted blood in her mouth as her teeth bit into the soft underside of her lower lip. 'I wish I'd never met you, I certainly don't wish to relive any of it!'

'But the past is still there. You can't escape it... any more easily than you can escape me. In the thirty years of my life, I have been the focus of female seduction routines more times than I can count,' Rafael told her with harsh amusement. 'Women who know what they're doing. You don't appear to——'

'I'm not really interested in your opinion.'

'Subtlety evidently doesn't come with maturity. A Mae West impression at this hour of the day could only make me laugh.' Rafael expelled his breath audibly, shooting her a forbidding look from hooded dark eyes. 'Then you always did make me laugh, *es verdad*? It was that streak of highly deceptive naïveté which blinded me for so long to your real nature. I should have been warned by the birth-control pills I saw in your bag——'

'The *what*?' Georgie broke in with a furrowed brow, and then she tensed with comprehension.

Rafael shot her a sardonic glance. 'I assumed they were for my benefit.'

'You would.' Embarrassment held her only briefly.

'It should have occurred to me that you had already been involved in a sexual relationship, but then, my romanticised view of you did not allow such reasoning at that early stage.'

A ragged little laugh, empty of humour, fell from her strained mouth. Rafael was so sharp he would cut himself some day, and wasn't it fascinating to learn that he had been ready to misjudge her right from the beginning? Such a tiny thing, an oversight, a glimpse of a packet of pills in her bag, from which he had drawn incorrect conclusions. She would have died sooner than admit that she had been put on the contraceptive pill to regulate irregular periods.

She stood up. 'I think I need some fresh air,' she said jerkily.

'Georgie . . . strange as it may seem, I do not hold you responsible for a liaison begun at so early an age. You were the innocent party,' Rafael drawled with grave emphasis, his hard jawline clenching. 'But, at the time, I found the discovery of that particular relationship deeply offensive. It contravened my every principle of family-life, though I knew he was not in fact your brother——'

'What the heck are you talking about?'

'Did you think I didn't know?' Rafael threw back his imperious dark head, his challenging gaze imprisoning hers by blatant force of will.

'Didn't know what?' Tension had sprung into the atmosphere, thickening it. Georgie suddenly felt cold and threatened.

'Is the habit of secrecy still so engrained that you cannot be honest even after all this time?' Rafael demanded with derision. '*Por Dios* . . . you live with him!'

Georgie went white by slow, painful degrees. Her tongue stole out to wet her dry lips. She could not believe that he would dare to suggest that she actually *lived* in the sexual sense with Steve or, indeed, that she had ever had an intimate relationship of any form with her stepbrother.

'I know,' Rafael repeated very quietly. 'I know that you began sharing his bed when you were seventeen.'

Her stomach curdled at the enormity of such a belief. 'That is the most disgusting thing anyone has ever accused me of,' she whispered strickenly, her distressed eyes clinging helplessly to his. 'And you can't believe it...you can't possibly believe it.'

Rafael rose fluidly upright, his hard golden features fiercely set. 'I prefer to have this out in the open between us. While I can appreciate your reluctance to face the fact that that liaison is no secret to me, I will *not* allow you to lie to me.'

He believed it. He actually believed that she had slept with Steve before she had even met *him*. Incredulous at the revelation, Georgie stared at him with wide, shocked eyes. 'You're crazy...absolutely crazy!'

Rafael stood back several feet from her, six feet two inches of darkly powerful masculinity. But, despite that distance, he had her cornered. Implacably obdurate dark eyes were trained on her. 'I am aware that my sister has no idea of that relationship, but surely your father and your stepmother cannot still be in the dark? Or are you telling me that it is now at an end and you remain just good friends under the same roof?' he derided.

'Steve doesn't even live under the same roof,' Georgie heard herself protest, her brain in too much turmoil for her to know where to attack first. 'He has an apartment now. He rents out the house to students at the college nearby. I have a tiny flat in the attic and I act as a sort of caretaker, keeping an eye on things...' Her voice simply drained away then as she wondered numbly why she was rabbiting on about something so utterly trivial.

'So it is over now——'

'It never began!' Georgie threw back with sudden wildness, her distress growing as the full connotations of what Rafael believed her capable of sank in. 'I've never had any sort of intimate relationship with Steve and I don't know how you can accuse me of something so disgusting! I've always thought of him as my brother——'

'That is all he ever should have been until you were old enough to know what you were doing. He took advantage of your youth and your passion, but you should have known that it was wrong,' Rafael delivered in harsh condemnation.

'You're not listening to me... are you? You don't believe me,' Georgie registered sickly.

Rafael vented a roughened laugh. 'I followed you home with him that last night. I didn't trust him with you. *Madre de Dios*... I didn't want to distress you with my suspicions about the exact nature of his feelings for you! Then, through the window, I saw you in his arms, lovers kissing passionately. Everything fell into place then. At last I understood.'

'You saw Steve kissing me?' Georgie echoed hollowly. 'But how...? The curtains weren't pulled,' she recalled abstractedly.

'Correct. I had a superb view...'

Georgie was deep in shock. Rafael had opened a locked door on the past, filling in details she hadn't been aware of then. But he had twisted the picture as she knew it and flung her into violent turmoil. 'It wasn't what you thought,' she burst out abruptly.

'The only acceptable response now is the whole truth and nothing but the truth!' Rafael delivered with murderous quietness. 'And I do believe I'm entitled to ask one question.'

Numbly she looked back at him, pale and shaken and unbearably tense.

'While you were seeing me, were you *still* sleeping with him?'

'Dear God...' Georgie was so appalled that her stomach responded with a nauseous lurch of protest.

'So you weren't. One small consolation,' Rafael breathed scathingly. 'Then I supplanted him. Were I generous, I should now excuse his every jealous attempt

to come between us, but I excuse nothing that he did
and I blame you for deliberately deceiving me into believing that you were innocent. Did it amuse you? Or
did you want to believe that you could carry the deception through to the bitter end?'

Georgie covered her face with her hands and turned
unsteadily away, desperate to escape that lethal accented
drawl.

'I believed you would marry him,' Rafael admitted
harshly. 'For years, I have expected to hear news of your
marriage through my sister. Instead, what do I hear?
One man after another—*friends*, María Cristina trust-
ingly calls them—but you and I both know that you lie
back on the nearest bed for your male "friends"...'

Suddenly Georgie just couldn't take any more, and
the very abruptness with which she dived past him took
him by surprise. She flew out of the house, running
without even knowing where she was going. Her heart
was thumping sickly in her throat, every sobbing intake
of oxygen rattling through her lungs. She wanted to take
off like a jet plane and leave everything that distressed
her far behind, but the torment of pain was remorse-
lessly trapped inside her and she was stuck with it.

The heat swiftly sapped her energy. She got a stitch
in her side and had to stop and bend over, struggling to
get her breath back, the dusty ground below her feet
tilting sickeningly up at her.

'Georgie!'

Her head whirled up. She saw Rafael moving with
long, determined strides towards her and panic filled her.
No more. Right now, she really couldn't take any more!
Her fevered eyes whirled round the cluster of buildings
near and far, passing blindly over the curious faces of
the people in the vicinity, and then she saw the pretty
little whitewashed church with its open doors and took
off again.

The coolness of the dim interior engulfed her in welcome. Her feet took her down the aisle into a seat in the shadow of a stone pillar. Wrapping her arms round herself, she attempted to catch her breath and banish the awful nausea threatening. Shock. She knew what was wrong with her. Shock and a kind of horrified disbelief that even Rafael could believe such things of her.

'This is not the place for you,' Rafael murmured in a stifled undertone from behind her.

'Go away,' she mumbled. Did he think she was going to desecrate his precious church by her mere presence? She wouldn't be surprised if he did. And even in the Middle Ages, Rafael wouldn't have allowed her sanctuary here. He would have dragged her out and thrown her to the crowd to be torn apart, no doubt, she reflected wildly. Rafael was a savage and, with anyone who fell into the whore category, he was a throwback to the Spanish Inquisition.

And then she heard another voice—very quiet, very calm—speak in Spanish, and there was one of those explosive silences which could be physically felt... It seemed to go on forever and ever before she heard the astonishing but unmistakable sound of Rafael's retreat. Only then did she appreciate that for once impulse had not betrayed her. The church was the one place Rafael Rodriguez Berganza did not rule supreme.

She knew her saviour had to have been the priest, and she waited shakily to be forced into speech, but no voice spoke and the silence stayed, slowly soothing the tumult of her emotional upheaval, enabling her to think again.

So now she knew why Rafael had refused to listen to her attempts to explain the platonic nature of her friendship with Danny. He had been suspicious of her morals long before that day. The pills—then what? Steve's dislike of him? Steve had not been jealous, for goodness' sake! Steve simply hadn't liked Rafael. And when Rafael had seen that embrace, he had forced every other fact to fit, choosing to assume that that accidental glimpse was merely the tip of the iceberg in a far more intimate relationship. After all, hadn't she been shamelessly encouraging towards him?

Had her passionate response to him been that misleading? Had she come across as some sort of nymphomaniac? He had a wild imagination... Or had he? Witnessing that embrace certainly would have been a shock, as much of a shock for Rafael as it had been at the time for Georgie. Rafael could never have seen a hint of such intimacy in her behaviour with Steve at any other time. And that fact alone might well have been the final confirmation of Rafael's suspicions. Clearly he had believed that she and Steve were polished pretenders at being simply stepbrother and sister in public view, an act they had put on to conceal their true relationship from family and friends.

Moisture dripped on her tightly clenched hands. She lifted an uncertain hand to her damp face, discovered she was crying. It was so very hard to try and be calm about an accusation so outrageous and so distressing. But that same accusation revealed so much about Rafael. She shuddered.

From the outset Rafael had been sickly prejudiced against her. He had probably fought hard against the attraction between them and, even in succumbing to that attraction, he had still been on red alert for any flaws that she might display. Desire had driven Rafael, and the price of fulfilling that desire had been marriage.

But intellectually, of course, he *hadn't* wanted to marry her. If it hadn't been for her connection with María Cristina, Rafael would just have taken what was on offer and slept with her, slaking his desire in the most basic way possible. Subconsciously, he must have fiercely resented that reality. So it must have been relatively easy for Rafael to begin to suspect that her innocence was an act, and fate had been wonderfully kind to him in serving up the kind of evidence he required to convince himself that she was a whore instead.

Rafael had run true to type, she reflected numbly. Hot-blooded, suspicious, jealous and melodramatic—the archetypal smouldering Latin lover. Yet it was so difficult to equate that image with the freezingly self-contained male who had rejected her at their final meeting. He had not mentioned Steve then. Why not? Had it been beneath his precious dignity to reveal the extent to which he believed himself to have been deceived? He had not called her a whore, either. Indeed, in retrospect, she realised that Rafael had been remarkably restrained that day. But it was almost laughable that he could have believed her steeped in sexual sin at so tender an age. But she couldn't laugh, had never felt further from laughter.

She felt agonisingly hurt and bitter and it was that incredible pain which she now feared most of all. Her pride and her principles revolted against the image Rafael now had of her. Yes, perhaps she would have liked the romantic illusion back, just as he had shrewdly divined. Being treated like a scarlet woman might have briefly appealed to her sense of humour when she put on an act that first night in an effort to hold her own, but with Rafael, she could never ever forget that once she had loved him.

The memory was just there in the back of her mind all the time, warning her that she was vulnerable, warning her that she still found him staggeringly attractive on a purely physical level, and that something inside her which she was deeply ashamed of made her behave more outrageously around him than she would ever have dreamt of behaving around any other man. Why was that? Was there actually a part of her which rejoiced in his desire for her body? Could she be that stupid? Hurriedly, she rose from the worn wooden pew.

She was walking towards the blinding sunlight flooding through the doors when the portly little priest appeared before her. 'I am Father Tomás Garcia,' he told her in perfect English, extending a polite hand that couldn't be ignored. 'And you are Georgie, María Cristina's friend.'

Taken aback by the assurance with which that statement was made, Georgie mumbled she knew not what.

'Would you like some tea? Or possibly some lemonade? This is the hottest part of the day and I think you must be very thirsty. You are a teacher, aren't you? A fine profession, but more challenging now than it was in my time,' he remarked, accompanying her outside and turning towards the small house in the shadow of the church. 'Primary or secondary level?' he prompted with interest.

Ten minutes later, Georgie was ensconced in a comfortable armchair with a glass of lemonade, in a cluttered but sparsely furnished sitting-room, and she didn't quite know how she had got there. 'You know,' she muttered uneasily, fearing that the little priest was acting on a false assumption, 'I'm C of E.'

Father Garcia chuckled. 'I'll forgive you. You were telling me about your history course,' he reminded her.

It was over an hour before she departed, and her throat ought to have been sore from talking so much. After all, when all her years at college had been exhausted, they had somehow moved on to her family and from there to London, which her companion had visited forty years earlier and never forgotten. She was astonished by how relaxed she felt as she turned uncertainly back.

'Thanks,' she said huskily.

'For what do you thank me?' Father Garcia's sparkling brown eyes, so lively in his round, peaceful face, rested on her intently. 'It has been a very great pleasure for me to make the acquaintance of Rafael's bride-to-be.'

'*Bride*?' Georgie couldn't help it; the repetition erupted helplessly from her startled lips and even to her own ears she sounded like a cat whose tail had been trodden on.

'Fiancée?' the little priest suggested with apparently unshakeable good humour that took no note of her shock. 'That is the modern term, I suppose.'

'I'm afraid you've misunderstood,' Georgie began, in an agony of discomfiture.

'It is supposed to be a secret? But how could it be *here*?' Father Garcia's expressive eyes twinkled merrily. 'Naturally we are all excited at the prospect of Rafael's marriage.'

And off he went before Georgie could unglue her tongue from the roof of her dry mouth. Dear heaven, did Rafael have any idea of the expectations he had raised by bringing her here? Father Garcia had spoken of their marriage as though it was one centimetre short of accomplished fact, and she had only arrived yesterday! Was he aware that Rafael had once planned to marry her?

In a renewed state of turmoil, Georgie headed back to the house, but this time she was abnormally conscious of the number of smiles and inquisitive looks she received on the way. Without hesitation she went off in search of Rafael, determined to demand transport off the *estancia* again. This farce had gone far enough! He simply couldn't keep her here against her wishes!

He was on the phone in the library, which he appeared to use as an office. As she burst through the door his gleaming dark head jerked round, an expression of astonishment briefly etched on his devastatingly handsome features. Presumably nobody ever entered the inner sanctum without a knock and official permission.

'I will be with you in a moment.' It was a cool aside.

Stalking over to the window, Georgie turned her back on him and jerkily folded her arms. She listened to him talk in fast, idiomatic French, his accent and inflexion flawless. It set her teeth on edge. He was rapping out orders like the feudal autocrat that he was. When the call was concluded, she spun round.

'I hear that Father Tomás has been entertaining you——'

'The grapevine is supersonic around here, isn't it?' Georgie cut in, throwing her vibrant head back and watching him with a bright little smile pinned to her sultry mouth. 'Did your little bird also tell you that he thinks we're about to get married?'

'What an extraordinary idea,' Rafael gibed without pause, betraying not an ounce of the discomfiture she had expected to rouse. Eyes dark as Hades raked over her and his sensual mouth twisted wtih cruel amusement. 'I may have gone overboard in my lust to possess you four years ago, but you will recall that I didn't ever get as far as a proposal. In short, *querida*, men like me don't marry women like you, unless they are suffering from temporary insanity.'

The angry flush on her beautiful face slowly receded, leaving her painfully drawn.

'You see,' Rafael extended indolently, 'I first met you at a time when I was bored with the easy availability of your sex. No woman was ever a challenge. Every woman I ever wanted came to me, shared my bed, did whatever it took to try and hold my attention. I wanted to be the hunter but I never needed to exert myself——'

'I don't want to hear this!' Georgie interrupted with sudden violence.

'I want you to hear it.' Rafael lounged gracefully up against his solid antique desk and surveyed her with hooded dark eyes. 'And then, one day, I met quite unexpectedly the most stunningly beautiful girl, who blushed with enchanting regularity and looked at me with what seemed to be her every thought written in her gorgeous eyes. But this stunningly beautiful girl was untouchable by virtue of her youth. And that for me was the very essence of the romance which every other woman had been so quick in her eagerness to deny me. Don't look so staggered...remember, I was only twenty-four,' he reminded her with sardonic bite. 'And, with hindsight, not one half as clever as I liked to think I was!'

'Don't!' Georgie was disturbed by his savage self-mockery, and her nails dug painfully into her palms.

'Men always want what is out of reach. That was three-quarters of your attraction,' Rafael asserted drily. 'And as I got to know you—or believed I was getting to know you—I also discovered that you were bright, amusing and apparently outspokenly honest, a trait which for me was on a par with your beauty. Having to wait for you undoubtedly increased your desirability tenfold. I had never had to wait for anything in my life before and, while I waited, I endowed you with every conceivable virtue.'

The contempt with which he cynically dismissed what he had felt then angered and hurt Georgie. He resurrected memories of those innocent days and those memories burnt her now like acid. 'I don't believe in looking back,' she said tautly. 'It's a mistake.'

Rafael spread long brown fingers in a gesture of careless disagreement. 'I'm not so sensitive,' he drawled. 'You were a learning experience for me. Different culture, different values. I was young enough to believe that things like that didn't matter...but they do, very much.'

'Why on earth did you bring me here?' Georgie demanded shakily, denying the creeping tide of mortification consuming her.

'An overwhelming desire to punish you, and so far, I have to confess, it has been an extraordinarily satisfying experience,' Rafael murmured without remorse.

'You swine... you utter swine,' Georgie whispered in a stricken rush.

A slanting ebony brow quirked. 'But not yet quite as satisfying as I anticipate. I want you lying under me, gasping with excitement, begging for release. And after I have had you, I will be entirely satisfied. Playing this waiting game merely adds an edge.'

Without even thinking about it, Georgie hit him, the crack of her palm resoundingly loud in the smouldering silence. He didn't even flinch. The reddened mark of her fingers darkened one savage cheekbone. He snaked out a powerful arm and yanked her between his spread thighs, reading the raw apprehension flaring in her wide eyes. Incandescent gold raked over her scared face and abruptly he laughed. 'I'll take it out of your hide in bed. That's a first, Georgie. No woman has ever struck me before.'

'I hate you!' Georgie launched, with a sob of distress snatching at her raw vocal cords. 'I don't know how you can do this to me!'

'So easily, it would terrify you,' Rafael shared almost conversationally. 'In fact, I could develop quite a taste for your tears. Poor Georgie, one last dangerous impulse backed you into the tightest corner of all!' Long fingers forced up her chin, quelling her attempt to evade him. 'So impetuous, so uncontrolled... so very different from me. I was raised to be intensely disciplined, responsible, serious——'

'I'm not interested!' she spat back at him, appalled by his insight into her character. 'Let go!'

'And you panic with such naked abandon,' he murmured flatly. 'I was a bastard after breakfast, wasn't I? But then I wanted the truth——'

'But it wasn't the truth! It was what you wanted to believe!' Georgie condemned hotly. 'What you'd like to believe so that you can excuse yourself for treating me like dirt!'

Rafael laced a hard hand into her tumbling hair and tightened his fingers with painful thoroughness. 'He was your lover. I know it and, before I'm finished with you, you'll admit it,' he swore.

'For heaven's sake, I've never had a lover!' Georgie slung back at him between gritted teeth. 'And I'm sick to death of you acting like I'm some sort of raving nymphomaniac!'

'You've never had a lover?' Glittering dark eyes raked hers with pitying derision. 'Georgie... do you think I believe in those mermaids upstairs?' he asked very drily. 'Why pretend? It doesn't matter any more. But lies infuriate me.'

It was useless. She saw that and regretted her honesty. 'Please let go of me,' she muttered.

Astonishingly, he released her and Georgie backed away on cottonwool legs, trembling in spite of her efforts to control that physical weakness.

'You are ashamed of your relationship with him now,' Rafael breathed with smouldering dark golden eyes pinned contemptuously to her. 'A little too late to impress.'

'Go to hell!' she spat, her throat choked up with tears. 'I detest you!'

'But it's the wanting that hurts most, *es verdad*?' Rafael dealt her a slashing look of cruelly amused comprehension.

'I'd sooner go to bed with a—with a total stranger!'

'Oh, I'm sure you've done that at least once,' Rafael drawled with laconic certainty. 'Exclusive, you're not.'

Outraged, Georgie stalked back to him. 'Well, then, you're not very fastidious, are you?' she hissed, in a tone shaking with red-hot fury and frustration at her inability to shut him up. 'But brace yourself for disappointment, Rafael. After this morning's little honesty session, I would be certifiably insane to let you anywhere near me.'

He reached for her and she bristled like a spitting cat, ready to claw as she went into startled retreat, registering her mistaken direction only as the wall connected with her taut shoulderblades. 'I will not stand for this!' she erupted in a burst of indignation.

As Rafael closed the distance between them, an appreciative smile slashed his golden features. 'You are so much more entertaining now than you were then. Four years ago, it was, "Yes, Rafael, no, Rafael, whatever you think, Rafael," and I couldn't understand where all your spirit had gone,' he confided, bracing a hand on either side of her head. 'Of course, it was an act put on to impress. Then you were playing for high stakes. You may not have guessed what was on my mind but your goal was certainly marriage——'

'Like hell it was!' Incensed by the scathing accusation, Georgie's every muscle clenched defensively as he deliberately moved closer. 'Now, back off!'

'But that is not what you want.' Rafael lowered his dark head, veiled eyes a shimmer of hot gold on her wildly flushed face, and she was entrapped by a curious stillness, her breath locked in her constricted throat. 'What you want with every fibre of your being is to possess me as thoroughly as I intend to possess you...'

CHAPTER SIX

GEORGIE was mesmerised by the savage brilliance of Rafael's sexually explicit gaze and the ragged edge of blatant need in his dark, deep voice. The familiar musky scent of him teased at her flaring nostrils as he dropped a hand to her hip and suddenly hauled her against him. Her heart raced crazily. The hard thrust of his masculine arousal pulsed against her abdomen and then he lifted her up to him with a powerful ease that exhilarated her. For a split-second she was looking down at him and hunger tore at her with cruel claws, ripping away every proud layer of pretence.

A desperate pain pierced her then, a terrible vulnerability. In all this time, all these years, no other man had ever drawn her as he did. In the dark of the night, in the secrecy of her dreams, she had tossed and turned and craved him, and despised herself for that treacherous yearning. But now, as she clashed with devouring golden eyes and burned, she felt the answering tremor of response snaking through his magnificent physique.

His arms tightened fiercely around her and he drew her down, taking her mouth in a deep, shuddering admission of need that sent her every sense rocketing to fever-pitch. And she knew then that the power was not his alone. Wrapped round him like a vine, Georgie kissed him back with all the fire he had awakened. As his tongue penetrated between her parted lips, her nails dug into his broad shoulders, a stifled whimper of excitement escaping her.

Rafael groaned something in his own language and swept her right off her feet with bruisingly impatient hands. She captured his hard cheekbones between her palms and stared up at him with dazed eyes, out of focus with passion. He succumbed to the lure of her swollen mouth again somewhere halfway up the stairs and control seemed to go out of the window at that point, because he braced her against the wall and took her lips with a driving, demanding sexuality which reduced her to mental rubble.

'*Madre de Dios*...' he swore roughly against her throat, struggling for breath, and then he carried her up into the bedroom, tumbled her down on the bed and pinned her there with a wildly exciting lack of cool.

He wrenched his jacket and tie off and ripped at his shirt without breaking the connection of their mouths once. Her heartbeat thundered in her ears like a pulse-beat of desire. His fingers found the neckline of her cotton top and tore it down over her arms. He curved his hands over the shameless thrust of her pouting breasts and she shivered in violent reaction, helplessly arching her back to increase the pressure on her unbearably sensitive nipples.

He seized on a taut rosy crest with his teeth and the explosion of sensation he released made her cry out, her teeth gritting, her throat extending.

'*Perdición*' he groaned, lifting his arrogant dark head to look down at her as he dealt at speed with the remainder of his clothing. 'So long...I have waited so long for this.'

So long, yes, she thought intensely, reaching back up for him with the single-minded motivation of a programmed doll. A relentless hunger seized her as he sealed his virile length to hers. Her whole body flushed with consuming heat and she turned to him, driven by something much more powerful than she was, and let her hands travel through the light mat of curling black hair across his muscular chest, glorying in the freedom to touch him at last.

Raising his head, he pressed her down to the pillows again, stilling her fluttering hands, the dominant male, sentencing her back to passivity. From below ebony lashes he dealt her a wholly predatory look that made her burn and quiver. He reached down and peeled off her shorts and panties in one impatient movement. He thrust a hair-roughened thigh between hers and fanned out her hair with his fingers so that the vibrant strands surrounded her exquisite face, tumbling in a fiery cascade across the white pillows. From somewhere he had found control again and now he contemplated her with an indolent air of possession.

Georgie trembled and met that look and suddenly remembered about *this* bed, *this* room. The significance of their surroundings and the recollection of his savage desire for revenge suddenly chilled her to the marrow. 'No,' she said shakily. 'Not here——'

'*Sí* . . . it is what I want,' Rafael said softly.

'But not what I want!' Georgie suddenly gasped, the ability to think returning by degrees in dangerous little warning spurts.

'All you want is me.' Rafael evaded her attempt to drag herself free of his intimate hold and flattened her back to the mattress with his vastly superior strength. He subjected her to a wolfish appraisal, golden hawk eyes scanning her shocked and confused face with a devastatingly cruel amusement. 'Your one virtue. All you ever wanted was me from the very first moment. It wasn't the limo, it wasn't the accent and it wasn't any schoolgirl fantasy either,' he asserted. 'It was far more basic. An intense sexual desire to possess and be possessed.'

'No.' Georgie sucked in air and shook her head back and forth in urgent negative.

His thumb pried apart her lips, brushed against her teeth. 'And you can't control it... unnerving, isn't it?'

The tip of her tongue brushed of its own volition against his thumb and then withdrew sharply as he laughed. 'Is it?' she whispered.

'You tell me... Here, now, you're *mine* to do with exactly as I please.' To illustrate that raw assurance, Rafael bent his head and circled a distended pink nipple with his tongue and then his teeth, and the entire conversation was, for Georgie, plunged into some dark limbo as her swollen sensitive flesh screamed with sensation and craved more.

He took her mouth with carnal expertise, slowly, tormentingly, denying her the greater force that her every skin-cell demanded, until her hands rose and speared into his hair and she held him to her, quivering with unabated need, surrendering to the incredibly powerful urges of her own body.

His fingers roamed over her flat, taut stomach and into the damp tangle of curls at the apex of her thighs and suddenly she couldn't be still any more, suddenly she was burning alive. He explored the moist tender flesh with a knowing eroticism that made her breath sob in her throat. Nothing could have prepared her for the intensity of the pleasure or the electrifying throb of primal excitement making her hips rise in supplication. There was an ache now, an intolerable ache, building down deep inside her.

'*Cristo*... you're so tight.'

She heard him groan, but no words could connect now. Her brain had shut down. Every response she gave was instinctive and out of control. She writhed as he cupped her hips and came down on her, was suddenly stilled by forceful hands, and then she felt him, the hot thrusting hardness of his masculinity alien against her. Her eyes flew wide with an intuitive fear of the unknown and she met the pagan stamp of intense desire on his dark features above hers. Another kind of ache stirred inside her, tugging violently at her heartstrings, making her lie back in helpless submission, trembling with the force of her own need.

'*Dios* ... you feel like a virgin.'

His hand pushed her thighs wider, higher, drawing her up to receive him. He entered her with one sure thrust and the piercing pain of his intrusion took her completely by surprise.

'Georgie...' Golden eyes abruptly swept hers, a frown of incomprehension drawing his arrow-straight ebony brows together. '*No... imposible*,' he groaned, black lashes dropping low on his damp, driven features as he moved again in an instinctive surge to deepen his possession.

Her teeth sank stoically into the soft underside of her lower lip, for beyond the pain was the most extraordinary pleasure at the feel of him inside her. Intimate beyond belief. Heat flooded her in a blinding wave. She could feel the force of the control he was exerting as he thrust slowly, carefully into the very heart of her. His breathing was ragged, his sweat-slicked body sliding against her supersensitive flesh, and she threw her head back, moaning his name as the pressure began to build again unbearably.

Every new sensation was torturously intense. Her heart slammed madly against her ribcage as he began to drive into her faster, harder, with shredding control and fierce, masculine domination. The pleasure took her over, rising to a shattering crescendo that plunged her entire body into quivering, indescribable ecstasy. Above her, she felt him reach the same plateau and shudder and groan as he sank deep into her one last time.

Afterwards she was in a state of prolonged shock, still lost in the intensity of extraordinary physical response.

He lay in the circle of her arms and she liked that so much, the weight of him, the feel of him, the so familiar scent of him that when he shifted away she felt disturbingly bereft as he flopped down on the pillows beside her in the thrumming silence. Her fingers curled into fists by her sides until she conquered the terrible urge to reach back for him, for that closeness her every sense craved.

Was she crazy? a little voice asked. They were not lovers in any sense of the word. There was no relationship, no tenderness, no love. Suddenly she felt empty and cold. But everyone had the right to sin at least once in a lifetime, didn't they? And Rafael was *her* sin. Just this one time and never again. They had made love—no, they had had sex, she adjusted, her troubled face tightening as she fought off a dismaying sense of vulnerability. He had not used her any more than she had used him, she told herself fiercely. She had always wanted Rafael Rodriguez Berganza...

'I'll buy you an apartment in Paris,' Rafael murmured smoothly into the silence. 'There will be times you will be able to travel with me...if you can be discreet, but you will never be able to come here again and you will have to break off your correspondence with my sister. You will live like a princess. I will give you everything but my name.'

It was like having a knife driven into her heart. Her stomach twisted sickly. He was so unemotional. Was this what she had waited for all these years? An invitation to be his mistress? A shudder of revulsion assailed her. So he didn't use you any more than you used him? Who are you kidding, Georgie? You are not up to this, you are way out of your depth.

'Say something...anything.' Rafael leant over her without warning and skimmed a surprisingly unsteady hand over the damp tendrils of hair clinging to her brow.

The nagging ache between her thighs felt like the greatest act of treachery she could ever have committed against herself. She clashed one fleeting time with brilliant dark eyes scanning her with probing intent, and hurriedly looked away again, hating herself.

'*Madre de Dios*!' The interruption to her frantic thoughts of shame and self-reproach was explosive. 'Georgie——?'

'I need a bath,' she mumbled, not listening, still glued to the edge of the bed and struggling for the act of courage it was going to take to walk across the room naked as a jaybird. But escape was definitely a necessity.

A hand like an iron vice closed round her forearm and turned her back abruptly to face him. Rafael stared at her with fierce demand in his eyes. His rigid facial cast and the pallor below his naturally golden skin betrayed his state of shock.

'What's wrong?' she questioned.

'Tell me that doesn't mean what I think it does...' Rafael urged in a ragged undertone.

Her brow furrowed, Georgie followed the direction of his gaze and saw the bloodstain on the sheet. She was appalled. She wanted to cover it again. But it was too late. He had seen it. She just couldn't believe that her body could have let her down like that. A keen athlete from an early age, it had never occurred to her that there could possibly be any physical evidence of her lost innocence.

'You were untouched,' Rafael breathed, driving a set of long brown fingers roughly through his tousled hair.

'Don't be ridiculous!' Georgie scoffed, lifting a pillow to hug.

'Look at me.'

Her sultry mouth set in a positively vicious line of mutiny. His shaken voice told her he was on the edge of extinction by severe shock.

'You were a virgin——'

'Nonsense! Now, if you don't mind, I'd like this bed back to myself.'

Abruptly, he snatched the pillow off her and flattened her back to the mattress with two very forceful and determined hands. 'I mind... I mind very much.'

Shattered, Georgie's eyes collided with tormented dark ones that devoured her every fleeting expression. 'Will you stop looking at me like that?'

'I felt the barrier... I told myself I was crazy... I just couldn't believe it!' Rafael vented unsteadily.

'I don't know what you're talking about——'

'Stop it, Georgie,' Rafael grated rawly. 'You were a virgin!'

'Will you stop saying that?'

'Admit it.'

'OK—big deal, I don't think—you were the first, so go and notch your bloody bedpost!' Georgie shrieked back, a boiling tide of embarrassing moisture dammed up behind her eyelids.

'*Dios*...but how is it possible?' Rafael demanded with a groan.

'Just leave me alone!'

Without warning, he pulled her into his arms. She could feel the raw tension still sizzling through him. She was as rigid as a mannequin in his embrace. Seemingly impervious to that lack of encouragement, he released his breath in a hiss. 'Forgive me... can you ever forgive me for what I have done?' he muttered unevenly. 'But to make such a sacrifice to prove to me how wrong I have been... How can I ever make that up to you?'

Cursing the reality that Rafael always cornered her when she was least capable of self-defence, Georgie was attempting to fight through the absolute turmoil of her own confusion. But that final incredible statement pierced the tumult and froze her. Rafael actually believed that she had made him a gift of her inexperience simply to prove that he had been wrong about her promiscuity all along. It was the most nauseating suggestion Georgie had ever heard.

'Well, you don't need to make it up to me, because I wasn't trying to prove anything! Your opinion of me, Rafael, is absolutely immaterial to my peace of mind.'

'You cannot mean that,' Rafael said with flat disbelief.

Georgie fought out of his temporarily loosened hold and grabbed the sheet round her. 'I'm sorry, I do mean it. Such an idea never once occurred to me,' she snapped, thoroughly fed up that he just wouldn't take the hint and leave her alone with the tumultuous mess of emotion that was sloshing around inside her.

'Not *that*,' he stressed. 'You cannot mean that my opinion means nothing to you after what we have just shared.'

'Wasn't exactly a communion of souls, was it?' Georgie heard herself say snidely. 'We had sex——'

'We made love——'

'We screwed,' Georgie broke in, determined to have the last word.

'Don't talk like that!' Outraged golden eyes raked over her.

'Oh, is that one of those expressions which you're allowed to use and I'm not? Tough,' Georgie muttered tightly, pleating the sheet between her fingers, recognising that she was hopelessly engulfed in bitterness. 'I really can't understand why you're going on like this about something so trivial.'

Long fingers curved round her arms, dragging her round to face him. 'After all that has happened between us, how could it possibly be trivial?' he demanded savagely.

'Not many women go to the grave virgins. For heaven's sake, I'm twenty-three and I just thought it was time...

Well, to be honest, I didn't think at all,' Georgie adjusted with essential honesty. 'But if I had realised there was going to be a heavy post-mortem, I wouldn't have bothered, I can tell you that!'

'You're upset, embarrassed...I am spoiling everything,' he breathed starkly.

'You generally do when you open your mouth. I ought to be used to it by now.'

'My conscience...it is eating me alive,' he confessed tightly, reaching for one of her tightly clenched hands and smoothing out the small fingers. 'I have hurt you so much. You tried to defend yourself four years ago and I wouldn't listen to you. Why won't you look at me? Why won't you speak?'

'I'll probably be a bit more slick the next time I have a one-night stand,' Georgie bit out acidly, but she could hear the tremor in her own voice, the thickness of tears she was holding back. She snatched her hand back.

'There won't be a next time.'

No, he was right there. Nothing like learning the hard way, Georgie! Do you ever learn any other way? The last thing she needed was Rafael's guilt. It made her want to scream and claw at him. She had her pride, like anyone else, but it seemed to her that he was set on depriving her of even that. The past was past. She had no desire to reopen that particular Pandora's box.

Or the even more recent past. All that shameless rolling about and moaning she had done for his benefit—well, that was so far in the past that it was pre-civilisation as far as she was concerned. The worst mistake of her life. He treated her like dirt beneath his aristocratic feet and she rewarded him by falling into bed with him. A single tear rolled down her cheekbone, stinging her tender skin on its passage.

'*Querida*...please...please don't cry,' Rafael groaned. 'Anything you want, anything it takes, I will make it up to you...'

'A flight to La Paz.' Escape. That was all that was on Georgie's mind.

'That isn't what you really want,' Rafael assured her with harsh emphasis.

And that was the last straw. Georgie looked at him, her facial muscles stiff with pure rage. 'How the hell would you know what *I* want?'

He slung her a thwarted look, raw with a kind of incredulous frustration, and sprang off the bed to stride into the bathroom.

Georgie flopped back down again. 'Good riddance,' she muttered out loud.

Then she rolled over and buried her convulsing face furiously into the tumbled pillows. Why wouldn't he just leave her alone? Didn't he have his own bathroom? She reined the sobs back, wouldn't cry, wouldn't have cried if he'd held her upside-down over a bonfire and tortured her. Making an outsize fool of herself once in one day was enough.

This was the end of something that had started four years ago—no, six years ago, when she had first laid eyes on Rafael Rodriguez Berganza. A terrifying obsession which had grown out of a teenage infatuation. It was finished now. The act of sex had finished it forever. But what a shame it was that she had to sacrifice her friendship with María Cristina on the same funeral pyre.

For she would have no other choice. The last connection had to be severed. There would be no more letters bearing continuous little snippets of information about Rafael... Sometimes Rafael's sister had written so much about him that Georgie had wondered if her friend's own life was so empty that she had nothing better to write about. On the face of it, what possible interest could Georgie have been supposed to have in Rafael's travels, his speeches and his business interests, with never an indiscreet word about the women in his life?

But those letters, she appreciated, had kept Rafael alive inside her mind and her memory. Well, she needed to go on with her life and leave him behind her where he belonged, and she couldn't possibly do that and still stay in touch with María Cristina! Her throat thickened with renewed bitterness.

In the midst of her turmoil, Georgie was scooped without warning off the bed. 'What are you doing?'

'I ran a bath for you.'

'Why?' Georgie demanded baldly.

'Because it would appear to be about the only thing I can currently do that might be right,' Rafael delivered shortly, whipped off the sheet which had been wrapped round her and slid her into the warm water before she knew what was happening to her.

In silence, Georgie hugged her knees, dead centre of the splendid marble bath, her tumbled head downbent as she stared blindly down into the water.

'As God is my witness, I will kill him,' Rafael intoned with a murderous quietness that was somehow explosive in the charged silence.

'Kill who?' she mumbled without much interest, too caught up in her own stark sense of failure and inadequacy.

'Nobody important,' Rafael murmured smoothly.

'I want to go home,' she said tightly.

'I thought you wanted to see María Cristina and...and George.'

Astonishment held her taut and then drifted away again. Nothing like a rousing dose of guilt for the Latin conscience, she reflected. 'No.'

'*No*?' Rafael repeated, his disbelief at the careless denial palpable.

'No,' she said again.

'Why? No, forget I asked...' Rafael urged in abrupt retreat.

Later she didn't know how long she had sat there before she mechanically washed and then dried herself, and padded back to the bedroom. The sheet had been changed. Her cheeks burned. Marvellous, now everybody would know! Well, that was it. She wasn't budging out of this bedroom until he had that flight arranged! Donning a nightdress with shaking hands, Georgie got back into bed, great rolling breakers of misery submerging her.

Now—now, why didn't she bring it out and face it? Just when had she fallen in love with Rafael? Six years ago, four years ago or just yesterday? Did the timing really matter? He had turned away from her after slaking his lust. Then, she had suspected herself but, by the time he got around to suggesting the life of a kept woman in Paris, suspicion had become painful fact. That had been the final humiliation. To love a man who had caused her this much pain was insanity.

Pride, self-interest and intelligence ruled against loving a complete bastard. But the fact of the matter was that she *did* love him, could still hate him with unvarnished energy and passion when he hurt or angered her, but underneath all that was the love and this truly paralysing longing to be loved back. It terrified her. What had he ever done to be worthy of her love? Nothing, not a single damned thing!

She fell asleep and was wakened by a tiny sound. Startled, she sat up, saw Rafael standing over her and visibly flinched, her natural colour draining away.

'I brought you up some dinner...you were asleep at lunchtime,' he proffered tautly.

Georgie was stunned. Rafael with a tray. As unnatural a sight as Rafael up to his elbows in a sink full of dishes.

He looked a little rough too, a blue shadow darkening his strong jawline, harsh lines of strain between his arrogant nose and hard mouth. His tie was loose at his brown throat, a couple of buttons on his shirt undone, revealing a whorl of black, curling hair.

She dragged her uncertain eyes from him. 'Thanks,' she said woodenly.

He strolled round to the foot of the brass bed and closed his brown hands round the top rail. 'I explained to Teresa that you had been taken ill . . . and——' he hesitated '—I changed the bed,' he added in a strained undertone.

He had changed the bed. What the heck was going on here? Why was he behaving in this weird way? She was willing to bet that Rafael had never changed a bed in his life before. Of course, he was hiding the evidence. She suddenly wished she were a corpse. Now, that would have given him a real challenge to get his teeth into, the sort of challenge he really deserved. She just bet she was on a flight home tomorrow.

'We need to talk,' he drawled, when it became painfully obvious that Georgie was not about to break the silence.

'No.' She didn't even lift her head.

'Then I will talk and you will listen.'

'You could have nothing to say that I could possibly want to hear.'

A lean hand abruptly slashed through the air in a raking gesture of raw impatience. 'I make no excuses for my behaviour over the past forty-eight hours. I must have been out of my mind,' he admitted in a driven undertone. 'I abandoned every principle. I behaved dishonourably. I went off the rails for the very first time in my life and it has been a sobering experience. I deeply regret everything which has happened between us.'

Georgie's appetite had vanished. She surveyed the exquisitely arranged meal through swimming eyes. She was
suffering from this truly appalling urge to leap out of
bed and put her arms round him. Lord, but she had it
bad! Here he was practically on his knees and she didn't
even have the gumption to feel any sense of vindicated
satisfaction. He had insulted her, threatened her, deprived her of her freedom, and now he was saying sorry
in the only way he could. And since humility came about
as naturally to Rafael as walking on water would come
to her, she knew exactly what this approach had to be
costing him in terms of pride.

'Fine. Apology accepted,' she said with forced
lightness.

'That is very generous of you.'

It suddenly occurred to her that, in giving way to her
shell-shocked emotions earlier, she had been childishly
self-indulgent. They had made love, a development she
now saw as inevitable. And Rafael had not swept her
off to bed without her enthusiastic encouragement. She
forced her head up, dealing him a glance from beneath
thick copper lashes, and shrugged a narrow shoulder.
'Least said, soonest mended,' she dismissed, quoting her
late grandmother.

Lustrous dark eyes rested on her with incisive intensity. 'You are taking this very well!'

I'll be out of here tomorrow.

'Why not?' Georgie contrived another shrug, even
managed a faint smile, and felt immensely proud of
herself until she realised that she was finding it incredibly hard to drag her gaze from his darkly handsome
features. Memory roamed relentlessly back a few hours
and a surge of heat dampened her skin, interfered with
her breathing and sent her heartbeat into shameless acceleration. In bed, he was her every fantasy fulfilled,

and the instant that thought came to her she drowned in self-loathing.

'*Bueno.*' Rafael expelled his breath in a hiss. Tension sizzled from his stance in palpable waves. From the foot of the bed he watched her, his magnificent physique visibly taut. His hard jawline clenched, a tiny pulse tugging at the corner of his unsmiling mouth.

The silence smouldered. Georgie fingered a prawn off her starter and munched defiantly at it, her cheeks still hot as hellfire from her last thought.

'Then allow me the very great honour of asking you to become my wife,' Rafael breathed, with an abruptness that brutally shattered the tense silence.

CHAPTER SEVEN

HALFWAY to success in pursuit of a second luscious prawn, Georgie stilled and looked up, met shimmering golden eyes fiercely pinned to her. She tried and failed to swallow. Her wide violet gaze clung to him in rampant disbelief.

'I'm an angel now,' she whispered in shock.

'*Que*?' Rafael stared darkly back at her.

'You're not serious?' Georgie framed weakly.

'I have already spoken to Father Tomás.'

Georgie blinked rapidly at the calm announcement. 'You've *what*?'

'Or if you would prefer I could contact an English minister I am acquainted with in La Paz.'

Numbly, Georgie shook her head. Rafael gazed steadily back at her, impervious, it seemed, to her disbelief. She drew in a slow, shaky breath, her heart thumping noisily in her eardrums. 'I just don't believe I'm hearing this... You don't want to marry me!'

'Had I had more faith in you four years ago, we would already have been man and wife,' Rafael drawled in a tone of finality.

'But that's got nothing to do with *now*.'

'Georgie... I want to marry you.'

Georgie dragged unwillingly fascinated eyes from his forceful gaze and sighed heavily. 'When you said we were from different cultures, you weren't joking. I suppose you think you *have* to marry me because—well—because we slept together.'

'I want the right to share that bed with you every night,' Rafael murmured softly.

Her skin warmed. She didn't question the overwhelmingly strong attraction between them but she sincerely doubted that in any other circumstances it would have prompted Rafael to offer marriage after making love to her. He was feeling guilty. Rafael, who prided himself on his principles, his sense of honour and his excellent judgement, had just weathered the discovery that he was human after all. Not perfect, not without flaw... and both his manner and his appearance told her just how savaging that revelation had been.

So here he was now, offering the only reparation he could. Marriage. He would marry her because he had slept with her. He would marry her because he had been her first lover. And perhaps he would also marry her because he had already told her that that had been his intent four years ago. Not for any other reasons. Not because any romanticised view of her lingered from the past. No such illusions could remain after what Rafael had believed about her for so long. But, regardless of all that, Rafael would force himself to make the ultimate sacrifice. He believed that he *owed* her that wedding-ring. For a split-second she felt so corrosively bitter that it physically hurt to breathe.

'We're just not suited,' Georgie muttered. 'But I do appreciate the thought.' It was a lie. Suddenly she hated him for his precious code of honour and decency, light-years away from the values of the more liberated society in which she had been raised. Such a proposal was no compliment. 'Thanks, but no thanks.'

'It wasn't just a thought,' Rafael rebutted tautly.

'No, I expect it took a lot of macho courage for you to ask a woman you don't like and don't respect to become your wife,' Georgie responded, equally tautly.

'But the point is, I don't want to marry you anyway, so it wasn't necessary.'

'That is not how I regard you now.' His retort was level. 'I made a very grave error of judgement four years ago——'

A knife-edged laugh was torn from Georgie. 'An error of judgement!' she repeated helplessly, and looked heavenward, unable to escape the recollection of how badly she had been hurt by the fall-out.

A dark rise of blood had accentuated his high cheek-bones, but he held her evasive gaze unflinchingly. 'Think of it from my point of view——'

'*Your* point of view?' she gasped incredulously.

'I knew that Steve did not look on you as a sister. I was aware that he was sexually attracted to you——'

Georgie threw her head back, her disgust unhidden. 'Are you still trying to twist the facts? That night, when Steve suddenly grabbed me and kissed me, he had had too much to drink. He was upset because he had had a row with his girlfriend. It was just one of those stupid, crazy things that people do sometimes on impulse and it meant nothing!'

Rafael dealt her a slashing glance. 'You only see what you want to see, Georgie...'

'And what's that supposed to mean?'

His expressive mouth flattened into a compressed white line. 'Steve,' he breathed tautly. 'You still love him as a brother, as a member of your family?'

Georgie frowned, unable to understand his need to state the obvious. 'Naturally, we're close. Why wouldn't we be?' she demanded.

Rafael was very still, his dark features oddly tense and austere as he studied her. There was a long pause. Then he shrugged a shoulder with a grim air of finality. 'When I saw you in his arms, how do you think I felt?'

Georgie compressed her lips. She was a little surprised by his continuing hostility towards her stepbrother in spite of the fact that he now knew the truth. Didn't he now appreciate that he had misjudged Steve just as badly as he had misjudged her? Then, no doubt, Rafael still blamed Steve for that stupid kiss he had witnessed. 'I expect you were as taken aback seeing it as I was when it happened,' she conceded grudgingly.

'I was in love with you!' Rafael bit out with raw emphasis, and her head jerked up, her eyes widening. ' "Taken aback" does not begin to describe my feelings that night or the following day!'

'I find it very hard to believe that you loved me,' she admitted.

'Don't be more stupid than you can help!' Rafael slung her a glittering golden glance of exasperation. 'For what other reason would I have wanted to marry you?'

She swallowed hard. The idea that he had loved her four years ago merely piled on the agony. If he had loved her, he hadn't trusted her, and he had walked away without a backward glance. 'Well, it doesn't really matter now, does it?'

'So you keep telling me.'

'We've got nothing more to say to each other.'

'Another platitude,' Rafael derided, a gathering storm of anger lightening his gaze to gold. 'And what platitude will you employ if you find that you are carrying my child in a few weeks? Are we all to be treated to the "Oops, gosh, I didn't think" response that you seem to believe covers every eventuality?'

Georgie stared back at him, pale as death.

Rafael absorbed her stunned response with grim eyes. 'No, I didn't protect you. An inexcusable omission, but in all that excitement the risk only crossed my mind for one second, and I foolishly assumed that you would still be on the contraceptive pill. The look on your face tells me you are not . . . and why should you have been?' he demanded with a sardonic edge. 'You had no reason to take such a precaution.'

Georgie licked at her dry lips in a flickering motion, briefly lost in a stricken vision of single parenthood, unemployment and family horror. Then her fevered imagination steadied as she performed some frantic calculations as to the date of her last period, but there was no great comfort to be found there. Whether she liked it or not, there was a slight risk of pregnancy. Not a large risk, she hurriedly consoled herself—at least, she didn't think so.

'It's not very likely,' she asserted breathlessly.

'But not impossible?'

'Nothing's impossible, but I would say the chances are probably slim to none.'

'The eternal optimist.' Rafael slung her a scathing smile and then he asked her bluntly when exactly she could expect to know whether or not she was pregnant.

'That's none of your——'

'If you're pregnant, it will be very much my business,' he cut in drily.

Tight-mouthed, she obliged the information.

'I would say computing a risk factor of slim to none is suicidally optimistic,' he returned drily. 'And I have no intention of waiting to find out!'

Exhausted by all the stress, Georgie sighed. Suddenly she understood another motivation behind his stated desire to marry her. The mere threat of a Berganza being born on the metaphorical wrong side of the blanket was a shattering one for a male of Rafael's breeding. And it was typical of him to look only on the darkest side of the equation. Where Georgie instinctively expected not to be further punished for her recklessness by an unplanned pregnancy, Rafael probably expected triplets.

'God couldn't be so cruel,' she mumbled helplessly.

'Every child is a gift from God,' Rafael asserted with ferocious bite. 'That is why we will get married as soon as possible.'

A hysterical giggle lodged like a giant stone in Georgie's throat. 'I went to bed with you. I didn't sign my whole life away!'

'It was my fault. I seduced you.'

Georgie's sensitive stomach heaved and she looked at him with incredulous eyes. 'Women of my age don't get seduced—revolting word,' she grimaced. 'I take responsibility for my own actions.'

'But you're dangerously impulsive. You always were.'

Incensed by the unwelcome seed of reality to that assessment, Georgie stiffened defensively. 'Fortunately, I'm not impulsive enough to agree to a marriage which neither one of us wants! I'm not wrecking my life over one stupid mistake!'

'It is a mistake which you will have to learn to live with,' Rafael told her, striding towards the door, his hard-edged profile unyielding.

'In a pig's eye, I will!' Georgie launched back at him. 'And don't think you can bully me into changing my mind.'

The door flipped shut. She slumped back on the pillows. He had proposed to her, which was rather a joke. After all, he had already embarked on arrangements for a wedding! Typical Rafael. He always ran a one-horse race. And presumably he had expected her to rush breathlessly into agreement. But he knew she had loved him four years ago, was undoubtedly aware that she would have married him like a shot had he asked her then.

Like any girl, she had dreamt about marrying the man she loved. But that was then . . . and this was now, when she was a whole lot older and wiser. Rafael was not in love with her. She found it so hard to believe that he had *ever* loved her, so icily controlled had he been at their final meeting. Wouldn't a man in love have raged and stormed at her in bitter fury and jealousy? Or were such base but supremely human emotions beneath Rafael and the self-discipline he prided himself on?

She remembered that last meeting in his apartment so well.

Rafael had been ice while she did all the humiliating things he had reminded her of just yesterday. She *had* wept and begged. She *had* pleaded with him to listen to her. She *had* begged him not to leave her. Why had she gone to such lengths without the smallest encouragement to do so?

She had been passionately in love with him, and what Rafael had believed he had interrupted at Danny's apartment had been so ludicrous. Then, of course, she had not been aware that Rafael had also seen Steve kissing her. And naturally she would not have referred to that embarrassing slip of Steve's. She had calmed down by then, was very fond of her stepbrother and, if family loyalty hadn't kept her quiet, discomfiture over that embrace certainly would have done. Looking back, it merely seemed a silly storm in a teacup. It would never have occurred to her that Rafael could have seen them.

When she woke up the next morning, she pulled on jeans and a tailored white shirt with roll-back cuffs. No more games. There was no longer any need for games in the cause of self-defence. There was a need for calm and common sense. Presumably Rafael, a decent interval after all that positively gothic talk about honour and principles, would now be calmer and more reasonable too.

But, as she descended the stairs, her carefully prepared cool was instantly smashed by Rafael's appearance in the hall. He was dressed for riding in skin-tight beige breeches and a black polo shirt. Every superbly fit line of his gorgeous body was smoothly delineated, his lazy stride laced with an utterly unselfconscious animal sensuality. Quite simply, his sheer physical impact stopped her in her tracks. Lean, mean and magnificent. Her mouth ran dry.

'*Buenos días, querida.*' Bracing a polished leather boot on the bottom step, Rafael treated her to a raking, overwhelmingly male appraisal which made her skin heat. 'Do you still ride?'

'Only a handful of times since I went to college. I couldn't afford it.'

'It isn't a skill you forget. I'll take you out with me tomorrow.' Somehow he contrived to make the invitation sound as intimate as a siesta in a double bed.

Georgie tensed. 'I won't be here tomorrow.'

'You think not?' Reaching out, he tugged her forward in one smooth motion and encircled her in his arms. Still standing a step higher, Georgie found herself facing him levelly.

'Rafael . . . no!' she gasped feverishly.

He penetrated her anxiously parted lips with his tongue and she shuddered, electrified by the intense eroticism of his opening assault.

'Closer,' he urged, his breath fanning her cheek, smouldering golden eyes burning down into hers as his hands cupped the swell of her buttocks and lifted her into intimate connection with the hard thrust of his arousal. '*Sí* . . . like *that* . . .'

He crushed her mouth under his and she was electrified by the hunger which leapt into response inside her. Keen and fierce as a knife, that voracious hunger cleaved through her flesh. Her breasts swelled and ached and her nipples pinched into painfully sensitive points. She arched her back like a sensuous cat, desperate for more sensation, her head thrown back, her hands wound round his neck.

'If you had been in my bed when I woke up, I wouldn't be suffering this way. I would be satisfied,' Rafael murmured huskily, rubbing an abrasive cheek intimately against the tender skin of her throat and then reaching up teasingly to tug at her ear-lobe with sharp teeth, and if he hadn't been holding her up at that point she honestly believed she would have folded into quivering female surrender at his feet. By that stage, her entire body was on fire.

'Ah . . . we have company.' Swinging her down off the step and turning, Rafael lowered her to the floor, but kept his arms linked round her, her spine welded to the warm, hard wall of his chest.

'Company?' Georgie echoed dazedly.

'Allow me to introduce you to my father's eldest sister, Tía Paola. I know she will want you to address her as one of the family.'

Georgie's gaze fell on a beaming, plump little woman with white hair and twinkling dark eyes. In spite of her shock that Rafael should be entertaining unexpected visitors, and relatives at that, she found herself smiling back. Tía Paola had that kind of face. She moved forward to clasp Georgie's hands warmly and murmur a greeting.

'And, of course, Tía's ward—Beatriz Herrera León.' Georgie's attention was drawn by the young woman coming down the stairs towards them, a tall designer-clad brunette of quite stunning looks and presence. Liquid dark eyes regarded her with faint amusement as the introduction was performed. And, all of a sudden, Georgie felt horribly aware of her casual clothing, swollen mouth and thoroughly mussed hair.

'I am very pleased to meet you, Señorita Morrison,' Beatriz said with cool formality.

'Miss León,' Georgie murmured.

'Your *novia* is very beautiful, Rafael.' The brunette's gracious smile embraced both of them but her eyes remained cold as charity.

'*Novia*?' Georgie parroted, that being one of the very few Spanish words she was familiar with, thanks to María Cristina. It meant bride or fiancée.

Rafael's arms tightened around her. 'Excuse me, we have some calls to make before breakfast.'

Georgie was dragged—there was no other word for it—into Rafael's library. He closed the door and swung round to survey her with hooded dark eyes.

'*Novia*?' Georgie said again, an entire octave higher.

'Tía Paola has arrived to act as your chaperon.'

Hands on hips, Georgie stared back at him, aghast. 'My *what*?'

'Whatever happens now, I naturally wish to safeguard your reputation. My family is very traditional,' Rafael drawled without apology. 'In bringing you here alone, I compromised you. Tía's presence will silence any adverse comment.'

Georgie pushed an unsteady hand through her mass of vibrant hair. 'They think I'm going to marry you, don't they?'

'You will,' Rafael responded with complete conviction.

'I told you last night that I wouldn't even consider it!' Georgie stalked across the room in turmoil, raw tension edging every bitten-out word. She spun back to him. 'And I'm not likely to change my mind. All you're going to do is embarrass yourself with your family.'

'Not at all. If no wedding takes place, they will sigh and say I've wriggled off the hook yet again——'

'Make a habit of that, do you?' Georgie couldn't resist stabbing.

'I have never raised expectations I had no intention of fulfilling.'

Once you raised mine. But she didn't say it. The biting pain still lingered, and with it a tortured vulnerability. She felt torn in two. One half of her, what she deemed to be the intelligent half, desperately wanted to go home to sanity, but the other half of her was savaged by the sure knowledge that she would never see Rafael again.

'I won't marry you,' she said stonily.

'I want you more than any woman alive,' Rafael intoned with a wine-dark harshness underlying his accented drawl. 'Your beauty glows like a vibrant flame in this dim room. You look at me with those passionately expressive violet eyes and that enticing sultry mouth and I burn for you. If such hunger isn't a basis for marriage, what is?'

A quiver ran through her slender length. The hair at the nape of her neck prickled. The very sound of his voice could make her ache. In the smouldering silence, the tension was suffocating. Sex, she thought in shame, as her breasts stirred in response beneath her cotton bra. Every skin-cell in her treacherous body was poised on the peak of anticipation.

'It's not enough for me,' she said jerkily, lifting her chin, forcing back a response she despised.

Blazing golden eyes clashed with hers, and for an instant she couldn't move, couldn't breathe, couldn't even think straight. He was lounging on the corner of his desk, as terrifyingly beautiful as a hungry tiger, ready to spring. Her heart clenched. The fierce primal power of him sprang out at her in an aggressive wave. Last night's humility hadn't survived to greet the dawn. The driving force of his strong will was stamped in every hard bronzed feature.

'I could make it enough,' he asserted.

But I would be the lover, not the loved. Her pride could not tolerate that mortifying image. A flush ran up beneath her magnolia-perfect skin. She would be the toy in his bed, just another possession to a male already bountifully blessed with life's richest possessions. She saw how his natural arrogance had altered the reasoning she had believed she understood mere hours earlier. Forget the reparation angle! Rafael was now telling her that he was freely choosing to marry her for the sexual pleasure he expected her to give him.

Maybe that had been what he called love four years ago. Desire. A desire honed to a fine lustful edge by her youthful unavailability when they had first met. Hadn't he admitted that himself? That he had never had to wait for anything he wanted before? And she hadn't distinguished herself by making him wait this time, had she? No, she had been an easy conquest, betrayed by passion and need and love. And, if she married Rafael, she would betray herself over and over again in his bed until self-loathing spread through her like a cancer.

Almost clumsily she folded her arms, as if to hold in the fiery emotions surging up inside her. 'No,' she said again, her voice taut with unbearable strain.

'And will you be able to live with that choice?' Rafael asked in a velvet-soft purr of enquiry. 'For I will certainly marry someone in the near future. I am of an age to want a wife and a family.'

Georgie turned deathly white. That one casually cruel statement was like a knife thudding into her unprotected breast.

Rafael held her darkened violet eyes with savage amusement twisting in his hard mouth. 'Sometimes, I am a primitive bastard, *es verdad*? But you're taxing my patience. Every jealous, possessive bone in that exquisite body of yours revolts at the mere idea of me marrying another woman——'

'*No!*' she gasped strickenly, shattered by his instinctive cruelty and the cool insight which had made him use that particular weapon against her.

Rafael lifted his handsome dark head and angled a sizzling smile over her. 'Had we more time at our disposal, I would have been more diplomatic, more sensitive——'

'You arrogant swine!' she shot from between gritted teeth.

'I will not allow your need to punish me to come between us.' Eyes black as night surveyed her impenetrably from below lush ebony lashes. 'Nor will I crawl. Remember this, *querida* you were not the only one to suffer four years ago, you were not the only one whose pride and emotions were injured...'

Georgie stiffened, deeply disturbed by the assertion. Honesty forced her to admit that she had been less than generous in her ability to see those events from his side of the fence. But then, deep down inside, she still believed that if Rafael had really cared about her he would have betrayed his emotions more and he would at least have *tried* to listen to her. Was that so unreasonable? And what did it matter now, anyway? she asked herself with helpless bitterness. Even if he had loved her then, to the best of his seemingly limited ability, he wasn't in love with her now. If it wasn't for the sizzling animal sexuality he emitted as naturally as some men simply breathed, Rafael wouldn't be half so keen to marry her.

'Breakfast,' he sighed with sudden impatience.

Only as he straightened and moved forward did Georgie see what reposed on his desk. She darted forward, an exclamation on her lips. 'My bag!'

'*Sí* ... I had informed the hotel manager of your loss. The driver returned the bag to your hotel and it was conveyed here late last night with my guests. Check the contents.'

Georgie was already in the midst of doing so. Her passport was there... and so was her money. She went weak with relief.

'Most people prefer the—er—convenience of travellers' cheques,' Rafael remarked.

'I just didn't have time to get them before the flight out...OK?' Georgie demanded with belligerence. 'I want to give that cab-driver a reward——'

'It's already taken care of.'

'I'm sorry I called him a thief,' Georgie muttered.

'He may well have been tempted, but the fear that you would describe him, and might even have the registration of his cab, may have influenced him. Who knows?' Rafael returned with rich cynicism.

Georgie drew in a deep, sustaining breath and lifted her head. 'There's no problem now. I can go home...'

'But before you leave I will naturally demand the certainty that you are not carrying my child,' Rafael decreed, his beautifully shaped mouth compressing into a forbidding line. 'And you cannot give me that assurance yet.'

Frustrated fury hurtled through her. 'Last night, you admitted that you regretted everything you had done!'

'That does not mean I now give you the freedom to behave with the foresight of a five-year-old,' Rafael delivered with sardonic bite.

Rage roared through Georgie in a blinding, seething surge. Her hands clenched into fists by her sides. 'Don't you dare put me down like that! I didn't ask to come here! I wanted nothing to do with you!'

'Then why when you woke up in that cell did you look at me with such hunger?' Rafael sliced back with indolent cool.

'I did not look at you like that!' Georgie seethed in outrage.

'And maybe you don't recall smirking and flexing those truly fabulous legs like offensive weapons on the drive back to La Paz either?'

'I do not *smirk*...and if you can't keep your lousy libido under control, that is not my problem!' she practically spat back.

'You got exactly the effect you wanted. I was ignoring you and you didn't like it.'

'How dare you say that?'

'Four years ago, you were exactly the same. A natural-born tease——'

'You bastard!' Georgie was so outraged that she could hardly get the words out.

'If I ended up with the wrong impression, ask yourself how much the act you put on for my benefit contributed,' Rafael retorted drily. 'If any teenage daughter of mine tried to walk out of the door on a date in a plunge neckline with a pelmet-length skirt, suspenders and an ankle chain, I'd paddle her backside!'

'I was trying to look sophisticated, you insensitive toad!' Her voice quivered with a mortification which merely increased her fury. 'I suppose you'd have found me more exciting if I'd been covered from throat to toe like a nun!'

'You would certainly have been more presentable in public. And less confusing in private,' Rafael completed in a strained undertone, his starkly handsome features taut with an amalgam of emotions she was too angry to read.

Georgie had worked herself up to such a pitch of ungovernable fury that she was beyond speech. Snatching at her bag, throwing him a splintering purple glare of sheer loathing, she headed for the door.

'Georgie...' Rafael murmured very softly to her rigid back, 'if you treat my aunt to a temperamental display, you will discover that my temper is far more dangerous than your own.'

Her teeth actually ground together. The note of cool warning in that assurance nearly sent her into orbit.

Without turning her head, she walked out of the room, across the hall and out of the house. Another minute, another single minute in contact with that hateful tongue of his and she would have been up for murder! Aflame with rage, she stalked across the beautiful gardens like a tigress on the prowl.

He had no right to keep her here against her wishes! With flaring eyes, she shot a glance at the bare helicopter landing-pad and stalked on. There had to be some other way off the *estancia*. Family and guests arrived by air. What about everybody else? On horseback . . . on foot . . . or on four wheels? Her attention fell on the four-wheel-drive parked over beside a couple of other toughly designed vehicles. Well, well, well, she thought, glancing around the vast deserted asphalt expanse surrounding her.

Obviously there was somewhere to go out there on four wheels. Strolling over, Georgie glanced in and saw the keys in the ignition. It took her one split-second to make her decision. Her only other hope of escape was making a scene in the presence of Rafael's aunt, and she was very reluctant to subject that sweet little old lady to the shocking revelation that her nephew was virtually imprisoning his supposed *novia* on the *estancia*.

Sliding into the driver's seat, Georgie wasted no more time. Rafael could send her clothes on after her, and if he didn't bother, escape would still be coming cheap at the price. She had her money and her passport and that was all she required. The engine fired and she checked the petrol-gauge. The tank was full and there was a bottle full of water lying on the floor in front of the passenger seat. She drove off down the asphalt lane with an almost crazed sense of release exploding inside her, her palms damply gripping the leather steering-wheel.

The lane came to an end only a mile out, but the lie of the ground in all directions as far as the purple snow-

capped Cordillera mountains in the distance was flat and
would provide no problems for a four-wheel-drive. Even
so, the lush grass of the savannah provided a less smooth
surface than she had expected and, where it was broken
up by scrubland, the going was even rougher, but Georgie
was nothing if not persistent.

The heat was intense, even with the air-conditioning
running full blast. Perspiration ran down between her
breasts and her lower body felt stifled in the jeans she
was wearing. The very occasional tree was all that interrupted the monotony of the landscape. A sense of her
own isolation began to creep over her. She stopped to
moisten her dry mouth and only when she had tilted the
bottle back did she discover that what she had gaily assumed to be water was, in fact, some form of tonsil-
searing alcohol. Choking, tears springing to her eyes,
she threw the bottle aside in disgust.

So far, her assumption that there had to be some form
of settlement within a couple of hours' drive of the
estancia had yet to be fulfilled. She kept a careful eye
on the petrol-gauge. If she didn't hit somewhere soon,
she would be forced to turn back and the realisation
galled her, flattening her foot down more heavily on the
accelerator. Then, far to her left, she saw a clump of
trees and something pink shimmering . . . a rooftop?

Damn, damn, damn, she thought a little while later,
watching the graceful flock of pink flamingos round the
lagoon take flight in a gorgeous spray of heady colour
against the deep blue sky. It was the most beautiful sight
and, even in the mood Georgie was in, she responded
to that beauty. Killing the engine, because she was in
severe need of a break, she slid out into the enveloping
heat, flexing her stiff muscles and tugging her shirt out
of her jeans in a vain attempt to cool off.

She was going to have to turn back. Rage had been
dissipated by exertion. Another one up to you, Rafael,

she reflected in raw frustration, strolling towards the shore of the lagoon. The water shimmered like a spun-glass enticement. She was so hot... Then something shifted in the corner of her eye.

'Oh, my lord...' Georgie watched what she had dimly taken for a floating log metamorphose into a big, ugly alligator heading her way. Her stomach heaved with a kind of sick, terrified fascination and then instinct shifted her frozen limbs and she ran like a maniac back to the car.

'You can keep the local wildlife, Rafael,' she mumbled, winding up the window as the creature was joined by another, their horrible little stumpy legs beginning to plough through the grass.

Without any further ado, she turned the car and started back. She had been driving about an hour when the engine began to make unhealthy spluttering sounds. Within a mile the vehicle coughed to a final halt, and none of her efforts could get it going again. The heat built around her and she was forced to take another swig of the noxious brew in the bottle. Liquid was liquid, she reasoned.

The emptiness of the savannah was surreal. It would have been terrifying had Georgie not had such immense faith in Rafael, who would find her if only out of a need to strangle her with his bare hands. She rested her head back, breathing shallowly, and waited miserably to be rescued. Another hour went by on leaden feet. Her optimism took a sudden dip on the recollection that the helicopter hadn't been at the *estancia* and finding her without aerial reconnaissance might be like looking for a needle in a haystack.

Better wed than dead, she thought, staggering out of the inferno-like heat of the car interior when she could bear it no longer. Severe sunburn as opposed to suffo-cation—not a lot of choice there. It was his fault. He had driven her to this. He had made her desperate. And yet what real effort had she made to escape before now?

Had she lifted the phone beside her bed to call Steve, who was almost certainly home again by now? Had she contacted the British Embassy? Had she tried to bribe his helicopter pilot? Had she thrown herself on Father Garcia's mercy? No, she had rolled back to Rafael like a homing pigeon...and gone to bed with him. At no stage, she realised numbly, had she made a single realistic attempt to free herself. Until now, and then it had taken naked rage to push her to the attempt.

In the shadow of the car, she sank down on the scrubby grass. When she first saw the speck on the shimmering horizon, she thought it was a bird, undoubtedly of the vulture variety, scenting a banquet. Then she realised it was a horse and rider. On a slope, they briefly stilled, silhouetted against the skyline. It was Rafael. She *knew* it, *felt* it in her bones.

Nobody else but Rafael could possibly look that good on a horse. A big black Arabian, which ploughed across the rolling plain with power, stamina and extraordinary natural beauty. Her heart rushed up into her torturously dry mouth. And I said no, she thought, deliriously impressionable as sheer relief washed over her.

CHAPTER EIGHT

GEORGIE rose shakily upright. The stallion thundered to a halt, reined back with powerful ease twenty feet from her. Incandescent golden eyes smouldered over her hot, crumpled length, patently checking out her physical condition. Rafael dug out a two-way radio and spoke into it in fast Spanish, but his compelling gaze didn't roam from her for a second. It was curiously like being handcuffed and tied up.

Immobile, Georgie looked back at him in the simmering silence that was laden with menace. He was mad, of course he was mad. So he would say 'I told you so' in a variety of cutting, utterly unpleasant ways, because nobody said that phrase with greater satisfaction than Rafael. Rafael loved to be proved right. And, like it or not, she would take it all on the chin for once.

Setting off on a whim into an unknown, hostile terrain as featureless as this one had been the behaviour of a total idiot and no doubt she deserved everything she had coming to her. But the main reason Georgie would let him shout at her was the intense and naked relief she had seen etched in those gorgeous eyes as he visibly reassured himself that she was unharmed.

Rafael had been worried sick about her safety, probably far more worried than she had been on her own behalf. That dark, brooding temperament of his did not have a shred of her own invariably sunny, optimistic outlook. Rafael always expected the worst. A fat alligator snoozing beside a heap of picked-bare bones

132

wouldn't have surprised him. That certainty sent a pained tenderness washing through her.

He dismounted in one fluid movement and tossed a water bottle to her without even needing to be asked. It landed on the grass at her feet. Lifting it with an unsteady hand, Georgie swiftly took advantge of the ice-cold precious water within. Then, beginning to feel positively intimidated by the continuing unnatural silence, she moistened her throat and her brow with the cool liquid.

'*Madre de Dios . . .*' Rafael growled in a seething tone of savagery she had never heard from him before. 'You are the most stupid bitch it has ever been my misfortune to meet!'

Gulping, Georgie nodded and wondered if it was too soon to test out a grateful smile.

'What do you have to say for yourself?' He strode forward, a dark flush delineating his sculpted cheekbones.

'My hero...?' Her voice emerged all squeaky and strange.

And that was it. Rafael went rigid, and then his narrowed eyes bit into her like grappling hooks and he reached for her with one savage hand, roughly grasping the front of her shirt to propel her closer. 'You think this is funny?' he splintered down at her from his vastly superior height, in a surge of such undisciplined rage that his diction was destroyed. 'Every man available has been engaged on an all-out search for you! And what do you dare to say to me when I find you?'

'Sorry... I am very sorry, but it's not my fault the blasted car broke down, is it?'

'It was in for repair.'

'Oh... Well, I didn't know that,' Georgie muttered weakly.

'Where were you going?' he demanded with raw aggression.

'I thought there'd be a village, another ranch... I didn't mean to cause anyone any inconvenience... I mean...' Sentenced to stillness, her stomach turning over, Georgie watched for some encouraging sign that his rage was levelling out, and failed to receive it.

'Oops...gosh...I didn't think.' His smouldering eyes flashed fierily over her drawn face as she visibly winced at the slashing derision he revealed. 'There is nothing for hundreds of miles——'

'*Hundreds* of miles?' With difficulty, Georgie swallowed.

'No drinkable water, no source of food, poisonous snakes——'

'I got chased by an alligator,' she told him, hoping that confirmation of his expectations would cool him down.

'An alligator... You got as far as the lagoon?' Rafael roared at her a full octave higher. 'You stopped, obviously you got out of the car... for what?'

'I was hot and——'

'You were going to swim with piranhas and electric eels?'

'It never crossed my mind for a moment!' Georgie swore vehemently, shuddering with horror.

He spat something at her in Spanish and shook her again. Two buttons flew off her shirt. 'You did,' Rafael condemned, in so much rage that he could scarcely vocalise the contradiction. 'You did think of swimming! It's written all over you! In the name of God, do you have an IQ in single figures? You need a baby-sitter and a playpen, not a husband!'

Trying with a trembling hand to hold the edges of her shirt together, Georgie went rigid under the onslaught of his abuse. Taking it on the chin as a policy of non-aggressive negotiation vanished.

'Now, you listen here——' she began hotly.

'Shut up!' Rafael seethed down at her, his golden features a mask of fury. 'You took off in a tantrum and I, Rafael Rodriguez Berganza, do not listen to a woman who behaves like a spoilt, reckless child!'

'Get stuffed, you superior SOB!' Georgie hissed.

'What did you call me?'

'Gone deaf suddenly? Lost that wonderful English?' Georgie threw back wrathfully.

Trembling, he stared down at her, the explosive tension in every line of his powerful body hitting her in waves of palpable heat. Burning eyes dug into her. 'If I had married you four years ago, you would have respect for me——'

'No doubt you would have beaten it in with a whip... just your style!' Georgie screeched back.

'I have no need of a whip with you.' His seething gaze dropped to the heaving curves of her full breasts, visible between the parted edges of her shirt. And then he dealt her a dark explicit glance that sent her heartbeat racing up the scale.

Georgie was not slow on the uptake. Instant awareness linked with disbelief assailed her. 'No...' she said thickly.

He coiled a booted foot round the back of her legs and tipped her down on the grass with such fluid ease and speed that she didn't have a hope of evading the manoeuvre. A second later, he came down on top of her, one hand reaching instantly for the snap of her jeans. 'We'll save the Ferrari for some other time... but here, now, on Berganza soil... this is for *me*!'

Georgie was so shocked that he had her halfway out of her jeans before she made even a partial recovery. 'Have you gone mad?' she shrieked.

Her jeans were cast aside. He knelt astride her and slid down the zip on his riding breeches. Georgie stared up at him with a dropped jaw. He shed his polo shirt, flexing powerful muscles that rippled smoothly across his hair-roughened chest. She shivered in the heat, her nostrils flaring at the musky male scent of him.

'Rafael...?'

'You are mine...like the land.'

The absolute possession in the statement was primitive in its intensity. Shimmering golden eyes flamed over her with devouring desire, and heat flooded her every skin-cell in a wanton burst of instant response. He might as well have lit a torch inside her. Her teeth gritted as what remained of sanity sought to be heard. 'No!' she protested as he lowered his arrogant dark head.

'You are my woman.' Lean but frighteningly strong hands cupped her cheekbones. His burnished gaze held hers fiercely. 'And by the time I have finished with you, you will know it too,' he swore with unapologetic savagery.

'I don't like it when you get macho,' Georgie said in breathless defiance.

'Liar...I excite the hell out of you,' Rafael derided. 'I'm still waiting to qualify for a knee in the groin!'

He very nearly did, but with a raw burst of laughter he evaded her furious attempt to make good that oversight. He stilled her with all the power of his superior strength. And then he took her mouth with a ravishing passion that stole her soul. She was stunned into submission by the white-hot hunger he unleashed on her. One hand fiercely knotted in her hair, he plundered her readily parted lips, every stab of his exploring tongue teaching her the depth of his need.

With his other hand, he wrenched her bra out of his impatient path, curving hard fingers over the exposed mounds of her staining breasts. With an earthy groan, he touched and tantalised the distended pink nipples which betrayed the extent of her response to him. The raw intensity of what he was making her feel excited her beyond bearing. Her fingers drove into his raven hair in ecstasy as he suckled strongly at her sensitive breasts. Her whole body was a melting river of liquid flame.

As his head lifted from her breasts, she drew him back to her, wild for the hot, hard possession of his mouth again. Her darkened eyes clung to his and her arms closed convulsively round him, adoring hands splaying across the long golden sweep of his satin-smooth back, and she knew it then—knew that whether it was madness or not he was everything to her, everything she had ever wanted, everything she had ever needed, everything she had ever craved in her most secret thoughts.

With a tormentingly light touch, he explored the moist silken heat of her, and tiny sounds she couldn't hold back began to escape her. Her fingers dug into his powerful shoulders, her entire body racked by an intolerable pleasure that only made her cry out for more. He pulled free of her and parted her thighs and she shivered violently, desperate for the ache he had aroused to be satisfied by the hard thrust of his masculinity.

Abruptly she tensed in shock as his silky hair brushed her taut stomach and she felt his mouth caress her in the most intimate way of all.

'No!' she gasped, her eyes flying wide.

His hands tightened inexorably on her slender thighs, preventing her withdrawal. '*Si*...I want you out of your mind with pleasure,' he murmured softly.

The experience fulfilled his every intention. One moment she was rigid with tension, the next lost in a world of physical sensation so intense that she was overwhelmed. She writhed and moaned, helpless in the grip of her own body's unbridled response. She gasped his name pleadingly at a peak of quivering urgency.

'*Ahora* . . . now.'

He lifted himself and plunged inside her in one devastating thrust of possession. Her every sense was
screaming for the release that only he could give. Her
nails dug into his back and then he was moving on her,
inside her, with every powerful stroke of his hips reinforcing his dominance. As the heat of passion spiralled
out of control, she cried out in ecstasy as he drove her
to a shattering climax.

Still in a satiated daze, Georgie lifted her heavy eyelids.
He reminded her of a primitive golden god, surveying
a pagan sacrifice spread out before him. An aching vulnerability swept her as she collided with tawny tiger eyes
that revealed nothing of his thoughts.

'Rafael?' Involuntarily her hand reached up to smooth
one hard cheekbone.

'*Enamorada* . . .' With a curiously harsh laugh, he took
her startled, reddened mouth with his own and it began
all over again . . .

What have I done? What have I done? The anguished
question rang in ceaseless refrain inside her head as she
fumbled her way back into her clothes with hands that
just weren't responding with their usual efficiency. She
felt shattered, drained, desperately confused, all at one
and the same time. Her mind touched on the raw passion
Rafael had employed to attain her submission, and
something shrivelled up and died inside her.

He strolled across the flattened grass and gently removed her hands from the crumpled shirt she was attempting to tie closed. He peeled the sleeves back down
her arms in silence and strode back to his horse. From
a saddlebag, he produced a polo shirt, similar to the one
he wore himself. Her cheeks burning, she caught it as
he tossed it to her, and hurriedly dived into its
voluminous folds.

He vaulted back into the saddle and reached down to pull her up in front of him. She was so tense that he had to flatten a hand to her abdomen to force her into relaxed contact with his hard body. She trembled, stricken by the sheer force of her physical awareness of him now.

'Is that why you want to marry me?' She couldn't hold the question back any longer, though the instant she voiced it she wished she had kept her mouth shut.

'*No entiendo, querida,*' he drawled.

He understood. He understood damned fine, but he would make her spell it out.

'The sex—is it worth a wedding-ring?' Georgie demanded, grateful he couldn't see the stinging tears lashing her eyes.

'You can be very crude...' he murmured lazily against her ear.

'Put it down to my lack of experience.'

'Sexually we are a match made in heaven—am I to deny that?'

If the past hours of fevered passion had taught her anything, they had taught her that she could not deny him. But she wanted more, she wanted so much more than the confirmation of the raw hunger she aroused in him. She wanted to be needed...she wanted to be loved. And that terrified her.

Because she couldn't live without him either. All along she had been playing a kind of game with him without even realising it. At no stage had she made a realistic effort to leave him. Today... That didn't count. One last-ditch attempt to do what her intelligence urged her to do, and even then she had run with the safe, sure knowledge that he would follow her. Only she hadn't dreamt that the resulting confrontation would be so cataclysmic.

Where was pride now? Rafael had smashed it, left no defence to hide behind. Her throat thickened. Quite deliberately he had employed her passionate response to him as a weapon with which to subjugate her. What price now all her angry assurances that she had no intention of marrying him? And that was exactly why he had done it. His patience had run out. Wasn't it an education to discover that when you pushed him hard enough, honour and principles simply took a hike? In a tight corner, Georgie was impulsive…but in the same position, Rafael was unrepentantly ruthless. She shivered.

His arm tightened around her. 'I would say the chances of slim to none have shortened considerably.'

Her spinal cord jerked into rigidity as his meaning sank in.

'And do you have an excuse this time?' she whispered shakily.

'None. I wanted you. I didn't give a damn.'

Georgie couldn't believe he could be that brazen. Her mouth dropped open.

'And, as you so generously assured me, a woman of your age takes responsibility for her own actions. Naturally, that freed me to be as irresponsible as I liked.'

'But you are not an irresponsible person, Rafael!' she hissed over her shoulder, very nearly giving herself whiplash, she was so indignant at having her own words thrown back at her as justification of his behaviour.

'But I'm versatile. You wouldn't believe how quickly I learn.'

She trembled with incredulous resentment. If increasing the odds of her becoming pregnant got him what he wanted, never let it be said that Rafael had shrunk from the necessity. And to think she had actually been dumb enough to believe that at the outset that frenzied lovemaking had been spontaneous on his side. Rafael? *Spontaneous*? He was a conniving, manipulative… And this was the man she loved? The anger ebbed. Yes, she did love him. Madly, passionately and probably into eternity.

She cleared her throat and took a deep breath. 'So,' she said, in what she hoped was a brisk tone. 'When's the wedding?'

He dropped the reins. Georgie twisted her head in astonishment at such clumsiness from a superb rider. The stallion had slowed to a ridiculous plodding walk anyway, without either one of them noticing, she abruptly registered. 'Rafael?'

He bent down to retrieve the reins but she caught the clenched jut of his jawline. The guy was in shock!

Georgie went white. 'Just joking,' she said in a high-pitched tone. 'You weren't really serious about marrying me... *Of course*, I guessed!' she improvised tightly. 'I just thought I'd have my revenge!'

He closed both arms round her so tightly that she could hardly breathe. 'Don't talk rubbish,' he breathed not quite steadily into her hair. 'I don't joke about things that serious.'

Plastered so close to him, she could feel the accelerated thud of his heart, the audible unevenness as he inhaled. For a split-second, when she had believed he didn't want to marry her, her entire life had metaphorically gone down a drain before her eyes and she had been ready to let the alligator snack on her, so bleak and dismal had been her future. 'I'm not sure I'm convinced,' she muttered uncertainly. 'You look shattered!'

'What an imagination you have,' he murmured, sounding reassuringly more like himself.

'You look shattered,' Georgie said again, although she had never been less keen to pursue a subject, for now that she had decided that she was going to marry him, the fear that he might have cooled off on the idea devastated her.

'Possibly I wasn't expecting you to surrender this—this...' Unusually, he hesitated.

'This quickly? This easily?' she inserted, burning with mortification. 'Expected me to be more of a challenge, did you? Suddenly discovered that when I gave you what you said you wanted, you really didn't want it at all? Well, let me tell you, I——!'

'Shut up,' Rafael snapped with a quaver in his usually level drawl. 'Because if I laugh, I'm dead in the water, *es verdad*? I'll go back to being a slimy, insensitive toe-rag... *Por Dios*, I have had enough of this peculiar conversation! I want to look at you...'

Impatiently anchoring his hands beneath her arms, Rafael helped her to dismount. He vaulted down in her wake and gazed at her with glittering dark eyes sharp enough to cut glass. He was perceptibly tense. Both disconcerted and confused, she looked back at him. 'Rafael, what——?' And that was as far as she got.

'Georgie, tell me truthfully—why, after all that I have done, are you prepared to marry me?'

Completely unready for so direct a question, Georgie flushed and glanced away.

'It doesn't matter what you say. It won't change anything,' Rafael stated, with a tautness at variance with the reassurance.

'You're very attractive,' she mumbled, loathing him for putting her on the hot seat without warning, miserably recalling everything he had said on the subject of marriage—emotion hadn't figured once either before or after he took her to bed and discovered she wasn't the bed-hopping tramp he had believed.

'I think we can take that as mutually understood,' Rafael retorted very drily, but with an edge of driven impatience. 'We should talk about this. Trust me and be honest. Why do you want to marry me?'

Did he suspect that she was in love with him? Did that make him feel guilty again? Did it worry him that she might be entering the marriage with expectations and demands he couldn't possibly fulfil? Slowly, Georgie lifted her fiery head, biting at her lip.

'You can give me the kind of life I've always wanted,' she answered after much frantic thought, her wide eyes eloquent of her inner turmoil.

He released his breath audibly and sent her a shimmering golden glance that was utterly impassive. '*Estupendo* . . . fine. I think I'll radio for the helicopter. You look tired,' he completed flatly.

In frustration she watched him use the radio. She took a couple of steps away. Evidently, she had said the wrong thing. But what did he want from her? She forced a stilted laugh and swung back from him. 'Rafael . . . what would you have said if I had said I wanted to marry you because I loved you?'

'I'd have laughed myself into the nearest asylum.' A sardonic smile curved his sensual mouth, hooded dark eyes gleaming over her as he threw his arrogant head back. 'And run like hell. In a marriage of—shall we say, convenience?—love would be a messy and embarrassing complication.'

He could have taken an axe to her and caused less pain. In the back of her mind she had thought that maybe in time, maybe when all the nasty ripples from the past had settled, maybe when he realised that she could make him happy, his emotions might become involved and he would contrive by some wonderful miracle to look on her as something more than a beautiful, sexually available bed-partner. But now he was telling her with brutal finality that he absolutely didn't want that kind of emotional attachment between them.

'Great . . . then we both know exactly where we stand.' With a smile a world-famous actress would have prided herself on, Georgie concealed the fact that in one smooth sentence he had demolished her every hope.

'And that is important,' he conceded, without any expression at all.

That seemed pretty much to take care of Rafael's desire to talk about their future. He didn't say another word until the helicopter landed and Georgie was too miserable and too busy hiding it to be anything other than grateful for his silence. Exhaustion was dragging her down by then, emotional and physical. Every bone in her body ached. It had been the longest day of her life and it seemed to her that she had worked through every possible emotion in her repertoire.

'You're ready to collapse.' Taking one hard look at her as she stumbled out of the helicopter, Rafael swept her up into his arms and, in spite of her muffled protests, insisted on carrying her into the house.

'I think it's also important that you know that there are times when I don't like you very much,' Georgie whispered in a choky voice against his broad shoulder, drinking in the familiar warm, sexy scent of him and hating herself for being so susceptible.

'That's mutual, too.'

'You mean you don't like you or you don't like me?' she prompted unsteadily.

'You,' Rafael supplied smoothly, as Teresa surged to open her bedroom door.

Georgie burst into a flood of tears. She certainly shocked him. She shocked herself even more. She hadn't even felt the tears gathering.

'Don't be such a baby... I didn't mean it. *Madre de Dios*,' he grated as he laid her down on the bed. 'I never know what the hell you're likely to do next! You open your mouth and I haven't a clue what to expect!'

'Read my lips, then,' Georgie sobbed, and mouthed something very succinct and rude, a phrase that told him to take himself off pronto, combined with a look that told him a jump off the balcony would be her preferred form of exit.

Rafael cast her a seething look of angry frustration. 'I think you are the most irrational woman I have ever met.'

'And s-stupid...don't forget that!' Georgie sobbed, rolling over and burying her face in the pillows, hating the way she was behaving but totally unable to suppress the need to hit out at him.

'I'm sorry.'

Her sensitive hearing suggested she was being treated to gross insincerity, an apology merely to silence her irrational exasperating behaviour.

He said it again louder, and his intonation was ice-cold.

She gulped. 'Accepted.'

'We will get married on Saturday.'

Saturday was only three days away. '*Saturday*?'

'The most convenient date in respect of my business commitments.'

Marvellous, she thought, in the mood now really to wallow in her misery. Convenient? The ceremony was to be slotted into his schedule like an appointment.

'Do you want your parents present?'

'They're on a second honeymon cruise of the Greek islands,' Georgie told him. 'Why spoil it?'

'It is your choice.' Temper back under iron wraps, he was equally dry.

Another sob snaked through Georgie. The mattress gave. 'You're overtired,' Rafael murmured tightly. 'And maybe I have seemed unsympathetic...'

Unsympathetic? What a typical Berganza understatement that was!

'This has been a very emotional day,' he persisted doggedly, impervious to the lack of encouragement he was receiving. He gripped one of her hands tightly before she could whip it under her like the other one. 'But I promise you that you will never regret marrying me. I'll make you happy... Perhaps you don't want to live here? We can live anywhere.'

Momentarily disarmed, Georgie found herself listening, quite astounded at the idea that he could be offering her a choice of where they lived when she had always believed that Rafael regarded the *estancia* as his only possible permanent home.

'Although it doesn't really matter where the bedroom is, does it?' That final softly derisive sentence swiftly put paid to any goodwill he might have reanimated.

Georgie snatched her hand away, cut to the quick. He didn't need to drive that message home any harder. She was already painfully aware of the sole value she had in his eyes. And, as the door closed behind him, Georgie wondered in an agony of doubt if once more she had foolishly allowed impulse to overrule sanity. What sort of a relationship could she possibly build with a man who regarded her in such a light?

And he had sounded bitter. What the heck did Rafael have to be bitter about? Right now, could he be feeling as confused as she did? Throughout the day, Rafael had lurched unpredictably from one mood to another. Was it conceivable that she had hit the nail squarely on the head earlier? Could it have been that, when she had finally agreed to marry him, Rafael had suddenly registerd that that really wasn't what he wanted after all?

Dear lord, how humiliating that would be... But she couldn't help remembering all that Rafael had said about the attraction of her unavailability in the past. Rafael liked a challenge. Rafael was a natural predator. For such a male, the hunt was often far more exciting than the catch. Right now, was Rafael bitterly regretting the trap he had dug for himself? Georgie simply couldn't live with that fear.

Teresa came and insisted on helping her into bed. A beautiful meal was brought up on a tray and everybody showed an embarrassing desire to fuss over her. Rafael's aunt came up to ask how she was in slow, careful English. Georgie squirmed, unhappily aware that she had caused a furore. And after that she fell asleep, waking up very late to darkness.

For a while she lay pondering her earlier misgivings, and railed at her own reluctance to face up to them. With sudden decision, she rose and pulled on her robe and tidied her hair. The lights were still on downstairs. She was aware that Rafael often worked late, being one of those individuals who seemed to thrive on little sleep.

She was on the last step of the stairs when Beatriz erupted with hot cheeks and wild eyes from Rafael's library. 'Never in my whole life have I been so insulted!' she hissed at Georgie. 'But I blame you, not Rafael. He is out of his senses with drink! What have you done to him? It is a disgrace that a man of his stature and education should be in a state of gross inebriation——'

'He's drunk?' Georgie whispered, having taken some few seconds to recognise this heaving-breasted, outraged young woman as the frigidly correct and controlled beauty she had met earlier in the day. '*Rafael*?' she stressed, almost as shattered by the idea as her companion was, but a good deal less judgemental.

'It is this ridiculous wedding... What else can it be?' Beatriz told her accusingly. 'I offered my sympathy but he was too proud to accept it. Rafael could not possibly want to marry a woman like you. You are nothing, a nobody...a social climber who used his sister as a passport into his acquaintance! Had you any decency or any respect for the name of Berganza, you would set him free!'

Leaving Georgie white and trembling in shock, Beatriz stalked up the stairs.

CHAPTER NINE

GEORGIE'S soft knock on the library door drew no response. Apprehensively, she opened the door and walked in. One light was lit on the desk. Rafael was slumped in the swivel chair behind it, his long lean legs planted on the desktop, the mess of papers there crushed indifferently by his booted feet. His face was in shadow but she could see that his eyes were closed and, surmising that he was asleep, Georgie moved closer.

He hadn't shaved for dinner, if he had had any, and hadn't changed either. His blue-shadowed jawline and tousled black hair gave him the appearance of a desperado. But the lush ebony lashes fanned down on his abrasive cheekbones were as long as a child's, and a tortured tenderness twisted through her. She didn't need Beatriz to tell her to set him free, she reflected painfully, her mouth downcurving at the sight of the low level on the bottle of malt whisky. If the prospect of marrying her reduced him to this level, Rafael could look forward to seeing the dust of her exit within hours.

And then she saw the gun lying beside the bottle. She had never seen a gun except on television. But there it was, a relatively small black metal article... a revolver? Dear God in heaven. Her stomach heaved. Rafael couldn't possibly be that desperate... could he? Anyone less likely to be contemplating suicide would be hard to find. Rafael was so strong... wasn't he? Then why was the gun there? a little voice screamed. Why, when Rafael was doing something so tremendously out of character as getting himself roaring drunk, did he suddenly have a gun sitting beside him?

Her heart in her mouth, Georgie tiptoed closer, intending to take possession of the revolver. Better safe than sorry, she decided. As she moved, a sheet of paper crunched beneath her toes, and she bent down and picked it up, intending to replace it on the desk. Her fleeting glance was caught accidentally by the lines of numerals with minus signs. Some sort of a bank statement, belonging to someone in an enormous amount of debt. Embarrassed that she had glimpsed a no doubt private document, Georgie hurriedly set it down on the desk.

'Beatriz... *vete a hacer puñetas*!' Rafael suddenly snarled.

Georgie flinched back and gasped, taken by surprise.

His lashes flew up on dark, dark eyes with a wild febrile glitter. 'What do you want?' he slurred in another tone altogether, as he visibly struggled to focus on her.

'What did you say to Beatriz to put her in such a tizzy?' Georgie asked in a falsely bright voice, to conceal her rampant nervous tension.

A sardonic smile briefly curved his taut mouth. He didn't reply.

'Rafael?' Georgie pressed worriedly.

'Leave me... I am drunk,' Rafael framed with obvious difficulty, and reached for the bottle again. '*Se acabo.*'

'What does that mean?'

Rafael surveyed her and emitted a harsh laugh. *No tengo nada... nada*!' he repeated savagely, raking her anxious face with embittered eyes which didn't seem to be quite taking her in.

I have nothing—she understood that all right. What did he mean, he had nothing? On the brink of forcing herself to ask him if it was the threat of marrying her which had prompted him to hit the bottle—and frankly, if it was, she felt more like hitting him than proffering comfort—Georgie was silenced by her confusion.

'What can I give you now?' he muttered indistinctly, tipping his glass to compressed lips.

A glimmer of devastated comprehension assailed her. Her shocked gaze suddenly stabbed back to the bank statement she had replaced on the desk. Of course, that statement belonged to him, she reasoned. Who else could it possibly belong to? He was in debt to the tune of millions. No wonder he was getting drunk!

She took a deep breath. 'Rafael... have you got business problems?'

'Business problems?' Now that did grab his full attention. His dark head fairly spun back to her, his glinting eyes narrowing intently.

'I have nothing... what can I give you now?' he had said. What else could he possibly be admitting to? She had been very slow on the uptake.

'What makes you think I might have these problems?' he contrived to enquire, looking a lot more acute and aware all of a sudden than he had a few minutes previously. He even raised himself up slightly from his slump in his seat to survey her better.

Georgie swallowed hard on the lump that had come out of nowhere into her throat. She didn't want him to think that she had been prying, so she decided not to mention having accidentally seen that damning statement. Rafael was so proud. Failure of any kind was anathema to him. Naturally he would try to cover up. But, oh, the relief of learning that his condition had nothing whatsoever to do with her or their projected marriage!

'You can be honest with me, Rafael,' she whispered tightly. 'I won't breathe a word to anyone.'

He breathed in deeply, still studying her with slightly glazed eyes. 'You think I have suffered—er—financial reverses?'

'You just told me you had!'

'I did?' Rafael pushed decidedly unsteady fingers through his black hair and seemed to be sunk in thought. Then, with startling abruptness, he glanced up again. '*Sí,*' he muttered fiercely. 'Naturally this worries you. You fear that I will not be able to supply this life of luxury you crave! And now you change your mind about marrying me, *es verdad*?'

'Rafael . . . how could you even think I would feel like that?' Georgie gasped, tears springing to her eyes, stricken for him, not for herself, because she could hardly begin to imagine what it must be like for someone like Rafael, fabulously rich all his life, suddenly to face a future deprived of the status and luxuries he no doubt took completely for granted.

'You don't think like that?' he prompted weakly, his voice just sliding away.

Georgie read that strained voice as being evidence of the depth of his despair. And she couldn't stand the distance between them any longer. Aching to offer him comfort and reassurance, she slid past the desk and threw herself on the carpet beside his chair so that she could wrap her arms round his lean waist, since she reckoned he was far too drunk to be capable of standing up. The slowness of his reactions certainly suggested that he was. As she made physical contact, he went absolutely rigid.

'Please don't push me away,' Georgie pleaded vehemently. 'Don't let your pride come between us.'

'My pride?'

'You really are drunk, aren't you?' she sighed, burying her head on his lap in a sudden surge of helpless tenderness.

'I *feel* very drunk,' Rafael confided unsteadily.

'I'll probably have to say all this again in the morning because you won't remember it. Now, listen,' she said, angling back her vibrant head with an air of stubborn determination. 'Your money has never been important to me. I don't care if you're broke or up to your ears in debt——'

'In debt?' Rafael repeated in a deeply shaken undertone.

'I suppose you don't know at this stage just how bad it's going to be, but what I'm telling you now is that it doesn't matter to me.'

'It doesn't?'

She gazed up at him, blinking back tears, absorbing only a tithe of his shattered expression through that veil of moisture. 'And I'm very hurt that you think that it could matter to me. Of course, I still want to marry you—I don't need a life of luxury to be happy.'

'You don't?'

Georgie groaned. 'I realise that you're drunk...but could you please try to stop repeating everything I say?'

A lean hand lifted and his forefinger traced the wobbling curve of her full lower lip. Instinctively, Georgie pressed her cheek into his palm and simultaneously she felt the raw tension ebb from his long, lean length. There was a long silence, violet eyes meshing mesmerically with gold.

'And do you think you could put the gun away now?'

'What gun? Oh...that one,' Rafael gathered abstractedly, with the utmost casualness. 'I must lock it away. Father Tomás learnt that it was in the possession of one of my most hot-headed *llaneros* and persuaded him to give it up before he was tempted to use it on somebody.'

Georgie's cheeks burned at the melodrama that had leapt right out of her own imagination. Rafael, still in the same uncharacteristic mood of complete relaxation, suddenly arrowed wondering dark eyes over her taut profile. '*Querida mía* . . . you surely did not think——?'

'Of course I didn't.'

'You crazy woman,' he groaned, abruptly bending down and gathering her up into a heap in his arms.

'You seem to be sobering up.'

'Shock.'

She supposed he meant the shock of the bad news he had presumably had. 'Do you want to talk about it?'

'Not tonight, *gatita*.'

She rested her head against a powerful shoulder, delighted by the reception she was receiving from him. He had been shocked that she was prepared to stand by him through thick and thin, but he had cheered up marvellously, so she was prepared to forgive him for holding so low an opinion of her.

'Your worries have been on your mind all day,' she reflected out loud, thinking of his positively insouciant manner before breakfast when he had clearly been trying to put up a macho front, and then the staggering changes of mood he had exhibited later on.

'Let us not even consider them now,' Rafael said soothingly.

She frowned. While she was no keener than he to face a presumably ghastly, stressful and horribly complex financial crisis, which was evidently destined to leave them ultimately as poor as church mice, she did feel it was something that had to be dealt with immediately. Then, what did she know about such things? What possible advice could she offer? No doubt Rafael appreciated that too and, equally certainly, he had within reach all the professional assistance he could require.

'I just wanted you to know that I'm here . . . to be supportive,' she added tautly.

'This I have noticed,' Rafael commented with a slightly dazed inflection from above her downbent head. 'After all, you are now showing some—some—er—affection for me for the very first time.'

Affection? What a milk-and-water translation of the ferociously strong feelings which were driving her! But then, she didn't want to overdo it, did she? Rafael was very proud. Very probably affection was the most he was prepared to accept until he felt in control of events again. Although she had to admit he had already made the most remarkable recovery from his apparent stupor of intoxication.

'I thought you might need it.'

'And maybe you find—er—losers more appealing?'

Her head flew up. 'Rafael...you are not a loser,' she protested emotionally. 'Just about anybody can get into trouble with money—it doesn't mean you're a loser! You've got to allow yourself to make mistakes. Nobody's perfect.'

'I used to think I was,' Rafael breathed with sudden austerity, his stunningly handsome features hardening as his mouth curled. 'And I'm starting to realise that I got what I deserved.'

'Please... It depresses me to death when you start getting all grim and self-critical.'

'But I have not been sufficiently critical of my treatment of you.'

Georgie looked levelly into lustrous dark eyes. 'This is a fresh start for us. I mean, it is...isn't it?' she pressed, with desperate hope that this wonderful new openness she sensed between them wasn't about to prove a flash in the pan by morning. 'As if we've just met for the first time?'

'Permit me to warn you, then, that you are in serious danger of being ravished on the very first date,' Rafael murmured slumbrously, delightfully willing, it seemed, to play along with the suggestion, his hands settling on the swell of her buttocks as she sat astride him.

'It wasn't like that, though, was it? Not back then,' she remarked, unable to silence the rueful observation. 'You were so cold.'

With a stifled groan, he leant his brow against hers and sighed. 'Georgie... don't you have any idea how much restraint it took for me to keep my hands off you? I was desperate to make love to you but you were so young——'

'Was that really why?'

'I didn't want to take advantage of you and I didn't want the hunger of our bodies to take over to the exclusion of everything else... as it so easily could have done. For me, marriage is a very serious commitment which I would want to last a lifetime,' Rafael stated with firm emphasis. 'I have seen too much of the misery which broken homes inflict upon children. Think well before Saturday, *querida*. Once we are married, I will not give you your freedom again.'

Georgie felt reassured rather than challenged. At the back of her mind, she had been afraid Rafael might choose to cast her off again when familiarity bred contempt in the marital bed, as she had believed it surely would if only the most basic sexual instincts had prompted him to marry her in the first place. But now he was telling her that he expected their marriage to last.

'I need a shower and some coffee,' he said wryly. 'And you should be in bed. Beatriz will be wide awake listening for creaking floorboards, and I'm very much afraid that, if she hears them, she will take great pleasure in telling you.'

'I don't give a hoot.'

Rising up, Rafael slowly slid her to the ground. He gazed down at her and his eloquent mouth twisted. 'But I do,' he told her with quiet finality.

Georgie reddened fiercely and recognised how much had changed between them. For just a little while Rafael had seemed out of control, but now he was back in the driver's seat again, instinctively reasserting his dominance. 'I feel pretty cut off now!' she said baldly.

And he flung back his handsome head and laughed with spontaneous appreciation. It crossed her mind that he looked incredibly light-hearted for someone who was facing the loss of a fortune, said to run into billions. Was he trying to save face or something? Or were things not as bad as she had innocently imagined?

Patently unaware of her thoughts, he guided her to the door and reached for her hand. 'Georgie...that your passion matches mine is a wonderful thing,' he said intently. 'In fact, it is a source of sublime satisfaction whenever I think about it.'

He drew her to him, extracted a driving kiss that she felt sizzle right down to her toes and back up again, and then set her back again, breathing hard. *'Buenas noches, enamorada.'*

Of course, of course—he was probably intending to sober up and sit up all night and work in an effort to sort the financial mess out. It dimly occurred to her that they couldn't have picked a worse time for a wedding. Surely he would need to travel abroad and have loads of serious meetings with banks or creditors or whatever? Abruptly, Georgie said as much, before he could vanish back into the library.

Rafael stilled, black lashes swooping down low on his suddenly hooded gaze. Colour darkened his blunt cheekbones. 'No...it is absolutely essential that I maintain a pretence of normality and that no word of this leaks out before I am properly prepared to deal with it,' he stated very abruptly.

'Can you really keep the lid on something like this? Won't it make it more of a strain—sort of pile on the agony?' Georgie reasoned anxiously.

Rafael drew in a long, deep shuddering breath. A tiny muscle tugged at the corner of his unsmiling mouth. '*Querida* . . . let us not spoil our wedding with such concerns,' he urged.

'Well, if you think that's best——'

'Believe me, I do.'

Biting at her lip, Georgie nodded, terribly touched that he should be putting their wedding ahead of all else. Up on the landing, she very deliberately bounced on the floorboards outside Rafael's bedroom, giggled, opened and closed the door and then crept like a mouse into her own room beside it. Her methods of dealing with Beatriz Herrera León were considerably more basic than Rafael's and nobody, least of all a nasty piece of work like the snobbish Beatriz, was about to make Georgie ashamed of the fact that she and Rafael were already lovers.

The next morning, Georgie leapt out of bed and realised how happy she was. Oddly enough, she had always scorned that old chestnut that a crisis often drew people together. If there were cracks in a relationship, the crisis was more likely to blow them wider apart. And yet look at what had happened between her and Rafael last night! Somehow all the barriers had come down between them. The hostility and the rough uneasy edges had miraculously vanished. Rafael had been really strong and tender and caring.

Anxiety flooded her as she heard the burst of voices over the breakfast-table. She was suddenly so scared that Rafael might have reverted again overnight. But the minute she entered the room, Rafael rose to greet her. With Beatriz looking on as though she was being forced to witness an indecent act, Georgie found her hand being carried to his mouth as he planted a kiss intimately to the inside of her wrist.

'You look fantastic, *querida*,' Rafael murmured in his dark, deep seductive voice while she hovered there in a haze of stunned pleasure. 'That colour is spectacular on you.'

Georgie skimmed a self-conscious hand down over her chain store-bought pink sundress and positively glowed. 'You think so?'

Hungry golden eyes clung to her vibrantly beautiful face. 'I think so.'

Georgie's gaze wandered dizzily over the open-necked white shirt and the close-fitting faded denim jeans he wore. 'You look wonderful too,' she whispered. 'I've never seen you in jeans before.'

'Your coffee is getting cold, Rafael,' Beatriz said flatly.

Beatriz discussed the price of coffee in the Third World, moved on to Bolivian politics and then did them all to death with her opinion of the British Welfare State. Absently impressed by her intelligence, Georgie ate and watched Rafael watching her and letting his coffee get cold, and she was so happy that it was like being on another planet.

'I have something for you,' Rafael informed her, pulling her chair back for her and generally behaving as though a slight draught might give her pneumonia. She loved it.

He carried her off into the drawing-room and ten seconds later he was sliding an incredibly opulent emerald ring on her engagement finger. 'Where it belongs at last.'

'You mean you bought it four years ago?' Her violet eyes swam. 'It's so *big*—I mean beautiful!' she adjusted hurriedly, biting back what he would probably consider a very tactless suggestion that, if it was as hugely expensive as it looked, he might be wiser to hang on to it and sell it.

He laughed softly, as though he could read her mind.

'Rafael?' She swallowed hard. 'I was so scared you would have changed again this morning——'

'Changed?'

'Never mind.'

'No.' Rafael tugged her slowly, indolently forward into his arms, bringing her into stirring contact with his superbly masculine body and she simply stopped breathing—she was so electrified, not only by that physical proximity but by the softened darkness of his gaze. 'From now on, I want you to share everything with me.'

'You're just so different...'

He smiled brilliantly. 'But so are you.'

That reality belatedly occurred to her. Last night, she had been all over him like a dose of chicken-pox, and this morning she had been floating around like a starstruck teenager again. And evidently he just *loved* that kind of response, she registered a little dazedly. Did it massage his ego? Was that it? Or had this miracle been solely worked by his shocked realisation that even though he had lost every penny, she was going to hang on to him like grim death?

'So I'm not going to be needing the old silver bullet again, then?' Georgie teased.

He leant forward and traced her sensitive lower lip with the tip of his tongue and she trembled, her lower limbs displaying all the solid capacity of cottonwool as a burst of heat slivered through her, swelling her breasts, pinching her tender nipples almost painfully tight. Low in her throat she moaned, and yesterday she would have been embarrassed about such instant susceptibility, but today she was ready to suggest she risked the alligator again so that they could have some privacy.

'*Por Dios,*' he whispered, in between explorations of the moist interior of her mouth which had her breathing in panting little gasps of anticipation. 'A silver bullet wouldn't stop me.'

In case she was in any doubt as to his meaning, he pressed a hand to her hip and locked her into raw connection with the hard bulge of his aroused manhood, and she grabbed at his shoulders to stay upright when every sense prompted that she lie down wantonly on the nearest available horizontal surface. He groaned in matching frustration, his big powerful body trembling against her. The knowledge that he was as close to the edge as she was made her feel incredibly proud of her femininity.

'I could come over all dizzy and go upstairs and lie down,' she whispered in desperation.

'We could saddle a couple of horses and get lost.'

'We could chuck the horses out and just go for the stables.'

'You are an incredibly sensual woman,' he muttered thickly. 'I want to be inside you again so badly...but we are going to wait for our wedding night.'

'OK.' Deciding on shock tactics, Georgie dropped her arms, eased free of his hold and strolled across the room to throw herself down on a *chaise-longue* where she extended her long tanned legs with flagrant provocation.

Incandescent golden eyes flamed over her with such a force of hunger that she ached and stopped playing. I love you, she wanted to say, I love you so much, but the awareness that that information would be seriously unwelcome silenced her. Keep it light, Georgie, keep it light, she urged herself angrily.

According to Rafael, marriage was a lifetime commitment. She had all the time in the world. The last thing she wanted to risk now was scaring him off before she got that ring on her finger. Were Rafael's emotions so disciplined that he was afraid of letting go and loving her, or had he merely been telling her up-front that while he might lust after her like mad, he just knew he wasn't capable of falling in love with her?

As he moved forward he frowned, and bent to pick up something from the carpet. 'Yours?' He extended a gold charm bracelet.

Georgie got up to accept it. 'It's always falling off. I should get the safety chain repaired.'

Rafael laughed. 'That might be a good idea.'

'Lucky it dropped off in here,' Georgie said, carefully clasping it back round her wrist. 'I'd hate to lose it. Steve gave it to me for my twenty-first——'

'Had I known, I would have dumped it in the trash.'

Georgie blinked and glanced up. Every shred of good humour had been stripped from Rafael's expression. He bristled with visible aggression, his expressive eyes cold and hard.

'Just because Steve gave it to me?' Georgie asked incredulously. 'Why are you still so hostile towards him? You know that nothing happened between us, and he is part of my family——'

'Not in my eyes, and he will never be welcome here,' Rafael asserted with grim emphasis. 'Nor will I permit you to meet him except in the company of your parents.'

Georgie was seriously tempted to giggle. It was so ridiculous. Did Rafael have any idea how ridiculous he sounded? Was he jealous? Was that the problem? Four years ago, he must have been eaten alive with sexual jealousy when he believed that Steve had been her lover and now, even though he knew what nonsense that had been, he was still stubbornly clinging to the same closed mind.

How could any sane man be jealous of a single embrace? Or was it that Rafael still suspected that she found Steve attractive, other than as a brother? Now, that idea really did worry her. If Rafael could *still* cherish such suspicions, he had a real problem. That kind of jealousy was neither amusing nor understandable...it was threatening and dangerous.

'Rafael...you know that night when Steve grabbed me and kissed me, I was really turned off,' Georgie confided. 'I do not find Steve attractive in that way——'

'I am now aware of that.'

'In fact, I was so upset and embarrassed—well, that's why I took off for Danny's for the night,' she completed.

'I have also worked this out for myself.'

'What a leap of faith that must have taken!' Georgie couldn't help her sarcasm. Her explanations had not altered Rafael's attitude one iota. Freezing austerity still stamped his set, dark features. 'I'm rather glad I've lost touch with poor Danny.'

'He was merely a friend. Naturally I accept that now——'

'But not my stepbrother, who is my brother in all but blood?'

Rafael sent her a smouldering look. 'I do not wish to discuss this matter further.'

Georgie tussled with her hot temper as Rafael banded an arm round her narrow back. 'We have so many other things more important to discuss,' he reminded her.

Instantly, Georgie was cooled and stabbed by conscience. Why on earth was she wittering on about Steve when she knew that Rafael was under great strain? Now was not the time to tell him that he was being unreasonable. 'I'm sorry,' she sighed. 'You must be really worried.'

Ebony lashes lifted on golden eyes. 'About what? Oh...*that*!' he grasped, contriving to look suddenly very grave again as his arm dropped from her. 'But didn't we agree that we would forget about that until after the wedding?'

'Yes, but——'

'No buts.'

'You must have nerves of steel. The way you've been behaving, nobody would even suspect that there's anything wrong.'

'It is in the back of my mind constantly,' Rafael sighed heavily. 'But I am depending on you to help me to be strong.'

He was standing over by the window, his back turned to her as if he couldn't quite bring himself to make such a demand and look her in the face. Georgie took the hint and closed her arms round him. He swivelled fluidly and pressed her face into the hard wall of his chest. A tremor ran through him. 'Let's get some fresh air,' he suggested.

It was a wonderful day. He showed her round the estancia, introduced her to everyone and made up ridiculous stories about all his illustrious but deeply boring-looking ancestors that had her falling about in hysterics. She had forgotten what a wonderful sense of humour Rafael had when he let his guard down. They spent the afternoon in the swimming-pool, and were still sitting talking at the dinner table long after Tía and Beatriz had excused themselves to go to bed. And even though Georgie slept alone, she slept like a log.

The second day was even better. The helicopter dropped them at the mouth of the Rio Tuichi, where they were met by a guide and a motorised canoe, and they cruised through a section of rainforest until it was time to go back, and Georgie wasn't a bit sorry that Rafael was lowering himself to a simple tourist excursion for her benefit. She was well aware that he usually travelled into the Amazon with various professionals in tow and camped out to rendezvous with Indians from the more remote settlements. She was equally aware just how much pleasure he was receiving from showing her a world she had never dreamt of sharing with him.

She went up to her room to change for dinner and was stunned to find the closets and cabinets in the dressing-room, stuffed full of unfamiliar garments. Bewildered, she fingered a shot silk top and palazzo pants outfit with a famous designer label.

'Like them?' Rafael grinned at her stunned expression from the doorway. She hadn't even heard him enter her bedroom.

'Everything is in my size.'

'It's yours. I had a selection ordered. Exquisite as you look in that white dress you wear every night for dinner, I thought you might enjoy a change.'

'But these kind of clothes cost a fortune!' Georgie gasped. 'And I thought you were broke!'

Rafael winced and actually paled. 'Things aren't quite as bad as that—not as bad as I initially imagined, that is,' he added, studying her frowning, surprised face intently.

'They aren't? Are you sure?' Georgie persisted in considerable confusion. 'Why didn't you say?'

'I was about to... Wear that for dinner,' he suggested in an intimate tone that quite sent her temperature rocketing and blitzed her reasoning powers. 'Turquoise and green will look stupendous with your hair, *querida mía*.'

Georgie threaded a self-conscious hand through her torrent of curls and smiled blissfully at him. 'You think so?'

'I think so.'

'Will you be able to keep your jet?'

Rafael's lustrous gaze narrowed. '*Perdón?*'

'I just couldn't picture you travelling economy class,' she confided.

He lounged back against the door-lintel and treated her to a devastating smile. 'I do believe that I will be able to save you from such a sight.'

The third day, the day before the wedding, Georgie went out riding with Rafael. When they returned to the house, Rafael was called to the phone, and she found herself seated alone with Beatriz, Tía having opted for breakfast in bed.

'You must be pregnant,' Beatriz said coldly, right out of the blue. 'Why else would he be marrying you?'

Georgie stiffened. 'I am not pregnant.'

'I was betrothed to Rafael as a child,' Beatriz told her with icy dignity.

'I'd be a liar if I said I was sorry it didn't work out,' Georgie managed after a long pause, belatedly registering why the brunette disliked her so intensely. She had been far too wrapped up in her own happiness to spare more than the most fleeting thought for Beatriz, who was the most snobbish, moralising bore she had ever met. The other woman was also beautiful, highly intelligent and very accomplished, she had to concede in all fairness, although it went against the grain to do so.

'His father died, and then mine. He would have married me had he not met *you*,' Beatriz said thinly. 'And I want you to know, before you congratulate yourself on your success on trapping him, that I intend to tell Rafael that your arrival in our country during his sister's absence was no accident.'

'I beg your pardon?'

'The whole family knows. It was a standing joke. Every time María Cristina made it known that she had issued another invitation for you to visit, she left the country soon afterwards!'

'Say that again,' Georgie invited breathlessly.

'She confided in Tía. That is how I know. In her innocence, María Cristina wanted to bring you and Rafael together, and obviously you persuaded her to do it!'

'Then how do you explain the fact that I didn't come to her wedding?' Georgie was in a daze, but a great whoop of laughter was mingling with her incredulity.

All these years she had believed that her best friend was entirely ignorant of her feelings for Rafael. But María Cristina had clearly known all along and kept quiet, perhaps out of respect for Georgie's apparent wish for privacy. And, in her own uniquely scatty way, María Cristina had tried to throw them together... by ensuring that if ever Georgie did arrive in Bolivia she would find herself stranded and forced to contact Rafael.

'And I was so very disappointed when you failed to show...'

Both female heads spun. Rafael was poised several feet inside the door, a curious half-smile playing at the corners of his sensual mouth as he looked at Georgie. 'Did you know that María Cristina knew about us?'

'But does she? Or was it just me—I mean my feelings—she guessed at?' Georgie stumbled awkwardly. 'I never told her anything!'

'Neither did I.'

'You don't understand, Rafael,' Beatriz put in with distaste. 'The woman you are on the brink of marrying plotted and planned to throw herself in your path——'

'How flattering,' Rafael drawled.

'And, what is worse, she manipulated María Cristina into doing her bidding.'

'My sister has the temperament of a mule,' Rafael said drily. 'I don't think anybody has ever manipulated her into doing anything she didn't want to do.' He switched smoothly to Spanish and, a moment later, Beatriz went puce, stood up, stalked out and left them alone.

'She said you were betrothed as children.'

'Our fathers certainly discussed it, but she was only a child at the time and there was no formal betrothal. However, when I remained single, Beatriz began to nurture certain ambitions,' he volunteered. 'She has a keen sense of her own many virtues and will undoubtedly make someone a splendid wife, but she lacks any sense of humour and, between you and me, I would as soon take a refrigerator to bed!'

A startled giggle erupted from Georgie, and then her face tightened worriedly as she searched his. 'I didn't do what she said...and I can't believe that María Cristina deliberately invited me here, knowing she would be abroad.'

'If my sister did, I should be very angry. To strand a young woman in a foreign country where she does not even speak the language is not a joke.'

'All the same, I think I could forgive her.'

'You may amuse yourself ferreting out the truth when she arrives this evening.'

'María Cristina's coming *tonight*?' Georgie flew to her feet. 'And I haven't even told her—I didn't even ask you for her phone number!'

'She doesn't know about the wedding. I swore Antonio to silence,' Rafael admitted mockingly. 'She doesn't even know you're here.'

'I really can't believe we're getting married tomorrow,' Georgie confided helplessly.

'What could possibly go wrong now?' Encircling her with his arms, Rafael eased her close and, briefly, she rested her cheek against his shoulder, drinking in the scent and feel of him.

'I'm not sure I can handle being so happy,' Georgie whispered unsteadily.

'Are you happy?' Narrowed dark eyes roamed over her upturned face. 'Is the past finally behind us?'

Georgie shrugged playfully, her fingers flirting with his silk tie and lingering to splay against the muscular breadth of his chest. 'What past?'

A lean hand clamped over hers, his gaze turning incandescent gold with hunger, his expressive mouth curling with amusement. 'I've been wondering...where did you pick up those moves you unleashed on me that night in the Ferrari?'

Georgie reddened. 'Magazines.'

He looked down at her for a stunned instant. 'What sort of magazines?'

'Perfectly respectable women's magazines...' Georgie shifted sinuously against him, eased her free hand below his silk-lined jacket and skimmed her fingers along his waistline, feeling the muscles in his flat hard stomach jerk tight in involuntary response. 'And you know something, Rafael...it was all true. You reacted like a textbook case and then you blew it,' she sighed.

'The next time you do that I want you to...' And as he bent his dark head down and told her in explicit language exactly what he wanted her to do next, she went hot all over and weak at the knees.

When his mobile phone buzzed and took him off to the library, Georgie felt bereft. She also felt a little embarrassed for herself. Every time she got within hailing distance of him, she behaved like a wanton. The intense sexual attraction between them just took over, but she couldn't help being aware that Rafael's control was far stronger than hers. Maybe she should be playing it more coolly. If she didn't, Rafael was likely to tumble shrewdly to the fact that she simply couldn't keep her hands off him because she loved him and that was the only way she had of expressing those feelings.

In the late afternoon, she was fixing flowers in the hall, cheerfully unconcerned by the knowledge that she had no hope of matching Beatriz's magnificent arrangement in the drawing-room. When she heard the helicopter flying in low, she didn't even lift her head. Helicopters came and went on a regular basis on the *estancia*. About five minutes later, however, Teresa came rushing in from outside. 'Your brother has come, *señorita*!' she gasped, out of breath. 'I not expect, nobody tell me he was coming. Where do I put a brother to sleep——?'

'*Steve*? Steve's here?' Georgie interrupted in astonishment, the flower she had in her hand dropping unnoticed to the polished floor.

CHAPTER TEN

GEORGIE flew across the gardens and sighted Steve's familiar, broadly built figure, the sun glinting on his thatch of blond hair. A delighted smile lit up her features as she raced up to him. 'How on earth did you know where I was?' she demanded.

Steve studied her with a tight mouth. He looked pale and strained, almost as though he had been bracing himself for a far less welcoming reception. 'I received a call from our mutual parents.'

'But I haven't been in touch with them——'

'Berganza is having them whisked off their ship and flown out here for the wedding, I believe.'

'Gosh…he thinks of everything, doesn't he?' Georgie shook her head slowly. 'I didn't like to mention them coming because I thought I'd left it too late. He must want to surprise me.'

'How sweet of him,' Steve sneered, his pale blue eyes cold with condemnation. 'Thanks for telling me you were getting married. You came out here just to run after him, didn't you? You never let on to a soul what you were planning!'

'Because I didn't *plan* it! It just happened,' Georgie muttered, taken aback by the attack. 'And OK, I know you don't like him but, for my sake, surely you can grit your teeth and be pleasant?'

'I'm hoping to take you back home with me.'

'No chance. I love him,' Georgie said baldly. 'Please don't spoil things, Steve.'

'You've been out here...what? A week? And you're marrying him? Have you lost your mind? Have you forgotten what he did to you the last time?'

'There was a misunderstanding which I don't want to go into,' Georgie said awkwardly. 'And I appreciate that you think I'm jumping in feet first, but maybe you should know that Rafael was going to ask me to marry him back then——'

'Like hell he was!'

'You haven't seen the mermaid taps.' For a moment, Georgie looked positively smug.

'I don't know what the blazes you're talking about and, to be blunt, I don't care! I'm taking you back to London with me right now.' A large hand clamped round her slender forearm.

Georgie gazed up at her stepbrother in disbelief. 'Have you gone mad? I'm getting married tomorrow.'

'He'd make you bloody miserable. He's a womaniser, Georgie. If he's willing to give you a ring, it's only because that's the only way he can get you!' Steve said unpleasantly.

'Don't be stupid... Look, what's the matter with you?' Georgie shot at him with shocked eyes. 'Why are you acting like this?'

'Get your hands off her.'

Georgie's head spun. Rafael was standing about ten feet away, both fists clenched. He wore an expression of chilling menace. 'Oh, no, don't you start,' she snapped in exasperation. 'What is the matter with the two of you?'

'You were safe,' Rafael drawled at Steve, his golden features set with blistering derision. 'You were safe, though you didn't know it. I had no intention of telling her.'

'Telling me what?' Georgie broke in, as Steve's fingers loosened their grip and finally dropped from her. She stepped back from him, her head spinning between the two men, both of whom were ignoring her. Steve was rigid and pale, breathing heavily. Rafael had an aura of violence she had never seen in him before. It scared her. Although the two men were fairly evenly matched in size, she sensed that Rafael had a killer instinct which Steve lacked. And she also knew, after one shocked glance at Rafael's shimmering golden gaze, that he had every intention of getting physical.

'Right,' she said, raising her hands in what she hoped was a strong, meaningful motion. 'I am not having this. If you lay one finger on him, Rafael . . . the wedding is off. Steve may be behaving like an idiot but you are not helping matters, and I would like him all in one piece for the photos——'

'You think I'm scared of that slimy bastard?' Steve seethed, striding forward and thrusting her roughly out of his path.

'Go back to the house, *querida*,' Rafael murmured in a flat aside.

Georgie shook her head vehemently. 'No way!'

'If you do not go voluntarily, I will have my bodyguards carry you back,' Rafael told her, with a sudden spurt of flaming impatience.

'Did you hear me tell you that I'm not marrying you if you touch him?' Georgie's voice wobbled with rage and pain. The threat hadn't made Rafael bat a magnificent eyelash.

'It's your word against mine, Berganza! Who do you think she'll believe?' Steve slung aggressively. 'There's a lot of family mileage in twenty-one years. Are you going to take that risk?'

'Oh, beat the hell out of each other . . . I'm past caring!' Georgie hissed at the pair of them in disgust, stalking off several yards, hoping that her stinging scorn would cool Rafael off. She just couldn't believe that he was behaving like this. And what were they talking about? Steve's word against Rafael's on *what*?

She glanced back over her shoulder before she realised that Rafael had actually taken her at her word. Appalled, she watched him take a swing at Steve. Her stomach clenched with nausea as the blow connected. 'Stop that... right now!' she shrieked, and began racing back, ready to throw herself between them, but someone caught her from behind, anchoring a restraining arm round her.

'What the——?' Craning her neck, she discovered one of Rafael's bodyguards gazing down at her with a mixture of embarrassment, apology and steel determination to do as he had evidently been told.

Georgie actually thought she was going to be sick when she saw Rafael hitting Steve again. She had never realised that the sight of two men fighting could be so brutal or so frightening. And she had been right in her estimation of the odds. Her stepbrother was on the brink of being hammered to a pulp and there was absolutely nothing she could do to stop it. Nobody was about to interfere.

'I'll never forgive you,' she screamed at Rafael, and she really meant it. The man was an animal. She didn't care what lay between the two men, could not imagine that there could be anything capable of excusing the savagery being enacted before her. And she was devastated that Rafael could behave in such a fashion. She saw her hopes and her dreams breaking into pieces in front of her. Seeing this side of Rafael terrified her. He was a maniac, subject to paranoid jealousy—that was all she could think.

Steve hit the ground and stayed down. Was he unconscious? Rafael spun on his heel and walked away, pausing with apparent calm to address some instruction to one of the hovering men, who had been watching the fight. The arm round Georgie dropped away. She sped over to Steve. He was already lifting his head with a groan.

'God...' he mumbled, wiping the blood away from his mouth. 'I hate to admit it but I'm glad you stayed. I think he'd have killed me if he hadn't had you as an audience.'

'The doctor will see to him,' Rafael murmured icily from behind her.

'The only person who needs a doctor around here is you!' Georgie gasped in quivering disgust. 'A psychiatrist! Tell Teresa to pack my clothes—*my* clothes, not those fancy rags you bought. I'm not going back into that house. I am not marrying you. And I never want to hear from you again... is that clear?'

Rafael raked diamond-hard dark eyes from Georgie's furious face down to Steve's emerging look of relief. He released his breath in a soft hiss. Four centuries of icy hauteur tautened his proud dark features. 'The loser takes all, *es verdad*? You take his side over mine...'

'It's one heck of a lot more complex than that!' Georgie vented not quite steadily, but she met his eyes in a head-on collision.

'But you are the woman I intended to marry and you have neither loyalty nor trust in me,' Rafael condemned.

'This is so painfully melodramatic,' Steve said snidely, picking himself up.

Rafael hit him again.

Georgie just couldn't believe it. Her stepbrother went sprawling back on the ground again, clutching his nose and groaning.

'Go with him. I no longer want you,' Rafael delivered. 'But you deserve to know the truth before you leave.'

'What truth?'

Rafael stared down at Steve's prone figure with burning loathing and contempt. 'Have you the guts to tell her, or must I do that as well?' As the taut silence stretched and her stepbrother made no response, Rafael emitted a harsh laugh. 'He was in love with you four years ago——'

'*No!*' Georgie interrupted sharply.

'And you rejected him that night. He was jealous and he was bitter,' Rafael continued in the same murderously quiet drawl. 'And when I came looking for you the next morning, he *confessed* all to me, but he confessed to lies. He told me you had been lovers since you were seventeen, that he loved you and wanted to marry you——'

Georgie started to tremble, her darkened violet eyes clinging to Steve's clenched profile. 'No, he couldn't have done that...'

'He was very convincing. He even told me how ashamed he was of taking advantage of your youth and inexperience, but that he just couldn't help himself!' Rafael spelt out in disgust.

A stifled sound of distress broke from Georgie. Suddenly she knew that she was hearing the truth. Steve couldn't even meet her eyes, nor was he making any attempt to defend himself. She was appalled.

'And, not content with that, he suggested that you had also slept with your friend Danny, and he told me how much he blamed himself for damaging your ability to tell the difference between real love and sexual pleasure!' Rafael completed witheringly.

'You couldn't have done that to me,' Georgie whispered sickly, staring at Steve.

'Wake up, Georgie. He did it because, as far as he was concerned, if he couldn't have you, he didn't want me to have you either!' Rafael scorned. 'Your rejection of him must have cut deep indeed. This man, who stood in the position of a brother to you—he thought nothing of voicing filthy foul lies which resulted in your pain and humiliation. I assume that was your punishment for not finding him attractive... and mine was having my faith and my trust in the woman I loved totally destroyed! Never would I have believed that a man who was a member of your family, who had watched you grow up and behaved as a brother towards you, could have stooped to such a level as he did. Or that any man would confess *falsely* to such shameful behaviour!'

Georgie was in deep shock, her anguished eyes clinging to Rafael's dark, driven features. She was appalled that she had never once suspected that Steve could have been in love with her then. Yet she dimly understood how fixed an image one could form of a family member, how easy it could be never to question what might lie behind that safe image. She had been very close to Steve but, in the absence of any form of sexual awareness on her side, she had been effectively blind to his feelings, translating his interest and concern for her as purely brotherly responses. Only now did she see so clearly that Steve had been too interested and too concerned ... and too hostile towards Rafael.

'It's all behind us now, for God's sake,' Steve muttered heavily.

'But you came here to take her away sooner than risk exposure. You didn't want her to know the truth,' Rafael asserted. 'And I was fool enough to keep quiet because I didn't want to hurt her.'

Georgie flinched and covered her hot face with cold, trembling hands. 'I didn't know... how could I have?'

But, looking back, she saw Steve at her shoulder playing devil's advocate, stirring the pot of her insecurity about Rafael, undermining their relationship at every opportunity by planting little darts where they would cause the most damage. She also grasped the full extent of Steve's deception, shuddered as she recalled his sympathetic response to Rafael's rejection of her.

'How could you do that to me? You knew I loved him!' Georgie burst out abruptly, and then she noticed that Rafael had already walked away, that she was alone with her stepbrother.

'I thought you'd get over him, maybe turn to me.' Steve rose upright, dug his hands into his pockets and looked back at her with rueful eyes. 'I had it bad. It was a long time before I accepted that I was beating my head up against a brick wall and that you were never going to feel the same way.'

'But to tell him *that*——' In distress she turned away.

'He didn't have to believe it,' Steve said defensively.

But Georgie understood exactly why Rafael had believed those lies. Rafael was fundamentally a very honourable man. He had known that Steve loved her, seen them kiss, been forced to witness her close ties with her stepbrother. No, she didn't blame Rafael for believing, she blamed herself for being so bound up in her love that she had been blind to what was happening around her. And ironically, four years ago, Rafael had actually protected Steve by choosing not to face her with what he had been told. Why?

Why had he continued to protect her from the truth about Steve? Rafael had known how much the truth would hurt, and hurt it had and did, but perhaps not to the degree which Rafael had assumed. The intervening years had eroded her close ties with her stepbrother.

'I'm sorry,' Steve said. 'I just couldn't face it coming out. I got over you. It's behind me——'

'But you still didn't want me to be with him——'

'I'm never going to like the guy, Georgie. What do you expect? What do you think it was like for me standing by on the sidelines watching the two of you together?' he asked with remembered bitterness. 'I'm not proud of what I did, but I didn't think he had any intention of marrying you. He put the weapon in my hand when he told me he'd seen us kissing, and I'm sorry, but I couldn't resist using it.'

Dully she nodded, for she could dimly understand that.

'Look...I'm off. I'd be distinctly *de trop* at the wedding,' Steve muttered with a grim smile. 'Maybe I'll make it for the first christening... OK?'

'There isn't going to be a wedding,' Georgie reminded him in a shaky voice.

Making his stiff and painful passage back towards the helicopter he had arrived in, Steve turned his head. 'Georgie...the fight was a *male* thing, if you know what I mean, and you shouldn't have interfered.'

'It was disgusting!'

'But oddly enough I feel better.' Steve grimaced at her look of disbelief. 'It's like it's finally finished now and, since I'm feeling generous, I'll give you another reason why he took until now to tell you what I did...and why he just walked away. I think he's scared.'

'Scared? Rafael?' Georgie parroted.

'Scared that once you knew how I used to feel about you, that fondness you *once* had for me,' he explained wryly, 'might just warm up into something more meaningful.'

Georgie froze, and turned an abstracted glance on him as he headed for his transport out. But all she had sought to do was stop the fight, naturally not wanting to see the two men come to blows. Then, she hadn't known just how powerful a motivation lay behind Rafael's need for physical vengeance. And then, afterwards, Rafael had said, 'The loser takes all,' when she had rushed to Steve's aid, believing Rafael to be the main aggressor and therefore underserving of her attention. Maybe she should have kicked Steve while he was down, she thought hysterically. In Rafael's presence she had not condemned what Steve had done...she had still been too shocked.

She hurried back to the house and was shattered to discover Teresa in her bedroom, laying out her clothes on the bed to pack them.

Teresa sighed, and shook her head. 'Ees very hard to understand this on, off, on, off wedding.'

Her heart in her throat, Georgie ran Rafael to earth in the drawing-room where he was standing moodily surveying an ancestral portrait with a large drink in one hand.

'Oops...gosh...I didn't think what I was saying when I said the wedding was off.' Georgie leapt in and tested the water straight off.

'I will put no pressure on you to remain,' Rafael retorted harshly.

'All right, if that's the way you feel about it...' Georgie drew herself up to her full height, her chin tilting, and then drew in a deep, shivering breath. 'Well, actually, it's not all right because I'm not going—not unless you tell me that you want me to go.'

'You have your mind of your own.' Hooded dark eyes flicked her a forbidding glance. 'Where is he now?'

'Steve? Probably airborne by now. He reckoned he would be unwelcome at the wedding but he might just make it for the first christening,' Georgie dared.

Rafael's jawline clenched. 'I forgot about that possibility.'

'Fancy that, and just a few days ago, that was all you could think about!' Georgie reminded him helplessly.

'No doubt that is why you insist that you are not leaving,' he drawled in the same unyielding tone.

'Franky, no. Whether or not I might be pregnant hasn't even crossed my mind and it wouldn't influence my feelings either way,' Georgie stated with perfect truth. 'It isn't a good enough reason to get married.'

'Then what have we to discuss?'

Georgie went white. Steeling herself, she had been trying to work up to telling him how she really felt about him. No more lies, no more half-truths to save face, she had told herself, no more room for misunderstandings. Pride urged her to agree the point and go with dignity, as she had not done four long years ago. But now she knew that, then, Rafael had undoubtedly been far kinder to her than most men would have been in the same situation. He had not thrown Steve's sordid revelations in her face and she still marvelled at that restraint.

'Rafael...I am very sorry that Steve lied like that——'

'It is not your place to apologise for him...or is it?' he growled, glittering golden eyes on her with almost physical force. 'Do you now defend him for what he did, even though it was your reputation he destroyed?'

'No...I don't defend him at all. I think it was a revolting thing to do and I was very shocked, but it happened four years ago,' Georgie stressed tautly, her violet eyes clinging to his hard, set features. 'And I can't get as worked up about it as you can because I didn't know about it when it really mattered. I also thought that we had overcome the past...but it seems I was wrong!'

'Your sole concern was for him out there——'

'And you've accused me of being childish,' Georgie suddenly launched at him, her voice nonetheless shrill with distress, for she wasn't getting through to Rafael. He had withdrawn to some remote place, outraged and offended. 'That was before I knew what you were fighting about and I thought Steve had been knocked out. You hate him and I can understand that now——'

'How can you understand what I feel? How can you possibly understand?' Rafael suddenly shot at her in savage surge. 'Thanks to him, I lost the woman I loved four years ago and, thanks to him, I have lost you again!'

'You haven't lost me.' Georgie licked her dry lips.

'I do not want you without love. It wouldn't work.'
Rafael stared down broodingly into his half-empty glass,
his strong features strikingly taut. 'I am already bitter—
how much more bitter would I become, thinking of what
we once had and lost? I cannot pretend that what we
have is enough, when I would always be wanting what
you could not give me,' he bit out with raw emotion.
'So, go while I am in this sane state. I do not want a
broken marriage between us and I see no way of us ever
overcoming the past.'

Sentenced to stillness by the savage edge to his
emotional delivery, Georgie was afraid in that welter of
bitter words, she had somehow misinterpreted what she
had heard. Her heartbeat was racing madly behind her
ribcage. 'Rafael,' she said weakly.

'I feel resentment now, even though I have no en-
titlement to it,' Rafael continued darkly. 'You were the
victim, not I. It was not you who lied, not you who were
stupid enough to swallow his lies, and I was the one who
walked away, so what right do I now have to demand
more than you are capable of feeling? You desire me,
and you have a naturally sunny and affectionate dis-
position and, for many men, that would be enough. But
is is not enough for me. If I cannot have it all, I am
better off with nothing.'

Tears swam in her eyes and she wrinkled her nose to
hold them at bay. She had never seen him so worked up
and, characteristically, he was looking solely on the dark
side, apparently unable even to consider the idea that
she might, after all, be capable of giving him what he
insisted he needed. She cleared her throat. 'Are we
talking about love?'

His beautifully shaped mouth tightened and she
realised that pride had permitted him to talk all the way
round the subject as long as the fatal word was not actually mentioned. 'What else?'

A surge of joy filtered through Georgie, restoring the colour to her cheeks, chasing off the strain from her vibrant face. 'Oh, well, if that's all, you've been unusually modest in your assumptions. And I would have said you were not the modest type——'

'What are you talking about?' Rafael demanded, with no diminution in his grim bearing.

'Let me give you this scenario, Rafael. You spirit me out here with the worst of gothic intentions. How hard did I try to escape? Why did I go to bed with you? Why did I finally agree to marry you? Why was I prepared to stay with you even though you might lose everything?' Georgie questioned with a helpless smile, although she had intended to keep him hanging to the end. 'And, if you're as clever as I think, you ought to be coming to one of two possible conclusions. Either I'm as limp as a wet dishcloth or I'm crazy about you.'

'*Es verdad*?' Rafael searched her bright, speaking eyes and suddenly dropped the cold front. He strode forward and gripped her shoulders. 'You are serious?'

'I'm beginning to think I never really stopped being crazy about you. I love you so much... How can you not see that?' she whispered ruefully.

'I didn't. I thought you felt sorry for me when you saw me getting drunk, and I was prepared to use that to hold you,' he confessed, a dark flush accentuating his handsome cheekbones. 'But it was a shameful thing to do.'

No, it had been an education, but she was tactful enough to keep that acknowledgement to herself. 'You were that desperate?' she couldn't help prompting.

'I wanted what we had back and I believed it was lost forever... but it was not lost for me,' Rafael muttered, with something less than his usual perfect English. 'You had not been here very long before I understood that even with all the unpleasant things I had believed of you, I still loved you.'

'You love me too?' Georgie was in seventh heaven.

'It was not only the desire which tore my heart out from the first day,' Rafael told her with satisfying fervour as he pulled her up against him and stared down at her with adoring dark eyes and a slightly stunned expression, as if he still couldn't yet believe that she loved him back. 'It was the liking and the laughing too. Your spirit, your sense of humour, the manner in which you stood up to me. I had turned you into a shallow bitch inside my mind over the years, and then instantly I was faced with the reality that, whatever your morals were, you were really still the warm, vibrant girl I fell in love with at the age of seventeen——'

'I love the sound of your voice,' Georgie confided honestly, 'especially when you're saying things like that. Did you really fall for me back then?'

'One look that first day and it was like being hit by lightning.'

'Lightning struck twice. I thought you were gorgeous. I couldn't take my eyes off you,' Georgie admitted unsteadily.

'*Te quiero, querida mía.*' Tired of talking, Rafael raked impassioned eyes over her and lifted her up in his arms to devour her mouth with an intense hunger he no longer tried to hide.

Some timeless minutes later, Georgie registered that what she was lying on was not a bed, but a rigid and hard sofa. Rafael's jacket was on the floor along with his tie, and his shirt was hanging open, revealing the glorious expanse of his muscular chest. She scratched her fingernails through the curling dark hair hazing his pectorals, smiling a very feminine smile of power as he shuddered in response and came back down to her again fast, sealing his hard body to hers in a movement that gave her no doubt of his ultimate intentions.

'You are wearing too many clothes,' he muttered raggedly, positively aflame with impatience.

'I thought we were waiting for tomorrow night,' Georgie gasped, as one lean hand closed over the mound of one swelling breast, frustratingly barred from him by the tight bodice of her fitted top.

'Forget that,' Rafael groaned. 'I cannot wait...'

'And to think I thought you were not a spontaneous guy,' Georgie sighed in delight.

Neither one of them heard the door open. They were far too busy kissing.

'Tía's no great shakes as a chaperon, is she?'

Rafael's head flew up in shock. Georgie froze. As Rafael sprang off the sofa, Georgie sat up and grinned from ear to ear. María Cristina was wearing a matching grin on her rounded, pretty face.

'This is going to take a lot of living down, brother dear,' Rafael's sister asserted, tickled pink at having surprised her very self-disciplined older brother in such a situation. 'And in the drawing-room too, where anybody could walk in.'

'Anybody else would have had the good manners to knock,' Rafael vented in a driven undertone.

Georgie flew across the room into her friend's arms. 'You already knew I was here!'

'I knew the day you arrived. I've been in cahoots with Teresa. I swear it was excitement which sent me into labour,' María Cristina chuckled. 'Go and meet your nephew, George,' she said to Rafael. 'Georgie and I have some catching up to do.'

Teresa brought coffee. Antonio, María Cristina's husband, wandered in briefly to be introduced. Teresa brought Georgie's namesake in and he was much admired before he closed his big dark eyes and went cheerfully back to sleep in his beribboned Moses basket.

'Of course I knew you were in love with my brother,' her friend laughed. 'And I thought he was in love with you. I even guessed when you started seeing each other. Rafael was so happy and you floated about as if you were on a cloud. Then you broke up, and ever since I've been racking my brains on how to bring the two of you together again. This time, when I invited you, I was really devious and I took an awful risk——'

'You knew you were going to California and yet you practically pleaded with me to come and stay with you?'

'Guilty...but it worked. You had to contact Rafael to find out where I was, and I knew he was still interested because he was always so keen to know what you said in your letters and what you were doing,' María Cristina confided. 'But I have to tell you, with a wedding arranged for tomorrow, the pair of you have more than exceeded my wildest expectations!'

'Are you pleased?'

'Georgie, I'm over the moon! I couldn't be more delighted—Rafael has been so gruesomely serious since you broke up...'

'Alone at last,' Rafael groaned, leaning back against the door as he locked it. *Por Dios*...what are you wearing?'

Sinuously sheathed in a peach satin and lace teddy, which made no attempt to pretend that its function was anything but pure female provocation, Georgie lounged back against the pillows on the comfortable bed and shamelessly basked in the reality that her new husband was riveted by the view.

They had had the most glorious wedding-day, with her parents and all Rafael's closest relatives in attendance. Georgie thought headily of the moment Rafael had slid that gold ring on her finger and of the expression of love in his rich dark eyes. Her toes curled, just reliving that moment of knowing that she was the most wonderful woman in the world as far as he was concerned.

'You haven't even asked where we are going,' Rafael said mockingly, dropping his jacket in a careless heap and coming down on the bed beside her.

Her heart raced at his proximity. The throb of the jet engines was not as loud as her own heartbeat. 'I'm expecting to be taken to heaven tonight,' she whispered, running wantonly possessive eyes over his magnificent length.

'I have the villa in the Caribbean.'

'I can't wait that long...'

Rafael leant down and extracted a devastatingly erotic kiss that turned her bones to liquid honey. 'Did you think I would ask you to?'

She linked her arms round his brown neck, weak with longing. Golden eyes merged with violet in the smouldering silence.

'*Te quiero, enamorada,*' he muttered feverishly, and drew her close. For a long time afterwards there was nothing but the heated rise of their breathing and her long, gasping sighs of pleasure. Satiated, they lay wrapped tightly together in an intimate tangle of limbs.

'I'm glad you didn't have to get rid of the jet. This bed is very convenient,' Georgie sighed.

Rafael tautened. 'I have a confession to make.'

'Anything bar murder, you're forgiven,' Georgie mused dizzily, running a worshipping hand over his smooth golden back.

'I lied about the financial reverses...'

'You *lied*?' Forcing him back from her, Georgie sat up and surveyed him in horror and bewilderment. 'But how could you have been lying? I saw a bank statement lying on the floor that night, and it must have belonged to you, and the account was in the red to the tune of six figures.'

'A bank statement?' Rafael frowned. 'In the red ... Ah, those statements I was studying that night belonged to a bankrupt company I was thinking of buying.'

'Really?' Feeling decidedly foolish, Georgie went very pink and dropped that angle. 'You were saying that you lied to me, which I consider quite unforgivable!'

Rafael started talking fast. 'But you warmed to me as never before when you thought I was having business problems,' he protested.

'You rat, you utter rat!' Georgie screeched at him, reflecting on her painful enactment of the stand-by-your-man routine.

'Think of our children ... you would not want them to be poor, surely?' Rafael reasoned in desperation.

'You must have been laughing your socks off at me that night!'

'No, for the first time I was encouraged to hope that I could win you back,' Rafael asserted. 'So I thought maybe I would be a loser for a little while and see what happened——'

'You played on my sympathy, you sneaky, conniving rat,' Georgie condemned afresh. 'What was all that guff about you having nothing left?'

'Without your love, I had nothing. That was why I was drowning my sorrows and feeling sorry for myself. You had told me you wanted me only for the life I could give you, and that cut deep ...'

'You deserved it—all that posturing about love being messy and complicating things. That was your pride talking.'

'Sí ...'

'Without your love, I had nothing.' And he really meant it. 'Maybe I can forgive you this once,' she sniffed, not surrendering too easily and keeping her distance. 'On the other hand, I could walk out...'

'We are sixty thousand feet above the ground.' As he made the reminder his striking features were slashed with helpless amusement. 'Not that I would expect a small consideration like that to stop you!'

'If you don't stop laughing at me, you're——' She was silenced as he jerked her back down on top of him and claimed her mouth hungrily again.

'Oh, yes...' she moaned several minutes later, the previous conversation having vanished from her mind. 'Thank God the alligator didn't get me,' she murmured, with heartfelt gratitude that she had been spared for a future of such unsurpassed ecstasy.

'Clearly he wasn't half as sneaky and conniving as me...' Rafael drawled, with rich self-satisfaction.

Charlotte Lamb was born in London in time for World War II, and spent most of the war moving from relative to relative to escape bombing. Educated at a convent, she married a journalist, and now has five children. The family lives in the Isle of Man. Charlotte Lamb has written over a hundred books for Mills & Boon® since 1973. She has had more than 45 million copies of her books in print, which have been published all around the world.

DYING FOR YOU
by
CHARLOTTE LAMB

CHAPTER ONE

ANNIE got the first phone call at midnight on a cold spring night.

'Remember me?' a voice whispered, and the hairs on the back of her neck stood up.

She had only just got back to her London flat, she was alone, and already on the verge of tears because her best friend, Diana, had just married the man Annie loved.

'Who is this?' she asked, then wondered if it was one of the band, who were all still drinking at the bar in the hotel where the wedding reception had been held. When they were drunk all five of them could do the silliest things.

But there was no reply. The phone went dead. She hung up, frowning, then switched on the answering machine. The last thing she needed tonight was crank phone calls.

She turned away with a swish of silk, comforted by the sensual feel of the sleek material against her skin. Annie loved good clothes. She had helped Diana choose her wedding-dress and had chosen the dress she herself wore as bridesmaid—almond-green silk, a colour which exactly matched the colour of her eyes. She would be able to wear it for parties afterwards. There was a faintly Victorian look about the style of the dress, as there had been about Di's wedding-dress; and Annie had put up her long black hair into a smooth chignon at the back of her head, carried a tiny Victorian-style bouquet of violets displayed on ferns.

She must take the best-looking flower and a spray of fern out of the bouquet, and put them between the pages of a book of poetry. She often pressed wild flowers in books; she liked finding them when she turned the pages years afterwards, being reminded of some special day, some important moment in her life. They always seemed to retain their scent, yet altered and nostalgic, a gentle, faded sweetness that gave her back instant memories.

However hurt she felt, she knew this had been a very important day in her life; she would want to remember it.

Yawning, she looked at her watch. Bed! she thought, seeing that it was way past midnight now. Annie kept strict hours when she wasn't performing on stage. She would be in bed by ten most days, up very early, and tomorrow was no different. Tomorrow she had to be up at seven. She had a photo call at nine at the recording studio where she was just putting the final touches to her new disc.

She took off her green silk dress and hung it up carefully in her wall-to-wall wardrobe, put on a brief nightdress and matching négligé, then sat down at the dressing-table and started to take off her make-up, and smooth a toning lotion into her skin. However late, however tired she was, Annie always went through the same routine before going to bed.

'When you're in the public eye all the time people notice everything about you, so never forget to look your best. You are always going to be on stage!' Philip had told her years ago.

She hadn't been sure then that she liked the idea. In fact, it had been her first premonition that fame and success were not going to be without their drawbacks.

Philip had watched her shrewdly. 'Not so sure you like that, kid? Well, now's the time to make your mind up, before you really get started. If you want to be a star you have to take the rough with the smooth; there's no two ways about it. If you want out now, you only have to say so. Nobody knows you yet; you can easily go back to your old life without anyone being any the wiser.'

She hadn't wanted out. She had looked at him with wide, melancholy green eyes and sighed.

'There's nothing for me to go back to,' she remembered saying. 'I want to be a singer more than anything else in the world.'

It had been that simple then; it was that simple now, and yet it got harder every year, although that was something Philip hadn't warned her about. The strain of being at the top and fighting to stay there was only a part of it; there was a more personal price to pay, because the public wouldn't give you any space. They ate you up if you let them, and you never knew whether you could trust the people you met; you couldn't be sure if they really liked you, or were starstruck, or wanted to use you in some way.

That was a hard lesson to learn. It hurt, and you were tempted to grow a second skin, toughen up; but Annie instinctively knew you couldn't let yourself get too tough or the music would lose something vital. Getting hurt sometimes seemed essential to the music. Some of her best songs had been written about her secret feelings for Philip, feelings of which he seemed blithely unaware.

He had always treated her the same way from the beginning: as if to him she would always be the seventeen-year-old kid he had met all those years ago. In the beginning she had been relieved to find she could trust him to keep his hands to himself, not to proposition her or make off-colour jokes. Philip was a tough businessman, but he was kind and thoughtful to her; he treated her as if she were his daughter or his sister, and at first that had been fine. Until she had realised she was in love with him, but that Philip simply didn't see her that way.

It was from that time that her songs had begun to have a deeper tone, she thought wryly, looking back. Until then she had just been pretending to write about love; like most people when they were young, she had loved sad songs, had acted out emotions she had never really felt. Falling in love with Philip had made her work far more personal, far more real, and in the past six months she had written some of the best work she had ever done, because her grief and loss when she heard that he was going to marry Diana had made the songs pour out of her, often two or three a week, a very high production rate, for her or any other songwriter.

It had helped to keep her busy. In preparation for her new disc and the forthcoming European tour she was to make, over the last six months she had been working so hard that she hadn't had time to think too much.

For eight years she had had Philip and Diana to rely on, for help, advice, comfort and companionship. Philip was her agent and manager, and to look after her when she first came to London he had found Diana Abbot, who was then a twenty-two-year-old secretary in Philip's office. Diana had gone on working for Philip, but she had also shared Annie's flat, made sure she got to the studio on time, accompanied her on tours, and dealt with the Press and any other problems Annie ran into. A tough, capable, streetwise girl from the back streets of Liverpool, Di had a kind heart, warm brown eyes that smiled all the time and an infectious laugh.

Annie was as fond of Di as she was in love with Philip. He wasn't handsome, but he had sex appeal. Tall and rangy, with steady, cynical blue eyes and hair the colour of toffee, he was always noticed by women. Annie had had to watch him dating other girls for years, a little comforted because none of his affairs lasted long. His life was too busy, too involved with work. The girls got bored with waiting for him to ring them, and moved on. Annie kept hoping Philip would finally realise that she was no longer a girl of seventeen, but a grown woman, but she had never once imagined that when Philip did fall in love it would be with Diana.

Three months ago a mix-up over luggage had meant that the two of them had missed a connecting flight during Annie's coast-to-coast tour of America. A blizzard had raged for two days, making it impossible for them to fly on to catch up with Annie and the band. It had been the first time Philip and Diana had ever spent a long time alone together.

'I really got to know him,' Diana had said later, telling a pale, stunned Annie that she and Philip were getting married. 'Funny, I'd known him for years without ever getting past the surface, but once we started talking it was like peeling an onion; there were layers I'd never suspected. We couldn't go out of the airport hotel: the wind was like a knife, and the snow was six feet deep in places. There was a power cut, and we had no TV, no heat and no light, so we huddled under quilts, in our overcoats, and talked and talked.'

'And fell in love?' Annie had said, pretending to laugh, and Diana had turned a face glowing with happiness to her, nodding.

'And fell in love. Crazy, isn't it, after knowing each other for years? It was as if there had been a wall between us, and suddenly it fell down.'

Annie had felt sick at first. She had been hurt and jealous, bitterly shaken by this blow, but because she loved them both she had managed to hide her real reaction.

Neither of them had an inkling what the news had done to her. That was one good thing. She had never confided her love for Philip to Diana, and she had never let Philip himself glimpse it, either. At least they didn't know how she felt, so all she had to do was go on acting, pretending to be delighted for them.

And in a funny sort of way, she was—she did love them both, and she wanted them to be happy, even if it meant that she was going to be left alone, after years of being the most important thing in both their lives.

She had first met Philip at a friend's party where she had sung a couple of songs. It had never occurred to her to think of a life as a professional singer. When Philip told her he could make her a star she hadn't believed him. She had no self-confidence and very little vanity, yet some instinct had made her trust him, and that instinct had been a sound one.

Everything he had promised her had come true, slowly at first, but over the last few years with dizzying speed. First she had worked in clubs, at night, while in the daytime she had had vocal training, stage training, dance lessons, and then Phil had got her that first recording contract, which really started her career. Now she was becoming known in America, and in two weeks' time she would open her tour of Europe with a big concert in Paris.

She was becoming a star in the UK too, which brought its own problems, including getting crank calls, but she didn't often get them now because her phone was no longer listed anywhere; only a handful of people knew her number. She had gone ex-directory several years ago when she started getting problems with fans ringing her day and night. At the same time she had moved to this flat in a rather exclusive district close to one of London's big parks. The street was lined with trees; there was no passing-through traffic, just the cars of wealthy residents, or visiting tradesmen. There were big houses set in large gardens, so that one got a sense of living almost in the country, there was so much greenery around and on warm days a delicious country smell of leaves and flowers.

Even more important than all this, the large block of luxury flats into which Annie moved had a very thorough security system. There was a uniformed guard, with a savage-looking dog, on patrol all night around the grounds, and the electronically controlled doors of the building only admitted you if you had a card which you fitted into the computer by the door. You had to tap in your personal security number. Only then did the door open for you.

This was one of those anonymous blocks of flats where everyone behaved in a civilised fashion, not playing TVs or radios at top blast, not having riotous parties, not having violent rows with each other. There had been two bedrooms, one for her, one for Diana, who had shared the flat with her.

Now Annie would be living there alone, and she was finding it hard to adjust to that. She had never lived alone before. Before she met Philip she had lived with her mother and stepfather and her two stepbrothers in London. The family had all been relieved when she moved out: the house had been overcrowded, and Annie had never got on with her stepfather. She had barely seen any of them since.

Living alone was faintly nerve-racking. She listened to the silence: the only sound was the low hum of the central heating system, of the fridge in the kitchen. There were people living all around her, yet they were so quiet that it was like living alone, on the moon.

Every flat was occupied, in fact. This was a very popular apartment block; there was a waiting list of tenants wanting flats. A number of celebrities could be seen coming in and going out; often they had other homes and only kept their flat in this block for trips to London. It was well managed, comfortable, with a swimming-pool, saunas and a very well equipped gymnasium.

Life was easy here: lifts whisked you up and down, there was always a porter on the door, your garbage was disposed of by simply pushing it into a chute next to the lift. There was even an underground car park so that if fans did ever find out where she lived and waited outside she would be able to drive out of the building without being stopped.

Annie had felt totally safe there. Until now.

But it was stupid to let the phone call prey on her mind. After all, it hadn't been obscene, just some stupid joke by one of the band, probably.

Yet as she climbed into bed she was still thinking about the call. If it was just a joke, why did it bother her so much? It did; she couldn't deny it. The words kept ringing in her head. Remember me. Remember me? Had it been a question, or a demand?

Whichever it had been the intonation had somehow been disturbing, no doubt because she was here alone, for the first time in her life, feeling abandoned, left behind.

Tonight she was an easy target for whoever had rung. But nobody could have known that. She had tried to fool everyone at the wedding, tried to be the life and soul of the party afterwards—at all costs, Philip and Diana mustn't guess at her real mood. They had every right to take happiness when they found it; she didn't want to ruin their big day.

She wasn't a teenager any more; she was twenty-five, for heaven's sake! She could look after herself; she had flown the Atlantic several times, could speak French and Italian quite well, was learning Spanish—these days, as Philip said, music was an international business and meant a lot of travelling. The more languages you knew, the better.

So stop feeling sorry for yourself! she thought crossly. You've got plenty of life skills; you can manage on your own.

She could drive a car, cook; she had even had self-defence training and could throw a man over her shoulder if the need arose. Surely to heaven she could learn to live alone, and she could cope with grief and loss. You could cope with anything if you had to.

She turned over and settled to sleep, and some time during the night she vaguely heard the phone begin to ring, then cut out as the machine took over, but she was beyond caring by then.

In the morning she was in a rush to get to work, so she didn't even bother to listen to the answering machine; she simply left it switched on.

The photo session was boring. She always felt like a dummy being arranged in a shop window, and her face ached from smiling by the time it was over.

'Try to look happy, love!' urged the photographer gloomily.

'Sorry, I hate having my photo taken!' she said.

'It shows,' the photographer told her. 'Relax. Look, just a few more and we're finished.'

The band lined up behind him and made elephant's ears with their hands, and she laughed naturally.

'That's better!' the photographer said.

The drummer, a huge boy of twenty called Brick because he was built like a brick wall, grinned at her as they all walked away. 'I read in a book once that primitive tribesmen think that when you take their picture you're stealing their souls—is that what you think, Annie?'

He was the band's leading joker; the others all chuckled.

'I just hate pictures of myself!' she muttered, wondering if it had been Brick who had rung her last night, and he looked down at her slanting vivid green eyes, her sleek black hair and the small, pale-skinned triangular face which some journalist had not long ago described as giving her the look of a kitten caught out in the rain. That had made the band laugh their heads off! But it had infuriated Annie.

'You can't be serious!' Brick said, shaking his head at her. 'You're amazingly photogenic, love! And you should be used to cameras by now; your face is always in some magazine or other these days.'

She shrugged without answering. Her dislike of cameras was another of her instinctive reactions, a gut feeling based on nothing rational, purely primitive, no doubt. People never understood; she rarely tried to explain any more.

'Did you ring me last night, Brick?' she asked, and he looked blank.

'Ring you? No. Did you ask me to? I don't remember anything much about the wedding after the reception started.'

The others all roared with laughter. Annie smiled wryly. No, it hadn't been Brick, or, from the expressions of the rest of the band, any of them, either. She knew them well enough to be sure she would have picked up a self-conscious expression if the phone call had been a joke by one of them.

She and the band rehearsed for hours, not breaking for lunch, just having a yoghurt and an apple some time during the day. Philip got angry if she put on weight. It ruined the image he had spent years building up.

He was always telling her, 'Image is everything in this business! It isn't what you are, it's what they think you are that matters, and you have to be certain always to look the way they think you should.'

The public saw her the way Philip intended they should—a street singer, small, sad, lonely, defiant.

She wore her long black hair down, framing her pale face. Her make-up highlighted her big eyes, her wide mouth. Her stage costumes were simple and inexpensive; she wore mostly black, accenting her slenderness, her frailty. And although the songs changed with the years, the mood of her singing remained the same. Her fans liked her that way.

Sometimes, though, Annie felt trapped inside a persona Philip had created but which she wasn't sure fitted her any longer, even if it had when she first began singing.

'Missing Phil and Di?' Brick asked her as they left the rehearsal rooms. 'Come and have a curry with us; we're going to that Indian place down the street.'

She shook her head. 'Too fattening. I'll eat at home; see you all.'

When she got home she automatically switched on the answering machine while she was slitting open her private mail, all of it from friends in the music business. There was a letter from Philip's office about the forthcoming tour, signed in his absence by his secretary, a telephone bill and a postcard from Budapest from a previous member of the band who had left to join another group, who were touring Hungary.

Annie read that first, smiling over the few scribbled words, and then her head lifted in shock as she heard the whispering voice on the answering machine. She had been so busy all day that she had forgotten last night's crank call, but she remembered now as he said softly, 'Remembered me yet?'

The phone clicked off again, but that wasn't the end of it. The recording whirred on again. He had rung a second time; this time he whispered, 'I remember you, Annie. I remember everything.'

Annie felt ice trickle down her spine. She stared at the machine, waiting, but there was nothing else on it; it clicked off.

Who on earth was it? Not Brick. It wasn't one of his silly jokes. These phone calls were no joke. They were too disturbing to be funny. Were they veiled threats? Some sort of come-on meant to intrigue her? She had no idea what was behind them, but one thing was certain. She had never heard that voice before.

She was sure she didn't know this man, that they had never met, or if they had it had been so brief, so casual, that she had simply forgotten all about it.

Why hadn't he? She shivered, frowning. It was scary to think that out there was a man who thought he knew her when he didn't. Was it some crazy fan who had started to believe his own fantasy? She had heard about things like that; it hadn't occurred to her that it might actually happen to her.

And that accent of his ... It was odd in some indefinable way, perfectly good English, but there was a faint note occasionally that made her wonder if he was a foreigner.

She was very aware of being alone in the flat. It was night again, very quiet. Was she the only person awake in the whole block of flats?

Walking over to the window, she looked out into the London sky, glowing with sulphurous yellow light from the street-lamps below. Annie gazed at the tall houses opposite, some rooms lit, others dark. There were people in all those houses, people in the other flats above and below her. Yet she felt intensely alone, and she was frightened.

The phone rang and she jumped violently. Swinging round, she stared across the room. She had forgotten to put the answering machine on again.

Well, she wasn't answering him. She would let it ring and ring; he would give up in the end, believing she was out.

She went to the bathroom and ran the shower full on to drown the sound of the phone, had a lengthy shower. As she switched off the jet of water and stepped out, wrapping herself in a towelling robe, the flat was silent again and she heaved a sigh of relief, but as she walked towards the kitchen in bare feet the phone began to ring again.

She angrily shut herself in the kitchen and made some supper: a small mixed salad sprinkled with chopped nuts and fruit. The phone still rang and rang.

He wasn't reacting the way she had thought he would. Why wasn't he giving up? Surely it must be obvious that she was out?

She wasn't, of course. But he couldn't know that. Could he? Her nerves jangled. Could he? But what if he was out there, somewhere, near by, watching her?

Her heart almost stopped. If he lived near here, or was down there in the street, he could see her lights on; he would know she was in the flat.

Suddenly a new idea occurred to her. What if it wasn't the guy who had been ringing her? What if this was Philip or Diana, ringing her from their honeymoon hotel, to check that she was OK? They would be worried if she didn't answer, at this hour of the night.

She ran out of the kitchen into the sitting-room, snatched up the ringing phone.

'Hello?' she breathlessly said.

'I wondered how long it would be before you answered,' the smoky voice said, and her heart skipped a beat.

'Why are you doing this? Stop ringing me; leave me alone—who are you?' she gabbled, hardly aware what she was saying.

'Haven't you remembered yet? Never mind, you will.'

'Look, it's very late, and I'm tired; will you get off this line? And don't ring again!' Annie shakily said.

'Are you ready for bed?' he whispered, and she began to tremble, almost believing he could see her. He knew she was only wearing a robe and was naked underneath it. 'You must be tired; you've had a long day,' he said, and her eyes stretched wide, in shock. 'I won't keep you up; I just wanted to say goodnight,' he murmured softly. 'I'll be seeing you soon, Annie.'

The phone went dead again, and she slammed her own down, panic pouring through her. He was coming here. What else had that meant?

She ran to the front door of the flat to check it was locked, stood in the hallway listening to the usual silence, waiting for the sound of his footsteps, for a ring on the door.

It was minutes before she remembered the security system in the flats. He couldn't get in; the night porter downstairs on the desk would ring her, wouldn't admit anyone until she said it was OK.

Yet somehow she wasn't entirely sure. She waited, her heart in her mouth. The minutes ticked by; nothing happened. No phone rang; nobody came to the door. She shakily retreated to the living-room, sat staring at the silent phone, waiting.

It was two hours before she realised he wasn't coming; not tonight, at least. She wondered then if she should ring the police, move out, go to a hotel, but she wouldn't let this crazy person drive her from her home. When Phil and Di got back they would be horrified if they heard about it; they'd feel guilty, think that she couldn't cope alone.

No, this was some sort of war of nerves. For some reason this man was trying to frighten her, but she wasn't going to let him. What could the police do if she told them about it? Monitor her phone calls? Maybe she should have her number changed again. But then how had he got this number in the first place, and would he get the new one too?

Who was he? How did he know so much about her?

She went to bed, and managed to sleep after a while. When she woke up next morning she had a confused memory of a dream; phones had been ringing, a voice had haunted her sleep, there had been strange, terrifying flashes of light, and for some reason she had kept hearing the sea.

It must have been the traffic of London in the distance, she decided as she got ready. It sometimes sounded like the sea when you heard it at night, and the flashes of light must have been headlights from passing cars.

She and the band rehearsed hard for eight hours that day. She had no time to think about anything else, but as she drove home that evening she began to wonder what messages she was going to find on the answerphone, and her nerves leapt as she switched on the machine.

There were none. Relief made her feel almost sick, but the next day she rushed to the answerphone as soon as she got back to her flat. This time there was a short message from Philip's office. No messages from the whispering voice. Perhaps he had got tired of playing cat and mouse with her, had given up the game or turned his attention elsewhere.

She got a card from Philip and Diana a couple of days later: blue skies, palm trees, a ludicrously blue sea and on the other side a message that made her laugh, ending with a reminder that they would meet her and the band in Paris in a week. They would need time to rehearse at the venue itself, and do Press interviews before the tour began, and Annie hoped to get in some sightseeing.

Annie was beginning to get used to living alone by the time she drove to Heathrow to catch the flight to Paris. The equipment was going overland, and then by sea, in large vans, and the band had all elected to go with it. Brick, in particular, had a neurotic fear of something happening to his amazingly expensive drums if they got out of his sight. Annie preferred to fly, though; it was quicker and more comfortable.

There had been no more of the weird phone calls; she was sleeping normally again and looking forward to seeing Di and Phil very soon. She was going to have to get used to the fact that they belonged to each other now, more than they did to her, of course. It would be painful, difficult at times; but Annie was determined to get over this first awkward phase of the new relationship. The other two meant too much to her for her to want to lose them. She would simply have to live with her feelings, as she had for years now, and maybe one day she would meet someone else, and get over Phil at last.

She would be the first to arrive in Paris, since the band would take quite a while to drive across France with all their equipment. They planned to stop *en route* at a hotel for the night, and they would join Annie at the hotel the following day.

Philip's secretary had arranged for Annie to be met at the airport by a chauffeur-driven car, and she had an escort on the plane, a couple of security men hired by Phil to make sure she had no problems on the flight. They all sat in first-class, the men on the aisle side, in case someone tried to talk to Annie, who sat by the window.

She was casually dressed in a black and scarlet skiing jacket under which she wore a white silk jersey shirt, and black ski-pants and boots. A few passengers walked past, staring, but she kept her face averted, staring out of the window, and when they landed she was whisked through the VIP channel at Charles de Gaulle and escorted almost immediately out of a side-door. A large black limousine was waiting. The two security men had words with the chauffeur in a dark suit, who got out as they approached. He held the door open for Annie, half bowing, murmured a greeting in French, and Annie climbed into the back and settled down in the luxurious, leather-upholstered interior, while her Gucci luggage was loaded on to the car.

The two security men weren't coming with her in the car; they were returning to England. A French security team would take over whenever required. The driver closed the door and got behind the wheel, then the limousine purred softly away and from behind smoked glass windows she watched the airport terminal disappear as they followed the unwinding ribbon on the auto-route.

It was some minutes later that she turned her gaze to the front again, and noticed the driver. She hadn't noticed his face when she got into the car, and now she couldn't see it, but he had smooth black hair and wide shoulders. She caught a glimpse of his neck, tanned and powerful above a white collar. He hadn't said a word to her since they set off, for which she was grateful, because now that she was in France she was nervous about practising her French. She had been learning it for years, and could talk quite easily to her teacher, but that was a very different matter from talking to French people in their own country.

She stared curiously out of the window at the boring, ugly environs of Paris, so similar to the outskirts of London and any other major city in the world, the typical urban sprawl of the late twentieth century. There was a lot of traffic, but the driver sped past it all, the effortless power of the car engine making her faintly nervous. She thought of leaning forward and asking him to slow down, but something about the powerful shoulders, the set of that dark head, made her decide against the idea.

She watched the city thicken around them on either side of the wide motorway: roofs, tower blocks, spires of churches. They passed familiar names on road signs: Neuilly, Clichy, St Denis, entry points for the inner city, but the car purred on past, and after a while it began to dawn on Annie that the driver seemed to be heading away from the city, out again into the suburbs on the other side of Paris.

Had he lost his way? Or been given the wrong destination? Or was he taking some route she didn't know about?

She was about to lean forward to ask him when they approached a toll barrier which stretched right across the motorway. The limousine slowed and joined a queue, and Annie looked up at the huge signs giving directions for the road ahead. Lyon? That was a city right in the centre of France—why were they taking a road that led there?

They reached an automatic ticket machine and the driver leaned out and took a ticket; the barrier rose and the car shot forward with a deep-throated purr.

Annie leaned forward and banged on the glass partition. 'Where are you going?' she asked in English, then in French, '*Monsieur—où allez-vous*?'

He still didn't turn round, but he did glance briefly into his mirror and she saw his eyes, dark, brilliant, with thick black lashes flicking down to hide them a second later.

'You're supposed to be taking me into Paris,' she said in her badly accented, agitated French. 'Don't you know the way? You'll have to turn back. Do you understand, *monsieur*?'

He nodded his head, without answering, but the car drove onwards along the Peage, so fast that Annie had to cling to the leather strap beside her, her body swaying with the speed at which they moved. He must be doing a hundred miles an hour, she thought dazedly, watching another road sign flash past. Versailles. Wasn't that about fifteen miles outside Paris? Where were they going? Then the black limousine began to slow down again, took a right-hand turn off the motorway, and joined a queue passing through another toll barrier.

Annie breathed a little more easily. 'Are you going back on the other side of the motorway?' It hadn't taken very long to drive this far past Paris; no doubt it wouldn't take long for him to drive back into the city, and she didn't like to tell him what she thought of a limousine driver who didn't even know the way from the airport to Paris. Or was this roundabout route a trick he often played on unsuspecting foreigners? Was he paid by mileage? Well, when Phil paid the bills he could deal with this man; she would make sure Phil heard about what had happened.

They reached the head of the queue, he leaned out and threw coins into the automatic machine, and the barrier lifted. The black limousine shot forward with a purr of power, like a panther going for the kill.

Annie leaned back in the corner, rather nervously looking out of the window, waiting for him to take the motorway link road to return to Paris on the eastbound road.

He didn't. Instead he turned on to a local road, narrow and winding, and began speeding along between green fields and woods.

Annie tried not to panic. She sat forward again and banged on the window, more forcefully. '*Où allez-vous, monsieur? Arretez cette voiture.*' And then, getting angrier, and forgetting her French entirely, 'What do you think you're doing? Where are you going? Please stop the car; let me out!'

There was still no reply; he didn't even look round, but as they approached a roundabout he had to slow, so Annie shot to the door and wrenched the handle.

That was when she discovered that the door was locked, and that she could find no way of unlocking it. The lock must be controlled from a panel in the front of the car. Before the driver could negotiate the round-about she rushed to the other side of the car, but that door was locked, too.

She sat down suddenly on the edge of the seat. She was a prisoner. Her heart began to race; she was very pale and yet she was sweating. She looked into the driver's overhead mirror, caught the dark glance reflected there.

Huskily she asked him, 'What's this all about? Where are you taking me?'

'I told you I'd see you soon, Annie,' he said in that soft, smoky voice, and her heart nearly stopped as she recognised it.

CHAPTER TWO

FOR a moment or two Annie was so shocked that she just sat there, pale and rigid, her mind struggling to cope with her situation, then she whispered, 'Who are you?'

He didn't reply, and when she looked into the driving mirror above his head she couldn't see his eyes, only the olive-skinned curve of his profile turned away from her, the gleam of black hair above that. He had a strong, fleshless nose, powerful cheekbones. It was a tough face; Annie searched what she could see of it, trying to assess the sort of man this was, what he might plan to do to her.

'Have we met before?' she asked, but there was still no reply. She pretended to laugh, trying to hide her alarm. 'I'm sorry not to recognise you, but I meet so many people, it's hard to remember all their faces. Fans are always waiting after concerts, asking for autographs, talking to me—is that where we met? Are you a fan?'

He didn't look like a fan, though. She didn't really believe he was. Her fans were usually in their teens, or early twenties; they wore the same sort of clothes, same hairstyles, immediately recognisable as the latest street trend. Many of the girls dressed like her, actually, even to having black nails and lipstick, although that was something she had only done briefly, a year or so ago, and no longer did. She'd got bored with that.

This man was too old to be one of her fans. He had to be in his thirties and she thought his clothes were old-fashioned: that dark suit, the white shirt, the dark tie. Now that she focused on his clothes she began to realise what good quality they were: the suit looked as if it might have been tailor-made. It was certainly expensive; it hadn't come off a peg in a shop. The shirt and tie, too, looked classy, from what she had seen of them.

The clothes puzzled her. Clothes usually told you something about the person wearing them, and the message she got from what he wore was that he was respectable, conventional, yet what he was doing was neither of those things.

So he wasn't a typical kidnapper, either, although who knew what they would look like? This might, in fact, be a clever disguise meant to make him invisible, anonymous, someone police would discount as a possible suspect.

His silence was unnerving. Swallowing nervously, she tried, again, to get him to talk to her.

'Why won't you tell me who you are?'

'Later,' he said without looking in her direction, his eyes fixed steadily on the road ahead.

She broke out, 'Well, where are you taking me?'

'You'll see, when we get there.'

'Tell me now.' She tried to sound cool, calm, unflustered, unafraid, but her throat was dry and her mouth moved stiffly.

He didn't answer.

She shifted on the seat and could see his hands on the wheel: firm, capable hands, long-fingered, the skin tanned. They had a strength that worried her. Annie looked sideways out of the window at the green French countryside. Spring was only just beginning, a few new leaves appearing on the trees. The sky was blue but the sun wasn't hot. Where had he been to get that tan?

And then another thought occurred to her. She had noted a faint foreign accent right from that first phone call—was he French? Or some other nationality? Had he just arrived from another country, somewhere hot? Sicily? she wondered. Hadn't she heard that Sicilian shepherds often kidnapped people and held them to ransom? That it was a family trade? She looked at the driver's black hair and olive skin. He could be Italian. But she was going to Italy later on the tour; why hadn't he waited until she got there? Why snatch her in Paris?

'Are you kidnapping me?' she asked, and caught the dark flash of his eyes again as he looked at her in his driving mirror.

He still didn't say anything, though, which in itself was disturbing, because not to answer was a sort of admission. It meant he wasn't denying it, at the very least.

She burst out huskily, 'People will soon be looking for me, you know.'

His face stayed averted; he didn't respond.

'There are a whole group of us coming to Paris—my agent, the band, the tour manger... If I don't arrive at my hotel they'll call the police.'

He shrugged indifferently, but she kept trying to make him see sense.

'You can't just snatch someone without anybody noticing! When they check up with the airport they'll find out that a car collected me. Plenty of people saw me getting into your car, including the security men who flew from London with me. They saw you; they'll have noticed the number of your car.'

Would they have done, though? They had talked to him, certainly, had looked at his car, but would they have thought of looking at the number of the black limousine? There hadn't been many other people around, either; if anyone had been watching they would have been looking at her, because she had been escorted out to the car by security men and airport officials eager to avoid any problems with the media.

She wasn't yet a big name in Europe, though. The Press wouldn't have been over-excited by her arrival. She was just starting to sell records there, so she wasn't likely to be big news, but with a concert tour starting a week later there might have been Press interest, so the airport hadn't taken any chances.

That reminded her of something. 'There was a limousine booked,' she said slowly. 'Was that you? Are you from the limousine firm? Because if you are, the police will track you down at once.'

He laughed.

Annie's nerves grated. 'Why are you doing this?' she asked him angrily, then something occurred to her and in a sudden pang of hope she asked, 'This isn't some elaborate joke, is it? I haven't been set up? Are you taking me to meet Phil and Di somewhere? Is this one of Phil's practical jokes?'

Phil was famous for practical jokes; the idea should have occurred to her before if she hadn't been so unbalanced by recognising the voice that had made all those phone calls.

'No, it isn't a joke, Annie,' he said, and the way he said it made the panic start up again.

She couldn't breathe; she lay back against the upholstery, fighting to keep calm, fighting to breathe naturally. She closed her eyes and tried to shut out everything else, to stabilise herself.

There was no point in losing control. There was nothing she could do at that moment; she was locked inside this car behind smoky glass windows which would hide her from anyone looking in from outside, so that she couldn't even attract attention by waving or screaming. She would just have to sit here and wait until they arrived at wherever he was taking her.

Her heart missed a beat. What would happen then? If only she knew what he meant to do to her. He didn't look like a dangerous lunatic, or a criminal; in fact she had to admit he was strikingly attractive, if you liked Mediterranean colouring: the olive skin and black hair and dark, gleaming eyes. She always had, but then she had French blood, through her father, who had been born in France, of French descent, although he had spent most of his life in England.

Annie had only visited France a couple of times herself. It had been the one country she wanted to visit as soon as she started travelling with the band. She had never been there while her father was alive, and she had promised herself she would one day go in search of the place where he had been born, in the Jura mountains, but there had never been time so far for such a long trip. When you were giving concerts you did the gig and moved on, unfortunately.

Her father had been dark and olive-skinned with dark eyes, like this man. He hadn't been tall, though; and he had been slightly built, not powerful. Annie's long black hair had been inherited from him, but she had been born with her mother's skin colour and green eyes. As a child she had often wished she had inherited her mother's blonde hair, too, but now she was glad she was a mix of both parents. She wished now that she were even more like her father.

She had adored her father, and his death when she was eleven had darkened her childhood, especially when her mother married again within a year. Annie had never liked her stepfather, and made no effort to hide her hostility; and Bernard Tyler had soon come to dislike her too. So had her mother.

Joyce Tyler knew her daughter condemned her for marrying again so soon after her first husband's death, and resented Annie's open contempt. She had twin sons a couple of years later, and became totally engrossed in them. She had always been a man's woman, never unkind, but largely indifferent to her daughter; now she was only interested in her sons.

When Bernard Tyler began slapping Annie around, Joyce Tyler did nothing to stop him. In fact she bluntly told Annie it served her right. 'If you were nice to him, he'd be nice to you. You only have yourself to blame.'

By then fourteen, Annie began staying out of the house as much as possible, because she was afraid of Bernard Tyler as well as disliking him. She started living for the day when she would be old enough to leave home for good. When she met Philip and he offered her a career in music she packed a case with everything she valued and left, knowing that her mother wouldn't even think about her again, and that Bernard and his two sons would be glad to see her go.

When she began to be well-known they had got in touch with her to ask her to lend them some money, offering a long, rambling story about financial hardship as an excuse, but Philip had dealt with that, as he did

with all her financial affairs. They had been given tickets
for a concert soon afterwards, and Annie had seen them
briefly that night, but then they had vanished again, no
doubt because Philip made it clear that he wasn't paying
them any more large sums of money; and she had been
relieved, yet that reminder of past misery had made her
unhappy for days.

Her life would have been so different if her father
hadn't died so young, her mother hadn't then married
Bernard Tyler. Annie's happy childhood had ended at
the age of eleven; until she was seventeen she had been
lonely and unhappy. Even to remember those years now
was to feel greyness steal over her. She frowned, pushing
the memories away.

'You're very quiet,' the driver said, and she started,
looking at him again, but all she could see was his profile
and the dark sweep of his lashes.

'I was thinking. My friends are going to be very upset
and worried when I don't arrive. They'll wonder what
on earth has happened to me.'

'They'll soon find out.' His voice was cool, dismissive, and she flinched.

'What does that mean? Will you ring them?' Saying
what, though? Telling them that she had been kidnapped and they would have to pay a large ransom to
get her back?

She wished she could see his face properly instead of
merely getting glimpses now and then. People's eyes
usually told you a lot about them, but that wasn't true
about this man. His eyes were like bottomless wells: deep,
lustrous, impossible to plumb. And yet she was beginning to feel an odd teasing familiarity...

Had they ever met before? she wondered. Or had he cleverly managed to plant the idea that she knew him in her head subliminally, with his phone calls, and ever since he picked her up at the airport?

The limousine slowed, turned at right angles, and left the road on which they had been travelling. Annie looked out and upwards, seeing that they were driving between deep, sunk green banks from which trees and bushes sprang, over a winding, unmade road.

No! she realised; this wasn't a road—it was a driveway leading up to a house. A moment later the house itself came into view: not a large house, but detached, with trees and a garden around it, two-storeyed, with mossy pink tiles on the roof, the walls painted white and the closed shutters over every window painted black.

As the car halted outside the front door Annie tried to make out whether there were any other houses in view, and felt her heart sink as she saw that the white house stood on the edge of some sort of wood, which lay behind it, and that there were only fields in front of it. It could hardly have been more isolated. She couldn't see another house anywhere.

Nerves jumped under her skin. She bit her lip, feeling real fear growing inside her.

The driver got out and came round to open her door. Annie stayed obstinately on the seat, her chin up, defying him.

'I'm not getting out; I'm staying here until you drive me back to Paris. Take me back to Paris and I'll forget this ever happened, but if you don't...'

He reached one long arm into the car, took her by the hand, and jerked her forwards. He took her by surprise, and he was even more powerful than he looked. She couldn't resist the tug he gave her. She almost fell off the seat, and the next minute had been scooped up by his other arm going round her waist, lifting her off her feet and out of the car, kicking and struggling helplessly.

He carried her up the steps to the front door, holding her under his arm as if she were a child, ignoring her increasingly wild attempts to escape. While he was unlocking the door Annie wrenched her head round and bit his hand; he gave a stifled grunt of pain, but didn't let go of her until they were inside the house and he had kicked the front door shut behind them.

Slowly he lowered her feet to the floor, his arm still round her waist, holding her tightly against him so that she helplessly slithered down his body, aware of every slow, deliberate contact, her breasts brushing his chest, their thighs touching, the warmth of his skin reaching her through their clothes. The effect was electrifying. She didn't want to feel it, but she did: a deep physical wrench that made her almost giddy. Breathless and shuddering, she tried to push away once she was standing up, on her feet, but his arm was immovable; she couldn't break the lock he had on her. Her long black hair dishevelled, a mass of it falling over her face, she watched him through it, her almond-green eyes like the eyes of a scared child in the dark.

He lifted the hand she had bitten, looked at it. So did Annie. 'I'm bleeding,' he said, sounding surprised. 'You have sharp little teeth.'

And then he absently put out his pink tongue-tip and licked the blood away. Annie watched him, her nerves prickling. The little gesture had an intimacy that shocked her, yet sent another of those quivers of response through her body.

It was at that moment that she really began to be afraid, to believe that this was actually happening, that she had been kidnapped for motives she didn't yet understand by a man who frightened her and attracted her at one and the same time.

Her insides collapsed, but she fought not to show how scared she was, throwing back her head and looking straight at him, hoping she looked calm and confident.

'Why don't you take me back to Paris now, before this gets really serious? Kidnapping is a very serious offence, you know.'

'Very,' he agreed, straight-faced.

Flushing at what she suspected to be mockery, she snapped, 'You could end up going to prison for the rest of your life!'

'They have to catch me first,' he pointed out coolly, brushing the tangled black hair back from her face with those powerful tanned fingers. The light touch of his hand sent a trickle of icy awareness down her spine, and yet there was something like tenderness in the gentle movement of his fingers. Even that made Annie afraid—afraid of what might be coming, what he meant to do with her.

'Why don't I show you the room I've got ready for you?'

Her stomach turned over. She wondered if he could hear the acceleration of her heartbeat, see the spring of perspiration on her face.

If he picked up her nervous reaction he didn't show it. 'Then we'll have lunch,' he added, and she bristled.

'I'm not hungry! I couldn't eat; I feel sick!'

'You'll feel better with some food inside you,' he said, as if she were a child. 'It won't be anything elaborate—

I'm no cook—but I've got plenty of salad and cheese and fruit. It was freshly bought this morning in the market; you'll find it's delicious. And I've got a bottle of very good wine.'

'I don't drink wine!'

He raised straight black brows at her, looking genuinely incredulous. 'You don't drink wine? You're missing out on one of life's great pleasures. I shall have to teach you to enjoy it while you're here. It will calm your nerves down, relax you.'

That was what she was afraid of, what she must not allow to happen. She had to stay on the alert, on her guard against him, and watchful for an opportunity to escape. If she could only get out of the house she might be able to hide among the trees until it was dark and then walk until she reached a village; there must be one somewhere near here!

'If you want to calm my nerves you might start by letting go of me!' she told him, and without a word he let his arm fall.

She took several steps away, looked around the small, shadowy hall from which a staircase led upstairs.

'Does this house belong to you?'

He didn't answer, but she sensed from the expression in his eyes that it didn't.'

'Look, Mr...? You still haven't told me your name. Or at least told me what to call you. I must call you something.'

He frowned oddly, hesitated, then said curtly, 'Marc.'

From the way he watched her she couldn't tell whether it was really his name but she didn't query it. 'Marc,' she repeated. 'You're French, aren't you?'

'How did you guess?'

He was kidding. Solemnly she said, 'A wild stab.' She put her head on one side, listened to the silence surrounding them. No sound of traffic from outside, just the constant murmur of the trees in the wood behind the house, yet there was something familiar to her about the noise. She couldn't track it down for a minute until she realised it reminded her of the sound she had heard in her dream the other night—a sound like the sea. This was it, not traffic, not the sea, but the rustle and whisper of hundreds of branches swaying and bending in the wind.

Why on earth had she heard that sound in her dream? There was something uncanny about it. It made her shiver. She had never been here before; why had this sound got into her dreams? Maybe he had rung her from here. Maybe the noise had been a background sound on the answering machine tape.

'Did you ring me from here?' she asked him, and he gave her a sharp look, shaking his head.

'The phone has been cut off.'

She was sorry to hear that, but maybe it had been telepathy. He must have had this sound in his head when he talked to her on the phone and she had picked up on it. Nothing uncanny about telepathy—she had several times had ideas leap into her head from Di or Phil when they were working together. If you were on the same wavelength it could easily happen.

But she wasn't on this man's wavelength! she hurriedly thought. She couldn't be.

'Why has the phone been cut off?' she asked, thinking that the house had the strange, echoing feel of a house which was always empty; it didn't feel like anybody's home.

'I didn't need it.'

'Then where did you ring me from?'

He didn't answer, eyeing her drily.

She noticed that from the hall several doors opened into rooms which were gloomy with shadow because of the closed shutters over the windows. She only got an impression of them, a fleeting glimpse of dark oak fur- niture and leather chairs, a wallpaper with trails of ivy and blue flowers.

'Is there anyone else here?' she asked huskily, listening.

He half smiled again. 'No, we're quite alone, Annie.'

She tensed, bit her lower lip, watching him and wishing she knew what went on inside his head. Or did she? Maybe she was better off not knowing! 'At least tell me what this is all about! Why have you brought me here? Do you want money? Are you going to ask my record company for a lot of money before you let me go?' Her mind worked feverishly. But even if Philip paid him whatever ransom he demanded, would he let her go? Alive?

She had seen his face now; he hadn't tried to hide it. Didn't kidnappers usually kill their victims so that they could never identify them? Fear made her stomach clench, sent waves of sickness through her.

'This has nothing at all to do with money!' he bit out, and she stared at him, afraid to feel relief. If he wasn't holding her for ransom, what did he mean to do with her?

'Then why have you brought me here?' She searched his face for a clue. The hard, insistent lines of it did nothing to lessen her tension. 'Are you sure you really know who I am? You aren't mixing me up with someone else, are you? Because you keep asking if I remember you, but I don't, and I'm sure we've never met before. I have a good memory; I'd remember if we had met.'

His dark eyes hypnotically stared down into hers. 'You'll remember Annie,' he said softly. 'I can wait; I've waited a long time already.'

A shiver ran down her back. If she wasn't careful, he would start convincing her! He didn't look it, but he must be crazy.

'Stop arguing, Annie,' he said. 'Come upstairs and I'll show you your room.'

She dug her heels in, resisting the hand that seized her elbow and tried to move her towards the stairs.

'You can't keep me here against my will and get away with it! I don't know what the penalty is for kidnapping in France, but you don't want to go to prison for years, do you? Look, if you just want to get to know me, I'll have lunch with you now, and then you can drive me back to Paris, and I'll see you again there. I'll get you a ticket for my concert and——'

He laughed harshly. 'You know you don't mean it; if you made a date with me it would be the police who kept it, I imagine. I'm not stupid, Annie. You're ready to promise me anything to get away. Do you think I don't know that?'

'What are you going to do to me?' She tried to hide her fear, but he would have had to be blind to miss that look in her eyes.

His brows met. 'I'm not going to hurt you, Annie; don't look like that!'

He sounded so convincing. She let out a long sigh, put her hand out to him. 'Then please let me go, Marc—please...'

Taking her hand, he looked down at the slight, pale fingers he held, slowly entwined his own tanned fingers with them. Annie felt her heart skip sideways in a little kick of awareness.

'Not yet,' he said. 'Just for the moment, you're my guest. You'll find the house very comfortable, and it's tranquil here, much more peaceful than you would have been in Paris. No media clamouring for interviews, no telephones, no fans waiting outside to hassle you. Why don't you stop worrying and enjoy it?'

Annie considered him soberly. If she kept her temper and was not unfriendly maybe she would be able to talk him round, get him to see sense and take her back to Paris.

She pulled her hand away; he let it go without comment. Annie began to walk upstairs, aware of him following close behind her.

'In here,' he said, throwing open a door on the landing above.

Halting on the threshold, she watched him walk across the darkened room to the windows. He opened them, flung back the shutters, and light flooded in, making her blink, dazzled, staring at him.

She felt a strange flash of surprise, a jerk of dislocation, like mental whiplash, and for that instant had the oddest feeling, and then it was gone, and she was watching him with wide, half-blind green eyes.

He stared back at her with a curious eagerness, as if he knew that something had happened to her just then, as if he could read her thoughts, or her feelings; and that bothered her. That could be very dangerous. From now on she must try to hide from him what she was thinking, or she would have no defences against him.

'Annie?' he whispered.

'Where's the bathroom?' she asked, trying to keep all intonation out of her voice.

She thought she heard him sigh. Then he gestured. 'Through that door. I'll go downstairs and start preparing lunch, so don't be long. I'll bring your cases in from the car later and you can unpack after lunch.'

She waited until she heard him reach the bottom of the stairs, then she went over to the window. How far was it to the ground from up here? If there was a handy drainpipe it might be worth risking the climb down. She peered down at the garden below and grimaced. No, that was out.

There was no drainpipe close enough—the nearest was outside the bathroom, and the bathroom window looked far too small for her to climb through it. From here, too, the ground seemed a very long way off. She wouldn't like to risk breaking a leg, or worse, by jumping out of the window. In films people knotted sheets together and climbed down them; maybe she could try that.

But not now. She could hear noises from the room below, a tap running, the sound of china clattering. That must be the kitchen. If she tried to climb out of here now he'd be sure to spot her.

She went into the bathroom and found it very pretty: the fittings a primrose-yellow, a pine shelf along the wall filled with French toiletries—bath oil, soaps, gels, shampoo, talc.

Annie washed, then deliberately left her face bare of make-up, brushed her long black hair up into a neat bun at the back of her neck, made herself look as unattractive as possible.

Looking at her reflection in the bathroom mirror, she saw the nervous awareness in her green eyes and turned away quickly. In this situation it was very dangerous to admit, even to herself, in the privacy of her own head, that she found him attractive. No, more than that, if she was honest. Ever since she first saw him she had been mesmerised; and that was scary.

He might keep telling her not to be scared, that he wouldn't hurt her, but the fact remained—he had kidnapped her, brought her here by force. Why had he done that, if not for ransom? What on earth was going on here? She was afraid to think about it.

Was he out of his head? Look at his obsession that they had met before! Yes, one of them had to be crazy, and it wasn't her. She was one hundred per cent certain she had never seen him in her life until today.

Then she remembered that fleeting dizziness when he opened the shutters, the feeling of *déjà vu*, and she frowned, bit her lip. What on earth had that been about? For a second she almost had thought she remembered...something...

Angrily she pushed the thought away. She was letting him get to her, that was all. She must not let him hypnotise her into joining him in his fantasy. That way lay madness.

Feeling calmer, she went downstairs, started looking into rooms, until she opened a door into a large, bright kitchen with golden pine fittings, white walls and red and white gingham curtains. There were bowls of hyacinths in bloom on the windowsill, and the whole room was full of their scent and the fragrance of fresh coffee.

While she hesitated at the door, Marc turned to look at her, his narrowed eyes skating over her face and hair, his brows rising sardonically.

'You look about fifteen! Is that meant to make me keep my distance?'

'I hope you will anyway,' she said primly, not meeting his eyes.

There was a long silence, and at last she had to look up. He was watching her seriously, his dark eyes level and frowning.

'I told you, you don't need to be afraid. I'm not holding you for ransom, I won't hurt you, and, I assure you, I won't leap on you suddenly. I won't force you to do anything you don't want to do.'

Red burned in her cheeks. 'You forced me to come here, and you're forcing me to stay here against my will.'

'It was the only way I could get you to myself for long enough,' he coolly told her.

'Long enough for what?'

'To get to know me,' he said. 'Now come and sit down at the table and we'll have lunch.'

Still absorbed in thinking over what he had just said, she didn't argue. She sat down automatically and looked at the food he had put out on the square pine kitchen table—a large bowl of crisp green salad tossed in dressing, black olives in a dish, some hard-boiled eggs, tomatoes, a gingham-covered wicker basket of sliced French bread, a platter of various French cheeses and a bowl of fruit.

Annie hadn't felt hungry until then, but the food looked so good that she felt a surprising pang of hunger.

'Help yourself,' he said as he sat down opposite her.

She took salad—a mixture of avocado, lettuces, cucumber, green peppers—a hard-boiled egg, a tomato, some black olives, a slice of Brie, some of the golden bread.

'I'm sorry there's nothing more exciting,' he said, and she looked up, her green eyes startled, then smiled.

'It's great food—I've always loved a picnic; that's what this is—a picnic indoors.'

'But picnic food tastes better in the open air,' he said, reaching over to pour white wine into her glass, and that was when Annie had another of those strange *déjà vu* flashes, a baffling sense of having seen him do that before.

As she drew a sharp, startled breath he looked up at her, his body stiffening, his face watchful.

'Annie?' he said again, as he had before, and she slowly lifted her own eyes to stare back at him, dazed.

He held her eyes. 'Tell me what you felt,' he softly said.

'I don't know,' she whispered. 'It was ... nothing ...'

'It was something,' he said, and his black eyes glittered. 'You're beginning to remember.'

CHAPTER THREE

'WHY don't you tell me when we're supposed to have met, and stop playing games?' Annie burst out.

Shaking his head, he gestured. 'Taste the wine.'

'Was it in England? In London?'

'There's no point in trying to guess. When you remember, you'll know.'

But she was beginning to read his expressions, the fleeting thoughts passing through those brilliant liquid black eyes, the way his mouth changed, softening, tightening, twisting. He might not have denied that they'd met in England, but something about his face just then told her that that wasn't where they had met. Where else could it have been? She was determined to make him tell her.

'America?'

He laughed, shook his head.

That didn't leave many other countries. Annie hadn't travelled very widely yet. So she came to the most likely answer.

'Was it here, in France?'

He didn't answer, but his eyes were as bright as black stars.

'It was, wasn't it?' she said slowly.

'So now you believe we have met,' he said, his voice deep, vibrating with a new note, passionate, excited. She felt her pulses leap, and this time it was she who didn't answer. She didn't have to; her sudden flush, the way she looked down, her dark lashes cloaking her eyes, spoke for her.

Huskily she finally said, 'I believe you think we did. But I really don't remember—I'm sorry. I've only been to France a couple of times—it must have been on one of those trips, I suppose. The last time I came here I spent two weeks in Normandy with my best friend and her sister. We stayed in a wonderful old hotel in Caborg, right on the sea. It was very hot that summer; we spent a lot of time on the beach—was that where we met?'

He shook his head, sipping wine and leaning back in his chair, his lids half down over his dark eyes, his legs stretched full-length sideways. Annie didn't mean to stare, but she couldn't help noticing that under his shirt she could almost see the ripple of lean muscled flesh every time he breathed. He had a very slim waist and hips, or was that a visual illusion because of the length of his legs? She couldn't deny that he was her type. His long, supple body was intensely sexy.

Her eyes drifted back upwards, and with a start of shock met his gaze. Annie looked away, her colour high.

'Well, where did we meet?' Her voice was husky, defying him to make anything of the way she had been looking him over. 'If I knew where we met I might remember it. Why don't you tell me?'

'Because you have to remember without any help from me,' he said coolly.

'Why?' she persisted.

He ignored the question, gesturing. 'Come on, eat some of your salad—you look as if your blood sugar is a little low. Maybe that's why you're so bad-tempered.'

'I'm bad-tempered because you've kidnapped me!' she retorted, but picked up her glass and drained the pale golden wine while he watched, his brows shooting up.

'Careful! If you aren't used to drinking wine it could go to your head if you drink it too fast.'

She reached for the bottle, which stood in a vacuum jug in the middle of the table, but Marc lifted it out before she seized it, poured her another half-glass, refilled his own, advising her,

'Eat your food before you drink any more; it's never wise to drink on an empty stomach.'

'Will you stop giving me orders?' But she began to eat all the same, and the food was delicious—the cheese, the bread, the salad with its tangy dressing tasting of lemon, vinegar and herbs and glistening with oil. All this tension seemed to have given her an appetite, or maybe it had been the wine, after all.

Later they ate fruit and then drank some of the most wonderful coffee Annie had ever tasted.

She told him so, and he grinned.

'Thank you. The secret is in the beans; you have to grind just the amount you need each time you make coffee or you lose a little of the flavour.'

'I make instant at home,' she confessed, and he grimaced.

'Instant? No comparison.'

'Probably not, but I don't always have the time or the energy to make fresh coffee. I work very hard most days. I'm dead tired when I get home and I just want to curl up and relax, watch TV, read magazines, have a long bath, anything to take my mind off what I've been doing all day. I suppose you have the same image of pop musicians that most people have—you think we just play around in recording studios, having fun, and that most of us can't actually sing, or play our instruments, but that isn't true of anyone I work with. We all know what we're doing and we work very hard—rehearsing the same tune over and over again, constantly breaking off to work on a particular phrase, and, even when we finally get around to taping it, often doing take after take before the recording people are satisfied. It's exhausting, believe me, and hell on the throat; and when you're on tour it can be even worse because then you not only have to rehearse every day, you're doing a live performance at night, and you have to travel across country, even across continents, which is another sort of drain on your energy.'

Mildly he murmured, 'I only said that freshly ground coffee tasted better than instant. It wasn't an attack on your lifestyle.'

Flushed, she laughed, relaxing again. 'No, sorry, it's just that I was interviewed by some journalist recently who had an axe to grind about women with careers who stop off and buy microwave dinners on their way home instead of cooking a real meal for their men. We had a blazing row and he wrote an article that tore me to shreds.'

He listened, his head on one side and his eyes half veiled by drooping lids. 'There isn't a man in your life, though, is there? Unless you've managed to keep him a big secret so far.'

She glanced at him and felt the intensity of his concentration on her, sensed the tension in his long, lean body. The back of her neck prickled.

This wasn't the first time someone had got totally hooked on her; fans often went through a phase of obsessive devotion, especially at first. For some of them their favourite star became an icon they could worship from afar, yearning all the time to get closer and closer. Annie had always found that sort of fan disturbing, but so far none of them had ever come this close; she had never needed to be physically afraid of what one of them might do, although now and then she had a recurring nightmare about the death of John Lennon. She knew with one part of her mind that that wasn't likely to happen to her, that she simply wasn't world-famous enough to attract that sort of craziness, but when she noticed one particular male fan hanging around outside her home, outside the studio, peering into her car as she drove out, gazing fixedly at her, she always felt ice trickle down her spine.

As she hadn't answered him, Marc repeated tensely, 'Have you got a lover?'

She meant to refuse to answer, but the darkness in his eyes drew the word out of her.

'No,' she whispered, and heard the intake of his breath, saw the satisfied flash of his eyes. Hurriedly she got up and began clearing the table. Marc helped her, showing her how to stack things in the dishwasher and put it on. When the kitchen was spotless again he said, 'I'll get your cases in from the car now, shall I?'

He had seemed so reasonable while they were working together, handing plates to each other, putting stuff away, that Annie went back to pleading with him, her green eyes, wide, coaxing, 'Please take me to Paris; don't go on with this. My friends will have started looking for me by now; they'll have called the police.'

'Nobody's expecting you until tomorrow,' he coolly informed her. 'The hotel has been told you're visiting a friend for a day or two.'

She drew breath sharply, her eyes very dark. 'Who told them that? You?'

He nodded. 'I rang your hotel from my car while you were upstairs.' He watched her face change, smiled wryly. 'And before you get too hopeful, my car has a security lock on it, and I carry the car keys on me all the time.'

'How long are you planning to keep me here?' she broke out.

'Just for tonight.'

She stiffened, her heart began thudding painfully behind her ribs. What did he have planned for her tonight? Her green eyes flickered as she stared at him, seeing him through a veil of disturbed awareness, a primitive rhythm beating in her veins as she faced what he was spelling out for her. He had kidnapped her, brought her here, and tonight he obviously meant to have her.

Annie felt her stomach clench. What chance did she have of stopping him? He was far too big, too powerful for her to fight. There would be no contest. Her only hope would be to hit him with something heavy before he knew what was coming, and the thought of physical violence made her feel faintly sick. Would she actually be able to do anything like that?

He might bleed. She might kill him. She bit her lip, shivering. Her throat husky, raw, she muttered, 'If my manager arrives and finds I'm not at the hotel he's going to start a panic, whatever story you've given the hotel. He knows I don't have friends in France.'

'Your manager is the guy on honeymoon at the moment, though, isn't he? Why should he cut his honeymoon short? You used to share your flat with Diana Abbot, the girl he married, didn't you?'

Annie was almost past getting a shock every time he revealed how much he knew about her, but hearing the cool way he said Di's name, talked about her marrying Phil, made her nerves bristle again, and made her even angrier.

'Yes,' she said curtly. 'I suppose there's no point in asking how you know all that.'

He gave her a sideways, amused look. 'I read newspapers. It was all in there—or don't you read your own Press? The wedding got quite a bit of coverage, and every newspaper mentioned the fact that the bride was your oldest friend, Diana Abbot, who had been sharing your flat for years, acting as some sort of secretary-cum-bodyguard, dealing with your fan mail and the Press and all the jobs you didn't have time to do. One or two papers speculated on what you would do now, whether you'd be living alone or whether someone else would take over her job.'

Slowly Annie said, 'You rang me for the first time that night...after the wedding...'

Nodding, he watched her, his dark eyes narrowed and intent, while she thought about that.

'You hoped I'd be alone when I got back to the flat, didn't you? You hoped that after a very emotional day, which most wedding days are for everyone concerned, I'd be wide open to your spooky little messages.' She looked at him contemptuously. 'It was a nasty, deliberate little campaign, wasn't it? It was meant to scare the life out of me while I was all alone in my flat and feeling low. What are you, some sort of sadist? Do you get your kicks from terrifying women?'

'I'd hardly call my message terrifying. It was only two words.' He held her gaze, softly said them again. 'Remember me.'

A shudder ran down her spine, just as it had the first time she heard him say it.

'What's so terrifying about that?' he asked, and of course he was right. Two simple little words could hardly be called terrifying—they weren't even a threat—and she could have listened, shrugged, walked away without thinking about the odd message again, but for some reason she couldn't explain even to herself she had been struck by the words, the tone, the voice. They had haunted her sleep, and next day there had been the other calls to reinforce the effect of the first one, and, finally, the promise that he would see her soon.

'It was mysterious, though; and I was feeling very strung-up,' she said curtly. 'Don't tell me you didn't guess the effect it would have, or mean it to have that effect, because I'm sure you did. You strike me as a man who works out every move he makes before he makes it, and doesn't miss a trick!'

'I chose my moment very carefully, it's true,' he admitted shamelessly. 'When I heard that your flatmate was getting married a short time before you started your European tour in France I saw that this would be the right time to get in touch with you.'

'Kidnap me, you mean!' she threw back at him, wondering how long he had been planning it, inwardly shuddering at the thought of what lay behind all this—his obsession, his private fantasy.

'There was no other way to do it,' he said coolly, and her over-bright green eyes watched him with apprehension, yet he still sounded rational, even reasonable, as he added, 'I had to talk to you. I knew your tour was just starting, that you'd only be in France for a short time, and then you would be off on your travels for weeks on end with very little spare time. This was a window of opportunity—just a couple of days when I could be alone with you before the rest of your entourage caught up with you.'

'Just a couple of days?' she repeated slowly, watching him. 'And then you'll let me go?' But she was still afraid to believe him.

'You'll be back in Paris tomorrow night,' he quietly insisted.

'Why should I believe anything you say?' she challenged, and he held her stare again, his eyes level, darkly brooding.

'You can believe that. I give you my word of honour. You'll be safely back in your hotel by the time your friends start looking for you. Whatever happens between us.'

The words hit her like gunfire. Whatever happened between them? Dry-mouthed in shock, she looked down, a tremor running through her, suddenly visualising what could happen, his tanned body naked, moving above her with the supple power she had been aware of from the start, his hands touching her, his mouth...

Appalled, she broke off the thought, pulling herself together. What on earth was happening to her? What was she thinking about?

But was it her mind that had been taken over, or her body? she wondered, very aware of him inches away, his black eyes watching her with that worrying intensity. If she was thinking about him making love to her it was because her body had begun to respond to him sensually. Mind and body were inextricably linked, after all; you couldn't separate them. Nerves and senses, blood and cells, were all part of the same entity; touch one and you touched them all.

This man was attempting to do more than get to know her, though; she felt sure of that. He wanted to take her over entirely, body and soul. She felt herself the focus of a desire that frightened yet excited her, even while she angrily resisted it.

'I'll get your cases and you can unpack what you need for tonight,' he coolly said, and walked out of the kitchen.

Annie followed him down the hall, but he turned at the front door and said, 'Wait upstairs. I'll bring the cases up to you.'

He didn't want her trying to escape, of course. She reluctantly began to climb the stairs and he stood, watching her, until she reached the landing and went into the bedroom he had told her she could use.

She heard him walk to the car, the grate of his heels on the path. She was tempted to make a run for it, but common sense warned her she had no chance of getting away before he caught up with her again, so instead she quietly began exploring the other rooms on the same floor of the house, starting with the main bedroom at the front, which was probably his room, she decided.

The shutters were closed and the dark blue shadows of the afternoon made the room dim, but she looked around it from the door with curiosity, only to stiffen almost at once as she saw her own face looking back at her from the opposite wall. It wasn't her reflection in a mirror. It was a huge, almost life-size coloured poster portrait given away a year ago in Britain by one of the teenage music magazines. He had stuck it up facing his bed.

But it wasn't the only picture of her in the room. As her stunned gaze slowly travelled round the walls she recognised her own face on every inch of available space—disc covers, photos from magazines, pencil drawings, newspaper articles, water-colour and oil paintings of her, black and white glossy stills signed by her, which meant he had got them from her own publicity people.

She had heard of fans who did this sort of thing, but she had never so far met any of them, and had always believed they were all teenagers, kids in that no man's land between childhood and adulthood who got obsessed with a role model, an icon. This man was no teenager. His obsession was far more disturbing. Shock made her icy, sent shivers through her. He had to be crazy!

My God, my God, I've got to get away, she thought. But how?

Then she heard him coming up the stairs, and her nerves jumped violently.

There was no time to run back into her own room. She could only stay where she was. She heard him pause in the doorway of the room he had told her to use. He would see immediately that she wasn't there. He dropped the cases; she heard the floorboards creak as he walked along the landing towards his own room.

A shudder ran through her as she sensed him behind her, picked up his scent, the fresh cold air which came with him, a smell of pine which was probably his shaving lotion.

'So you found my bedroom,' he murmured. 'Let's have the light on, then you can see it properly.'

He switched on the electric light. She blinked, dazzled.

'I've got every recording you ever made,' he said, gesturing.

She looked at the music equipment along the wall below the window: expensive looking, with huge speakers, she noted, set between shelves full of compact discs, singles, audio tapes and video tapes.

'Those aren't all mine?' She hadn't made that many! There were dozens on the shelves, and she didn't recognise them all.

'Different language versions of them, the French, Spanish, Italian, German... and the American versions, but they're mostly the same cover as the British edition.' His voice was casual, almost professional, as if he was an expert on this subject. 'I like the English versions best—obviously they are the original, and they work best—but I enjoy listening to the French ones almost as much. Why don't we put one of the French discs on now?'

'No, please don't!' she burst out.

'Don't you like your own work?' His face was quizzical, but unsurprised. She wondered bitterly if he had read that somewhere among all the other details of her life he had cut out from newspapers and magazines.

'That's what it is—work!' she said shortly. 'And when I'm doing it I enjoy it, but I'm not working at this moment, so I don't want to be reminded of it.'

'How do you like my room?' he asked softly, and she knew he was really talking about the pictures of her that lined the walls.

She didn't want to answer, but by now she knew too much about him. He would go on asking until she answered.

'Who did all the paintings?' she asked, and wasn't surprised when he said,

'Me.'

Taking a closer look at one of the small pencil drawings near by, which was obviously a sketch for the largest oils canvas, she said reluctantly, 'You're good. Is that what you do for a living? Are you an artist?'

He looked down at her sideways through dark lashes, grimacing slightly. 'I went to arts school for a year, then decided I was never going to be good enough to make it my life, so I gave up the idea, but I still enjoy doing the odd sketch or painting.'

While he was talking, her eye was caught by a silver-framed photograph standing on the low cabinet beside his bed. There were a group of people standing outside a gabled cottage which had a Swiss look to it, and behind the building green meadows against forested hillsides steep enough to be mountains.

Annie went over there and picked it up, took a closer, longer look. There were three people in the photograph—one of them clearly Marc himself, looking younger, maybe in his early twenties, so that the picture must have been taken some years ago. The other two were a man and a woman in middle age, dark-haired, weather-tanned, smiling. Annie looked hard at them both and decided the man resembled Marc, although the older man's hair was silvering. Were these his parents? And where had the photo been taken?

'What a lovely place,' she said. 'Where is it? Switzerland?'

His voice was low, husky. 'No. It's France. The Jura region.'

Her head swung, her green eyes startled and enormous. 'The Jura? But...how extraordinary. My father was born there.'

He inclined his head. 'I know.'

She should have known he would. Was there any part of her life he didn't know about? She looked back at the photo. 'Are the people you're with your parents? There's a strong resemblance.'

He smiled. 'Yes. I'm told I'm very like my father when he was younger.'

'What were you all doing in Jura? Having a holiday? Do you do hillwalking, or climb?' He looked as if he might, and his parents had a tough, outdoor look about them. Had he gone there on holiday because he knew she had a family connection with it? Actually, she'd never visited the Jura region, although she vividly remembered her father nostalgically talking about his childhood home among the hillsides thick with pine forests, their scent on summer days overpowering, and running between them the valleys rich with fertile green alpine meadows, full of cows and wild flowers in the spring and summer.

'I was born there.' He said it so flatly that for a second she didn't take it in; she just stared at him, her lips apart, her breathing irregular.

Then she repeated it incredulously. 'Born in the Jura?' He nodded.

'What a coincidence,' she said slowly, wondering if it was anything of the kind. Had he become far more interested in her after he found out that her father came from the same region of France as himself? Music fans seized on such tiny details and blew them up out of all proportion, made them omens, signs and portents.

Coolly he said, 'No. It isn't a coincidence. It's part of the pattern.'

She gave him a wary look. 'Pattern?'

'Of destiny,' he said. 'Don't you believe in destiny, Annie?'

'I've never thought about it,' she hurriedly said, but she was not being strictly truthful. Of course she had thought about destiny, or fate, or whatever you called the strange way life worked out for you, often without your own volition. Her own life had been full of such inexplicable, surprising collisions. Her career had happened by accident, not design on her part. She had been cheerfully living day to day without any real plans for a future, and Phil had walked into her life and taken it over, forged a career for her, and was now building her up into an international star.

Phil's destiny had happened by chance, too. Oh, it had been Phil who found Diana to look after her; but after that, for years, he hadn't taken any real notice of Di, only for fate to intervene again, strand the two of them in the middle of snow-bound America, just long enough for them to fall in love.

Of course she believed in fate and destiny, but she didn't want to admit it to a man she was afraid might be crazy. She didn't want to encourage him to believe they might be fated for each other, although she suspected that that was exactly what he believed.

A new idea hit her. Sharply she said, 'I've never been to the Jura, you know. If that is where you think we met.'

The deep, dark eyes held hers. 'It *is* where we met, Annie.'

'I tell you I've never been there!'

'You'll remember,' was all he said, and Annie flushed angrily.

'I tell you we've never met, and I have never been to the Jura.'

CHAPTER FOUR

ANNIE said it with angry vehemence, but that was only because she was terrified that any minute she would start to believe him. He was compellingly sure of himself, and Annie kept getting flashes of uncertainty. Could she have forgotten meeting him? Had she ever been to the Jura? How could she have forgotten anything so important? But people did, didn't they? They had blackouts, lost whole days, weeks, months of their lives without ever being aware of what happened until suddenly the amnesia ended and they remembered everything. What if that was what had happened to her?

She looked back over the years since she'd left home and begun working with Phil and Diana, and couldn't think of any time, however brief, when she was not with one or the other of them. If she had vanished from sight, even for a few hours, they would surely have said something.

Oh, stop it! she told herself wildly. Of course you haven't blacked out any memory of him. You haven't had amnesia. This is all nonsense. Stop letting him get to you.

That way madness lay. She had to stay sane, rational, bring her common sense to bear on everything he said to her.

She turned and fled, along the landing, to the room he had told her to use. She had forgotten the cases he had brought up from the car and had left just inside the door of the other bedroom. Running without looking where she was going, she went straight into them, was unable to save herself, and fell heavily.

'What have you done to yourself?' Marc was there before she could get back on her feet. He knelt beside her, pushed the spilt black hair back from her face, staring at her forehead, a dark frown on his face.

Annie felt wetness trickling down her cheek and thought for a second that it was tears. She tried to wipe them away, looked at her hand, and was startled to see blood on her fingertips.

'How on earth did you manage to cut your head?' Marc demanded, helping her to her feet with one arm around her.

'I don't know,' she said crossly, childishly sorry for herself all of a sudden.

He looked down at her suitcases, whistled impatiently. 'Look at that! Somehow or other the metal strip along the edge of the top case has become detached; it looks like a serrated knife! You must have cut your head on that when you fell. I'll see if I can knock it back in place later. Next time you might not get off so lightly.'

Steering her across the room, Marc pushed her into a sitting position on the side of the bed.

'Stay there while I get some water to sponge your head with,' he said, walking away, and although she resented being ordered around like that Annie couldn't have disobeyed him if she tried. Her head was swimming, she felt giddy, and closed her eyes entirely.

The bruise had begun throbbing; she tentatively explored it with her fingers, wincing. It felt enormous, pushing out from under her skin like a small boulder, hot and hard to the touch.

'Don't touch it!' Marc told her, returning with a bowl of water, a natural sponge, a towel. He knelt down beside her, gently sponged the blood from her head before looking more closely.

'Hmm. Yes, it isn't serious—the cut is tiny, and the bleeding is stopping already—but you're going to have a nasty bruise there. You'll have to hide it with your hair once the cut has healed up.' He dabbed her head dry with the towel. 'I could put a dressing on it for tonight.'

She still felt dizzy, but the sensation had changed. The odd whirling of her senses now had more to do with Marc being so close, on his knees beside her, his body half leaning on her lap while he attended to her head. She had never been so conscious of anyone in her life. He was having a devastating physical effect on her. She was appalled to feel her breasts swelling, round and full, the nipples hardening on them as he invaded her body space even more, his face inches from her, his body moving against her knees.

'Shall I put a dressing on?' he asked again.

She had difficulty speaking, her voice was breathless, husky, but she tried to sound calm, sensible; she fought to hide what his nearness was doing to her.

'I'd rather let it heal naturally. If you put a dressing on it the air can't get to it.'

He nodded. 'You're probably right.' He gently pushed her silky black hair back from her temples to leave her forehead bare for the time being, and Annie kept her eyes down, fighting to steady her breathing.

'How's that?' he asked. 'Any other injuries, while I'm playing doctor?' He laughed as he asked, and she forced a faint smile, shaking her head.

'No, that's it.'

'Good.'

He dried his hands, his eyes lowered, his thick, dark lashes brushing his olive skin, making it safe for her to watch him and be sure he wouldn't catch her. The gentleness and concern he had showed her just now was puzzling, a contradiction. This man who had brought her here against her will, and kept talking like a crazy man, had such a tough male face and body, but could yet be as gentle as a woman when he chose, showing a tenderness, a caring, that surprised her.

He looked up at that moment, too quickly for her to look away. She heard him draw an audible, fierce breath, and saw darkness invade his eyes. Yet they were brilliant, lustrous, glowing. She couldn't look away from them; she felt as if she had fallen into them and was drowning.

'Annie,' he whispered, and laid the palm of one hand along her cheek, caressing her.

A quiver ran through her, but she was transfixed, unable to move.

He slowly leaned forward, and she watched his mouth, scarcely breathing, waiting.

When his lips touched hers she half groaned, shutting her eyes. His mouth had a heat that spread right through her body. She liked it too much; she was afraid of how much she liked feeling his mouth against her own. She must not let him kiss her. She knew how it would end, if she did. Suddenly terrified, she pulled away.

That was when she realised Marc had had his eyes shut too, because a few seconds later he opened them, with a sound like a deep, wrenched moan, and she saw their dark irises, the deep, glowing centres like a black hole in space.

He got to his feet, pulling her up too, his hands gripping her shoulders.

'Don't,' she broke out, shuddering as she saw the look on his face. No one should feel that much. It was terrifying to be the object of such a need, so much emotion. Annie was aghast.

He didn't seem to hear her. His head came down, seeking her mouth with a blind hunger that made her heart crash helplessly against her ribs.

She twisted and turned to escape, but finally his mouth caught hers and his hands drew her closer, one of them sliding down her spine, pressing her against his body while the other began delicately exploring her from her throat to her waist, each light caress of his fingers sending waves of wild feeling through her. For the first time in her entire life Annie discovered the erotic capacity of her body. Her skin was burning; she felt as if she had a fever which made her ache from head to foot, made her bones feel as if they were melting inside her over-heated skin.

Her fingers curled into his shirt, holding on to him to stop herself falling down.

She had never been kissed like that in her life before. It wasn't even like being kissed. It was like being absorbed, taken into him. She didn't know how to respond; she just shut her eyes and held on to him, light-headed, almost delirious.

He began undoing the buttons on her white silk jersey shirt; she felt his fingers shaking as they slid inside and touched the lacy bra underneath the shirt, pushed the lace aside and found the warm, smooth flesh of her breasts.

Annie's body arched helplessly, a hoarse, wordless sound of pleasure moaning in her throat.

'Annie, Annie,' he whispered, and she felt him shudder, then he broke off the kiss and lifted his head.

Pleasure still reverberated inside her; it was hard to come back from where he had taken her, but she slowly opened her eyes and looked up at him.

'Have you ever been to bed with anyone?' he asked in a low, rough voice.

She instantly prickled with resentment. 'How many times do I have to tell you? My private life is nothing to do with you! Stop asking me questions like that!'

He went on watching her closely. 'I have read the odd hint that your manager was your boyfriend.'

A flush crept into her face. 'Newspapers are always inventing stuff like that!'

His eyes narrowed, penetrating intelligence in their darkness. 'But was it all invention?'

She couldn't hold his stare; she looked away, her chin lifted, conscious of a quick-beating pulse at her temples, in her throat. 'There was never anything between me and Phil.'

It was true, after all. Phil had never had a clue that her feelings were anything more personal than a warm affection. She was sure he had never guessed. He would have betrayed awareness if he had, because although Phil was a hard-headed businessman he was hopeless where feelings were concerned; and Annie could never remember so much as a self-conscious glance. Phil had always been blind about love; that was why it had taken him so long to realise how he really felt about Diana, how she felt about him. Those feelings must have been buried beneath the surface for years before fate took a hand and brought them together, and suddenly Annie was grateful that she had never betrayed herself by look or word. At least she had no painful memories to forget.

'How did you feel when he married your flatmate, though?' Marc persisted.

'I was their bridesmaid! I wouldn't have been if I hadn't been very happy for them!' Defiance made her eyes very green. He wasn't getting any more personal revelations out of her, if that was what he was angling for! 'What are you, a reporter?' she sarcastically asked, and as she said it the idea suddenly made sense. She looked sharply at him, wondering if she had hit the nail on the head, but he just laughed.

'No, I'm not a journalist, Annie.'

'What are you then? You must have a job.'

'I'm a businessman.'

'What business?'

He shrugged. 'Never mind that now...'

'If you can ask questions, so can I!'

'If you can evade answering, so can I!' he mocked, laughing. 'Tell me about this manager of yours... he's attractive, and from what I've heard he runs your life and has done ever since you were seventeen. Is it true that he was very possessive with you, didn't allow you to date, wouldn't let you go anywhere alone, kept you locked away when you weren't singing?'

Angrily she snapped, 'Of course not! All that was just dreamt up by media people Phil wouldn't allow to interview me! They couldn't get to me, so they invented spiteful gossip. That's the way they operate. If you don't co-operate, they get their own back another way.'

'He changed your entire life, though, didn't he? You must have been grateful; maybe a little in love with him?'

'Maybe a little, once.' She heard herself admit it with fury and amazement. How had he got that out of her? She hadn't meant to tell him anything. Hot colour rolled up her face, she bit her lip.

'It wasn't serious, though?' He sounded as if he cared, as if her answer mattered.

She had to answer; she couldn't let him think she was seriously in love with Phil. 'No, it wasn't! But I still say it's none of your business! It was never serious, anyway. I just had a thing about him for a while. Way back, before he started dating Di.'

Marc nodded, as if the answer was what he wanted, or had been expecting. 'And was there ever anyone else?'

Her temper flared again. 'Don't you ever give up?'

'No, never.' His face was intent, pale; his voice deepened, husky and not quite steady. 'Annie, I must know if I've been your only lover.'

She gasped. 'You aren't ever going to be my lover!'

'I was, and I will be, Annie,' he said in that deep, smoky voice.

For a moment she simply didn't take it in, and then she flushed to her hairline, her green eyes wild. 'What are you talking about? You haven't been my lover! I've never slept with you.'

'Sure about that?' His black brows arched and she had that same flicker of recognition, *déjà vu*, whatever you called it. She had seen him look like that before, seen the crooked charm of that smile, heard the deep, vibrating note of his voice in passion.

She swallowed, trying to drum up her anger again. 'Stop trying to confuse me, because it won't work. There's nothing wrong with my memory. Since I was seventeen every day of my life has been accounted for— I've never been anywhere without either Diana or Phil, and they would have told me if I had had any sort of blackout, or vanished, even for a few hours.'

'Annie, listen——' he began and she furiously broke in before he could finish whatever he'd been going to say.

'No, you listen to me! Whatever you're trying to pull, you can forget it. I know I never met you before, and you certainly haven't been my lover.'

She began fumbling with the buttons on her white silk shirt, forcing them back, clumsily, through their buttonholes, aware of him watching her with those intense black eyes.

'I was, and I will be,' he said again.

Annie turned on him with something like desperation. 'You said I needn't be afraid of you, but how can I trust you now? There isn't even a lock on the door of this room. After what you just tried, how do I know you won't walk in here in the middle of the night, and rape me?'

'I won't,' he said, his mouth hard. 'But you can always move some furniture in front of the door if you're really scared. You don't have to be afraid of me, though, Annie. When you go to bed tonight you'll be as safe in this room as if it were your own flat.'

She made another appeal to him, green eyes pleading. 'If you really mean that, take me back to Paris tonight. Please, I can't stay here. I have to go back.'

'Tomorrow,' he said stubbornly. 'I need a few more hours.'

'For what? Why are you keeping me here? Why won't you let me go?'

'I told you. I just want to talk to you, Annie. One day you'll understand, but I can't explain yet. I want you to remember without being prompted; I'm convinced you will. Just a few more hours, that's all I ask.'

She sagged down on to the edge of the bed. 'I'm so tired. This is a strain for me, can't you see that? I don't need it just before I begin a major tour. I should be resting, relaxing, not being put under stress like this!'

'Then lie down now, on the bed, and sleep for a couple of hours,' he suggested gently. 'Would you like to change into something else?' He looked at her suitcases. 'Shall I unpack for you while you rest?'

'No!' she said with force. 'I'm not unpacking my cases; I'll just get a few things out of the smaller one. And if you won't take me back to Paris, then get out of here and leave me alone, for God's sake. I'm exhausted, but I won't get any rest with you in the same room.'

His face hardened, his eyes obsidian, withdrawn. He turned away and walked out. Annie ran to close the door behind him and began moving furniture in front of it— two chairs, a little table piled on top of them. They might not keep him out forever, but shifting them out of the way would slow him down and give her good warning that he was coming in here.

'I'll be back in a couple of hours!' he called, making her jump.

He had been listening. He knew she had moved all that furniture behind the door.

Well, good! she thought defiantly, opening the smaller of her cases and taking out what she thought she might need. She laid a long, lace-trimmed Victorian-style white silk nightdress and matching négligé across the end of the bed, then went into the bathroom and washed. She brushed her hair down again, looked at her reflection angrily, with dismay at the flush on her face, the feverishness in the green eyes.

She looked so different. She had changed too much too fast. He had only had her here for a few hours, but she could actually see the difference in herself, and she was afraid he could, too. Her eyes held secrets; her mouth seemed fuller, the colour of it richer after his long kisses.

She looked at her face in dismay, remembering the heat, the desire, he had aroused inside her. She still felt it. I wanted him, she admitted, shuddering. For the first time in my life I wanted a man—and he knows how I felt. Why did he stop making love to me? I didn't want him to stop, and he knows that, too.

She was bewildered. He was a puzzle, not least because of the way he seemed to know so much about her. How did he? He could have picked up facts from newspaper articles, but how did he know what was in her head? She was beginning to be afraid he would always know what she was thinking, feeling.

She turned away from her reflection and what it told her, and hurried out of the bathroom. She needed to forget, to recover from the shock of everything that had happened since she arrived in France. She had only been here for a few hours; it felt like weeks. The day had been like a wild ride on a fairground switchback. She was drained, exhausted. She couldn't remember ever being this tired.

She kicked off her shoes, took off her silk shirt and ski pants, and, wearing only her fragile camisole and lace-trimmed briefs, got into bed. Dusk was gathering in the room, birds were calling sleepily in the garden. Annie began to feel warmer as the weight of the quilt reached her. She slowly fell asleep.

Afterwards she realised she must have been asleep for several hours before the dream began.

She dreamt she was wandering into the edge of a pine forest. She was alone, but she was looking out for someone, expecting someone to come. The air was full of the scent of pine and green fern, yellow-starred gorse. A slanting sunlight came down through the tall trees, twigs and pine-cones crackled underfoot, and a few birds flew past, but further in there was darkness, deep black shadow and a brooding silence.

Annie walked slowly until she reached a little clearing. Someone moved among the trees and she turned to watch, her pulses racing.

A tall, dark figure came out into the sunlight, into the clearing, and she saw his face.

Her heart lifted; she began to run, filled with joy, holding out her arms. He caught her, lifted her up into the air, and began kissing her, swung round and round with her held tightly against him, her feet off the ground, flying in a circle.

The dream dissolved, the way dreams did, without rhyme or reason, and she found herself in another dream, but still in the pine forest, this time at night.

She wasn't walking through the trees; she was climbing upwards along a hill track, carrying a string bag which was very heavy. Reaching the summit of the hill she plunged into the forest along another track until she came to a small wooden hut built in a little clearing.

As she saw it she felt the same joy, the same lifting of the heart. She began to run, but when the door of the hut opened there was no one inside; the place was empty, dark, silent. It looked as if nobody had been there for years; there was no sign of anyone having set foot inside it.

Almost before she had time to take that in, she found herself running, sobbing, through the deepest part of the forest, among the darkest shadow, the profoundest silence. She was filled with a sense of loss. She was calling someone's name; she wasn't sure who she was looking for, only that she was very afraid.

Suddenly the night was split open with noise and blinding light. There was a sound of machine-guns, flashes like lightning, voices shouting. Annie couldn't see anyone, but she was overwhelmed by a grief so powerful that it was like dying. She began screaming. Screaming. Screaming.

A voice began to shout her name. 'Annie, Annie...' There were heavy thuds, the sound of wood splintering, heavy objects crashing down. Light dazzled her and she woke up, struggled up on to her elbow, looking wildly around the room.

Marc had forced his way into the room. The table and chairs had been knocked over, and one chair leg had broken. The electric light had been switched on; by it she saw Marc running towards her.

He bent down over her, his face pale. 'Are you OK? Annie, that noise...did you have a nightmare?'

Trembling, icy, white-faced, she whispered, 'I had a dream...a terrible dream...'

Marc pulled the quilt up around her bare shoulders, wrapped her in it as if she were a child, sat down on the bed next to her, and held her, rocking her.

'It's over now, though. All gone. You're safe, don't worry. I'm here; I would never let anything bad happen to you, you know that. I'd die for you.'

It was such an emotional promise; he couldn't mean it. She hated hearing him say things he couldn't possibly mean. Annie's common sense would never let her believe he could mean it.

She had grown up in a world where people did not love like that, did not say such things. Nobody had ever loved Annie with such passion. She was scared of the very idea of it, afraid of the consequences of believing it, in case he was lying, or exaggerating, or just using words without meaning them.

She was trembling so badly that she had to lean on him, her face buried in his shirt, feeling the warmth of his body close to her.

'Tell me about your dream,' he said, holding her.

She needed to talk about it. It was still so vivid, so real. 'I was in a pine forest,' she said, beginning to think more clearly, putting her dream in context, recognising where it had come from. 'That must have been because you talked about the Jura, about the forests and the alpine valleys.' Her brows knit together. 'I think you were there, although I don't remember your face, just that there was a man...'

But she wasn't being strictly truthful. She knew it had been him in her dream. She couldn't remember seeing his face, but as she ran into his arms she had known who she was kissing, although she wasn't telling him that.

Marc was very still, listening intently, his hand automatically stroking her tumbled black hair.

'And then...' She swallowed, her eyes shut, remembering with horror. 'It all got mixed up. I was running, crying; and then there was machine-gun fire, headlights, men shouting...in a foreign language; it sounded like German... God knows why I dreamt that. What put that into my head? Some film I saw recently, I suppose.'

Marc didn't comment; his hand went on stroking her hair.

'Someone was running among the trees, trying to get away,' she said slowly. 'I think he was shot, I didn't see, but I was so terrified, I started screaming...'

There was a long silence, then Marc asked, 'Was that all of your dream? Was that when you woke up, screaming?'

She nodded, felt her face was wet, ran a shaky hand over it, then gently pushed Marc away, pulled a paper hanky out of a box of them beside the bed, and blew her nose.

Only then did she remember that she was only wearing a little silk camisole, with shoe-string straps, which left her arms and shoulders bare. The silk was so fine that she might as well have been naked, and Marc was looking down at her, breathing thickly.

She hurriedly pulled the quilt around her again and turned angry green eyes on him. 'I can't remember when I last had a nightmare. I don't think I've ever had one that terrifying—but it isn't so surprising, is it? I'm on edge, after what you've put me through—no wonder I'm having nightmares. Maybe now you'll take me back to Paris! I shall be too scared to go to sleep tonight, after having those dreams. They might come back.'

'They probably will,' Marc said quietly, and she did a double take, staring at him.

'How can you be so calm about it? I tell you it was terrifying...I can't go through that again tonight! You don't know what it was like!'

'I do,' he said, and Annie sat still, her green eyes wide and startled.

'What do you mean, you do?'

'I had those dreams over and over again for years, Annie. I still have them.'

Slowly, trying to understand what he meant, she said, 'You have nightmares all the time?'

'*Those* nightmares,' he said.

'Those?' She was at sea, lost. 'What are you talking about?'

'The dreams about the forest, the hut...'

Annie froze. She hadn't mentioned the hut when she told him about her own dream.

Her eyes searched his face. He was serious, his dark eyes grave as he looked back at her.

'What hut?' she whispered.

He sighed. 'You didn't dream about the hut? Among the trees? A woodman's hut, piled with timber around the sides?'

She was silent, only then remembering the logs piled up against the hut walls. She had absorbed the way the place looked without thinking about it because she had been so eager to get there, to reach the man waiting for her.

Marc watched her. 'You did dream about it, didn't you?' he pressed huskily.

'Yes,' she breathed. 'How do you know? What's going on?' She tried to think, to work out what was happening, but panic and fear made her so jittery that she couldn't think straight. 'Are you conducting some sort of experiment on me? Is this one of those paranormal things? Have you been trying to put ideas into my head, using telepathy? What are you doing to me?'

'I'm not doing anything,' he assured her, but how could she believe what he said?

'Then how else could you know what I dreamt about? You must have done something to make me have those nightmares. What was it? Did you hypnotise me? People can do that, can't they? Put a post-hypnotic suggestion into someone's head, make them do things, say things, when they wake up, without knowing why they're doing it, and tell them to forget it ever happened, afterwards— even forget that they were ever hypnotised.'

He shook his head. 'I didn't hypnotise you, Annie.'

'Then how do you know what I dreamt?'

'I told you, I've had the same dreams.'

She stared into his eyes, her brows knitting. 'I don't understand. What are you talking about? How can you have had the same dreams? Why should you have the same dreams as me, and how can you know about it, even if you do?'

'Because both of us get our dreams from the same place, Annie.'

'I know that. Dreams come from the unconscious,' she retorted. 'And my unconscious isn't the same as yours!'

'We dream about our lives, Annie. About what we did today, yesterday, last year. We go backwards and forwards in time, dream about the present and the past; we mix time up, to make sense of our lives.'

Her green eyes impatient, she snapped, 'But those dreams I had just now weren't about my own life! I didn't recognise the place, except that . . .' She broke off, biting her lip and he gave her a wry little smile.

'Except that you knew you were dreaming about the Jura?'

Crossly she said, 'Well, you had put it into my head with your photo and your talk about the region! But I've never been there, and don't try to tell me I'll remember it, because there's nothing to remember. It's true my father was born there, and his family had all lived there for generations, so he said, but he never took me there, and although I've often thought of going there one day I haven't got around to it yet.'

'Annie, you don't understand——' he began and she angrily interrupted.

'I tell you I've never been there. Never in this life.'

There was an odd, echoing silence. She looked at Marc quickly, struck by something in that silence, something in the expression on his face.

His voice low, he murmured, 'Never in this life, no, Annie. But you have been there and you're starting to remember. I was sure you would, with the right stimulus. You've started following a path I've already been along. What you dreamt about just now really happened, you see. It was all real—the hut, the forest paths, the darkness and then the blazing lights, the threatening voices, the machine-gunning. I have dreamt about that for years now. I remember every tiny detail, with very good reason. That's how I died.'

CHAPTER FIVE

FOR a minute Annie was dumbstruck. She couldn't believe her ears. What he had said kept echoing inside her head, making no sense at all. She stared at him, her green eyes widening and stretching until her skin hurt, and Marc stared back fixedly, not qualifying what he had said, or explaining. She took a long, harsh breath.

'You're mad! Absolutely out of your tree.'

'Annie, listen——'

'I've listened long enough,' she furiously told him. 'I'm not listening to any more of this crazy talk. You need help; you've got a serious problem. But I'm not a therapist and I haven't got any interest in letting you play out your fantasies at my expense.'

She pushed him aside and scrambled out of bed, no longer caring that she was only wearing the silk camisole and briefs. There was only one idea in her head now. She had to get away from him.

Barefoot, she raced to the door. Marc was on his feet too before she reached the other side of the room; he came after her, caught her shoulder, and swivelled her round to face him.

'This is not a fantasy, Annie! Any more than your dream was a fantasy.'

'You put that into my head somehow! I don't know how yet, but I'm sure you did.'

'Oh, come on! Nobody has ever invented a way of influencing the way other people dream.'

'I told you—you must have hypnotised me!'

'And I swear to you, I didn't!' His face was intensely serious, his dark eyes glittering. 'Annie, everybody's dream life is private, personal. So where did that dream come from? Ask yourself that.'

'I don't know and I don't care!' she angrily said, struggling to get away again. He held on tightly, leaning towards her.

'Annie, it was a memory. Of something that happened, to us.'

He was so horribly convincing. Annie was afraid she would start believing him. She reacted in pure panic, looked around for something to hit him with, and her eye fell on the larger of her two suitcases, still standing near the door. Annie seized the handle, turned, and threw the case right at Marc. It hit him in the stomach. He gave a thick grunt of pain and shock, stumbling backwards, and fell, sprawling across the carpet.

Annie didn't wait to see if he had been hurt. She ran as fast as she could, across the landing, down the stairs, two at a time. In the hall, on a chair, she saw her black and red ski jacket, which Marc had taken off when they first arrived. She snatched it up without pausing on her way to the front door, didn't even dare risk stopping to put it on.

It was pitch-dark outside and there was rain in the wind, making her shiver convulsively. She let the front door slam behind her and began to run round the house towards the wood she had noticed from her bedroom window, shouldering into her ski jacket as she ran, grateful for a little warmth. There were clouds across the moon and she couldn't even see any stars, but there was enough light from the house to make it possible to see the garden paths and the wood crowding in around the garden.

She headed for a wooden gate she had observed from the window earlier in the afternoon. She had thought then that that must be the gate into the wood. Once there she would be able to hide among the trees until Marc got tired of looking for her, gave up, and went back indoors, and then she could make her way through the wood until she found a village. There had to be one. This was not an isolated part of France. Distances were always deceptive in the country. There might be a village hidden just out of sight, in any direction; but a rise in the ground, a clump of trees, could be hiding it from her at the moment.

It wasn't as far to the gate as she had expected, but as she reached it and pushed up the metal latch she heard Marc running somewhere behind her. Fear leapt up in her like adrenalin. She put on a fresh spurt, ran faster, all out, her heart beating far too hard, her breathing beginning to come in harsh gasps.

She had to get away. Had to. He must not catch up with her. Behind her she heard him getting closer. He had longer legs; he was covering the ground faster. They were going uphill now, she sensed; it was harder to keep going. Sweat had begun to pour down her body. She couldn't see in the blackness within the trees, kept brushing against them, felt branches tearing at her long, dishevelled hair.

Cramp in one leg made her double up with a stifled groan. God, that hurt. Worse, it made it impossible for her to run another inch; she would have to stop for a minute. In agony, she stumbled sideways, off the track, behind trees, leaned on one, shuddering, while she massaged her cramped leg with one hand, her breathing painful, so loud in her own ears that she didn't hear Marc's pursuit for a moment. Only when her breathing began to slow slightly did she hear the cracking of twigs and pine cones under his feet, the pounding sound as he came closer up the winding track between the trees.

She waited for him to run past her, but to her horror he slowed too, stopped. She felt him listening to pick up the sound of her; she could hear his ragged, torn breathing.

Annie tried not to breathe either. She leaned her face on the rough bark, hoping to stifle the sound of her intake of air. She was trembling violently.

'Annie!' he called. 'Annie, you can't stay out here. It's far too cold; you'll catch a chill.' There was a long pause, then he called again, 'Annie! Don't be stupid. This is ridiculous. You could get hurt out here in the woods, in the dark. There's an old quarry somewhere in there; you could tumble into it, and get killed, and if you didn't do that, you might trip over a fallen tree and injure yourself, and lie there for days in agony.' Another silence. She heard him listening, waiting for her to betray herself, then he said furiously, 'I'll find you, if it takes all night, you know! I won't give up and go away.'

She trembled violently, believing him.

He waited again, then she heard a loud crack as he moved; but he didn't go on up the path, through the wood, although the next sound seemed further away, but level with her. He was stealthily exploring the trees on the far side of the path from her, she decided.

She risked raising her head, peering round the tree sheltering her. It was too dark to see very far, and before she actually saw Marc the darkness was split by a broad yellow beam which flashed round the wood in an arc.

Annie screamed.

In that instant her dream seemed to come true. She was in a state of mindless panic, waiting for the shouting, the machine-gun fire. She didn't even think of ducking back behind the tree, and the light which had been flashing over her came back to stay still, pinning her like a dazzled moth on the background of the wood.

Marc began running towards her. The light bounced away from her, made circles in the dark; and she snapped out of her terror, stopped screaming, began running too, wildly, without thinking where she was going, just knowing she had to get away.

He caught up with her before she got far. Above her own tortured breathing she heard his, rough and dragging, right behind her. She couldn't help looking back to see how close he was, and that was a bad mistake. As she turned her head a branch hit her across the face.

She gave a yelp of pain, thrown off balance again, and Marc leapt forward, hurling himself at her in a rugby tackle. Their bodies collided. He brought her down heavily, so winded by the impact that she couldn't move for several minutes. She lay on the damp earth, breathing thickly, face down, forcibly inhaling the scent of pine cones, leafmeal, fungus. Marc was on top of her, the weight of his body making it impossible for her to move. He was breathing as raggedly, his chest heaving.

After a minute or two he shifted, but only just enough to take her shoulders and turn her face upwards. She was too exhausted to try to escape.

He lay beside her, leaning over her, their bodies touching. When he turned the torchlight on her she blinked, shuddering and dazed, unable to see anything at all suddenly.

'You're blinding me!'

'I wanted to see your face.'

'Well, you've seen it!' she resentfully muttered. 'Now turn that damned torch off!'

He didn't turn it off, but he moved the beam slightly so that it no longer shone right into her eyes.

'Your face is filthy,' he told her. 'You look like something out of a horror film; you're covered in leaves and spider's webs, and there are twigs in your hair.' He lightly brushed his free hand across her cheek, picked a twig, some leaves, out of her hair.

A tremor ran through her. His touch was beginning to be so familiar, carrying a physical intimacy that dismayed her, as if she had always known the way it felt to have him caress her, run his fingers through her hair, as if their bodies had a shared past.

And that was what he wanted her to think, wasn't it? But how was he managing to plant these suggestions in her brain? She wouldn't have thought she was the suggestible type. She would have described herself as sensible, down to earth, not easily talked into folly.

Well, you learnt something about yourself all the time, she thought grimly.

His fingertips trickled across her mouth, and to her fury she felt her lips parting, quivering with reaction. Marc looked down at her intently and she looked back in nervous awareness, her green eyes cat-bright in the torchlight.

The torch went out; darkness swamped them.

'The battery must have run out,' she huskily said.

'No, I turned it out, to save the battery,' Marc told her, and distinctly moved closer.

'I'm cold, we'd better get back to the house,' Annie said in a hurry, her nerves prickling uneasily. The warmth of his body was much too close; her ears began to drum with aroused blood.

'You always liked lying in the forest, in the dark, with me,' Marc whispered against her ear.

'Don't start that again! I told you—I don't believe a word of it; you're wasting your time!'

'But it was summer-time then,' he said, pushing his hand into her hair, stroking the thick tumbled strands back from her face. 'Long, warm summer nights...'

He was lying on his side, his other arm across her, their bodies touching closely all the way from their shoulders to their knees.

'It isn't summer now, and it is cold,' Annie said, trying to see his face against the cloudy sky. All she could see were his eyes, glittering back at her, and behind his head the race and tumult of the spring night, the wind driving pale clouds across the moon, and behind the moon the blackness of the vault of the sky.

His eyes came closer, glowing in the dark. Annie was shaken as her mind tilted again in one of those strange flashes of *déjà vu*, a wild instability making her doubt her own sanity.

This had happened before. It had.

It had happened before, in the dark, in a wood, lying on the damp earth together, with the night sky wheeling overhead. A warm summer night, the scent of wild garlic and crushed grass...

She reached for the memory, but it was already slipping away. Maybe she had never experienced anything of the kind. Maybe he had implanted the memory in her head a moment ago with his talk of making love on long, warm summer nights.

She wished she knew. Was she being subtly brainwashed? Was she so fragile of identity that she was putty in his hands, taking any impression he wanted to make on her?

While she angrily, almost desperately, tried to understand what was happening, Marc came down on top of her, his mouth finding hers before she could turn her head away, evade him. He parted her mouth, kissing her with such hunger that she lost all sense of who she was, what was happening. Her mind clouded; she gave way entirely, her arms going round him, her body shuddering with pleasure as Marc's hand slid down over her, pushing inside her ski jacket, warm on the thin silk and lace of her camisole, the only barrier between his hands and her flesh. She was breathing so fast that she was almost afraid her heart would stop. She wanted to cry; the intensity inside her was so great.

What was happening to her? She caught his head in her hands, felt his hair sliding through her fingers, clinging to her skin, warm and vital.

His hand was still travelling slowly, tormenting her, down her hip to her thigh, his fingers sensually exploring upwards again, caressing her skin, along her inner thigh, inside her tiny silk panties. As his fingertip brushed the warm moistness between her thighs Annie felt a shock like an earthquake hit her.

Gasping, she pulled back. 'No! Don't!' she groaned, cold with shock, shaking as if she had a terrible fever.

Marc lifted his head. He was breathing in sharp, hurried bursts, like someone in pain, in agony.

'Annie...'

His voice was as deep as the ocean; the desire in it spiralled inside her until she thought she would scream.

'No. I can't.' Each brittle sound was forced out of her. Her throat was as dry as ashes. She couldn't swallow.

At that instant the moon came out from behind the clouds and a pale white light filtered down through the trees, showed them each other's faces.

He was darkly flushed, his skin tight over his cheekbones, his eyes glittering with passion, frustration in the reined tension of his mouth.

Annie was white, dark-eyed, her mouth trembling and her body shuddering in the after-shock of recognising how close she had come to letting him take her.

'Let go of me!' she shakily whispered.

For a second she thought he would refuse. She was terrified of what he might do next.

Then he shut his eyes, breathed fiercely for a moment, then got up stiffly and helped her to her feet. She was shaking too hard to be able to walk. She staggered against a tree and leaned there, very close to tears.

Marc bent and picked up the torch he had dropped, turned it on, and when she made a wordless protest flicked the beam off again. As if that had reminded him, he asked her,

'Why did you scream when I started using the torch?'

'You startled me.'

'For God's sake, Annie! Tell the truth!' he snarled, and she jumped about a foot in the air.

'If you're so sure you know the truth, why are you asking me?'

'I want you to tell me. You're still trying to pretend I'm lying, Annie, and I want you to face up to the fact that I'm not, and that you know I'm not. Now why did you scream?'

She could have refused to answer, but somehow she didn't want to. She was too bewildered by everything that had happened since he met her at Charles de Gaulle airport and brought her here. The hours since then had been a waking nightmare, shock after shock; she was almost past being surprised. She had begun to need to know what this was all about; she wanted to talk about it.

'It broke my dream,' she muttered. 'All right? When you shone that torch on me, it was as if I was dreaming again... It was all there—the trees, the darkness—and I was running, being hunted... When you turned on your torch I suddenly didn't know if I was dreaming or it was really happening. I was disorientated; I went into a panic.'

She shivered, and Marc switched on the torch again to look at her, frowning.

'Come on, we'd better get you back indoors, before you catch pneumonia.'

He put his arm around her waist, and she was too weak to push him away again. She leaned on him and let him start to guide her back down through the trees to the garden of the house.

'Are you OK?' he asked as she stumbled beside him in the light of the torch.

She gave him a sideways look, her voice prickly with resentment. 'Oh, of course, I feel just great. It's been such a lovely, peaceful day, and it's ending up with me running around a pitch-black wood, falling over brambles and gorse bushes, getting whacked around the face with branches. Why shouldn't I be OK?'

'You shouldn't have run away, Annie. I told you I'd take you back to Paris tomorrow, and I will. Believe it.'

The harsh timbre of his voice was convincing. She sighed.

'I had to get away. Marc, what you said to me was so...'

'Crazy,' he supplied. 'I know. You said.'

Her temper flared. 'Well, it was! I don't know what on earth you think you're talking about, but it's scaring the life out of me. I don't like things I don't understand. Stop coming out with such weird stuff.'

'We'll talk back at the house,' Marc tersely said, and began hurrying her along the uneven path, towards the garden gate.

The lights of the house seemed so welcoming that Annie could almost have cried at the sight of them, which was stupid, considering the urgency to get away from the place that she had felt just an hour ago. Then it had felt like a prison, a madhouse; now it looked like home. She was too drained to look closely at the wild swings of mood she was experiencing; it was just another aspect of the bewildering situation she had got herself into.

When they got back inside Marc pushed her up the stairs towards her bedroom.

'Take a hot bath,' he urged. 'I'll cook our supper. How about an omelette? I could cook an *omelette aux fines herbes*; there's a little herb garden right outside the kitchen door. Chives, chervil, tarragon, parsley... you used to make a superb *omelette aux fines herbes*.'

Shivering, she gave him a hollow-eyed stare and didn't argue, although she felt like denying it, saying she had never made a herb omelette for him, he was lying again, but what was the point? She had simply come to the end of her ability to keep denying things. For the moment she was going to let remarks like that wash over her head.

In the bedroom she collected clean underclothes, a sweater and jeans from her suitcase, and went into the bathroom, grateful for the bolt on the inside of the door. She ran a hot bath, sprinkled in bath salts, and while she waited for the bath to fill stripped with trembling hands.

Her teeth were chattering. She tested the water, quickly climbed into it, groaned as heat invaded her chilled flesh again, lay there with her eyes shut, not moving.

She tried not to think, but her mind led a life of its own. It kept reliving what had happened in the wood. She felt her stomach churning; she was pierced with a desire so sharp that it was like a burning knife.

'Oh, God, what is happening to me?' she said aloud, opening her eyes. She was burning hot now. She stared at the tiles on the walls, began frantically counting them to stop herself remembering the way she had felt in the wood. She still couldn't believe it. She must be going crazy; it must be infectious, a madness she had picked up from Marc. She hadn't even known him yesterday. How could she feel this way about him, so fast!

For years she had thought she was in love with Philip. Just a couple of weeks ago she had been suffering because he was marrying Diana; she had thought her heart was broken.

At least what had happened to her today had exploded that little myth. Her feelings for Phil had been mere affection, she saw that now. She hadn't been in love with anyone else so she had convinced herself she must be in love with the man who had rescued her from the grey misery of her home life. She owed Phil so much.

Of course it was easy for her to believe the gratitude and affection she felt meant that she was in love with him. He and Di were her dearest friends, always would be, but she wasn't and never had been in love with Phil.

She didn't know what it was she felt about Marc— but she knew it was dangerously explosive, an emotional dynamite she couldn't handle and was afraid might blow her sky-high if she made the wrong move.

'Five minutes, Annie!' Marc called from outside, and she jumped like a frog in the water, sending a wave splashing over the side of the bath.

'Are you OK?' he asked close to the door.

'Yes,' she hoarsely said. 'I won't be long.'

His voice sounded calm and gentle. People could be so deceptive. 'Omelettes spoil if they aren't eaten at once, so hurry up!'

Reluctantly she sat up in the bath, caught sight of her face in a mirror and grimaced. She looked as if she had been down a coal-mine! She hurriedly washed her face, then ducked her head under the water, rinsed her hair free of any remaining leaves, then stood up, water running down her body, wringing her hair with one hand as she got out of the bath.

She towelled herself rapidly and dressed, feeling much warmer and more relaxed as she went downstairs.

Marc looked round as she walked into the kitchen. 'Only just in time!'

As he turned back to the stove his eyes flicked over her from head to foot; she tensed, waiting for him to make some comment about the way she looked. She had tied her damp black hair with a piece of ribbon at her nape and was wearing a jade-green sweater which clung to her like a second skin, and tight, smooth jeans.

He didn't say anything, however, and she felt oddly
let down.

Marc lightly flipped the golden semi-circle of the
omelette on to a warmed plate and put it on the table,
gesturing. 'Sit down and eat it while I cook mine.'

She pulled her chair up to the table. 'This looks wonderful, a perfect omelette. Are you a chef, or something?'

He laughed. 'No, just a Frenchman.' He poured more
beaten egg into the pan, began making magical passes
with a fork, sprinkling chopped herbs into the centre as
it formed.

Annie began to eat, her stomach clamouring for food
as she smelt the fragrance of the egg and herbs. The
table was laid with salad, sliced French bread, fruit,
again. She took some lettuce and a slice of bread, forked
up more omelette.

The kitchen looked different tonight. He had lit
candles, turned down the ceiling lighting; the room had
a romantic glow.

Marc joined her at the table as she was halfway
through her food. 'Why didn't you pour the wine?' he
complained. He picked up the bottle of white wine,
poured some into her glass, then filled his own.

'Did your mother teach you to cook?' asked Annie.

'Yes, I used to help her in the kitchen after school,
but my father cooked too sometimes.'

'This was in the Jura? Did you live in a village?'

'A very small one, just a few houses, a very old
church.' He was eating, but she felt him watching her
secretly from behind his lashes. 'St Jean-des-Pins.'

Annie had almost begun to expect it. All the same, it
was like being hit in the stomach. She caught a sharp
breath, put down her fork.

'My father was born there.'

'Yes. I knew him.'

Her green eyes opened wide, stunned. 'You knew my father? Where did you meet him? I'm sure he never went back to the Jura after he left there.'

'I knew him when he was a small boy.'

She laughed. 'You mean, when you were a small boy!'

His head lifted and he looked levelly at her, unsmiling. 'No. I meant what I said. He was seven years old when I knew him.'

Her ears were whirring with alarm and confusion. 'What are you talking about? How can he have been! He was born in...'

'1936.'

He could have checked up on her father's date of birth easily enough; she wouldn't let the fact that he knew that throw her.

'Yes, 1936,' she said angrily. 'And his mother took him to England with her in 1945, and he never went back to the Jura, so you can't have met him there; you can't have been born until he was...' She did sums in her head, said fiercely, 'Twenty-four! He must have been at least twenty-four when you were born.'

'Eat your omelette,' was all he said, though.

Annie was no longer so hungry, but she finished her omelette and drank some wine without thinking, only realising suddenly that she hadn't meant to drink it after she had drained her glass. Marc leaned over and refilled her glass for her.

'Did your father ever tell you anything about his mother?'

'Now and then,' she warily admitted. 'But I was only eleven when he died; my memory of him is a bit fuzzy, and my grandmother was dead before I was born. She came to live in England after the war; I've never known quite why. I think she may have been involved in the Résistance during the war; anyway, when she first arrived in London she had some sort of Government job, translating. My father didn't talk about her wartime experiences often; he just let the occasional remark drop.'

Marc laughed, white teeth flashing in his tanned face. 'Typical of Pierre. He was always a quiet, stubborn, secretive boy. He took after his father, apparently. You know your grandfather, Jacques Dumont, was killed during the first days of the German invasion in 1940?'

'I know my grandmother was widowed early on in the war.' Annie had never been able to ask her mother questions about her father's family. Her mother never wanted to talk about her dead husband, and after she remarried it was impossible to mention her first marriage any more. Annie soon learnt that it drove her stepfather into a vicious rage if she did, and she was far too scared of him to risk it.

Marc was watching her as if trying to read her expression. 'Your grandfather joined the French Army as soon as war broke out, went out one day without saying anything to his wife, came back and calmly told her he was going at once to join his regiment, and was killed a few months later, without her ever seeing him again, leaving her with a small shop in the village to run, single-handed, and just one son, Pierre, your father, who was four then.'

Annie had never heard this family history; she listened intently, without doubting for an instant that what he told her was true. It all fitted what she did know about her father and grandmother's lives.

Marc sipped some wine, staring at the candle-flame flickering between them, his eyes deep and glowing.

'She wasn't like most of the other women in the village; she had had an English grandmother and had grown up speaking English as a second tongue. She went to university and took a language degree before she married her husband. That had been arranged when she was eighteen, that marriage; her parents wanted it. They were fond of Jacques Dumont; his parents were their closest friends. They were related distantly, in fact. Annie had known him all her life. She was fond of him, too.'

She started at the name Annie, flashed a look at him, but he seemed unaware of her, his face darkly dreaming in the candle-light, his head propped on one hand, his black hair tumbling over his forehead.

'She was never in love with him, though. Nor was he in love with her, she told me; they simply agreed to get married because it made everyone happy and neither of them had met anyone else. She was twenty-one; he was a few years older. They had very little money, but it was a good marriage, because they were friends, fond of each other. There were no ups and downs in their life, no passion; it was all very calm and down-to-earth.'

Annie wasn't sure she wanted a marriage like that. Marc met her eyes and smiled, as if reading her mind.

'But when he was killed she was deeply upset. She missed him badly, as she would have done a brother. She told me once that he was her best friend, and she was angry because he had died. That was why she got involved in the Résistance after the fall of France. It helped to take her mind off her grief, and it made her feel she was taking her husband's place, as well as hitting back at the enemy. There was a lot of activity in the Jura, naturally, because it was a border area, close to the Swiss and German borders.'

'It must have been very dangerous,' Annie thought aloud.

Marc laughed. 'Of course. Oh, yes. The whole area bristled with German soldiers. The Free French Government controlled the area of France southwards from just north of Vichy, but of course the Germans insisted on being in control of the border territory; they didn't intend to let anyone go back and forth through Switzerland.'

'But people did get through?'

'The local-born Résistance people knew every inch of ground, every forest track. They saved the lives of people who had to get out of France. Escaping British airmen, for instance, who had crashed in German-controlled territory and been rescued by local people, were sent on roundabout routes into Switzerland, travelling secretly by night through the mountains and forests. They passed from hand to hand throughout that area, from one safe house to another, with guides to get them where they had to go by night. The local Résistance people often risked their own lives to get them through the passes, over the border, down to the lakes.'

Fascinated, Annie asked him, 'Were your family in the Résistance?'

He looked at her, his mouth crooked, wry. 'I was one of those British airmen, Annie.'

CHAPTER SIX

ANNIE hadn't been expecting that. She got up in a lunge of agitation, pale and shaken.

'Oh, no! Don't start off again... One minute I think you're quite sane and normal, the next you come out with something so unbelievable I know you've got to be nuts! I don't want to hear any more. Come on, I'll help you clear the table and make coffee, then I'm going to bed.'

'No, Annie,' he said harshly. 'I've said I'll take you back to Paris tomorrow, and I mean to keep my word, but that means that time is running out. You've got to listen to me tonight!' He took her by the arms, looking down at her with insistent dark eyes. 'I realise how it sounds; I can't blame you for thinking I'm crazy, but I assure you, I'm not. I think if you just let me tell you the whole story you'll start to understand, even if you still don't believe it all. Will you at least let me finish my story?'

She bit her lip, frowning. She did not want to hear any more. Indeed she was beginning to be quite frightened, not so much by what he was telling her as by what was happening inside herself. Those weird flashes of *déjà vu*, the dreams she had had, the intensity of her feelings about him, the sense she had of knowing him, intimately, in a way she couldn't possibly do—she had been trying to give herself rational explanations for all that. But however hard she tried to believe those explanations there was still a secret residue of uncertainty inside her. She kept thinking, What if...?

What if it was all true? What if she had known him once, and simply didn't remember? What if it was she who was crazy, not he?

But what he had said a moment ago had wiped out everything that had led up to it. He had dropped the odd disturbing hint, made cryptic remarks, but now he had come out with something too far-out to believe. Now she knew he had to be crazy. There was simply no other explanation, was there? Annie had never believed anyone remembered their past lives; she wasn't about to start believing it now.

'I've gone to a lot of trouble to get you to listen to me,' he said in deep, husky tones. 'Please, Annie, just sit down again for a little while. I'll make coffee, then I'll tell you the whole story.'

She looked at him, ruefully accepting that however crazy his story might be she had to hear it or she would never stop wondering what he had been going to tell her.

'I must be almost as crazy as you are,' she muttered, giving in.

He laughed, his dark eyes vivid with relief. 'You're curious, admit it. You want to know the rest of the story.'

'OK, maybe I do, even if I can't promise to believe a word of it. I have to admit, you tell a good story.'

She sat down at the table and he began making coffee with the practised speed of someone who went through the process all the time. Annie watched him move around the kitchen, her eyes intent on him, her senses reacting with intensity to the way he moved, the black hair falling over his face as he bent across the stove, the ease and suppleness of his long, lean body.

Little flames of response kept igniting inside her. Her mouth was dry, her throat hot. She kept remembering what had happened in the wood, the feel of his body on top of her, the heat of desire. It was unbelievable—that she had only known him for a matter of hours, that she kept forgetting that he had kidnapped her, was holding her here against her will, that she could be swept off her feet by a man she knew so little about.

She would never have believed herself capable of such immediate and devastating passion. It had been a shock to her, to her idea of herself, and a revelation of aspects of herself that had been hidden until now.

The coffee was bubbling noisily, black liquid hitting the glass sides of the percolator. Marc put out cups, saucers, spoons, a bowl of brown crystals of sugar, a little jug of cream, a plate of fondant mints covered with dark chocolate.

He did everything with careful precision, placing the spoons exactly at the right angle, his fingers long and deft.

'You still haven't told me what sort of business you work in,' Annie casually murmured, and got a sideways glance that turned her heart over.

He had no right to be that sexy. She wished she had met him some other way, she wished he weren't so disturbing, so different from every other man she had ever met. He wasn't going to be easy to forget.

'I'll tell you later,' he promised, taking the coffee off the stove, and bringing it to the table. 'Do you want to drink this here, or shall we go and sit in the lounge?'

'How long is your story?'

'Long, I'm afraid,' he said drily.

'Maybe we should move somewhere more comfortable, then. I wouldn't want to sit at this table for much longer.'

Moving the candles on to the tray of coffee things, Marc said, 'I've got a log fire burning in the lounge, so we'll be warmer, too.'

He lifted the tray and carried it out of the kitchen. Following, Annie watched as candle-light sent huge black shadows leaping up the walls as they walked along the hall to the lounge, which, so far, she hadn't really seen, merely glimpsed, shadowed by the blue afternoon light through closed shutters over the windows.

Tonight the room was full of the golden glow of fire-light; in the hearth burned chopped pine logs, crackling with resin, wafting fragrant scent into the air. Annie sat down in a green-velvet-upholstered chair, by the fire, holding out her hands to it, while Marc put out the candles, on a low coffee-table, began pouring coffee.

'Cream?'

'No, thanks.'

'Sugar?'

'No, thanks.'

He gave her a cup of strong black coffee.

'Thank you.' She inhaled the fragrance, sighing. 'It smells delicious.'

'Have a mint,' he said, offering them.

'Thank you.' She took one and nibbled it slowly, staring into the flames. The back of the fire was filled with a firebrick stamped with a phoenix with spread wings, the grate was a pretty black ironwork basket and the hearth itself was immaculately tidy, even though sparks kept spitting out of the heart of the fire on to the wide stone hearth.

Marc sat down in another armchair, his long legs stretched out towards the fire, his coffee-cup clasped in his hands.

'How lovely to see a real fire,' Annie said dreamily, still gazing into the flames. 'In my flat I have central heating. There's something so comforting about a real fire, though, isn't there?'

'Yes, but fire can be terrifying, in a forest,' Marc said, a grim frown etching his forehead. 'We get them in hot summers, in the Jura; they can destroy acres of trees that have taken twenty years to grow. That's bad enough, but what's even worse is the feeling you get when a fire rages out of control. You're so helpless to stop it. It leaps from place to place, tongues of orange flame, floating on the wind, trailing drifts of dark smoke, consuming everything in its path. War is like that, too. Once it takes hold it rages out of control. It takes people over, makes them do terrible things they would never have done in peace time; it changes the nature of things, blackens and ruins whatever it meets. The temptation is to run away, get out of its path, but unless you're going to abandon everything you love you can't do that.'

'Have you ever fought a fire?' she asked, trying to keep the talk on a practical level for as long as possible.

'Yes. One summer when I was in my early twenties, I was staying with my family, in the Jura, when a forest fire started. Some teenagers were having a picnic on the edge of the forest. They made themselves a makeshift barbecue site, a spark ignited some dry grass, and suddenly a fire was raging out of control. The village all turned out to help the fire brigade; we had planes bombing the fire with water from the air, but the wind was sending the fire towards the village. We thought for a while we were going to lose everything. Luckily the wind dropped and we got the fire under control an hour later. But I didn't know that until much later. The burning branch of a pine fell and knocked me out.' He pushed the heavy fall of black hair back, and she saw a slight indentation in the bony structure of his forehead. 'I've had this ever since. I deliberately grow my hair over it to hide it. I was lucky not to get badly burned too.'

'It isn't very noticeable,' she comforted. 'I would never have seen it, if you hadn't shown it to me; your hair covers it entirely.' But her mind was working on what he'd said. 'Was your head injury bad?' she asked very casually. 'Did you have concussion?'

'They said I did.' He sounded as if he would dispute it, though. 'All I know is that that was the first time I remembered everything.'

Annie had guessed as much, but she drew breath sharply, her green eyes widening.

He smiled crookedly, reading her mind. 'No, Annie, you can't put it all down to concussion. I had remembered bits of my past life ever since I was a child. I would be doing something very ordinary, like watching rain falling outside, or a kettle boiling, or someone laughing, and suddenly I would have this flash of a memory, very fast, but very clear, like a snatch of a film replaying in my head.'

Annie tensed, paling.

'You know what I mean?' he prompted, watching her, as if he had always known when she had those moments of déjà vu.

She didn't answer. She didn't want to admit it had happened to her, too, since she met him.

He went on flatly, 'It was as if an ordinary event could trigger a memory of something similar which had been followed by something dramatic. Once, for instance, after I watched rain trickling down through the leaves of a tree in a garden, I suddenly remembered seeing a woman with long, dark hair tied up in a scarf, coming through the forest, in the rain, to meet me, and I was both terrified and intensely excited.'

'That could be a scene from a film you'd seen but didn't consciously remember.' Annie was still looking for common-sense explanations.

'Yes,' he agreed in a reasonable voice, 'except that I was only seven at the time, and the emotions were so intense, Annie, far too real for them to be memories of a film. They were very personal. I knew that that had happened to me. I had nightmares that night. I dreamt I was in a forest at night, trying to escape from people who were trying to kill me. I kept running, dodging between trees, but they trapped me—the dream ended when I was shot.'

She sat rigidly, staring. 'Shot?' He nodded, and she moistened her lips with her tongue-tip, shivering. 'In my dream I heard...' She broke off, hating to remember.

'I know,' he said in a quiet, flat voice. 'You heard machine-gun fire, and you knew someone had been killed. That was me.'

Annie jumped up, sending her coffee-cup over, hot black liquid splashing her legs, making her gasp.

'What have you done to yourself now?' Marc was up on his feet too, looking down at her jeans, scowling. 'Did you hurt yourself? Was the coffee scalding?'

She brushed the wet material, grimacing. 'No, it wasn't that hot; it will dry in front of the fire.'

She moved her chair closer to the fire, sat down with her legs spread across the hearth, and watched steam rise from her damp jeans as the heat reached them.

Turning her head, she crossly told him, 'It was your fault, anyway, for making me jump out of my skin! Stop saying things like that.'

His face was sombre, his eyes deep, dark wells of feeling and sadness. 'I can't. However crazy you may think I am, I believe it. Throughout my life I've remembered tiny fragments of a past life, and after I had concussion I found myself reliving that life all over again. You can say I was dreaming, if you like, and maybe I've been dreaming those dreams all my life, but I never remembered the whole dream when I woke up, just had fragments of it embedded in my memory, which were then triggered by some outside event, like rain, or hearing someone whistle, or hearing gunfire.'

She was very frightened. In a voice like the rustling of dry grass she whispered, 'Or maybe you had very bad concussion and you've been imagining this ever since!'

He shook his head, his hair a dark mirror to the light, reflecting glints and sparkles of flame, and Annie stiffened as she was hit by another of those brief flashes of *déjà vu*. She had seen him sit by a wood fire before, watched the flames reflected on his black hair, felt... Emotion overwhelmed her; she wanted to cry, and was shaken by the depth of her own feelings.

She had never imagined she would ever experience an emotion that cataclysmic. It was like dying, a sense of despair and sorrow that kept echoing inside her.

'No, Annie,' Marc said. 'I didn't imagine it. It happened; it's well documented. He was a real man. His name was Mark Grant.'

She drew startled breath at the name, but Marc went on talking.

'Everyone knew about him, the British airman who was shot in the forest, trying to escape. He's buried there, in St Jean-des-Pins, in the little cemetery on the hill in the middle of the village. There's a very plain marble cross on the grave, with his name on it and the date when he died. That was put up long afterwards by his family when they finally managed to visit his grave, and when I was a kid we had it pointed out to us on Sundays, after church. The village was proud of the grave, of him; he was part of our village history. It was considered lucky to name a son after him. There were four boys called Marc in my class at the village school.'

Annie burst out, 'Well, good heavens, no wonder you've always been obsessed with him! Was his the only British war grave in the cemetery?'

He nodded.

'And it had become the centre of a local legend? A dramatic story like that, it must have fascinated the local children, seemed far more exciting than anything that was happening to them, especially those who had been given his name! The war must have seemed very long ago, yet romantic; history, without any sting any more. Like English children playing at being Robin Hood and his Merry Men, not really understanding the misery of life at the time. History turns into fairy-stories, in a way. I bet you played at being the English airman being hunted through the forest, and shot!'

He was frowning. He didn't answer. She watched him, her green eyes troubled, sympathetic.

'Marc, don't you see? You already had that story buried in your unconscious, from a very early age, and

when you got concussion fighting the fire in the forest
you transferred the fire-fighting to another sort of war.'

His face was dark, shuttered, unreadable. She wished
she could see inside his head, find out if she was getting
through to him, or if he preferred his own fantasy to her
common-sense version.

Coaxingly she added, 'You had had a blow on the
head; you'd lost consciousness. You know how dreams
work—in your dream you were in the forest being fired
at by Germans, and you died. I bet the British airman
was shot through the head, too! Don't you see how it
all fits?'

Marc smiled wryly. 'Except for one thing. Nobody in
the village ever told us who had been looking after him,
in the little hut in the forest—nursing him, because he
was injured when he crashed and was not fit to travel
for weeks, feeding him, visiting him whenever it was safe
and there were no Germans in the area. Nobody could
tell me what happened between the Englishman and
Anna Dumont, because she never told anyone; nobody
ever knew. Oh, one or two Résistance people would have
known she was looking after him, but not that the two
of them had fallen in love. She was an intensely private
person. So when I was a boy there was nobody in the
village to tell me about Anna Dumont, or her son. The
two of them left years before I was born. Most of her
family were dead, or had moved away. All I was ever
told was that the British airman had been helped by the
Résistance, but he had been caught and shot.'

Her lower lip caught between her teeth.

The dark eyes watched her, a question in them. 'So
tell me, Annie, how did I know about the dead airman
and Anna Dumont?'

Slowly she said, 'You must have heard something, some time, and put two and two together.'

She refused to admit the alternative; it was too disturbing. She clung to her common-sense explanations, her belief in the rational and explicable.

He sighed. 'No, Annie.'

Crossly she said, 'If nobody told you that my grandmother was involved with the dead airman, maybe she wasn't. Maybe you made that up yourself. You probably knew she was in the Résistance; you knew she had moved to England before you were born—you mixed the two facts up and dreamt up the rest.'

He shook his head.

She eyed him impatiently. 'And if you were British in your past life, why did you come back as a Frenchman?'

'I don't know why; I only know I did. Maybe because I died in France? You came back as an English woman, maybe because you died in England.'

She drew a sharp breath. She had been expecting that for some time now; it had become obvious that he believed that, but all the same it was another shock.

'So I'm my grandmother reborn!' She began to laugh, close to hysteria. 'Marc, for heaven's sake, can't you see how utterly insane all this is?'

He moved suddenly, taking her by surprise. She looked down and he was kneeling at her feet; he caught her hands and held them, looked up at her fixedly.

'You're her living image, Annie. Surely you know that? You must have seen photographs of her when she was young. Years after I had concussion, I saw your face on an English record sleeve. I recognised you immediately, even though you were younger than Anna when I met her. She was thirty-two that summer. When

I first heard of you, you were only twenty-two. That was Anna's age when she married; the ten years after that were difficult for her. A lot happened to her.' He grimaced. 'A lot happened to the world during those ten years. In France, as well as Britain, there was a depression, unemployment, worry about the future, about the possibility of another war, and then the reality, when it began. Anna had suffered a good deal before I met her, and it showed in her face. She was thin and lined; her eyes and mouth told you a lot about what she had been through. But she was still lovely.'

Stupidly, Annie felt a sting of jealousy. His face, his voice, when he talked of her grandmother held such feeling; he glowed darkly with it, a man possessed. He was in love with a dead woman he had never met, and it was folly to let it hurt her, but she couldn't reason herself out of being jealous, any more than she could reason him out of these fantasies.

Marc looked at her, his eyes glittering in the firelight. 'And so are you, Annie, quite lovely.'

Quickly she said, 'So you do know I'm not the same person!'

'Any more than I am,' he murmured, his mouth unsteady. 'My life has been very different from the one Mark Grant led, just as yours has been wildly different from the life your grandmother led. But that's just surface difference, Annie, the small details of day-to-day living—where you're born, whether you're a man or woman, how your life works out. In a sense that's all to do with the envelope of flesh you're posted back in—what's within is what matters. There's an inner core of spirit which remains, eternally.'

She was struck dumb. He smiled at her.

'Now you look even more like your grandmother. She wasn't a talkative woman. She was given to long silences; she was very thoughtful. She had long black hair, like yours, which fell almost to her waist; she used to tie it up in a chignon at the back of her head. Most of the time she wore a black dress; they did in rural France in those days, if they were widows, wore black for years, even for life, some of them. She used to sing, too, did you know that? Her voice was untrained, but it was true——'

'You can't know all this!' she broke out, shaking. 'You've invented it! Even I don't know much about her, and she was my grandmother!'

'I loved her more than life itself,' he said deeply. 'And I mean that literally. I died for her.'

Annie drew a long, harsh breath.

'She was with me when the Germans arrived. If they'd found her she would have been shot too, but they'd have tortured her first to get information about the Résistance in that area. I couldn't let that happen. She didn't want to leave me, but she knew the dangers if she was caught, not to her, but for her comrades. She was very brave, but she was afraid of betraying her friends under torture. I made her go, and then I started off, making as much noise as possible, to lead the soldiers in another direction, giving her time to escape back to the village. They had dogs and searchlights; it was only a matter of time before they caught up with me. I could have surrendered, but I knew they would probably torture me too, to find out who had been helping me escape, so I kept going until they shot me.'

Annie was furious to feel tears spring into her eyes. She did not want to be moved by his story. That made

it too real, and she didn't want to believe it. Oh, obviously it was completely true that an English airman
had been killed in the forest near his village in France,
and was buried in the village cemetery, and it was
probably true that Marc had been named after him, but
as to the rest...well, how could she possibly believe him?

'It all sounds very romantic,' she said offhandedly.
'But you don't really expect me to believe it, do you?'

He didn't answer, just watched her with those dark
wells of eyes.

'Because it's too far-fetched! You have a very vivid
imagination; you've persuaded yourself it happened, but
I'm afraid you haven't convinced me.' Trying to seem
calm, Annie looked at the clock on the mantelpiece above
the sinking log fire. 'And it's getting late. I'm very tired.
I would like to go to bed now, please.'

She got up, and Marc did too, so that on her hurried
way to the door she collided with him. Her breathing
almost stopped as their bodies touched. She flung a
startled, wide-eyed look up at him.

'Annie, don't go,' he said hoarsely. His face was pale;
a muscle jerked beside his mouth.

'I must,' she said, starting to shake. 'I must, Marc!
This has been a very long day and I'm exhausted.'

'You've got to believe me,' he said in a harsh, strained
whisper. 'Time is running out. Don't shut your mind to
it, Annie. I'm convinced you're halfway there already.
I've been watching you all day and I'm certain you're
beginning to remember, but you mustn't fight it. You
have to open the door and let it in——'

A wave of terror broke over her. 'I don't want to end
up as crazy as you are!'

She pushed past him to get to the door. Marc came after her, caught her by the shoulders, pulled her backwards until she was lying against his body as he stood behind her.

'Let go of me, Marc!' she pleaded, but he simply ran an arm around her waist and held her firmly, to make sure she did not break away from him again.

His cheek moved softly against hers; she felt the warmth of his flesh through his clothes, his chest rising and falling right behind her shoulderblades, the muscled power of his body a wall against which she could lean, but which, she knew, she would have little chance of fighting if she ever tried.

'Don't be scared, Annie. I wouldn't let anything hurt you, I would never hurt you myself, either. How many times do I have to tell you? You're safe here, with me.'

His head turned into her throat. She felt the heat of his mouth on her skin and shuddered, with alarm, but, even more worryingly, with fierce response, as he moved closer, his body pressing into hers.

'Don't!'

Marc's mouth softly moved upward, and Annie turned her head away to stop him reaching her lips.

'Stop it! Let go of me!' she muttered, struggling.

The arm around her waist shifted. Suddenly she felt his hand slide caressingly over her breast, and gasped in shock. As her lips parted Marc whirled her round to face him, and before she could stop him he began kissing her hungrily, her face clasped between his two hands, and Annie was helpless to stop the deep, painful wrench of answering desire which tore her apart.

She closed her eyes and kissed him back, trembling violently, but her stupid mind wouldn't let her give in to her emotions. It kept pushing questions at her, insisting that she stop feeling and think. Think. Think.

It isn't really you he's kissing! It's her. His dream woman, the woman he's been obsessed with for years, the woman he believes he died for half a century ago. His hunger, his passion, was all illusory, self-deception. She was the focus for it now because she was alive and the woman he really loved was dead and beyond his reach.

Your grandmother! her mind reminded her scathingly. Marc is in love with your own grandmother.

Crazy, she thought. This is crazy. Marc's fingers caressed her neck, and fever ran through her veins. She couldn't breathe.

'Annie, Annie,' he whispered, his mouth sliding down her throat. His hand was moving up inside her sweater, caressing the warm flesh of her breast. She moaned, eyes closed, the pleasure of his touch so piercing that it had become pain.

This is madness, she thought; when I know he doesn't even realise who he's touching, it's sheer insanity! Why am I letting him do this to me?

Because you're stupid. Because he's almost brainwashed you. But if you don't stop this, you'll soon be nearly as crazy as he is! He's kissing you because you look like her, or at least look the way he believes she looked when she was young, so he's pretending you are her. It is her he's kissing, but it's you who is going to get hurt, because you're halfway to being in love with him already.

She felt a grinding shock as the admission hit her. No! she thought in horrified protest. I'm not. Not in love. Not that.

Only a week ago she had thought she was in love with Philip. No, she hadn't just thought she was; she had been convinced she was in love with Philip! On the day Marc first rang her and said, 'Remember me?' she had been depressed, she had felt abandoned, because Phil had just married Di. Looking back, she couldn't believe it was such a short time ago—time had stretched, twisted, contorted, over the last twelve hours. She found it hard to remember how she had felt before she met Marc. It was almost as if she was someone else now, with a new view of life, of herself, of everything.

'I want you, Annie, I need you,' Marc muttered, breathing thickly, and it was like being doused in ice-cold water.

Her eyes flew open. She stiffened from head to foot. If she didn't stop him now she was going to end up in bed with him tonight. He was going to talk her into it, she knew it. That was what was on his mind, what he meant by saying he needed her. Maybe he had always meant to get her into bed, in spite of all his protests. He was using seduction, not force, but it came to the same thing. Marc intended to sleep with her tonight.

Her stomach clenched in panic and fear. She had to get away, to stop him.

He had his eyes shut, his face buried in her neck. He was off guard now. She wouldn't get a better chance.

Annie broke away from him with all the force she was capable of, shoving him violently, sending him staggering away across the room. Before he could recover she was running up the stairs. She heard him coming before she reached her room, but she was able to get inside and start dragging a chest of drawers in front of the door before Marc could get there to stop her.

He was running so fast that he almost crashed into the door, making the panels shiver. 'Annie, let me in!' he grated, and she leaned on the chest of drawers, which was finally in position, her lungs heaving, her body shaking.

'Go away, Marc!'

'Why did you panic? Did I scare you? You don't have to be scared of me—I thought you realised that now. I wouldn't harm a hair on your head.' His voice deepened to a rough murmur, passionate, urgent. 'Don't you know how I feel about you, Annie?'

'I'm not my grandmother!' she bitterly spat.

There was a silence. She couldn't even hear him breathing for a few seconds.

Tears stung Annie's eyes. Wearily she whispered, 'Oh, go to bed, Marc, and leave me alone. I've had enough for one day. Whatever it is you need, look for it in those dreams of yours. You aren't getting me to stand in for her.'

She stumbled away across the room, heard him saying something quietly, and covered her ears with her hands.

'I'm not even listening!' she yelled, and fell on to her bed, face down, tears rolling down her cheeks, shuddering with sobs she stifled in the bedclothes. The last thing she wanted was for Marc to hear her and realise that she had been hurt. Hurt badly. It was far too late for her to stop herself falling in love. Somehow, some time, during the twelve hours since they first met, she had fallen in love with him, like Alice falling down the rabbit hole, plunged abruptly into darkness, tumbling helplessly, endlessly, as if to the very centre of the earth.

CHAPTER SEVEN

ANNIE slept heavily that night, but she dreamt, and kept waking from the dream, sitting up in bed, her heart crashing inside her chest, her breathing fast and shallow. Each time, she couldn't remember where she was for an instant, listening to the silence in the house, the sound of the wind in the trees outside, perspiration on her skin. Remembering at last, her hand trembling, she switched on the bedside lamp, looked at the clock, closed her eyes and groaned because it wasn't morning yet. She was so tired, though, that once her heart had slowed down and she felt calmer she lay down again, turned off the light, and almost immediately fell asleep once more, only to dream again and wake again an hour or two later.

It was a long night.

The last time she woke up it was from a rather different dream, hot, sensuous, erotic. They were in the forest, in a small clearing, lying on the grass. She was in Marc's arms; they kissed, their bodies moving urgently. She was aching with pleasure, needing to be closer, to be part of him. And then the dream stopped.

Annie woke up so suddenly that it was like falling off a cliff.

As her eyes opened the dream was still playing inside her head. She was groaning in disappointment and frustration, and at the same time trembling and dazed, feeling like a deep-sea diver who had come up too fast and was totally disorientated.

It was a moment before she registered what had woken her up, and snapped fully awake, eyes wide with shock.

Somewhere in the house someone was shouting.

Annie turned pale. What on earth was going on? She slid out of bed and ran to the door, listened tensely for a minute.

Was that Marc? The voice was so harsh, shouting, yelling. But it sounded like him.

Was he being attacked? Had someone got into the house? A burglar? Marc might get badly hurt. She couldn't stay safely behind her barricade; she had to help him.

Annie struggled for a minute with the chest of drawers, finally pushed it back and got the door open. As an afterthought she snatched up the broken chair leg which Marc had put to one side on another of the chairs. Armed with that, she ran out on to the landing.

The yelling had stopped by then, but she could still hear Marc's voice, muttering thickly, words she couldn't quite catch.

The noise came from his bedroom. She went in there and looked hurriedly around, her crude weapon ready, her heart beating fast.

There was no sign of a stranger in there, or of any fight having taken place. Marc lay face up on the bed, his arms flung wide across the covers, tossing and turning with restless energy, making sounds that froze the blood in her veins.

Annie crept up to the bed, suddenly afraid of what she might see. His eyes were shut, a bruised look about the lids, his mouth moving, quivering, moaning, but there were no signs of any injury.

She dropped her chair leg on the floor, pain knifing through her. As if she could see inside his head she knew what he was dreaming about and couldn't bear to watch. Bending over him, she urgently said, 'Marc! Marc, wake up!'

His cries cut off with a deep intake of breath. He lay very still for a beat of time, then in the grey dawn light she saw his lashes flicker, thick and black, stirring against his pale skin; the gleam of dark eyes showed, and he let out a long, shuddering sigh.

'Annie?'

She sighed, too, with relief that those terrible sounds had stopped. 'You were having a nightmare.'

His face was pale, beaded with sweat. She was horrified by the way he looked; as if he had been ill for days. Annie had a terrible urge to stroke the tumbled black hair back from his temples, cradle his head in her arms, rock him and comfort him like a child.

'Was I yelling my head off?' His mouth twisted wryly. 'Sorry; it doesn't happen often, just on nights when the dream's too real.' He looked sideways through the pale light at the clock on his bedside table. 'What time is it?'

'Just gone six.' She didn't ask what he had been dreaming about and he didn't tell her. Tonight, she was certain, they had had the same dreams. She didn't know how or why, but she didn't doubt that it was true, and the last thing she wanted to do was talk about them. Remembering them was bad enough; the terror and grief she had felt still darkened her mind, and Marc's dreams must be worse.

'Sorry to wake you up so early!' Marc gave her a wry half-smile, sat up, pushing back his tousled hair. That was when she realised he was sleeping naked. She hadn't taken on board the fact that his arms were bare until that moment. Shaken, she looked away hurriedly from the bare, tanned shoulders, the deep, muscled chest with the curly black hair growing down the centre from the midriff, disappearing beneath the sheet still covering the lower half of his body.

Deep inside her own body a drum began to beat—heavy, rhythmic, dominating.

Her mouth dry, she said in an unsteady voice, 'Why don't I make some coffee?'

She had to get away. If she didn't he might pick up on what she was feeling, and she would die if he did.

Flushed and flustered, she began to back away, but Marc moved faster than she did. His hand shot out and caught her arm, jerked her backwards so that she tumbled down on to the bed, giving a wild cry of shock.

When she tried to struggle up again, he held her shoulders down on the mattress and arched over her, looking down into her wide, feverish green eyes.

'I've been dreaming about you all night, Annie.'

'Don't tell me!'

Remembering her own dream, she felt her face burn, and her breathing came fiercely, hurting her throat.

Marc was watching her, his eyes quick and intent.

'Annie,' he said hoarsely. He was going to kiss her; she tried to push him back as he came down towards her, but when she touched his bare skin the impact sent a wave of desire crashing through her and she cried out wordlessly.

His mouth was on hers a second later and her half-formed protest died in her throat. His tongue moistly invaded her mouth, the heat and hunger of his kiss clouding her mind. She was lost, confused, no longer knowing if this was real, or a dream. They were so close, the present and the past, echoing within each other. Her eyes shut; she didn't know whether they were lying on a bed, or on the sweet, crushed grass of a forest, whether this was a cool spring dawn, or a long, hot summer night. She only knew that this man kissing her was the man she loved, had loved once, would always love; their bodies moved closer in remembered passion, intimate and sweet and familiar.

Her fingers ran up his chest, feeling the vibrating beat of his heart deep inside the hard ribcage, his breathing irregular, rising and falling rapidly. Marc's shoulders were as smooth as silk, as powerful as the body of a stallion, his muscles clenching as she touched him, his neck tense with awareness of her caress. The very thought of him dying made agony twist inside her. He was so strong and alive. She saw the dark forest, the flare of searchlights, heard the staccato rattle of machine-gun fire, and a scream of pain silently formed in her throat.

I love him, she thought, clasping his head in her hands, the thick, warm black hair prickling under her palms, her own head lifted to meet the driving demand of his mouth. If he died I'd want to die.

Was that how her grandmother had felt when the English airman was killed in the forest?

What am I saying? she thought, stricken. I believe it; that's the truth. I have started to believe every word he says—but what proof do I have? How do I know he isn't a liar, unbalanced, that every word he has told me isn't pure imagination?

'Annie,' he groaned against her mouth. He was lying on top of her now, the weight of his body deeply satisfying. Every time he shifted she shuddered at the pleasure of feeling his body move against hers and remembered her broken dream, the frustration that had raged inside her when she had to wake up just as they had been about to make love.

It was raging now, biting into her, making her ice-cold one second, on fire the next.

Marc suddenly broke off his kiss, breathing with heaving confusion, looked down at her as if he was being torn apart, his dark eyes glistening as if with tears.

'In a minute I'm not going to be able to stop, Annie, so make up your mind now... I said I wouldn't force you, and I won't, but I want you so much it's killing me. Let me make love to you.'

'I hardly know you,' she whispered. 'We only met yesterday. What do I know about you? I don't know what you do for a living, where you live, who you really are. You've said so much, yet what proof is there that anything you said was true? You could be the biggest liar unhung. You could be crazy. How do I know?'

He looked into her troubled green eyes. Quietly he said, 'I'm the only proof I have, Annie. Either you believe me, or you don't. Life isn't a court of law; there's no giving of evidence, no lawyers, no jury and no judge. We all have to rely on our own instincts about people. I am convinced I lived before. I believe I remember some of that life, in flashes, especially the last months before I was shot. I can't prove it, though, any more than I can prove that you are a reincarnation of your grandmother, or that we were lovers for a while. You have to make up your own mind whether you believe it or not.'

Annie gave a long, quivering sigh. He was right, of course. It all came down to whether she believed him or not.

No. It all came down to feelings, instincts, emotions—those vague, insubstantial things that weren't even easy to identify, let alone prove: thistledown floating on the summer air, moonshine, flickering shadows. She didn't understand them, but she knew what they told her.

She couldn't find the words. Words were too clumsy for what she wanted to say to him. Trembling, she turned her face into his neck and kissed the warm, beating pulse at the base. Her eyes closed, she blindly began to explore, slowly slid her mouth along his smooth shoulders, following every curve of bone, every hollow in the flesh, before her kiss trickled down to his deep, muscled chest, the moist flick of her tongue tasting his salty skin. This was what she had been doing in her dream; she was dying to go on from where she had left off when she awoke.

She wanted to touch him with utter intimacy, know him as she had never known another human being, as well as she knew herself; she wanted their bodies merged, one, completed at last.

She heard Marc groaning, felt the tension in his muscles as he touched her long, flowing hair, lifting it, letting it drift through his fingers, breathing in the fragrance of the soft strands, his arms across her back, enclosing without holding her.

'Annie...my darling...' he whispered, and then his body arched and he gave a piercing cry of pleasure and shock as her head went lower.

This was how they had made love in her dream. Dream and reality merged. She abandoned herself to sensuality, unafraid, without inhibition, and Marc's groans grew wilder, more intense.

He suddenly knelt up, looking down at her with leaping eyes. 'We don't need this!' he muttered, unbuttoning her long, silky nightdress.

She lifted herself up to let him pull it over her head. As he tossed it to the floor with one hand, he never took his eyes off Annie.

She lay on the pale sheet, her skin even paler, satin-smooth, trembling, and yet tense with desire as Marc's eyes moved down her body, from her small, rounded breasts with their hard pink nipples, down over her flat midriff and the smooth belly to the curled dark hair between her slender, white-skinned thighs.

Feverishly, Marc slid his hands underneath her, lifted her buttocks off the bed while he slid back between her legs and began to enter her.

Annie gave a cry of pain a second later, tensing.

'Did I hurt you?' Marc froze, looking down at her.

'No, go on,' she muttered, her arms round his body, pulling him down again. She was so hot that it was like being on fire. Instinct was driving her, an urge for satisfaction that wouldn't give her any peace until she found release.

Marc tried again, and Annie bit down on her lower lip to stop herself yelling out, but her body was eloquent enough to give her away, her muscles turning rigid, locking him out even while she tried to pull him closer.

Marc lay still on her for a moment, tremors running through him. 'You're a virgin, aren't you?' His voice was low, rough.

'It doesn't matter... Don't stop, please, Marc...' she half sobbed, holding him tighter.

'Darling, I'm hurting you.' His voice was distressed, uneven.

'I don't care; don't stop...'

He lifted his head and looked wryly at her. 'If it hurts you, it won't be much of a pleasure for either of us, Annie.' He rolled off her, lay down beside her on the bed, giving a long sigh.

Annie curled round to face him, her face unhappy. 'Well, I have to stop being a virgin some time; why not now?'

'Because, my love, I'm afraid I couldn't do much about it just at the moment,' he said in a dry tone, and she looked down his body and gave a little gasp of surprised laughter.

'Oh. I see what you mean. Was that because you couldn't...? Oh, Marc, I'm sorry.' Her lashes lowered, she smiled, put her hand out, murmuring, 'Couldn't we do something about that, though?'

Marc caught her fingers, took them to his mouth, laughing, his eyes dancing with amusement. 'You learn fast. I suspect you have a naughty streak. Another time, Annie, with pleasure, but not now. You're going to have to be patient about making love—it isn't going to be easy for you at first. It would be stupid to rush it; it could put you off for ever, and we don't want that, do we?'

'No, but——'

'We'll have to take it one step at a time, slowly.' His eyes glimmered at her. 'That will be fun, too, Annie, don't worry, but the technique will need lots of time, and the right mood.'

Frustration ate at her, and Marc's dark eyes flicked sideways, taking in her expression.

'Poor Annie...you want it badly, don't you?' he said gently.

Heat flamed in her face, but she nodded, trying to smile.

'Love's like music,' Marc whispered. 'Sometimes you have to improvise, try new variations...'

He rolled back closer, leant over to kiss her, and she gave her mouth up to him openly, passionately, regret in the way she clung.

Marc's hand began to touch her softly, tormentingly; she gave a little gasp of pleasure, her eyes tight shut.

He kissed her neck, her breasts, went on downwards, his mouth warm, brushing, teasing. Annie trembled, a husky moan in her throat as she felt his hair brushing her inner thighs, the moist invasion of his tongue probing the secret places that had resisted him a few moments ago.

Annie had discovered the stranger paths of sensuality; she had lost control of her body's responses, a wild, driving rhythm taking her over, her head turning from side to side, her skin glazed with heat, her mouth open in a low moan as she came towards the cliff edge of satisfaction, trembling and lost to everything but this fierce need.

As the screw turned for that final time she almost lost consciousness, the intensity was so great. Her cries of pleasure went on and on until she slowed and stopped, lay there, like a drowned creature, empty and still and pale.

Marc lay down beside her again. Annie almost went to sleep; she felt she could have slept for a hundred years, like the princess in the fairy-tale, except that there was no thicket of thorns around her, and no spell on her, and the prince was here, on the bed, beside her.

They lay together in silence for a long time, until she roused herself to whisper, 'Thank you.'

'Oh, I enjoyed it, too,' Marc said, laughing huskily.

She turned her face into his chest, her lips apart, warm and moist on his skin. 'Let me do that for you now...'

'Next time, Annie,' he said, his hands playing with her hair. 'I hate to say it, but we don't have the time. We must have breakfast and start out for Paris.'

Her head swung, her green eyes startled. 'At once?'

His smile teased. 'You were desperate to get there yesterday.'

'Was it only yesterday?' She seemed to have been with him forever, and she didn't want to leave.

'Only yesterday,' he gravely said, watching her.

She sighed. 'Time's so strange, isn't it? We haven't even known each other twenty-four hours, and yet I feel I've known you all my life.'

'All our lives,' he corrected, and she did a double take, her heart turning over.

'Oh, Marc...I wish I knew...'

'Whether it was true?' Marc's dark eyes glowed, lustrous, filled with certainty. 'It is, Annie.'

She was afraid of hurting him. Gently she said, 'I know you're sure, but I'm not, although I'm beginning to wish I were. I'd like to believe it, Marc. There's just some very down-to-earth part of me that can't accept it could be true.'

His face stayed calm and assured. 'It doesn't matter any more, Annie. I brought you here because I wanted to convince you we'd known each other before, but now I realise it doesn't matter. All that matters is this moment in time, not any others. If we have lived before, and forgotten our past lives, that was what was intended. To remember would make it very hard to start again, wouldn't it? I may be a freak, an accident—if I really do remember my previous life. But maybe you're right and I'm the victim of my own over-vivid imagination, and a childhood obsession.' He shrugged, his smooth bare shoulders rippling. 'It doesn't matter.'

She leaned over and kissed him softly on the mouth; their lips clung, warm, open, passionate.

As they drew apart, Marc said with a sigh, 'Well, we'd better hurry—you're due to lunch with the managing director of the French record company and some of his executives at one o'clock today, and you have a photo call in the hotel ballroom after that.'

He slid off the bed and picked up a striped gold and black robe from a chair, shrugged into it, and tied the belt around his waist.

Annie was stunned. 'What are you talking about? I don't remember having appointments today—and even if I do, how do you know about them?'

On his way to the bathroom, he coolly said, 'The French record company have a media manager—he set up an agenda for you to meet the Press before the concert. I've seen the schedule that's been sent out to the media, giving all your appointments.'

'How did you get hold of it?' Annie asked, but he just smiled at her over his shoulder as the bathroom door closed on him.

Who was he? she wondered, going back to her own room. What wasn't he telling her? She had realised from the first moment they met that he must have some inside track, a way of finding out very private information about her. He had said he wasn't a journalist, but she was beginning to be certain he was in the media. How else would he have got hold of the information pack on her European tour which had been sent out?

She showered, dressed with some care in one of the outfits Di and Phil had chosen for this tour's meetings with the Press—like all her stage clothes it was deliberately designed to match her public image as a sad and lonely waif, a street singer. She never wore the glittering costumes other singers wore. She came on stage in jeans, usually black, often barefoot or in old trainers, wearing a black tank top or sweatshirt. At first she had bought all her gear off the peg, but now Phil insisted that she wear outfits created especially for her by a young, modern London designer. The look was basically the same, but it had been co-ordinated to make exactly the right statement, and the designer was making a fortune these days by selling high street versions of her 'look' to kids at bargain basement prices.

Today the black top she put on was a midi version, cut short at the midriff, leaving her waist bare above black jeans which fitted snugly around the hips, but since it was quite a cool spring day she decided to wear a white sweater over her thin black top until it was time to meet the media.

Marc knocked on the door just as she was dealing with her hair. 'Coming down to breakfast? I've laid the table and made the coffee.'

'I have to pack my case again, but I can do that after breakfast, I suppose,' she said, opening the door. He was wearing the dark, smoothly tailored suit again, with a blue and white striped shirt and a dark blue silk tie. He looked elegant, but the toughness was undisguisable.

'You look wonderful,' he murmured, smiling at her. 'But I thought you always wore just black for photo calls.'

'That's the gimmick Phil dreamed up,' she said, laughing. 'And under this sweater I'm wearing a little black top—I'll slip the sweater off before I meet the Press.'

They had freshly squeezed orange juice, coffee and hot croissants for breakfast. Annie couldn't believe when he opened the oven and took the tray of perfect golden-glazed crescents out, filling the kitchen with a delicious scent of hot pastry.

'You made these?' she incredulously asked.

He laughed. 'I could have done—my mother taught me how—but there wasn't time. I put the oven on as soon as I got downstairs, took half a dozen croissants out of the deep-freeze, and when the oven was the right temperature popped them in; they only take twelve minutes to cook.'

'They're wonderful,' Annie said, taking a bite of flaky, buttery pastry. 'Mmm . . . I shouldn't eat this—it must be full of calories—but I can't resist. The French do have the best food in the world.'

'I won't argue with that.' Marc grinned at her, sitting down opposite and sipping his juice. 'Tell me what you remember about your father. How did he feel about living in England, instead of France? Didn't he ever want to come back home? He was so very French.'

'Maybe he had thought of it, once, but by the time I was old enough to notice anything he had a good job and was very settled in England.'

'I suppose when you're married, with a family to take care of, you tend to be more careful,' agreed Marc.

She shot him a glance across the table. 'You've never been married?'

'I never met anyone I wanted to marry.'

'But you must have had some relationships over the years. How old are you, by the way?'

His dark eyes teased her: 'I told you that yesterday, have you forgotten? Thirty-four, just ten years older than you are, Annie. And yes, of course I dated women now and then, and I have to admit I slept with several of them, but it was never serious, either for me or them. You can like someone a lot, be very attracted, yet never fall in love, never feel that if you lose them you're going to be badly hurt.'

Annie refilled her coffee-cup, poured some for him too. Frowning, she said, 'I wouldn't really know. I've never had any love-life, except the odd, arranged date with another pop star, which Phil set up, and he made sure that never went any further.'

'He really controls every aspect of your life, doesn't he?' Marc ironically murmured.

Annie grimaced. 'I was so young when we first met that Phil felt he had to keep a close eye on me, protect me. That was why he got Diana to share my flat, go everywhere with me, especially at first. He'd been around the music business all his life; he knew the sort of things that could happen to naïve kids who hit the street without knowing what they were doing. He'd had other young stars who got hooked on drugs or drink, and one who died of Aids. He was determined to keep me safe from all that, and I'm grateful he did now. From time to time I got rebellious and shouted at him over not having enough freedom, but I was so busy most days that I never actually had time to brood over it. And anyway...'

Her voice died away, and Marc watched her, dark eyes narrowing.

'And anyway, you were a little in love with him?' he supplied in a dry voice.

Pink colour flowered in her face. 'I had a crush on him for years,' she admitted. 'I think he took my father's place. I'd always loved my father more than my mother, and I missed him. Phil wasn't like him, but he was protective, and... well, fatherly. I loved that. I was angry with my mother for remarrying so soon after my father died, and I hated my stepfather. He didn't like me much, either. I was a nuisance; I reminded him that he wasn't the first man in my mother's life. He was jealous about that, and because I resented him and argued with him he had an excuse for beating me up every so often.' She grimaced. 'I suppose, to be fair, I was a typical awkward teenager, and could be a pain in some moods. So he could always justify what he did to me, and if I complained to her my mother said it was my own fault.'

His face grave, Marc said, 'You had a bad childhood.'

'Miserable,' she said, pulling a face. 'From the minute my father died, my home life went downhill.'

'Until you met Phil,' he thought aloud, and she nodded.

'Yes. Phil found me just at the right time. God knows what would have happened to me if he hadn't come along. I'd probably have run away from home, lived in London, ended up on the street; it makes me shudder when I think of it.'

Marc took her hand and held it, lifted it to his lips. 'I won't be jealous of Phil, then,' he said lightly.

She gave a husky laugh. 'You don't need to be.'

She heard the intake of his breath, then he looked at the kitchen clock and turned brisk and businesslike again. 'We'll have to be on our way soon. You go up and pack your case again, Annie, while I tidy up in here. I like to leave the place tidy.'

'I'll help,' she said, getting to her feet, but he shook his head.

'I can manage; it won't take me five minutes. Give me a shout when you want me to bring your cases down and put them in the car.'

Annie went upstairs, feeling like a child dragging her feet when she doesn't want to go somewhere.

She didn't want to go back to Paris, back to her busy working life, back to the hurly-burly of publicity, rehearsals, performances, endless travel from one gig to another. Being here had been like stepping out of time, arriving on another planet and seeing the world from an entirely new angle, distanced and with new eyes. So much had happened during the last twenty-four hours; she felt as if she had been away for weeks. Nothing would ever be the same for her, she was certain of that.

Slowly she packed her case, looked around the bedroom, remembering with a shock her feelings when she first saw it. She spent some time tidying up, stripped the bed, put the sheets into the bathroom linen basket.

'Are you ready, Annie?' Marc called from downstairs.

'Yes, OK,' she said huskily, and he ran up to collect her cases and take them out to the car, which was now parked right outside the house. By the time she joined him Marc had stowed her luggage and was waiting for her.

'Do you want to ride in the back in stately isolation, or will you sit in front with me?' he teased.

She made a face at him and got into the front. As
they drove away she looked back over her shoulder, a
long sigh wrenching her.

Without looking at her, Marc said softly, 'You'll see
it again.'

'Oh, you can read the future, as well as the past?' she
mocked him, and he grinned.

'I hope so.'

Annie's heart turned over. It was at that instant that
she knew she hoped they had a future, too. There was
so much against them. The way she felt might not last,
his obsession with her might fade now he had really got
to know her, her career might whirl them apart and keep
them away from each other until their feelings withered
and died... Anything could happen. She was afraid to
be too optimistic. Yet hope glowed inside her like a light
in darkness. She didn't want to stop feeling this way.
She was happier than she had ever been in her life before.
Every time she looked sideways there he was, driving the
car, his profile carved and intent, tanned skin stretched
over austere bone-structure, lids half down over those
glittering dark eyes, his mouth a warm, relaxed line.
Annie got the same stab of feeling every time. She wanted
to laugh out loud; joy bubbled through her veins. She
felt she could fly, if she tried.

'Tell me some more about your childhood,' she murmured. 'Is it cold in the winter, in the Jura?'

'It certainly can be! Some winters there's snow on the
ground for weeks on end,' Marc said, smiling. 'I used
to love winter when I was a boy; we all did. There was
always so much to do—skating, skiing, tobogganing.
Boys were always getting their front teeth knocked out,
or turning up at school on Monday with black eyes or

a broken arm. I never understood why my parents used
to complain about the snow; I thought they were
spoilsports.'

'I expect your mother worried about you.'

'I'm sure she did. She was very family-orientated. In
fact, she wasn't interested in anything else. She spent
most of her day in the house and garden; she was a great
gardener. She didn't grow many flowers; she preferred
vegetables. A very practical woman, my mother.'

'And she taught you to cook?'

He nodded. 'When she had time and I was around. I
was more often out with my friends, playing rugby,
fighting, climbing trees.'

'She was a great cook?'

'Oh, yes. She insisted on the best ingredients...
everything fresh, preferably grown by herself. She had
a little herb garden, and a small orchard—she rarely
bought fruit or vegetables in the market, even in winter.
I often used to be sent out to bring in winter cabbage
for dinner, on days when I had to dig for it in deep snow.
My fingers would be freezing by the time I got back to
the house.'

Annie didn't notice time passing. She was too
interested in what Marc was telling her about his
childhood, his family, the life in the Jura mountains and
valleys. It sounded warm, romantic, a wonderful life,
and she was aching to get there and see the place for
herself. She had a deep sense now that she would feel
she was going home when she did.

Suddenly she saw a road sign and realised they would
soon be in Paris; and at once she got jittery, her nerves
on edge. Marc had said that her absence wouldn't be
noticed, that nobody would look for her, but she couldn't

help wondering if he was right. What if Phil and Di had rung up, or someone from the French recording company had been in touch, only to discover that she wasn't at the hotel, had never even checked in, was, in fact, missing? She could imagine the panic and uproar that would have caused.

What if Marc was arrested as soon as they arrived? She shot him a look, chewing her lower lip.

'Marc, maybe you should drop me somewhere, instead of taking me to the hotel. I can get a taxi.'

He gave her a warm, amused look. 'Why on earth should I do that?'

'The police might be swarming all over the hotel!'

'They won't be.'

'Marc!' she began in agitation, but he just put a hand out, patted her knee.

'Stop worrying. I told you, everyone believes you've been staying with friends.'

They drove into the chaos of Paris traffic, the storm of cars whirling around them so fiercely that Annie kept shutting her eyes, terrified. There was a continuous blare of hooting; tyres screeched. Cars swerved past, almost hitting them, the drivers leaning out to bellow hoarse insults in French. She was glad she never had to drive in these conditions, but Marc didn't turn a hair, as if he was totally used to it, drove here every day.

Maybe he did she thought, frowning.

'Do you live in Paris?' That was one thing he hadn't touched on as he talked about his background. He had told her all about the past, nothing about his present.

'All week. On Friday evening I usually head for the country.'

Her eyes widened. 'Was that your house we just came from?' She had been sure he had rented it for a week or so.

'Yes,' he said coolly. 'I spend weekends and summer holidays there; I prefer life in the country, but I need to spend the weeks in town, because my work keeps me very busy until quite late each day.'

'You still haven't told me what work you do!'

'Later,' he said, slowing as they drove along a wide boulevard lined with smart shops. A moment later he turned into a narrower street and pulled up outside one of Paris's grand hotels. A uniformed porter hurried to welcome them, came round to open Annie's door and help her out.

Marc tossed him the car keys, smiled, and said in French, 'Park the car for me, would you, please, Jean-Pierre? And see that Mademoiselle Dumont's luggage is taken up to her suite.'

The porter nodded, smiling cheerfully. '*Bien sûr, Monsieur Pascal.*'

Annie registered with a little shock that the man knew Marc well. Marc was clearly a frequent client, which meant that he must have quite a bit of money. This was an expensive hotel.

A second later another, bigger shock hit her as she realised where she had heard the name Pascal before. It had come up a number of times in recent conversations with Phil and Di. Marc Pascal was the managing director of the French recording company who put out her discs. She had come back to Paris to have lunch with Marc himself!

CHAPTER EIGHT

'I DIDN'T tell you who I was because I wanted to crash through all the usual barriers,' Marc said a little while later, when they were alone again, in her elegant top floor suite with a breathtaking view of Paris from every window.

'Well, you did that all right!' Annie muttered, glowering at him.

He sighed. 'If you had known from the start that you were perfectly safe you wouldn't have listened to a word I said. You'd have laughed at me, thought it was all a big joke. I had to give you a shock, Annie, focus your mind, if I was to make you receptive to my story.'

'Brainwash me, you mean!'

His black eyes flashed. 'No, Annie. That isn't true! I couldn't think of another way of reaching you. I didn't know whether or not you had any memories of a past life, but you looked exactly like your grandmother, like the woman I kept dreaming about. When I first saw a picture of you it nearly made my heart stop.'

Her own heart turned over violently at the way he looked at her, the note in his voice.

Huskily he said, 'For a long time, believe me, I'd wondered if I was just imagining this woman in my dreams; I'd never seen any photos of your grandmother, you see. I didn't know for sure that the Annie I dreamed about was the same Anna Dumont who had once lived in my village. I'd asked around, I'd tried to check up, but nobody seemed to remember her very well. A few old women did, but they were very vague. I was certainly never told she had anything to do with the dead airman in the village cemetery. Then I saw a picture of you and realised you had the same name, and of course I wondered ... could you be her granddaughter? I knew she had gone to England after the war, and when I found out that your father's name had been Pierre Dumont I was certain who you were, but a strong family resemblance didn't mean you were the same woman reborn.'

'No, it doesn't!' she quickly said. 'I'm glad you do realise that, Marc!'

'I'm as rational as you are, Annie; I'm not crazy,' he drily said. 'But you know what Shakespeare says in Hamlet: "There are more things in heaven and earth, Horatio, than are dreamt of in your philosophy". However incredible it seems, it is possible. It seemed to me that, if I was a reincarnation of that Englishman, why shouldn't the woman he loved be somewhere in the world? I just had to find her, and after I'd seen pictures of you I knew I had to find out if there was more than just a physical resemblance.' He paused, his mouth twisting in self-mockery. 'I suppose I secretly hoped you might have had the same dreams.'

'Well, I didn't,' she said coldly, still angry with him for frightening the life out of her by making her think she had been kidnapped, when all the time her stay at his country home had been arranged in advance with Phil's office. Marc had told her coolly that she hadn't been informed because it was planned as a 'surprise' for her when she got to Paris. It had certainly been that, and it would be a long time before Annie got over the surprise.

'But you have now,' he said softly, and she gave him a hard glance.

'Why don't you admit you hypnotised me? Those dreams I had at your house... you planted them in my head, and before you woke me up you told me to forget I'd ever been hypnotised, didn't you?'

'No, Annie,' he broke out fiercely. 'That isn't true.'

'I don't believe you! Why should I? You pulled the wool over my eyes when you made me think you'd kidnapped me. How do I know you aren't lying about those dreams?'

'Hypnotising you into believing me would have been a pointless exercise,' Marc said in a deep, angry voice. 'I needed to know if you were the woman I had loved before. I took you into the country alone with me to set up the conditions I thought might trigger off any memory you did have... Why on earth would I cheat, by hypnotising you?'

'You've admitted how much you wanted to believe I was my own grandmother, born again. You were obsessed. You'd have done anything to make me believe I was her, wouldn't you?'

'You're wrong, Annie,' he said deeply. 'I wanted you to be her—but only if you really were!'

They stared at each other fixedly, Annie's green eyes accusing, bright with rage, Marc's dark gaze insistent, compelling.

'And if I wasn't?' she whispered. 'What then? You'd have lost interest, I suppose.'

The telephone rang. They both started, the noise breaking the mood. Scowling, Marc turned abruptly and snatched the phone up.

'Yes?' he snarled.

Annie was trembling so much that she had to sit down on the nearest chair. She still hadn't got over the surprise of finding out Marc's real identity and realising the charade he had been playing for her benefit over the last twenty-four hours. She couldn't remember when she had ever felt this angry before. She felt he had made a fool of her.

To take her mind off her feelings, she forced herself to look about her, appraising the sitting-room of the luxury suite she would be occupying during her stay in Paris. It was charmingly furnished, in Empire style, with green satin brocade chairs and sofas, a pale yellow carpet, wallpaper printed with elegant scrollwork on a cream background. A chandelier hung from the centre of the ceiling, elaborate cascades of glass droplets tinkling every time someone walked around the room. Long green satin brocade curtains hung at the windows, which ran almost from the ceiling to the floor, tied back at the moment with silken gold cords.

Marc put the phone down with a crash and Annie stiffened, her head turning towards him again.

'We're expected downstairs,' he said curtly. 'My people have arrived and are in the bar, waiting. We want to get lunch over in good time, before you have to face the cameras.'

'You go down. I need to do something about my make-up and hair.'

'No, I'll wait.' He looked at his watch. 'Five minutes, Annie, that's all you've got. Hurry up.'

Her teeth clamped together. Without a word she got up and walked into the bathroom, aware of him watching her, violently conscious of him every second of the time, and bitterly angry with herself for that. Any attraction she had believed she felt had to be suspect now. He had planned it all so carefully, gone to such lengths to deceive her.

As he himself had said, he had intended her to be 'receptive' to what he told her. How did she know just how far he had been prepared to go?

Her imagination came up with wild ideas of mind-changing drugs, subliminal interference, if not hypnosis itself.

Oh, it was crazy! she told herself, brushing her long, silky black hair and winding it up again into a sleek chignon at the back of her head. Every explanation she came up with seemed too unbelievable to be true.

But something had to account for the instant attraction she had felt from the minute she set eyes on him. She'd never had anything like that happen to her before. It was true that she hadn't dated many men in the past, but she had met plenty of them, on tour with her band, and when she was recording. Nobody had ever hit her like an avalanche before.

Yet Marc had. Even when they were driving towards Paris, that first day, before he so much as said a word to her, she had felt a strong physical attraction. She remembered sitting there staring at his black hair and olive skin, the wide shoulders, the dark eyes, thinking that he was one of the best-looking men she had seen in a long time.

She'd never been that struck by anyone before, and as for what was to happen later... Hot crimson colour flowed up under her skin as she looked at herself in the mirror, remembering the way they had made love, in the wood, in the bedroom. She shut her eyes, groaning. How could she have let that happen? She couldn't even comfort herself by saying he had used any sort of co-ercion. She had wanted him; her mouth went dry as she admitted she still did. How had that happened to her? She'd have sworn she wasn't the type to go overboard for a complete stranger, be ready to go to bed with him only hours after meeting him.

She didn't know how Marc had done it, but if this had been another century she would be accusing him of putting a spell on her!

She delicately brushed silvery green eyeshadow over her lids, renewed her glossy red lipstick, considered her reflection with her head to one side, sighed. That would have to do. She would obviously get another chance to do her make-up before the photographers arrived for the picture opportunity. First she had to have lunch with Marc and his executives, and that was going to be nerve-racking enough.

She emerged from the pale lemon and green tiled bathroom to find Marc pacing up and down the room impatiently, that lean, powerful body vibrating with tension.

He swung, his tanned face grim.

'Oh, there you are! I was beginning to wonder if you were planning to stay in there all day!'

She had taken off her white sweater and was now wearing the outfit Phil had picked out for her to wear for her first meeting with the media. Marc's narrowed gaze absorbed it, his black brows jerking together in a jagged line as he took in her plunging neckline, which revealed the deep valley between her breasts and the be-ginning of the round, smooth-skinned breasts them-selves. The black top clung to her like a second skin, but ended just above the midriff, leaving a bare expanse of pale skin.

'Is that what you're wearing?'

'Obviously!' she retorted, lifting her chin, her green eyes defiant. 'Don't you like it? The band thought it was very sexy.'

'I'm sure they did,' he said through his teeth. He looked at his watch, his forehead still corrugated. 'Well, there isn't time to look for something else. Come on, we'd better go, but I'll take a look at the other outfits you're planning to wear. We've been selling you over here as a sad little street singer; you've never had a sexy image.'

'Maybe I haven't in the past, but I think I will have in future,' she said aggressively.

Marc threw her a barbed look, black eyes glittering. 'Oh, do you? We'll talk about that later.' He threw open the door of the suite, and gestured. 'Come on, we're going to be late!'

She was in a mood to be annoying. She took her time swaying past him, not even glancing his way, her expression as calm and contained as she could make it, although she was very conscious of Marc staring at her, even more aware of the rigidity and tension of his body.

They made an odd couple; Annie caught sight of them both in the polished wood of the lift door. Herself in her sexy black top and sleek, tight-fitting black jeans; Marc looking authoritative, not to say autocratic, very formal and remote, in that elegantly tailored dark suit.

It was hard to associate what she knew about his dream world with the man standing beside her in the lift as they went down to the ground floor. Anyone seeing him from outside would be struck immediately by his good looks, his physical power, the hard bone-structure and the restless energy. Nobody would suspect that Marc was the type to believe in reincarnation or take any note of his dreams, let alone have such a complex and unusual mind. He looked so conventional, so sure of himself and his lifestyle.

If I'd met him today, looking like that, I'd have flipped over him! thought Annie as they walked out of the lift into the busy ground floor of the hotel. He didn't have to put me through that bizarre mock-kidnap just to get my attention. He must know what an effect he has on women.

Of course, it would have taken a lot longer to get to the same point in their relationship. She had to admit he was right there. If they were meeting today for the first time, they wouldn't be alone; they would have Marc's executives at lunch with them. And within another day or so Annie would be fully engaged in Press and publicity interviews, rehearsals, sound checks and all the paraphernalia of getting ready for a performance. And when she had done the Paris gig she would have moved on to the next venue, with the whole circus of musicians, backing singers, tour workers. She wouldn't have the time to see Marc, and he wouldn't have been able to get very close, make any deep or lasting impression.

A few people in the hotel foyer had suddenly recognised her; she heard the hush, then whispering broke out. People stared; a handful of them began hurrying towards her.

'Oh, dear,' she said helplessly, trying to recall a little French, in case she had to talk to people.

'What?' Marc asked, then followed the direction of her gaze and grunted. 'We haven't got time for fans; they'll just get in the way. Come on.'

He put an arm around her and rushed her away, through the doors of the hotel dining-room, saying drily to the head waiter as he met them,

'Anton, we're being chased. Keep them out, would you?'

The head waiter gave an unsurprised, soothing smile. '*Bien sûr, Monsieur Pascal.*'

While Annie and Marc walked across the dining-room to a large table by the window, looking out into a courtyard garden, the head waiter moved to intercept a couple of the bolder spirits of those on their trail, saying firmly but politely, 'Unless you are booked in for lunch, I'm afraid you cannot come in here!'

'*Salut!*' Marc said to the half a dozen people seated at the table, who all hurriedly got to their feet, smiling, answering him.

'*Salut.*'

'*Bonjour.*'

Several even said, 'Hi!' but with strong French accents.

They were busy inspecting Annie, too. She was used to being stared at by now, but she still found it a bit of a problem. Her colour rose; she had butterflies in her stomach. She would have liked to turn tail and bolt back to her bedroom. She was not so much shy as self-conscious, afraid of being a disappointment. People had such fixed ideas about you; they expected you to be miraculous, a cross between a saint and a raving beauty. The sun was supposed to shine out of you. And Annie knew she was very ordinary: a little, skinny girl with long black hair and sometimes mournful green eyes. The only thing about her that was not ordinary was her voice. She could sing. That was her one gift; it had changed her life. She was grateful to God every day for giving her that voice.

'Well, here she is,' Marc said lightly, his arm still round her.

Could he feel the tremor running through her? she wondered, and didn't dare risk meeting his eyes.

He introduced his staff one by one. 'This is Raoul, head of A and R.'

Annie shook hands with the short young man who headed the most vital area of any recording company, the artist and repertoire department. Raoul could be her age, and looked, she thought, rather like a very young Napoleon: olive skin, black hair cut with a fringe, a slightly full face, but an aggressive chin. But he wore very modern clothes: Jean Paul Gaultier, she suspected, from the extreme styling. He must be earning a good salary!

'These two are his chief talent-spotters,' Marc briskly said. 'Simone and Gerard.'

They were even younger, the girl about twenty-two, with a tousled bob of black hair and dark eyes. The boy was any age between eighteen and twenty-five, skinny, serious, and also dark-eyed and dark-haired. They both wore black trousers, black shirts, pink ties. They looked like twins.

'Spotted any great new talent recently?' asked Annie cheerfully.

They shrugged. Looked at each other. Shook their heads, unworried by their admission.

'We look at a lot of people every week...' Simone said.

'But almost never find anyone really new, or different,' said Gerard.

'Well, you must know how it is,' said Simone.

'It's a tough business to break into,' said Gerard.

Annie wondered if they went around together all the time, talked in unison—it was an act, carefully worked out, she decided, amused.

She said, 'I had a lucky break right at the start, or I wouldn't be here today.'

They both nodded. 'Right!' they said in English in unison.

'This is Francine,' Marc said, moving her along to meet the last two guests, who were from the marketing department. 'She's the head of the art department; she's responsible for the covers on your French recordings, so if you have any complaints about them she's the one to make them to!'

The tall, long-legged blonde girl laughed, but her blue eyes were frosty.

'I hope you don't have any complaints,' she quickly warned Annie.

'None,' Annie said, knowing she wouldn't have dared voice them if she had, not faced with that expression. 'The French covers are gorgeous.'

Francine thawed a little. 'Thank you. We think so. I've just seen your new logo—I love it, by the way.' She looked down at the fat folder on the table in front of her. 'I think it's gorgeous; especially against the black.'

The cover of the folder was black; Annie's official logo stood out brilliantly against it—an embossed pair of slanting green eyes, cat-like, naughty, with a fringe of thick black lashes.

'I thought it was silly when they first put the idea up,' confessed Annie, 'but my manager loved it.'

'We all do, too,' Francine assured her.

The logo was going on all her publicity releases and on the backs of records. It was the most recent development from the English recording company's image department, who had been working on a logo for her for months before settling for this one. Successful recording stars mostly had a logo these days, a simple symbol which would tell fans at a glance, without needing words, that a record was by her, or an article about her.

The last of the executives turned out to be the head of publicity for the company, Louis, a very elegant young man who at once started telling Annie some of his plans for the French part of the tour.

The head waiter appeared. 'If you are ready, *monsieur*, may we begin serving?'

'Yes, right away.' Marc nodded, and held a chair back for Annie to sit down between himself and Raoul, the head of A and R.

'We ordered the meal beforehand, as there were quite a few of us, to save time,' Marc told her. 'If there's anything you don't like we can always order you something else. I asked your people in London if there was any food you hated to eat, but they couldn't think of anything.'

'I eat most things,' she agreed.

The first course was terrine of rabbit and prunes, served with toasted brioche, a sprinkling of pickled gherkins, sliced tomatoes and spring onions with crisp lettuce.

'Delicious,' Annie said to Marc's lifted eyebrow of enquiry, and he smiled.

'We eat it all the time in the Jura.'

'That's where Marc comes from,' Raoul told her, and she nodded.

'So he keeps saying.'

Raoul laughed. 'He's very proud of the place. Have you ever been there?'

Annie shook her head, avoiding Marc's sideways glance, the glinting amusement in his eyes.

'Neither have I, but Marc makes it sound like the out-skirts of paradise.' Raoul laughed loudly; Marc didn't.

'Where do you come from?' asked Annie.

'I'm a Parisian.' Raoul's tone made it clear he felt it was far better to have been born in Paris than in the Jura.

'You have to understand,' said Marc drily, 'that France is two countries. Paris, and the rest. You are either a Parisian, or a Frenchman; they're not necessarily the same thing.'

Raoul laughed loudly again, appearing to accept this entirely. 'But we're very cosmopolitan,' he drawled. 'We eat the best of French provincial cooking in Paris.'

'Even *poulet au vin jaune*,' Marc said, as the waiter removed their plates and a heated trolley was wheeled towards them, loaded with food. 'This next dish is another speciality from the Jura—chicken, cooked in the yellow wine of the Jura region, with cream and *morilles*, a dark brown honeycomb-like fungus. The variety that grows in the Jura pine forests near my village has the best flavour, in my opinion.'

Raoul winked at her and Annie laughed, watching her portion of *poulet au vin jaune* being spooned on to a warm plate, to which was added boiled wild rice faintly coloured with saffron, and French *petite pois*, cooked with fragments of lettuce and onion.

Marc said softly to her, 'If you can't come to the Jura, I thought I'd bring the Jura to you.'

Her pulses leapt as she met his dark-eyed stare, the intent, intimate gaze which rarely left her.

Had any of the others noticed the way he kept watching her, the way his voice changed every time he spoke to her? She hoped they hadn't. It was a relief to be sure that they couldn't know that under the table he kept moving his knee against hers, that every so often his hand would brush lightly over her fingers, her arm, her thigh.

The tiny contacts made her breathless, made her heartbeat quicken, her mouth go dry, but she wished he wouldn't. She still didn't know what to think about him, what to make of what he had been telling her. She needed time to work out exactly what was happening inside her. He mustn't rush her any more. He had already rushed her quite enough.

She couldn't say any of that to him, though, over lunch with all those strangers around the table, listening, watching.

She moved her knee away from his, pushed his hand down, avoided touching him whenever she could, but her tactics simply seemed to amuse Marc, whose dark eyes glinted teasingly whenever she met them.

After lunch, Louis and Marc escorted her to meet the Press. Annie was used to being photographed by now, but it was still always exhausting, not to mention boring, being treated like a living doll, pushed and pulled into different positions, asked to smile, turn her head this way and that, to sit here and there.

She was relieved at being released from all that and allowed to go up to her suite to rest. Marc came with her, but stayed in the sitting-room of the suite, making quiet telephone calls in a very low voice, while Annie locked herself into her bedroom and lay down on the bed, closing her eyes with a sigh of relief.

It only seemed like five minutes later that she heard loud ringing from the front door of the suite, then Marc running to answer it, yanking the door open and muttering angrily, 'Stop ringing that bell!' Then his voice changed. 'Oh! It's you!'

Annie wasn't asleep. Not any more. Yawning, she listened, and then snapped wide awake as she heard Phil's voice.

'Tired already, is she? And we haven't even started yet! I hope this isn't going to be one of those tours! Well, never mind... Hi, Marc, how are you? Everything OK so far? Any problems? No? Good. You haven't met my wife, have you? Diana, this is Marc Pascal, the MD of the French recording company.'

Annie almost fell off the bed, running to unlock her bedroom door, and burst out just as Marc ushered the new arrivals into the suite. Diana and Phil looked round, smiling.

'There you are! What's all this about you being tired before we even hit the road?' scolded Phil, his eyes skating over her. 'I hope you haven't been burning the candle at both ends while we've been away. Let's look at you!' He kissed her on both cheeks, took her hands, assessed her with those cynical blue eyes, his head to one side. 'Hmm... you look different, somehow! Or maybe it's just that we haven't seen you for a couple of weeks. Have you been OK?'

'Fine,' she said, laughing. 'I'm a big girl now, Phil. I managed just fine on my own.' She turned to hug Diana. 'You've both got such great tans! It's wonderful to see you both. How's married life, Di? Do you think it will ever catch on?'

'So far so good,' said Di, her brown eyes warm and glowing. 'At least he doesn't snore. How does it feel to have the flat to yourself? It wasn't too lonely, was it?' Her voice was light, but Annie saw the faint anxiety in her eyes, and smiled reassurance, shaking her head.

'It felt a bit odd at first, but I'm enjoying being independent. No more arguments about what to watch on TV! And I don't have to turn my music down, either!'

Diana laughed. 'I can see there are going to be complaints from the neighbours!'

'Do you think this hotel can produce a good pot of tea?' Phil asked, wandering into the sitting-room, and they all followed him.

Marc looked doubtful, wrinkled his nose. 'Tea? I imagine they often get asked for it by English visitors, but whether they make it well or not I wouldn't like to guess.' He picked up the phone. 'Tea . . . for how many? Two? How about you, Annie?'

'I'll have tea, too.' She nodded.

Di watched him make the call to Room Service. She whispered in Annie's ear, 'Now he's what I call sexy. Didn't he take you to visit his country house? What was it like?'

What on earth was she supposed to say in answer to that? Annie swallowed and tried, 'Remote; a peaceful sort of place.'

'Is he married?'

Annie shook her head, and got a sharper, more curious look from Diana.

'Who else was staying there, then?'

Annie's nerves prickled. She should have realised that question was bound to be asked, sooner or later. Marc was putting down the phone; he caught the plea for help she silently threw him, and came over to join her and Di, saying blandly, 'Is she telling you about my friends? They were all dying to meet Annie; I had a problem keeping the numbers down.'

Diana frowned. 'I thought it was supposed to be a restful break for her, before she began the tour.'

'Oh, I made sure she had plenty of rest. I have a big stake in the success of this tour, remember? We're hoping to sell a lot of discs during the next week or two, and make our fortunes. She already has a big following over here, but I'm certain she's going to be a very big star by the time this tour is over.'

Diana was distracted, as he intended; she smiled delightedly. 'Of course she is! And not just in France—all over Europe.' She put an arm round Annie and hugged her. 'Aren't you?'

Annie laughed. 'Let's hope so!' But she was thinking, Oh, Marc was convincing, cool as a cucumber, covering up the truth without a blink. Watching that display of mental sleight of hand had made her wonder just what sort of man he was! How much truth had he ever told her, for a start?

Marc watched her, his eyes hard, probing her face. She realised he was trying to read her mind, tune into her mood, work out what she was feeling.

Phil and Diana's arrival had changed everything, and he had picked up on that, no doubt. Their return had called her back into the warm, familiar circle of their long-time relationship, split her off from Marc, made her deeply aware of how short a time she had known him, how little she knew about him, compared to the length and closeness of her friendship with Di and Phil.

Alone with Marc for hours, she had had no polite public mask to wear, no armour of social manners or pretences to hide behind. She had had to face him as herself, unadorned, stripped to the bone of her own nature, the woman she really was, not the layers of acquired personality written about in newspapers, talked about by disc jockeys, gossiped about by fans. That Annie had been largely invented by the media and her record company's image-builders and was nothing like the real Annie.

She suddenly realised that she probably knew herself better now, after twenty-four hours alone with Marc, than she had ever done in her life before.

It was so easy to start believing your own publicity, so easy to forget how much of your public persona was invention, or exaggeration.

For years she had been kept too busy to think about the increasing split between her real self and the mask put on her face by her media people. When she was seventeen they had answered questions for her, made up answers that suited the image they had for her. Annie had never argued about it. She never had the time, in fact. When could she ever stop and think, Who am I? What do I really think? How do I really feel?

She had opened her mouth and said the words Phil and Diana told her to say. She wore clothes they chose. She went to places they thought she should be seen at— nightclubs, restaurants, hotels, resorts. She had never resented being manipulated, treated like a living doll; she had been only too happy to please them both. She owed them both so much, after all; and she was fond of them, grateful to them.

But all the same, it was time now that she started running her own life, did her own thinking, made her own decisions.

Marc had helped her see that—which made it all the more ironic that the first thing she decided for herself was never to let him get too near her again.

She stared back at him, her green eyes glittering with defiance—and let him see what she was thinking, said to him silently across the room, Stay away from me, Marc. It's over. I don't believe you and I never want to see you again.

CHAPTER NINE

THAT first gig, in Paris, was a sell-out. Annie hadn't thought she was big enough in France yet to make that sort of impact, but Marc and his media people had done a tremendous job for months in advance creating the right atmosphere, an awareness of her that had been built up until the tour began, with Press hand-outs, constant gossip items placed in the right newspapers and magazines, on cable and satellite TV, posters pasted up in public places, but more especially, of course, interviews with her given out to the music and fan magazines.

'You haven't been out of the media for weeks past,' Louis, the PR guy from the record company, told her with satisfaction and an obvious sense of pride in his own achievement. 'Tickets sold out within days of the box office opening. I think this tour is going to be a smash hit, and France isn't the easiest market for foreign singers, as you know. We have too many great bands of our own. I must admit, I didn't expect to do this well with a first tour.'

'You've done a terrific job!' Annie congratulated him, and he grinned, well pleased with the compliment.

'Thanks. I'll be with you all the time, throughout the tour, to cope with any problems that come up, so don't hesitate to be in touch if you need me.'

'I won't,' she promised, aware that Phil or one of his staff would deal with any problems, anyway. She never had to bother with problems that came up, thank heavens.

She was up at crack of dawn, had a light Continental breakfast, and drove out to the stadium to start rehearsing early on the day of the gig itself.

The sound stage was largely built by then, although a few last-minute hammerings were going on, and men were crawling up and down the steel struts, tightening connections, checking for safety. There had been occasions when a stage fell apart under the gyrations of a big band, or seating collapsed when fans stampeded. Nobody wanted that this time!

Below the stage electricians were busily working away too, testing their circuits. Microphone leads festooned the air; from the mikes themselves came the occasional crackle or buzz as someone tested them.

A band of large, muscular young men had begun humping the instruments into place. Keyboards and drums took up a lot of room, and there were massive amplifiers littering the stage already. Every so often someone would drop something and a loud crash would echo and re-echo in the stadium.

'Watch it!' the guy in charge of the roadies would bellow. 'That stuff costs money!'

'Sorry, Jack!' the offending roadie would mumble, or mutter sulkily, 'He tripped me up!'

'Where's this going?' someone else would shout, and Jack would shout back.

The little group of backing singers stood in front of a row of mikes to the back of the stage, rehearsing, stopping, doing it again.

Annie, her band and the dancers who had joined them now began practising their moves; every movement they would be making on stage had all been planned down to the tiniest detail by a stage choreographer, and rehearsed back in London, in a big hall. Now they had to transfer those moves to the great, open-air stage on which they would perform, taking care not to trip over trailing electric wires or fall off the edge of the stage.

The band was largely static: they would be pinned down by their electronic instruments, taking just a few steps this way, a few back again. Annie could move about far more, and would be going on and off throughout the evening, and all of her moves had had to be planned and rehearsed. The dancers had elaborate routines to perform, sweeping back and forth across the stage like a glittering tide.

While the choreography rehearsals went on the electricians began their lights checks—counting down through the various changes of lighting for the evening, making sure all the circuits were working.

'It's a madhouse,' Brick said to Annie, grinning with enjoyment. 'Don't you love the build-up to a gig? I can feel it working down through me to my toes...'

'What?' she absently asked, watching the dancers flash past, arms whirling, leaping high.

'The adrenalin, stupid!'

'You never get stage fright, do you, Brick?' Annie envied him his cheerful exuberance.

'Not on your life! I can't wait to get out there tonight!' He made drumming gestures, eyes bright. 'Once we get going and the drums are building up I get so excited I feel I could fly if I tried. A live performance is the one time you can drum as hard as you like, and make all the noise you like, without worrying about anyone complaining, or being asked to turn it down! Drumming is like good sex; you can't have too much of it, but other people are always trying to stop you getting it or enjoying it.'

The band thought that very funny. Annie wasn't listening; she was watching Marc talking to Phil at the other end of the stage. The two men were staring up at the heavy lights arranged in batteries overhead. A man on a crane was busy adjusting them, while a man beside him took instructions on a walkie-talkie in his hand from a man standing down on the stage.

Marc was wearing a black sweater and blue jeans; he somehow managed to make the casual gear look elegant and very sexy.

Mouth dry, Annie looked away. She must not let him catch her watching him. She had managed to keep out of his way for the last few days, and once tonight's gig was over she and her circus would be moving on to do the next gig, in Lyon. He would hardly go with them.

The long day wore on; she was getting tired now. She had been on her feet for most of the day; her energy was running down.

'Go and take your rest. You're coming apart,' Di said, putting an arm round her as she broke off in the middle of a rather ragged version of one of her most popular songs.

'That was terrible!' she agreed, grimacing. 'I lost it halfway through. I'd better take it again before I go off.'

'Stop right now, Annie!' bellowed Phil from the seating at the front of the stadium.

She looked round, and as she caught sight of Phil below, with Marc standing next to him, the electricians turned on the full battery of lights in the fading afternoon light, and Annie was blinded by the flash.

For a second she was transfixed, dazzled, in her ears the rattle of machine-guns, the sound of a woman screaming.

'Good God, Annie! What the hell's wrong?' Di broke out from somewhere, invisible to her at that instant while her eyes were filled with all that watt power.

'Get those lights off!' Marc yelled from down below.

The electricians hurried to obey. The lights went out. Darkness seemed to come down.

Annie stood there, shuddering, tears in her eyes. Diana put both arms round her, rubbing her shoulders and back instinctively, murmuring puzzled reassurance.

'OK, OK, I'm here... You're safe... What was it?'

Marc had leapt up on to the stage; over Di's shoulder Annie looked into his face and saw the understanding in his dark eyes, the awareness of what had happened to her just now, what she had seen, heard, experienced.

She quivered, closing her eyes against him.

'Take her back to the hotel,' Phil said quietly to Diana. 'She's out of it. We should have sent her off a couple of hours ago; she's been pushing past the limit. Give her some hot milk and a couple of aspirin, then put her to bed in a dark room. No noise, no TV, no music. Stay in the next room; you can rest on the sofa, but don't go to sleep.'

'I'll take her,' Marc said, and Phil and Di looked at him in amazement.

Diana smiled politely. 'That's kind of you, but that's my job. I look after Annie.'

Marc didn't argue, but Annie felt the vibrations of his impatience with them.

'Let's go,' Diana said, steering her off stage, her arm around her. Annie was glad to get away from Marc's dark gaze. Would she have had that flash of vision if he hadn't been there, watching her, willing her to remember?

Back in her hotel room she slept heavily, a sleep punctuated by dreams from which she woke now and then, dazed, shuddering, not remembering where she was for an instant as she stared around the strange, dark bedroom, only to fall back and slip straight into sleep again.

She was exhausted. Even bad dreams couldn't stop her sleeping. Perhaps she was having bad dreams because she was so tired she wondered, hovering on the cloudy edge of sleep.

Diana woke her up with a cup of tea in good time to dress and get ready to drive back to the stadium. They were going in a caterer's van. The fans might not notice that slipping past the chanting ring around the stadium entrances, and, even if they did, they wouldn't see Annie inside; the windows had been blacked out.

'Food?' asked Di.

She shook her head, stomach heaving.

'Ought to eat a sandwich,' Di said, unsurprised, but still trying to persuade her, for once, to eat before a concert, knowing she never did, couldn't keep food down.

'Don't even talk about it! Let's go!'

They got past the crowds without anyone suspecting a thing, and Annie was bundled out of the van down a private entry which led to the dressing-rooms far below, in the maze of rooms and passages under the stadium. She found the band sitting about looking edgy and pale; only Brick was cheerful. A roadie brought him a vast hamburger while he was talking to Annie. The lead guitarist looked at Brick's mouth opening, the wedge of food going in, and dashed for the bathroom.

'You've got no nerves!' Annie accused Brick, averting her own eyes from the sight of his jaws.

'I'm hungry. I've been working like a dog,' he justified.

'You're always hungry!' the others in the band chorused, throwing magazines, old shoes, a couple of books, at him.

He ducked, chuckling. 'Collection of mental cripples, the lot of you!'

'Nervous, honey?' asked Phil, coming up to kiss Annie.

'Petrified.'

'Once you're out there you'll be fine, you know that!' he comforted, and she grimaced, hearing a full-throated roar from up above in the stadium, which was now pulsating with a full audience and the metallic twang of guitars, crashing of drums, from the French band which had gone on first.

'I know. Doesn't help. I haven't got butterflies in my stomach; I've got man-eating tigers.' She glared at Brick, now starting on some shoe-string fries. 'And it doesn't help to have the human garbage muncher over there eating his way through Paris. I'm shocked that the French have junk food like the rest of us. I thought they had better taste.'

'They make great hamburgers!' Brick happily told her.

'Probably made of horse!' the lead guitarist viciously said.

Brick looked horrified. 'You're kidding. They don't eat horses, do they?'

Everyone nodded. Brick turned green.

Phil laughed. 'Well, not long to wait, darling. The warm-up guys are doing a great job, getting them ready for you.' He looked at his watch. 'Another few minutes and the band can go up, then you can follow on when you get your cue.'

Annie dashed into the bathroom, sweat on her forehead. She didn't throw up, but she had to splash cold water on the back of her neck before the turmoil in her stomach calmed down. She stayed in there for a while, working on her make-up, until someone knocked on her door.

'Annie?'

She tensed. It was Marc's voice. What was he doing here? She hadn't expected to see him. She had to swallow twice before she could answer.

'Yes?'

'The band have gone up. You've only got five minutes.'

'Oh...' Her stomach started acting like a washing-machine again.

The bathroom door opened. 'Can I come in?'

'No! Go away! Where's Phil? Where's Diana?' She was feverish, agitated. She couldn't stay still; she was in a state of total witless panic.

'Stop it!' Marc's voice was cool and firm; he caught her, held her, his arms tightly folding her, in spite of her struggles.

'Let go of me! Why isn't Di there? She always stays with me... And Phil... Where are they?' She pushed against his strength, fighting a terrible desire to lean on it.

'They're upstairs, waiting for you. I said I'd bring you up. Here in France you're my star, so I told them I'd look after you until you went on...' His hand smoothed her hair, slowly stroking, caressing, gentling her as if she were a frightened animal.

'I'm used to them,' she said, sulky. 'I need them.'

'No, Annie, you don't,' Marc softly murmured, his mouth against her temples. 'You said it yourself: you're a big girl now; you don't need to have Phil and Di around all the time.'

'I don't need you either!' she said, but she ached to turn her face into his neck. She was quivering at the scent of his skin now, her pulses wild. She remembered the dreams about him being shot, dying, and tears burnt her eyes.

'Don't you, Annie?' he whispered, his hand moving up and down her spine, pressing her closer. 'I need you. As I need air and light and the sky overhead.'

She trembled. 'I had those dreams while I was resting at the hotel,' she whispered. 'Over and over again... Why did you make me start dreaming about it? I never did before, not till I met you. Now I suppose I'll have them for the rest of my life, dreams about something I don't even remember.'

He kissed her eyes, closing them. 'Don't think about them now. You have to go on and sing.'

'I can't!' she wailed, clutching him.

'Of course you can,' he soothed. 'I'll be there. You'll sing for me, Annie. This time you'll be singing for me.'

She heard the possessive note in his voice and her heart clenched in answering emotion.

Marc's mouth searched for her lips. She had stopped fighting it. She gave them up to him, her arms going round his neck, pulling him closer. She had lied. She did need him.

Marc pulled away first, breathing thickly, face darkly flushed.

'Time to go!' he muttered, and led her to the door. Outside in the passage people thronged, watching her, smiling, patting her as she went past for luck, saying it in French or English. She didn't hear a word they said; she just smiled automatically, nodding, her legs moving, one after the other, without her knowing what she was doing, like someone going to the scaffold.

They halted at the edge of the stage, just out of sight. Marc still had his arm round her. Phil came and kissed her, so did Diana, but Marc went on holding her in that possessive grip. She was vaguely aware of the curiosity, surprise, questioning in the looks Phil and Di gave them, but they didn't ask any questions.

Out on the centre of the stage a compere in a glittering red and silver lamé suit was doing a build-up for her. The audience were restless, chanting, 'Annie! Annie! Annie!'

At last the smiling compère gave her cue. 'And here she is now...' There was a long drum roll. 'The lady you've all come to see—here in France, for her first big tour...' Another long drum roll, and cheers. 'So let's hear you; I want to hear you loud and clear... Let's show her how much we love her... that wild and wonderful little-girl-lost...' Another final long drum roll. 'Annie Dumont!'

The crowd erupted into cheers. Marc kissed the top of her head and then pushed her gently forward. Annie automatically began to go through the rehearsed movements, ran out into the black centre of that enormous stage, with that storm of sound deafening her. A blue spot circled her and she stood there in the gesture with which Phil liked her to begin and end each gig—feet apart, arms flung wide, as if to take the whole audience to her heart, hands open, palms up.

The cheers rolled round and round her. She smiled, coming out of the chill daze in which she'd begun.

'*Salut! Ça va?*' she shouted into the microphone.

'*Salut, Annie!*' the audience roared back.

'*C'est formidable de vous voir!*' she told them, easily going into the script Phil had written for her.

By the time she began her first song they were eating out of her hand; she felt them out there, in the dark, barely breathing, giving her all their attention. Her adrenalin was flowing. Her nerves had all gone. She was living on a mountain peak as she finished the song and whirled across the vast stage, the spotlight following her.

The dancers flashed on, glittering in the dark, sequinned and diamond-bright. Annie called out their names, and the audience broke into tumultuous applause. She danced too, then sang again; you could have heard a pin drop as the melancholy notes sighed out. The audience sighed too, before they applauded.

Later, Brick did a long solo, the sound of his drumming rising into the deep blue Paris night sky, and the audience loved that too. Brick was popular. They loved his name, chanted it on and on when he had finished, and he took bow after bow, grinning.

It was a triumphant evening for all of them. Annie sang again and again; the audience would have kept her and the band there forever. Every time they tried to leave, the hoarse, demanding cries broke out again, but at last they left the stage and refused to go back, laughing, flushed, so high that they were almost flying. Champagne corks popped; glasses bubbled over. Everyone was kissing everyone else, but especially Annie. She was hugged so much that she was sure she would be a mass of bruises next day.

Phil and Di were there, lit up, over the moon with excitement. They kissed her, told her she had been marvellous, wonderful, never sung better, sheer magic.

On the far side of the room she saw Marc, his dark eyes fixed and intense.

He didn't come near her, but as their eyes met she felt her whole body shudder.

The noisy, crowded hubbub in the room faded briefly. She remembered the house on the edge of the forest, the silence, the remoteness. She remembered lying in Marc's arms in the darkness under the trees, overwhelmed by an emotion she hadn't expected, didn't understand.

She was used to singing in public, in front of big crowds, used to confusion and screaming fans, the crash and roar of decibels around her. She wasn't used to the way Marc made her feel. It scared her.

'Come on, time you got out of your stage gear and showered. There's a party laid on back at the hotel,' Diana said beside her.

Annie jumped, green eyes wide. 'What?'

'Don't worry, just a few hundred people,' said Di, laughing.

They were always too high after a performance to be able to calm down. Brick was almost walking on the ceiling. He had drumsticks in his hand and kept drumming on people's heads, on tables and chairs and walls. He wasn't drunk or on drugs, just pumped so full of adrenalin that he was crazy.

Usually Annie felt the same. She loved being on stage, performing, giving out. All the energy flowing out of her came back tenfold from the audience. For hours after a gig she couldn't think of anything else. Not tonight. Tonight she couldn't think of anything but Marc.

She took her shower, towelled dry, dressed in a party dress—one of the few she owned, a glittery green and silver thing, with a low neckline and almost no back, thin straps, a tight waist and short flared skirt that showed off her slender legs.

When she emerged again everyone whistled. Brick began singing in his rough, funny voice: one of their own songs, one he'd written. 'She's too sexy to be good...too sexy, that's too bad... Just watch the way she walks...'

Annie threw a cushion at him.

A few minutes later the security men took her and the band out along one of the secret passages, to be smuggled out in another van and taken to their hotel. They were whisked up to another suite, a larger one, already full of people and the throb of recorded music. Annie was handed more champagne, but only sipped it; she didn't need it to take her any higher.

Marc was there, but he never came near her. She kept seeing him, looking at him. He looked back at her, his eyes compelling, dragging her into their depths as if she were being drawn helplessly into a black hole in space.

Then someone would talk to her; she would have to answer, look at them, and Marc would get lost in the crowd again. But Annie had him on her mind all the time. She was throbbing with feeling, a deep, burning sensation inside her, a desire that hurt.

She had sung for him tonight. Not for the audience. For Marc; aware of him all the time, singing to him, for him, all of herself given in the music.

Slowly she began to come down from the elation that had filled her ever since the concert ended. That was when Marc came over to her. She stiffened as she felt him approach. He looked down at her and said quietly, 'Time you were in bed.'

The others protested, yelled, 'Hey! It's still early! Don't break the party up!'

But Annie nodded, her face very pale now. 'I am tired.'

'I'll escort you back to your suite,' Marc said.

She caught Diana's quick, searching look, felt Phil's frowning attention. They didn't say anything, but she knew they were looking from her to Marc and back again, working out what was happening between them. Usually it was one of them who took care of her, and any minute now, no doubt, they had been meaning to tell her to go to bed, just as it would have been one of them who stayed behind with her before the gig and ushered her upstairs on to the stage. Tonight, though, Marc had usurped their usual place, and they were watching her with surprise and no doubt a little alarm.

To reassure them she went and kissed them good-night. 'You two stay at the party, enjoy yourselves. I'm having trouble staying awake.'

She saw from their faces that they wanted to argue, insist on going with her, but with everyone else listening they didn't like to make any sort of scene, so all their questions would have to wait.

Marc didn't say anything as he walked her through the quiet hotel to her suite, but he followed her inside.

She turned on him in a flurry of agitation. 'Good-night, Marc!'

He caught hold of her shoulders and drew her towards him, kissed her possessively, lifted his head and looked down into her flushed, drowsy face.

'You sang for me, didn't you?'

'Yes,' she breathed, staring at his mouth and aching to kiss it again.

He smiled. 'Goodnight, Annie.'

She instinctively, without thinking, stood on tiptoe to meet his mouth as it came down again, but the kiss was brief, gentle, and a moment later Marc was gone, closing the door softly behind him, leaving her dying for him.

Next morning she was nervous as she first saw Di and Phil, but although it was obvious they were longing to ask questions she soon realised that they had decided on a policy of ignoring the subject of Marc. Every time his name came up Annie felt the prickle of awareness in the air, saw Phil and Diana exchange looks, bite back questions. She almost wished they would ask. It might clear the air. But what could she say, if they did? She didn't know herself what was happening.

They had to be moving on to Lyon that afternoon. Nobody got up before noon, and when the band surfaced they were all drained and pale. Even Brick was flat and hardly said a syllable, didn't even tap out a drum roll on his saucer with his spoon as he usually did at mealtimes, just yawned and stared at nothing, giving an occasional groan when he moved too fast or someone spoke too loudly.

The luxuriously fitted coach which was taking them on to Lyon turned up at the hotel at three and they all climbed into it. Brick fell asleep as they left the Paris suburbs behind and headed along the Péage.

There had been no sign of Marc before they left.
Would he turn up in Lyon? wondered Annie, staring out
of the smoked glass of the coach window, lying back in
her reclining chair. As the next hours passed she began
to need to see him. He was in her mind all the time; she
kept closing her eyes and seeing him, daydreaming about
him, remembering what he had said, how he had looked
at her, the touch of his mouth. Minutes dragged; time
was endless. She felt as if it was weeks since she last saw
him.

He appeared just before she was about to go on stage
for the next gig. Annie felt her heart turn over at the
sight of him. She had been feeling tired and depressed,
in no condition to sing up a storm that night, but instantly her mood changed; her adrenalin shot up, her
green eyes brilliant as he smiled at her.

'I'll take her up,' he told Phil and Diana, who were
by then her only companions.

They stirred, faintly resentful, looked at Annie, who
was barely conscious of them, watching Marc with her
heart in her eyes.

Any protest they might have made died on their lips.
They kissed her and went, wishing her luck for the gig.
They were hardly out of the door before she was in
Marc's arms.

'Missed me?'

She didn't bother to answer. He knew. She clung,
kissing him, and Marc sat down on the small couch in
the dressing-room, pulled her on to his lap, and kissed
her again.

Sometimes when they were alone she forgot the darker
side of their relationship: the dreams, the over-
shadowing past, of which Marc was always aware.

The present was all that mattered to Annie: now, this moment, Marc kissing her, holding her.

'Sing for me again tonight, just for me,' he whispered, and she did.

She sang with such passion and attack that she felt the band staring in amazement, and the audience went wild. It was the best gig she had ever done in her life.

Afterwards she was in tears, and everyone hugged her and told her how good she'd been, but she only had eyes for Marc, feeling his response across the room throughout the party afterwards. It was Marc who told her the party was over for her, again. It was Marc who took her back to her suite in the grand Lyon hotel, in the centre, between the Rhone and the Saone.

By then everyone knew about them. The band had begun making jokes, grinned at her, lifted eyebrows, but only if Marc wasn't there, because they were nervous of him; he was formidable, not a man to risk annoying.

Diana finally came out with what had been bothering her and Phil, her face and voice tentative, uncertain. 'Is it serious, Annie? Because...well...he's a lot older than you, and he's...well, French...'

Annie laughed a little wildly. 'What does that mean? Of course he's French; what has that got to do with anything? So am I—well, half French, at least.'

Di looked taken aback, as if that had never registered. 'Yes, I'd forgotten, I suppose you are...but you've never lived here...'

'I'm still half French, and Marc's only ten years older than me. That isn't too big a gap.'

'But with men like him, well, there must have been a lot of other women. He's far too sexy not to have had a busy love-life.'

'I know all about his past,' Annie said with conscious dryness. 'You'd be surprised how much I know about him.' Very surprised! she thought, and a lot more worried.

'You can't be sure he's told you everything!' Diana said, flushed and irritable. 'Annie, you've led a very sheltered life. I can't help wondering if you're up to coping with a man like him!'

'I'm learning,' Annie said, suddenly laughing. 'Di, I'm twenty-four! Time I made my own mistakes. Just let me do that, will you?'

Diana didn't know what to say, worried her lip with her teeth, frowning. 'You're so different suddenly. Ever since we got back from our honeymoon...' She broke off, watching her uneasily. 'You didn't resent it when Phil and I got married, did you?'

Annie had, but that seemed a long, long time ago. It no longer mattered to her at all. She shook her head, smiling at Di. 'I'm glad for both of you; I can see you're happy together, and that's great. It's true it changed things, but I think they had to change, don't you? You and Phil took such good care of me that I was far too comfortable to think of living a life of my own. Now, I can, and I'm discovering all sorts of things about myself.'

Diana looked taken aback, even more unsure, but she managed a smile. 'That's great, Annie, but...oh, do be careful, won't you? Marc Pascal is very sophisticated and experienced—and you're not. We just don't want you to get hurt! Maybe Phil should talk to him, check his background out, make sure he isn't married!'

'He isn't,' Annie said with confidence.

Diana gave her an impatient, almost pitying glance. 'Annie, he may have told you he isn't, but he could be lying. You only just met him; you can't be certain you can trust him. You've known Phil for years; you do know you can trust Phil.'

'Yes,' Annie said slowly, confusion sweeping over her.

'Let Phil find out more about him,' Di coaxed. 'After all, you never know! Men can be very deceptive.'

Annie hesitated, then sighed and nodded. 'OK.' She was used to letting Phil handle all her affairs, and she did trust him. Yet, looking back over the past few weeks, Annie saw how much she had changed since Di and Phil got married, or was it only since she met Marc? she suddenly wondered. How much influence had he had on her?

'Don't let him split you off from us!' Diana pleaded. 'You've been with Phil all these years, since you were a total beginner—it doesn't seem very fair to let a total stranger come between you and Phil now that you're a big star, does it?'

'I wouldn't,' Annie said, but uncertainly, because Marc was coming between her and Phil now, and she knew it.

'He's trying to,' said Di shortly. 'He's no fool, is he? If you become a big international star, you could make millions. As soon as he met you he wanted a piece of that, I've no doubt.'

'No, he isn't like that!' protested Annie, but she wondered, in her heart—was he? What did she really know about him, after all?

'You can't be sure of that, can you?' said Di, and it was true. She couldn't be sure of Marc; she had only known him such a short time. How did she even know that his tales about remembering his past life, and having

known her before, were anything but fairy-tales? Was
Diana right? Was he only really interested in the money
she would be making in the future, in the powerful role
of star-maker to one of today's big names? He was un-
questionably trying to take her over, acting possessively,
always there when she looked round, waiting for his
moment to move in and snatch her away from the others,
make it clear that she belonged to him now.

'Keep him at a distance until Phil has checked him
out,' Di begged, and she bit her lip, then nodded
reluctantly.

'OK. Now we're moving on out of France, I doubt if
I'll be seeing much of him anyway.'

Phil made a few phone calls at once, and came back
to shrug and say, 'Well, so far he checks out OK. There
don't seem to be any skeletons in his cupboard, but we'll
dig deeper, and see what we come up with.'

'You won't come up with anything,' Annie said defiantly, crossing her fingers behind her back in a childish
gesture.

'Don't get too serious about him, Annie,' pleaded Phil.
'Wait until we know more about him.'

After the gig at Lyon they were due to drive over the
border into Switzerland and on to Germany, where they
were to play at several venues, but that afternoon, just
before they were all to board the coach, Marc arrived
in a red Ferrari, roaring up while the band admiringly
coveted the sleek sports car.

'D'you think he'd sell it to me?' Brick asked her. 'Hey,
ask him if I can take it for a quick spin. I'd give my
drumsticks to get my hands on that steering-wheel.'

She told Marc, who laughed, shaking his head, telling
her in quick, dry French, 'I never let anyone drive this

car, and certainly not a twenty-year-old kid who has already smashed up a couple of his own cars!'

'Brick is reckless,' she had to admit, and turned to tell Brick he couldn't drive the Ferrari.

'Selfish swine!' Brick yelled at Marc, who grinned.

'I'm probably saving your life. She's a killer.'

That just excited Brick even more. 'I love dangerous cars and dangerous women,' he moaned as his friends dragged him on to the coach.

'So do I,' Marc said softly, looking down at Annie.

Flushed and uneasy, remembering what she had promised Diana, she said, 'I'd better board the coach, too.'

'You aren't going with them,' he informed her. 'You're coming with me.'

She stiffened, shook her head, her black hair loose around her face. 'I'm sorry, Marc, I can't come with you. I have to go with the band. They would be hurt if I didn't. They'd sulk for days. They expect me to travel with them, not go waltzing off alone, as if I'm special, and they're just the hired help!'

His face was tight, determined. 'You can travel with them for the rest of the tour, but just for a couple of days I want you with me. You aren't due to start rehearsing for your next gig until Wednesday; that gives us plenty of time.'

'What for?' she asked, agitated.

His arm went round her and he urged her into the passenger seat of the Ferrari. She resisted. 'Marc, I can't... My luggage is on the coach...and Phil and Diana will wonder what on earth has happened to me!'

They had gone on ahead some hours ago to make sure that everything was OK at the other end—that the hotels had rooms ready, and the stage and seating was well under way.

'The band can tell them you're with me.' Marc had got her into the car; he closed the door, turned, and called to Brick and the others, 'I'm taking Annie with me; we'll join you all in good time to do the gig.'

'Hey, what do you mean? What's going on?' Brick shouted, looking alarmed.

Marc jumped into the Ferrari and turned the ignition key; the car gave a dramatic roar, and as Brick came running towards them the Ferrari shot away.

'Buckle your seatbelt!' Marc tersely told her as she stared helplessly back at Brick's angry face.

'Where are you taking me?' she asked shakily, suddenly realising that they were alone again. What was he planning? Was Diana right about him? Was he ambitious, scheming, a clever man who had seen the way to get control of a coming big name? What did he have in mind for her now?

'The Jura,' he said, and her lips parted in a silent gasp. Marc shot her a look as they fed into the horrendous traffic passing through Lyon's choked and crowded motorways. 'I'm surprised you didn't guess!' he murmured, and of course she should have done. She might have done, in fact, if she hadn't been distracted by Diana's defensive worry about Marc and his possible threat to Phil's management of her career.

'But...isn't it hundreds of miles away?' she huskily asked.

'You have no sense of direction, do you?' Marc was drily amused. 'No, Annie, it isn't that far from here to the Jura. We should get there by this evening, in time for dinner. I've booked into a small local auberge I know,

near my village. They do great food, regional special-
ties; it's a simple place, but comfortable, and the people
are kind.'

'Are you taking me to meet your family?' Her heart
was beating suffocatingly fast. He had to be serious if
he was taking her home, and, even more important, obviously Diana was wrong: he wasn't married, or he
wouldn't risk introducing her to his family.

'Tomorrow,' he promised. 'You'll love them, and I
know they're going to love you. Don't look so worried.
You're tired; you haven't caught up with your sleep yet.
Lie back and close your eyes; rest for a while.'

She didn't argue. She was too surprised, for one thing,
and, for another, it was true. She was very tired; she
had used up so much energy over the last week, and had
little real rest. She shut her eyes and leaned back in the
seat, letting her mind drift. She was going to the Jura.

Home, she thought, with a start of surprise. I'm going
home. She had never really had a home since she was
eleven and her father died. From that moment on she
had been very conscious of being alone in the world.
Her mother had never loved her; she had never felt she
belonged, and everyone had a deep need to find a place
in which they belonged.

Maybe she would find she belonged in Jura.

She slept, and dreamed of green forests and green
valleys, crisp, cool air, wild flowers in every pasture,
below every stone wall, the sound of church bells ringing
across the miles, climbing peaks of blue-hazed foothills
with behind them white-capped mountain ranges. It
wouldn't be strange to her, this place she had never visited
before—her father had talked about it when she was very
small, Marc had told her all about it during those hours

alone together, and she had seen it in dreams many times before. She knew it was going to be totally familiar to her when she saw it in her waking hours too.

As they began to climb towards the Swiss border the air grew colder; the sky was blue and as clear as crystal. Annie was grateful for Marc's spare sweater, which he unearthed from a case in his car.

'I've got spare pyjamas, too, for you to borrow,' he said. 'We'll buy you a toothbrush.'

'You should have let me get my case off the coach.'

'You wouldn't have come with me if I'd given you time to think!'

She gave him a wry look. 'Why are men always so bossy?' Then she sighed. 'Phil and Diana are going to be very anxious.'

'They resent me,' he said drily.

'Well, they don't know much about you!'

'They're afraid I may take you away from them.'

She couldn't deny that, startled by his perception. He had got on to that quickly.

He gave her a long, dark-eyed stare, his mouth crooked. 'And I will,' he said, sending a tremor through her. His desire excited her. Yet Phil and Diana's warnings sounded inside her, too. Did he want her because he loved her, or because she was going to be a big star very soon, if Phil's assurances came true?

It was still daylight as they reached the edge of the village of St Jean-des-Pins. Marc slowed as they passed a small, gabled white-painted auberge with a swinging sign showing a silver fish among green reeds. The name 'Auberge des Pêcheurs' was printed in curly red letters below the picture.

'That's where we'll be staying,' Marc said. 'A lot of anglers come up here to fish our rivers, and people heading for the Swiss lakes often stop off for the night, too.' He drove on along a straight, seemingly endless road, running through pine forest, with dark rows of trees on either side.

'Where are we going?' Annie asked nervously, peering into the shadows beneath the pines. 'It will get dark soon.' The light was falling fast; inside the forest it seemed to be as black as night already.

Marc drew off the road and began driving along a narrow, unmade track with trees very close.

'No!' Annie said, suddenly panic-stricken. She knew this track; she knew where they were going. 'I can't! Marc, don't take me there; don't make me go!'

His hand slid sideways, gripped hers. 'Don't be frightened, *chérie*. I'm here; I'll take care of you.'

She reached for the door-handle and struggled to get out. He stopped the car. She opened the door and jumped down, and Marc leapt out too and ran round to grab her, his arms going round her.

'Why are you so scared? There's nothing there now,' he soothed.

'You know it's there,' Annie babbled, fevered and trembling. 'I've dreamt about it... I know it will be worse when I'm actually there, where it happened. It will be too much. I can't bear it.'

Marc held on to her, his face against her windblown black hair. 'Listen, Annie, listen to the forest...'

It breathed all round them, stirring in the wind, rustling, hissing like boiling water, crackling as twigs snapped and fell. It was never still.

She was fascinated, terrified.

'Trust me,' Marc pleaded. 'All I want you to do is walk up that track over there...'

'To the hut,' she broke out, shaking. 'I know where it goes. It will be dark in there... I hate dreaming about it... There's such a bad feeling about it. It's empty; he's gone, gone forever.' That sense of terrible loss came over her again, as it had in her dreams.

'I'm here,' Marc whispered, kissing her cheek, and she felt time dislocate again, swerve back into the present. Dazedly she looked up at him, put her arms around him, as if he might be snatched away from her again.

'Oh, Marc! What's happening to me? I'm terrified. Am I going mad? I can't go up there. I don't need to go; I know what it looks like.'

'I want you to see,' he insisted gently. 'You must see with your own eyes that it's all true.'

She hesitated, shivering in the wind, then sighed and gave in. He was right. She had to see, with her own eyes. She had to know.

The walk was a steep climb, in growing darkness. Annie jumped at every sound, kept looking round, eyes dilated. When she saw the hut she stopped in her tracks, her heart turning over and over.

'It's... exactly as I remember... saw it...' In those dreams, she thought. She had only seen it in dreams, and who was to say that Marc hadn't somehow managed to make her dream like that?

But could he make her remember like this? So vividly? Because she knew this place as if she had seen it all her life. She recognised every detail: the way the logs were piled around the outside, under the overhang of the wood-tiled roof; the door; the shuttered window; a covered wooden water barrel; the clearing around the hut; the pine trees stretching endlessly on either side; and even an old mountain ash growing near by, with new green leaves showing on the creaking old boughs.

Annie looked at the hut door, shuddering.

'I can't go inside! Don't try to make me!'

'Even with me?'

Annie looked up at him, into his deep, dark eyes, gave a long sigh. 'Oh, if I must...' With Marc beside her she felt she could face anything.

'Now where's the key hidden?' Marc said, and without needing to think Annie replied.

'Under the doorstep.'

Then she froze, turning white. How had she known that?

Marc was breathing audibly. Without looking at her, he bent down and felt slowly along the under-edge of the wooden doorstep, straightened with a key in his hand.

Neither of them said a word. He put the key in the door and there was a metallic grating, then Marc pushed the door open.

Annie stood on the threshold, stiff and tense, looking inside. The air was damp and cold, smelling of earth. There was an old wooden chair, a fixed wooden platform bed in one corner, on which a straw palliasse might be spread, a rusty old stove in the centre of the hut, with a round chimney going up into the roof, a shelf with a few mugs, plates, a saucepan hanging from a nail and another pile of logs along the wall, kept dry out of the wind and rain.

Nothing had changed. She recognised it all. Instantly. Even the saucepan hanging there in the same place, the old, battered tin plates once painted white with a blue

DYING FOR YOU 183

rim, all so familiar that she might have seen them yesterday.

Tears came into her eyes. She turned her face into the wooden wall and leaned there, shuddering, overwhelmed with a rush of memory which was like being in a speeding train and seeing fields, stations, people, flash past. Faster and faster they came, faces looming out of the mist of time, scenes, images.

'Oh, no, oh, no,' she kept saying.

Marc stood closely behind her, holding her. 'Ssh ... darling, don't ... don't cry; we'll go, if it's going to upset you like this!'

She didn't even hear him. She was somewhere else, back in the past, in his arms, not here, in this hut, but out in the forest, under the trees, on a warm summer night, making love on a bed of ferns which rustled every time they moved, the fresh scent of the crushed leaves and grass so strong that Annie could smell it now. She had her eyes shut, breathing in that scent, which brought with it all the intensity of pleasure she had felt in his arms. Her hands moved with tactile sensuality over his skin, his broad shoulders and the long, deep indentation of his spine, feeling the power of his body at her fingertips, hearing the rough torture of his breathing as he moved on top of her. She held him closer, pulling him down into her, wanting to hold him like that forever.

Moonlight dappled their pale bodies, rippled over them like silent water. Knowing the danger they were in gave a deeper, wilder note to their cries of pleasure. They made love with desperation, a hunger that could never be satisfied, always aware that it might be for the last time. In an uncertain world only love had meaning, but love was so fragile and death was always just around the corner. They couldn't have enough of each other.

Suddenly the image changed, startling her, like a blow in the face. She gave a low moan, doubling up in pain. Somehow she knew that this was the very next time she had seen him. A day later. When he was brought down to the village by his killers, who were demanding that he be identified, threatening reprisals, wanting to know who had been sheltering him, accusing the villagers. Annie had stood in the doorway of her shop, had seen him carried past: white, horribly rigid, dappled now with dry, blackening blood.

She couldn't bear any more. She dragged herself back to the present, to the hut, sobbing, shaking.

'Oh, why did you make me come here?' she muttered to Marc. 'I don't want to remember… It hurts too much.'

'It was all a long time ago, Annie. It can't hurt us now,' he said softly, his hand stroking rhythmically over her hair and down her back. 'Tell me what you just remembered… You did remember something, didn't you?'

She was silent for a moment, then she whispered shakily, 'We came back here, after making love in the forest that last time. We came back here, to the hut…'

She felt him listening, everything in him intent on her and what she was telling him. His hand soothed, comforted her, the warmth of it seeping into her chilled body.

'You said you wished we could have had a child,' she remembered, and at once saw it all again, playing in her head, saw his face, heard his voice, wanted to weep because he was dead. But he wasn't. He was here, listening to her. Confusion made her head swim. She shook her head, stumbling on, 'But you said we shouldn't…things being the way they were; it would have made my life a misery in the village... Country people have such fixed ideas; they'd never have forgiven me. You said you wouldn't do that to me. If we both survived the war, you said, you would come back and find me, and we would get married, but in case we didn't survive, never met again, you said we mustn't just go out like a candle-flame and leave nothing behind, as if we'd never been here at all.'

She stiffened at that instant, went dead white, gave a gasp.

'What?' Marc asked quickly, at once aware of a change in her.

Annie looked up at him, turned, looked round the hut, biting her lip. Marc waited, his face pale and tense.

'What is it, Annie?'

Annie stared at the piles of logs near the window. 'Over there... It was over there...' She began pulling the logs aside to expose the wall behind them, and after a brief pause Marc came to help her. It was hard, dirty work, but Annie hardly noticed the effort she had to make.

Five minutes later she stopped dead, breathing hoarsely. She fell on her knees and put out a shaking hand to touch deeply cut initials which had been carved into the lowest board of the hut wall. They had faded now, but could still be clearly read: the first letters of their names, A and M, entwined, and underneath the word FOREVER. The passing of half a century had not wiped them out. Forever, she thought. Was that why they had both come back? Had they somehow reached into eternity with the intensity of their feeling?

Marc knelt down beside her and touched the letters too, with a fingertip, staring at them.

'Oh, Marc...' she breathed, turning to look at him. 'They're still here.'

He looked into her eyes, his eyes glowing. 'So are we, Annie.' He was breathing very fast, his skin darkly flushed. 'I love you,' he said in a deep voice roughened by feeling, then his mouth was on hers, hot and insistent.

Any doubts she had ever had were gone. She knew with utter certainty that she loved this man once long ago, loved him now, just as she had loved him before, in another life and time. They had been cheated of that love last time; death had snatched him away. But they had another chance now.

Marc reluctantly lifted his mouth, stared down at her passionate face. '*Chérie*...' he whispered. 'I've loved you for so long. I knew I'd find you again one day, from the moment I began remembering. And ever since I saw that photo of you and recognised you, I only had one idea in my head—finding you again. I'd have come to find you at once, but I had to wait and plan it. I was afraid you would think I was crazy...'

'I did,' she said, half smiling, half sighing.

'But you believe me now...' His eyes were brilliant with assurance and belief.

'I've been remembering bits on and off ever since we met,' she confessed. 'I didn't want to... I thought I might be going mad, too, but just now it was all so vivid and real that I knew it wasn't just imagination. I was remembering something that had really happened...'

'I knew you would; you had to,' he said huskily. 'What we remember are bits of eternity. They come and go. Some things are clear, others aren't, but one thing I'm certain about: we belong together. We've been given our chance to make a life together, to have the children we never had before.' He broke off, gave her a quick, frowning look.

'What is it?' asked Annie, at once alert.

'I couldn't live anywhere but France, Annie,' he said abruptly. 'How do you feel about that? I suppose we could compromise, live six months here, six months in England...but...'

'I'll be happy living in Paris,' she said, her eyes brilliant with feeling. 'Have you forgotten I'm half French? And wherever you are is my home. We'll work something out with Phil and Di—there's no reason why he shouldn't go on being my manager, is there?'

'None at all,' said Marc. 'I have my own business to run. Phil's OK; I like him. I'm sure we can come to a friendly agreement. We'll make it work, don't worry, Annie, my love.' He caressed her cheek with his mouth, kissed her lashes and lids, whispered, 'All that matters is that we're together.'

She pulled him closer, began kissing him again. She could have stayed there in the cold little hut forever, kissing him, their bodies warm and breathing in that close embrace, but Marc pulled back, sighing deeply, after a long moment.

'It's getting late; it's pitch-black out there. We'd better get going, back to the auberge.'

He helped her up and they left the hut, their arms around each other. Marc smiled at her, his face glowing with the same joy she felt.

'Tonight we'll have dinner together, and talk, talk about everything, Annie. I want to know just what you remember. Then in the morning I'll take you to meet

my family, and tell them that I've met the woman I have
been waiting for all my life, that I am going to marry
her—as soon as she has said yes!'

'Yes,' Annie said.

Robyn Donald has always lived in Northland in New Zealand, initially on her father's stud dairy farm at Warkworth, then in the Bay of Islands, an area of great natural beauty, where she lives today with her husband and one mostly Labrador dog. She resigned her teaching position when she found she enjoyed writing romances more, and now spends any time not writing in reading, gardening, travelling and writing letters to keep up with her two adult children and her friends. Robyn started writing for Mills & Boon® in 1977, and twenty years on, in 1997 her fiftieth romance was published.

PRINCE OF LIES
by
ROBYN DONALD

For Sharon Wade Beeson, who asked, 'And what about Stephanie?' And for Sam McGredy, rose-breeder extraordinaire, for his kindness and for making the world a more beautiful place.

CHAPTER ONE

SOMBRE fir trees crowded against the small stone crypt constructed in the living rock of the mountain, concealing it from all but the keenest eyes.

The man who threaded his way so quietly that even the deer didn't sense his presence had such eyes, strange, colourless eyes that refracted light like shattered glass. At a muffled sound in the still silence he froze, his big body somehow blending into the gloom, that fierce gaze searching through the trees and up the mountainside.

A hundred years ago an eccentric English gentleman had built a little castle high in the Swiss Alps, but it was his wife who decided that the estate needed something extra, a romantically outrageous touch to set it off properly. A couple of ruined follies sufficed for dramatic impact in the woods, but the *pièce de résistance* was the crypt, never intended to be used, constructed solely to induce the right mood.

During the past century the carefully laid path had become overgrown, scarcely noticeable, but the crypt had been built by good Victorian tradesmen, and it still stood in all its Gothic gloom, the rigid spikes of an elaborately detailed iron grille barring steps that led down to a solid wooden door.

Frozen in a purposeful, waiting immobility, ears and eyes attuned to the slightest disturbance, the man decided that as an example of the medieval sensibility admired by many Victorians the hidden crypt was perfect. Not his style, but then, his self-contained pragmatism was utterly at variance with the romantic attitudes of a century before.

In spite of the fugitive noise that had whispered across his ears, no birds shouted alarm, no animals fled be-

tween the trees. His penetrating gaze lingered a moment
on stray beams of the hot Swiss sun fighting their way
through the dense foliage.

He hadn't seen anyone since entering the wood and
his senses were so finely honed that he'd have known if
he'd been followed, or if the crypt was being watched.
The waiting was a mere formality. However, when a man
lived on his wits it paid to have sharp ones, and the first
thing he'd learned was to trust nothing, not even his own
reactions.

A small, bronze butterfly settled on one broad
shoulder. Not until the fragile thing had danced off up
the nearest sunbeam did he move, and then it was
soundlessly, with a smooth flowing grace very much at
variance with his size. Within moments he was standing
at the dark opening in the shoulder of the mountain.

The iron door looked suitably forbidding, but the old-
fashioned lock that would have been, for all its ornate
promise, ridiculously easy to pick, had been superseded
by a modern one, sleek, workmanlike, somehow threatening. After a cursory glance he fished in his pocket and
pulled out a ring of keys. No clink of metal pierced the
silence. Selecting one, he inserted it, and as the key
twisted and the lock snickered back a look of savage
satisfaction passed over his hard, intimidating face.

He didn't immediately accept the mute invitation. Instead, his eyes searched the stone steps that led down to
another door, this one made of sturdy wood. For several
seconds the cold, remote gaze lingered on what could
have been scuff marks.

Eventually, with the measured, deliberate calculation
of a predator, he turned his head. Again his eyes scanned
the fir trees and the barely visible path through them,
then flicked up the side of the mountain. Only then did
he push the iron door open.

Although he knew it had been oiled, he half expected
a dramatic shriek of rusty hinges. One corner of his
straight mouth tilted in mordant appreciation of the

horror films he and his friends used to watch years ago, when he was as innocent as he'd ever been.

Moving without noise or haste, he slipped through the narrow opening between the iron door and the stone wall, relocked the door, and turned, his back pressed against the damp, rough-hewn stone. Now, caught between the grille and the wooden door, he was most vulnerable to ambush.

Still no prickle of danger, no obscure warning conveyed by the primitive awareness that had saved his life a couple of times. Keeping well to the side where the shadows lay deepest, he walked noiselessly down the steps. Some part of his brain noted the chill that struck through his clothes and boots.

A different key freed the wooden door; slowly, he pushed it open, his black head turning as a slight scrabble sounded shockingly in the dank, opaque darkness within. 'It's all right, Stephanie,' he said in a voice pitched to reach whoever was in the crypt. Grimly, he locked the door behind him. A hitherto concealed torch sent a thin beam of light slicing through the blackness to settle on a long box, eerily like a coffin, that rested on the flagstones. The man played the light on to the box until the keyhole glittered. For the space of three heartbeats he stood motionless, before, keys in hand, he approached the box.

Inside her prison she was blind, and earplugs made sure she could hear little. However, another sense had taken over, an ability to feel pressure, to respond somehow to the presence of another living being. For the last few minutes she had known he was near.

Almost certainly he was one of the two men who had abducted her on the road back to the chalet. The memory of those terrifying moments kept her still and quiet, her shackled limbs tense against the narrow sides of the box.

After the initial horrified incredulity she had fought viciously, desperation clearing her brain with amazing speed so that she was able to use every move Saul had taught her. She'd managed to get in some telling blows, scratching one's face badly as she'd torn off his Balaclava. She had been trying for his eyes, but a blow to her head had jolted her enough to put off her aim.

Not badly enough, however, to stop her from crooking her fingers again and gouging at his face, so clearly seen in the moonlight.

Then the second man had punched her on the jaw.

Two days later the man whose face she'd seen had hit her again in exactly the same place when she'd refused to read the newspaper.

Half-mad with terror, convinced that she was going to die in the makeshift coffin, she had managed to shake her head when he'd forced her upright and thrust the newspaper in her hand, demanding that she say the headlines.

She'd known what he was doing. Saul must want some reassurance that she was alive before he paid any ransom. The torches that had blazed into her eyes had made it very clear that her assailant intended to video her.

Her refusal had made her gaoler angry, and he'd threatened to withhold the food and water he'd brought. Still she'd balked, folding her mouth tightly over the cowardly words fighting to escape, words that were pleas for freedom, craven offers to pay him anything he wanted if only he would let her go.

So he'd hit her, carefully choosing the site of the bruise he'd already made when he'd knocked her out in the street. Pain had cascaded through her but she'd only given in when he'd told her viciously that he was prepared to send a video of him beating her up to her brother if that was what it took.

It had been the only thing he could have said to persuade her. Saul must never know what had happened to her in that crypt.

And now, after an unknown number of days, someone else had returned to the crypt. Her jaw still ached, but that was the least of her worries.

Shuddering, she bent her attention to the person in her dungeon. It was a man; was he the man who had forced her to dramatise her own misery so that her brother Saul would know she was alive?

She lay still, trying to pick up with subliminal receptors some indication of his identity. Strangely, she felt, with a hidden, atavistic shrinking, a strong impression of power and intensity, and beneath that a controlled menace that made her shiver with terror.

The muffled sound of his voice again, low, oddly compelling even through the planks of her prison and the earplugs, sent quick panic flooding through her, humiliating, loathsome, unmanageable. She tried to breathe carefully, counting the seconds, but it didn't help.

He spoke once more; although the words were somewhat louder they were still distorted by the physical response of her body. Her first reaction had been to will him to go away, but she suddenly wondered whether he was a passer-by who had merely stumbled on her prison. If that was so, he wouldn't know she was in the box on the floor. He might be her only chance to get out of here.

Nevertheless, it took a real effort of will to move, and when she did she moaned soundlessly at the pain in her cramped muscles. Clenching her teeth, she lifted her hands and hit the manacles sharply against the top of the box, hoping that the noise would be enough to attract his attention.

Strung taut by fear and foreboding, she screamed into the gag as the lid came up silently, yet with a rush of air that hurt her skin and proclaimed a violent energy in the man who stood above her. Ever since she had been locked in this coffin she had been desperately trying to get free, rubbing her wrists raw against the unyielding metal of the handcuffs, yet now she shrank back because the impact of the stranger's personality—intense, lethal, forceful—hit her like a blow.

Danger, her instincts drummed; this man is dangerous! Some primal, buried intuition warned her that he was infinitely more of a threat to her than either of the men who had kidnapped her. She sensed an icy, implacable authority, a concentrated will that beat harshly down on her.

But when he spoke his voice was level, almost impersonal. 'Just lie still for a few seconds, Stephanie,' he said, his voice pitched to pierce the earplugs.

So he was no casual passer-by.

Stephanie made herself stay quiescent as the gag was removed. This man knew exactly what he was doing, and did it as though he'd been wrenching off gags all his life. Life pulsed through him, an intensity of vigour, of purpose, a sheer, consuming energy that bathed her in white-hot fire.

Get a grip on yourself, she commanded. He still might come from the kidnappers. She said rustily, 'Who are you?' and strained to hear his answer.

'I've come to take you out of this. How do you feel?'

Relief was a slow, reluctant warming. 'I'm all right. Just numb all over.'

'You'll hurt like hell when the feeling starts to come back,' he said.

Her kidnappers had left nothing to chance; they hadn't intended her to escape. When he felt the steel manacles on her wrists and ankles the unknown man cursed roughly, but his hands on her body were warm and deft and gentle, and after a bit of manipulation the steel fell loose.

Nevertheless, it seemed an aeon before she was out of her coffin. Her legs wouldn't support her, so her rescuer held her with an arm around her waist and then all she could think of was that she was filthy and naked and that she must smell and look disgusting. She put up a fleshless, quivering hand to remove the plugs from her ears.

'I'll do that,' he said. In a moment the echo of her pulses that had been her sole companion for so many anguished hours was replaced by a rush of silence.

She didn't have time to appreciate it, for the numbness that held her body in thrall was overwhelmed by an agony so intense, she thought she might faint from it. Biting her lips to hold back mortifying whimpers, she clung convulsively to his broad shoulders as returning sensation surged through her with accelerating agony.

'How long have I been here?' she mumbled, trying to keep her mind off the torment.

'Three days.'

Free from distortion, his voice was deep and infinitely disturbing, detached, yet threaded by an equivocal undertone. English, she noted automatically, although there was something else, some hint of another country's speech; not an accent, more an intonation, a slight inflexion...

He sounded as though he could have spent enough time in New Zealand or Australia to be affected by their special and particular way of speaking.

Giving it up as too hard, she set her jaw and forced her shaking legs to straighten, her knees to lock so that she could stand upright. Sweat stood out along her brow, settled with clammy persistence into her palms. When the torture receded a little she managed to mutter, 'I tried to get free, but I couldn't.'

'It's almost over, princess.' His arm around her shoulders tightened. For several minutes he continued to support her trembling body, until at last he asked brusquely, 'Can you walk? Here, you'd better get rid of this——' Hands touched the blindfold.

Jerking her head away, she said, 'No,' because it gave her some sort of protection from his gaze. Not even when she had been stripped naked to the lewd sound of one of the kidnapper's comments had she felt so exposed, so helpless.

'Yes,' he said relentlessly. 'We're not out of the woods yet—literally. I don't think the men who snatched you will come back today, but if they do while we're still here you need to be able to see, and this half-darkness will give your eyes time to get accustomed to the light.'

Ignoring her panted objections, he stripped the blindfold from her shaggy head. Obstinately, Stephanie kept her eyes closed. 'Have you got any water?' she asked, running her dry tongue around an even drier mouth. 'I'm so thirsty.'

'Don't drink too much. It will make you sick.'

A metal flask pressed against her lips, and the blessed cool thinness of water seeped across her tongue. She gulped greedily, making a quick, involuntary protest when he took it away.

'No,' he said laconically, 'you can have some more later.' At her small sound of displeasure he went on, 'If you have any more now you'll be retching before you've gone fifty yards. Trust me, I know.'

An odd note in his voice coaxed her eyes slightly open. The torchlight barely reached the dank stone walls of her prison, but in its golden glow she saw a big man, tall and well-built, with a dark, angular, forceful face.

Shock hit her like a blow, followed by a strange, compelling recognition, as though she had always known he was out there, waiting. She would never forget him, she thought dazedly. He had rescued her from hell, and until the day she died she'd remember his warrior's countenance, stark in the earthy dampness of her prison, as well as his curt, understated consideration.

'That's better,' he said bluntly. 'Put these on.'

He had brought clothes—jeans and a shirt in muted camouflage colours. Gratefully, she struggled a few moments with limp hands and weak wrists, before saying on a half-choked note of despair, 'I can't.'

Without impatience, he said, 'All right, stand still.'

Competent hands pulled the clothes on to her thin body; he even managed to fit a pair of black trainers on her feet. Although the garments felt amazingly good after the soaked blanket she'd been lying on, she knew that she wouldn't feel clean until she had washed herself free of this place.

In a hidden recess of her mind she wondered whether she would ever feel really clean again.

'Let's get out of here,' he said.

Nothing in his tone indicated a need for hurry, but Stephanie suddenly realised that the longer they stayed in the crypt, the more dangerous it was.

Compliantly she tried to follow him across to the door, but her feet refused to obey her will. She began to shake.

'I can't walk,' she said angrily.

'You'll have to.'

Although the words were completely unsympathetic, he grasped her hand in his lean, strong one, and somehow she could move once more. Each step felt like knives in her flesh. Abruptly the story of the little mermaid and the sacrifice she had made to gain a human soul flashed into Stephanie's mind. When her mother had read it to her she hadn't liked the tale, finding it too sad, but until that moment she hadn't understood what a truly awful torture Hans Christian Andersen had devised for his heroine.

Tightening her lips, she held back any expression of pain. But when her rescuer switched off the torch and the blackness pressed in again, she couldn't prevent a choked cry.

'If you can't keep quiet I'll have to gag you again,' he said, each word stark with the promise of retribution. 'Walk softly, and *don't talk*. If anything happens to me, climb a tree and stay there. Most people don't think to look upwards.'

The next second she was stumbling behind a man who moved without sound. The door swung open silently, letting in a flood of dim light. At first it hurt her eyes,

but as she squinted tearfully she saw stone steps leading
up to bars, and beyond them a forest of firs, their trunks
and thick foliage blocking out the sun.

Closing the door behind them, her rescuer locked it
before leading her carefully up the steps, his back to the
wall, his head turned towards the entrance so that all
she could see of his face was the stern line of jaw above
a hint of square chin, the sweeping angle of cheek, the
dark, conventionally cut hair. His hand still engulfed
hers; although it was warm and insistent, she understood with a purely female recognition that it could be
cruel.

At the top of the steps he waited so long that she began
to drift into a kind of trance. Then, apparently satisfied
that the woods held no lurking enemies, he unlocked the
bars and slipped through, shielding her with the graceful
bulk of his body.

It was like all the thrillers she had ever read—the
gallant, aloof hero, the abused heroine, the dangerous
trek to safety. Perhaps if she could have viewed the situation as popular fiction she'd have been able to cope
with the sick dismay that washed through her when he
turned up the mountain and began to climb, half pulling
her along behind him.

Gasping within seconds, exhausted in minutes, she
knew she had to keep going, so she gritted her teeth and
ignored the pain. He helped, hauling her over rocks,
stopping occasionally to let her regain her breath. Her
heart was thumping too heavily in her chest for anything
but its erratic beating to be heard, and in a very short
time she was engulfed by a headache and a spreading
nausea that almost subdued her.

But anything was better than being locked in a box,
unable to free herself. With the characteristic doggedness
that came as a surprise to most people, Stephanie
scrambled behind her unknown rescuer, grateful for the
trees that sheltered them.

At last the steep slope levelled out. 'Stay here,' he said in a quiet, almost soundless voice, pushing her unceremoniously into a crevice beneath a rock.

Stephanie collapsed, peering through the bushes that concealed the narrow cleft, but he disappeared before she had time to query him, so she put her head on her knees, stiffened her jaw to stop the shameful whimpering she could barely control, and let her body do whatever it needed to recover. She was still panting when he slid back through the whippy, leafy branches with as little fuss as an animal.

Still in the same low voice he asked, 'How are you feeling?'

'I've felt better,' she said quietly, avoiding the cold clarity of his gaze. 'On the other hand, just recently I've felt worse. I'll be all right. How much further?'

'About a mile.'

As she struggled out he said, 'I think it should be safe enough to carry you,' and in spite of her automatic recoil he picked her up and set off.

Keeping her face rigidly turned away, she wondered why liberty didn't taste as good as she'd imagined it would in those nightmare days of imprisonment. She should have been ecstatic, because she'd expected death, and now there was a future waiting for her. At the very least she should have been relieved. Instead, an icy chill eddied through her, robbing her of everything but a detached recognition that she had been imprisoned and was now free.

Freedom was easy to say, she thought with a scepticism that hurt. Common sense told her that her body would mend quickly enough, yet as she lay there in the powerful arms of the man who had released her she wondered whether some part of her mind would be incarcerated in that box for the rest of her life.

'My car's not too far away. When we get there I'm going to have to put you in the boot,' her rescuer told her, his voice reassuring but firm enough to forestall any protest. He still spoke as though they could be over-heard. 'It will be bloody uncomfortable, but it's necessary, and I've put a mattress in there to make it a bit easier. I'm almost certain no one's been watching me, but we'll be going through several villages and the last thing we want is someone remembering that I had a passenger. So you'll have to stay hidden.'

Although her skin crawled at the thought of further confinement, Stephanie understood the need for caution. Mastering the flash of panic, she said, 'Yes, all right.' She thought his words over before asking slowly, 'Will S—will my brother be there?'

'No.' He paused before explaining, 'He's busy dealing with the men who did this to you. You and I will have to lie low for a while until it's over. I can't even get a doctor for you in case they have a local contact, but I have some experience in this sort of thing.'

'I'll be fine,' she said automatically, wondering where he'd gained this experience. First-aid training? A book on how to look after kidnappees?

Being rescued, she decided, closing her eyes, must have addled her brain.

He climbed for what seemed ages. Mostly Stephanie lay in a kind of stupor, accepting without thought the novelty of being carried, the controlled, purposeful toughness of the man. It did occur to her that he must be immensely strong, for he moved without any visible signs of exhaustion. And although he might not think there was anyone watching she could feel his alertness, a fierce concentration on every signal sent by the world around them. Several times he stopped and listened.

Whenever that happened she made herself still and quiet, trying to slow her heartbeat, calm her racing pulses and the rattle of air in her lungs, the interminable thud and throb of her headache. Although she too listened hard she could hear nothing but the sounds of the forest—an occasional bird, the soft rustling of a breeze in the trees.

Once she roused herself to whisper, 'Are we there?'

'Not quite.' When he went to put her down she surprised herself by clinging. 'It's all right,' he said gently. 'I'm just going to scout around and make sure no one is about.'

'Don't leave me.' Although she despised the note of panic in her voice, she couldn't control it.

'I'll be keeping a good eye on you.'

A small, childish noise escaped her lips.

'That's enough,' he said sternly, bending to thrust her into a cleft beneath a rock that broke through the bushes. 'I haven't gone to all this trouble to lose you now. Just sit there, princess, and I'll be here again before you've had time to get lonely.' He stepped behind a tree and disappeared, far too silently for a man of his size.

Disgusted by her feebleness, Stephanie waited, wishing she could point her ears like an animal to get a better fix on his whereabouts. A tangle of summer-green leaves hid her from any stray passer-by, but not, she knew, from a determined searcher. Her rescuer's familiarity with this mountain slope surely meant that he had spent some time reconnoitring.

Fighting exhaustion, she peered past the leaves, trying to identify a glimmering patch of white that danced in the sun beyond a belt of trees. At first she thought it was a waterfall, but by narrowing her eyes she could see that it was too regular for that. Slowly, it coalesced into stone, a waterfall of stone—no, columns of stone.

There, some hundreds of yards away through the trees, was what looked to be a temple, chastely, classically Greek. Her eyes blurred; she blinked to clear them, but a cloud had passed over the sun, and the tantalising streak of white was gone.

Perhaps it had been a hallucination.

His return startled her. It was uncanny; he seemed to rise out of the ground like a primeval huntsman, so at one with his surroundings that the trees sheltered him in their embrace.

'Not a soul in sight,' he said. 'Let's go.'

His arms around her were intensely comforting, like coming home. Sighing, Stephanie leaned her head against his shoulder. He smelt slightly sweaty, so it wasn't as easy carrying her as he made it seem. Another scent teased her nostrils, faint but ever present, evocative, with a hint of salt and musk. Masculinity, she decided dreamily.

She knew that she must smell hideous, reek with the stale odour of confinement. A pursuer, she thought with a wry twist of her lips, wouldn't need to search for her; all he'd have to do was follow his nose to find her.

She was still wondering why this seemed so especially unbearable when he said, 'Right, here we are.'

However, he didn't go immediately to the car that waited in the heavy shade of a conifer. It wasn't hidden, but few people would notice it, for it was painted a green that blended with the long needles of the trees.

Just inside the confines of the wood he put her against the trunk of a tree, and stood blocking her from anyone who might be watching, his whole being concentrated on a hawk-eyed, icily patient scrutiny of every tree, every blade of grass, and the big, dark car.

When at last he did move it was with a speed that shocked her. Within seconds she was deposited on the mattress in the boot, choking back a moan as he firmly closed the lid.

The engine sprang into life; with no delay the car drew away from the picnic spot and turned down the road.

Even on the mattress Stephanie was soon profoundly uncomfortable. Her bones seemed to have no fleshy covering to protect them; she ached all over, and she was shivering. She was also worrying. So great had her initial relief been that suspicion hadn't had room to take hold. Now, cramped like a parcel, trying to ignore the thumping of her head and the tremors that racked her, she began to recall things she had noticed but not questioned. Whoever her rescuer was, he had keys not only to the crypt and the coffin, but also to the handcuffs that had manacled her in the coffin.

Saul, her brother, had an excellent security department, but it was highly unlikely that even the most skilled operative would have been able to get those keys. So unlikely that she had better stop believing that the man driving the BMW had anything to do with Saul.

Her quick, instinctive stab of revulsion warned her that she was halfway into the Stockholm syndrome— falling in with the wishes of her captor.

Think, she adjured her pounding brain. Think, damn it!

There had been no indication that she was a target; if her intensely protective brother had heard the slightest hint that she was in danger, he wouldn't have let her come to Switzerland without a bodyguard. Or with one, for that matter. The close relatives of billionaires were sometimes at risk; she had long ago accepted the constraints of her world, and co-operated, so Saul had no reason to keep her in ignorance.

If Saul didn't know, if he hadn't been warned, then none of his agents would have been alerted. According to her rescuer, she'd been imprisoned for three days. She had no way of checking the accuracy of this, but if it was true, was that time enough for one of Saul's men to discover who the kidnappers were and get close enough to them to be able to copy the keys?

It didn't seem likely, unless the kidnappers had left clues the size of houses. And somehow she doubted that; they had been frighteningly efficient.

It seemed important to know exactly how many keys there were. Even understanding that it was a mechanism to push the truth away didn't stop her from counting them: the keys to the box, then to the handcuffs, keys to both doors. Four sets of keys. And he had them all.

She dragged a deep breath into her lungs. All right, don't panic! What sort of person was he, this man who had walked into her life?

Although she hadn't looked at him carefully, so she couldn't recall the colour of his eyes or even his colouring beyond the fact that he was dark, that first swift glance had seared his features into her brain: a blade of a nose, high, arrogant cheekbones, eyes that had something strange about them. Did he look like a criminal?

Not, she thought bitterly, that looks were any indication. The man whose face she had seen under his torn Balaclava hadn't looked like a criminal. If he'd been any type at all, it was a small-time shopkeeper.

Whatever, until she knew for certain, it would be much safer to work on the assumption that either her rescuer was one of the kidnappers who wanted all of the ransom, not merely a share of it, or an associate who knew what they had done, was trusted by them, and had decided to cut himself a piece of the pie. That would explain why he was being so careful not to be seen by the original kidnappers.

It sounds, she thought feverishly, like the instructions in an Elizabethan play: *Enter first kidnapper with gag, blindfold and coffin, exit first kidnapper. Almost immediately enter second kidnapper, a large, athletic man with keys and strong arms.*

If that was so, she was in just as much danger as before. He could quite easily plan to keep her safe as long as Saul demanded reassurance that she was alive, then kill her when the money had been paid over.

Her heart skittered into a rapid cacophony while her brain veered off towards the messy heights of hysteria.

Calm down. Panic isn't going to get you anywhere.

With an effort of will that made her teeth chatter she began to breathe slowly, regularly, forcing herself to count the seconds. Eventually the churning flood of fear in her stomach subsided, and with it her inability to think.

Paradoxically, the only thing that comforted her was that he'd used the keys quite openly. If she'd been less of a cynic she might take that to mean he was legitimate.

Of course, he could well be devious enough to use them deliberately so that she'd be confused into accepting him as completely above-board. It wouldn't be the first time someone had imagined that because her brother was one of the richest men in the world Stephanie Jerrard was incapable of logical thought, with nothing but clothes and jewellery and gossip in her mind.

He could have fallen into that trap. However, in the few moments she had spent talking to him she had gained the impression of a keen, razor-sharp intelligence, the sort of mind that didn't make obvious mistakes. Apart from the keys, what else was there to base suspicion on?

The tension clamping her muscles began to ebb as she realised how little there was. He'd been evasive when she'd asked about Saul. Or had he?

Questions jostled around her aching head, forcing their way through to her conscious mind, battering her precarious self-control. How long was this journey going to take? She felt as though she'd been in the car for hours. Although they were now climbing quite steeply she couldn't smell any exhaust fumes. Perhaps when you travelled in the boot of a car you left the fumes behind. No, she told herself, don't get side-tracked. Think!

While the car twisted and turned smoothly around corners, she decided to do nothing. Her suspicions could be entirely wrong, and anyway, common sense told her she wasn't going to be able to do any running or hiding until she'd regained some strength. The two men who had kidnapped her were around somewhere, and if she ran away and they caught up with her again, she thought with a shudder, they might kill her outright. After all, she could identify one of them.

So she'd eat and rest, and she'd probe as subtly as she could. If her rescuer was a villain she might be safe while she pretended to take him at face value.

Of course, there might be a perfectly logical explanation for those keys. All she had to do was ask. And if she didn't like the answer, she could fake belief until she found an opportunity to get away from him.

As the car slid to halt, she froze. Striving to look weak and pathetic and entirely brainless, she coerced her muscles into looseness, wondering despairingly whether she should try to get away now, when he would be least likely to expect it.

Before she had time to make up her mind the lock on the boot clicked. 'We're here,' he said, reaching in and gathering her up.

She said raggedly, 'Where's here? And what happens now?'

'This is where we're staying.'

'It looks old,' she said inanely.

'Not very. It was built last century.' He set off for a door across the garage.

Frowning, she looked around. 'It doesn't look like the stables.'

'It's not. This is the old laundry, which was converted into a garage some time in the thirties.'

Apparently he wasn't given to fulsome explanations. She said stubbornly, 'What's going to happen now?'

'I'm going to carry you upstairs, where you can shower and go to bed. Then you eat, and after that you sleep.'

It should have sounded wonderful but the greyness she had fought so long and vehemently had finally caught up with her. Blankly she said beneath her breath, 'Thank you.'

Some emotion sawed through him, but his voice was steady and deliberate as he said, 'It's nothing. Think of me as your doctor.'

Her doctor was forty, a married woman wearing her sophistication with cheerful cynicism and an understanding heart. Stephanie smiled wearily.

'Shower first,' he said. 'I'll have to stay with you, I'm afraid, in case you fall.'

A week ago she would have refused point-blank, but it didn't matter now. She didn't think she would ever be modest again.

She forced herself to look around as he carried her across a high, mock-Gothic hall and up some narrow stairs.

'This looks like a castle,' she said.

'Seen plenty of them, have you, princess?' His voice was dry.

'A few,' she admitted. It couldn't hurt. He knew who she was. What he might not know, she thought vengefully, was how formidable Saul was. On the first suitable occasion she'd make sure he learnt.

However, not even Saul was invincible, and she'd have to try to get herself out of this situation. So, she decided with an odd lurch in her heartbeat, she had better take a good look at the man who might well be her greatest obstacle. Fractionally turning her head, she sent a sideways glance through her lashes.

He wasn't handsome, but strength and a compelling and concentrated authority marked the slashing lines of his face. Not a man you would forget, she thought, wishing her head didn't ache so much that she couldn't think clearly. Surely kidnappers didn't look as though they strode through the world forcing it to accept them on their own terms? The two who had snatched her certainly hadn't. The one she'd seen was short and thin, inconspicuous except for his flat, emotionless black eyes, and the other had behaved with all the flashy arrogance of a small-time criminal.

This man couldn't have been taken for a small-time anything.

Stephanie felt physically ill; her whole body was screaming with pain, she was tired and hungry and frantic with thirst, and in spite of her efforts to keep a calm head she was terrified with the sort of fear that only needed a touch to spill into panic, yet her first reaction to eyes where the light splintered into scintillating

energy was a sensation of something heated and unmanageable racing through her with the force of a
stampede. Some hitherto inviolate part of her shattered
in a subtle breaching of barricades that left her raw and
undefended.

Eyes locked on to his face, she was thinking dazedly,
What's happening to me? when the corners of that
ruthless, equivocal mouth tilted a fraction. 'Do you think
you'd recognise me again?' he asked, his tone imbuing
the words with a hidden meaning.

'I'm sure of it.' Self-protection impelled her to add,
'I believe it's a well-known syndrome; people do tend to
remember those who rescue them from durance vile. Incidentally, how did you get into that cellar?'

He shouldered through a small door off a landing at
the top of the stairs, walked across a room dimmed by
heavy curtains, through another door, and stood her on
her feet, turning her at the same time so that she had
her back to him.

They were in a bathroom, neat, white, with a start-
lingly luxurious shower, all glass and modern fittings.
As his hands supported her for the first agonising moments, he said calmly, 'It's not a cellar, it's a fake crypt.
The locks on the doors are not brand-new, and the men
who put you there didn't bother to change them. Your
brother wields a lot of power, and it didn't take long for
me to get a complete set of skeleton keys.'

'And the handcuffs?'

His mouth tightened, but his eyes held hers steadily
as he said, 'There are techniques for picking them.'

Stephanie almost sagged with relief, her reassured
brain spinning into dizziness. Of course; she had read
of skeleton keys often enough; she should have thought
of them herself. And hadn't Saul's chief of security told
her once that there was no lock invented that couldn't
be picked, given time, equipment and a deft hand?

Before she had time to say the incautious words that
came tumbling to her lips, the man who had rescued her

began to strip her as efficiently and swiftly as he had dressed her.

'No,' she muttered, trying to stop his hands.

'You can't do it yourself.' He unzipped the jeans and pushed them down around her hips.

He was right, but in spite of her previous conviction about her lack of modesty she actually felt intense embarrassment. She had her back to him, but there was a mirror, and for a breathless second she saw their reflections, her pale, thin, hollow-eyed face beneath a wild tangle of rusty curls, the swift movements of his long-fingered hands unbuttoning her shirt.

Hastily she looked away, confusion and shame battling for supremacy. Although he was gentle, those tanned fingers branded her skin, leaving it hot and tender, connected by shimmering, glittering wires to her spine and the pit of her stomach. A lazy, coiled heat stirred there, as though his touch summoned something forbidden but irresistible.

Stephanie bit her lip, trying to use pain to drown out those other, treacherous sensations. It didn't work, and in the end she gave in, her eyes caught and held by the strange power of his.

'You have eyes like cornflowers,' he astounded her by saying. 'That brilliant, rare, clear sapphire. It must be a Jerrard trait.'

So he had met Saul. Stephanie's suspicions fell from her like an ugly, discarded shroud. Bewitched by the new and unusual responses of her body, pulses jumping, she waited until he moved away to turn on the shower before shrugging off the shirt and stepping out of her jeans. A quick flick of her wrist hooked a towel from the rail to wrap around herself.

She stumbled, and he caught her, pulling her against the solid length of his body. Stephanie flinched, that insidious, unwanted awareness reinforced by his nearness. Although she was tall and not slightly built, against him she felt tiny, delicately fragile, an experience intensified by the unexpected burgeoning of a languorous femininity.

Her rescuer's austere face was intent as he juggled with the shower controls, but that concentrated attention was not bent on her; he showed no signs of a reciprocal response.

You're mad, she told herself as steam began to fill the shower stall. Look in the mirror—your bones stick out, you're filthy, and you smell. The sort of first impression no one ever overcomes. Who in their right mind would be anything but casual and very, very detached?

'There, that should be right,' he said, urging her into the big, tiled, warm shower with its glass doors now tactfully obscured by steam. He didn't move away from the door, but at least he couldn't see much through the hazy mist.

A singing, surging relief persuaded her to release the bonds of the obstinacy that had held her together for so long. Only for a few hours, she thought as with eyes tightly shut she tried to wash herself. She could give up for a few hours and use some of this man's strength until she regained her own.

The water was like nectar over her skin, but its heat drained her waning energy, and her hands shook so much that she couldn't get soap on to the flannel. As tears squeezed their way beneath her lashes she continued grimly on, aware of the man who stood so close, a large, dim figure through the glass doors.

The cake of soap plummeted between her fingers and landed on her foot. Unable to prevent a soft cry of pain, she cut it short and crouched to pick up the wretched thing. It took a vast effort to push herself upright, and when she got there she could feel her legs trembling. Refusing to look at the man who watched, hating him for not leaving her alone, she gripped the flannel and passed it over the cake of soap.

He asked tonelessly, 'Do you want me to wash you?'

Lethargy enmeshed her, but she said, 'No, I can do it.'

Only she couldn't. Her arms ached, and her fingers wouldn't obey her, and her legs felt as though the bones had been replaced by sponge rubber.

He waited until she dropped the soap again, then said curtly, 'Here, give me that flannel. When you've as much strength as a cooked noodle courage and determination will only get you so far.'

Stephanie turned her face away, saying stiffly, 'I'm all right——'

'Shut up,' he said, interrupting her by taking the cloth from her lax fingers.

CHAPTER TWO

HOSTILITY flared brightly inside Stephanie, matched by a crackle of antagonism from him. A searing glance from those colourless eyes warned her that she wasn't going to win this one. Squeezing her eyelids shut, she stood mutinously while the flannel slipped slowly, gently over skin that was stretched and too sensitive.

Her blood gathered thickly in her veins. No matter how much she tried to concentrate on relief at being safe, all she could feel was the elemental nearness of the man who had brought her out of hell. His presence was a sensuous abrasion on her skin, electric, tingling, charging the shower stall with a fierce, primal vitality, setting acutely responsive nerves alight. Dazed, she set herself to endure what she couldn't change.

He didn't hurry. The flannel laved her body in subtle, diligent torture. He even shampooed her hair, working suds through the rust-coloured strands, seeming to understand that she needed it rinsed over and over until it was glowing against her head. Luxuriating in the purifying spray of water, she thought that he was surprisingly patient. She suspected that it wasn't an inherent part of his character, but had been hard-won by the exercise of will. Whatever, she was grateful for it.

Sudden exhaustion robbed her bones of strength, and she swayed, her hands whipping up to grab his forearm as she fell. Unwillingly her eyes popped open. A wide, bare chest filled her vision, fine wet hair slicked in a tree-of-life pattern over olive skin clearly in the best of health, a shocking contrast to her own sunless pallor.

Without her volition her gaze travelled down; she realised he still had his trousers on.

'You're getting wet,' she said foolishly, trying to curb a harsh, unbidden response, elemental and unwanted.

'I didn't think you'd like it if I came in without any clothes on,' he returned, a satirical note edging his tone.

Blood stung her cheeks and throat. Feeling much younger than her eighteen years, she stammered, 'No— well, no, I wouldn't.'

She had wanted to stay beneath the water until her skin was wrinkled and pale, washing off the results of being locked in a coffin for three days, scrubbing herself free from the taint and the terror and the evilness of it. But now she needed to get out of there.

Quickly, she said the first words that came into her head. 'I'm cold.'

'All right.' He turned off the spray.

Swallowing a lump that obstructed her throat, and apparently her thought processes too, Stephanie watched through lashes beaded with drops of water as he pushed open the glass door and stepped out on to the mat. Muscles moved in his back—not the smooth, sculptured works of art nurtured in a gym, but tautly corded, with the flowing vigour and hard, tensile power of rigorous work.

'Here,' he said, handing her a large, warm white towel.

Battling the treacherous feelings that surged through her, she accepted it and began to dry herself. He pulled another towel from the holder and started to wipe the glistening water from his arms.

Her last vestiges of energy evaporated as fast as the water on his skin. Stumbling once more, Stephanie would have fallen if he hadn't sensed her predicament and whirled around to catch her, moving with a speed and accuracy that obscurely frightened her. For the second time in as many minutes, she was supported against a taut male body.

'My legs won't hold me up,' she muttered, unable now to hide her panic with anger. Sensation bludgeoned her; acutely aware of the heated, silky dampness of his skin, the potency barely leashed in the tall body that supported her, she swallowed.

'Stand still,' he said in a cool, crisp voice, and began to blot the water from her shoulders.

Beneath the white towel his hands were careful yet completely impersonal. By the time she was dry Stephanie was shivering, engulfed by a fatigue that was only partly caused by her ordeal. Dimly she realised that she was being put into a huge T-shirt, thick and soft and enveloping, before being lifted and carried and lowered into a bed, and then sheets were pulled over her and she sank gratefully into the sleep that claimed her...

Until the nightmares came like evil wraiths, tormenting with the terrors she hadn't allowed herself to feel while imprisoned, slyly sneaking through the unguarded gates of her unconscious mind and into her brain, vivid, horrifying, so real that she could feel herself screaming.

'Stop that right now,' a masculine voice ordered, compounding her fear.

A reflex action filled her lungs with air. Opening her mouth to scream again, she flung herself on to the other side of the bed. The sound was cut off instantly by a hand clamping across her mouth. Bucking with terror, she lashed her tired limbs to greater efforts, wrenching at iron fingers, trying to bite, to claw, to scratch.

'Stop it, you little spitfire,' he commanded.

It was the impact of his body rather than his voice, low and gritty and threatening, that restored her to her senses. Suddenly she realised where she was, and that this man had taken her from darkness and horror and cleaned her and soothed her, as well as giving her water several times already that night when she'd woken gasping for it.

A convulsive shudder shook her and she stopped fighting. Amid the fading panic and confusion she registered the change in his tone as he repeated, 'Stop it,

Stephanie. You're safe, and no one is going to hurt you again.'

Silenced, the only sound the heavy pounding of her heart, she nodded feebly. The hand across her mouth gentled, relaxed, and slid down to the pulse that beat ferociously in her throat. 'Poor little scrap,' he said, his deep voice vibrating with a barely curbed anger.

Somehow the simple remark called her back from the frightening world of her memories. She didn't want to be pitied, pity weakened her, yet for a moment she let her craving for security pacify her back into childishness.

'I'm sorry,' she whispered. 'It was just a dream.'

Perhaps because that long walk in his arms had de-sensitised her, or perhaps because of his total lack of response to her nakedness in the shower, she forgot any reservations she had and followed her simple need for reassurance by burrowing into him. As his arms tightened her panic eased into a strange contentment. She pressed her cheek against a bare chest, the slight roughening of his hair on her skin a profoundly comforting sensation.

He moved, but only to switch on a small bedside lamp. The light and his heat and solidity eased the chattering of her teeth, reached through her defences in some sub-liminal way and soothed her, as did the quiet rumble of his voice reverberating from his chest to her ear.

'You're safe,' he said again. 'No one will hurt you here.'

She could remember her father holding her and saying the same words. He had been proved wrong, and she knew that the man who held her so sweetly couldn't guarantee his words either, but for the moment she allowed herself to believe him. Tiredness and the heart-warming feeling of being sheltered and protected combined to make her yawn.

'I'm sorry I'm such a wimp,' she said in a slurred voice when she could speak again.

'You're allowed a couple of episodes. Go back to sleep,' he said. 'If the nightmare comes back, try telling it you won, you triumphed. But sometimes they're actually good for you, even though they scare the hell out of you. It's one way the brain can try to make sense of what happened.'

'I *know* what happened,' she said grimly, resisting the possibility of any more dreams.

'Oh, intellectually, but I'm willing to bet that in your heart you're wondering how anyone could be so cruel as to put you through the particular hell they organised for you.'

'Money. That's what it usually is. Some people will do anything for money.'

'You're very young to be a cynic.'

'I'm eighteen,' she said.

He gave a ghost of a laugh. 'And I'm twenty-five. I'm still considered young, so where does that leave you?'

'Childish,' she retorted almost on a snap, pulling free. The quick spurt of defiance exhausted her and his comment forced her to realise that he wasn't her father. He was a total stranger, and a rather frightening one, because beneath the feeling of safety engendered by those strong arms there were other emotions, deep and bewildering, that combined to produce the subtle, wild attraction calling to her with a honeyed, siren's voice.

Trying to speak without any indication of her runaway reactions in her tone, she said, 'I'm all right now, thank you. I'm sorry I woke you.'

'Princess, you didn't wake me.'

She huddled back under the warm duvet, averting her face so he couldn't see it. 'Why do you call me that?'

'Princess? That's what you are, isn't it? A genuine eighteen-carat-gold princess, with everything but the title. And your brother could probably buy one of those for you if you weren't too fussy about its origins.'

As she thought this over, wondering how an amused voice could be so detached, the mattress beside her sank, and to her appalled astonishment she felt the covers twitch. Sheer shock jackknifed her upright.

'What the hell are you *doing*?' she demanded in a high, shrill voice, staring with dilated eyes as he turned to look at her.

'I'm making myself comfortable,' he said mockingly, crystalline eyes gleaming. 'You can't expect to hog the covers, you know. It's bad manners.'

'You're not——'

He interrupted with unexpected curtness, 'Stephanie, you're quite safe. I'm *sleeping* here, that's all.'

'But what—then why——?'

He said reasonably, 'Although I'm almost certain no one is watching this place, I believe in caution, so I'm working on the assumption that we're under surveillance. The last thing we need is for anyone to realise that there are two people living here now. So we act like one person. We sleep together, we move around the house together; when you're in the bathroom, I'll be next door with the light out. I'm going to stick as close to you as a shadow, princess, closer than a lover, but I'm not going to touch you.'

When Stephanie gathered her wits enough to object, he didn't let her get more than a word out before finishing with a steely authority that silenced her, 'Rules of the house, princess; don't knock them—they might save your brother a lot of money and both of us quite a bit of trouble.'

The problem was that she understood. Having grown up in a small English village, she knew too well just what a hotbed of gossip such places were, and how by some osmosis everyone learned in an astonishingly short time all about everyone else.

But although his logic made sense, a wary feminine apprehension rejected it. The close, constant proximity he insisted on was going to be an enormous strain on her. She pulled the duvet around her body, trembling in spite of the mild temperature. 'No! I'll be very careful——'

'I'm not suggesting this, or giving you power of veto. You have no choice, so you'll avoid unnecessary stress if you just accept it.'

His voice remained cool, almost indifferent, but she heard the curbed irritation buried in the words as well as the implacable resolution. She gulped. 'I don't want to!'

'Stephanie, if you're afraid that I won't be able to control my lust, rest assured that I am not attracted to thin, gangly schoolgirls, even when they have indecent amounts of money as well as big, innocent cornflower eyes and a mouth as soft as roses.'

No contempt coloured his voice, nothing but that steady detachment, yet each word was a tiny whip scoring her skin, her heart, as it was intended to be.

She retorted obstinately, 'I'm not sleeping in this bed if you are.'

Unimpressed, he said, 'Then sleep on the floor; I don't give a damn. But just in case you're stupid enough to run around the house putting lights on, I'll tie you to the bed-leg first.'

Stephanie bit down on a gasp of outrage. Her gaze flew to his face; she read an implacable, unwavering purpose there. He meant every word. If she made up a bed for herself on the floor he would shackle her. At that moment, ensnared in the ice of his eyes, she hated him with every part of her soul.

However, two could play the game of threat and counterthreat. Her lips tightened. 'Saul won't like that.'

He directed a hard, level stare at her. 'Your brother will have to accept that I know what I'm doing.'

Flinging caution to the wind, she said rashly, 'He can ruin your career.'

As soon as she'd said the words she'd realised it wouldn't work, but she hadn't expected the deadly silence that followed. When he spoke his voice was slow and even and truly terrifying.

'Perhaps we'd better get one thing straight,' he said.
'I am not afraid of or intimidated by your brother. I
never have been, and I don't plan to be in the future.
In your world, princess, money might mean power. In
mine it doesn't. Now lie down and shut up before I say
something I might regret.'

More than anything in the world she needed to make
some gesture, prove that he couldn't make her do what
he wanted, but something in his stance, in the way his
crystalline gaze met her rebellious eyes, something in the
remote, chillingly indifferent face with its angular bone-
structure and complete absence of softness or compassion, warned her not to try.

Defeated, she shuddered, almost swamped by the fear
she had fought so valiantly. He was as callous as the
kidnappers, finding the right buttons, pushing them
relentlessly.

'Very well,' she said, striving for dignified self-
possession, 'but using physical strength is just as des-
picable as using money to force anyone to do what you
want them to.'

'I suppose it's your privileged upbringing,' he said
conversationally, 'that means you don't know when to
stop,' and before she realised what he was doing he
caught her wrist in a grip just short of painful and leaned
over and kissed her with a merciless mouth, crushing her
objections, her worry and fear to nothing.

It was over in a moment. As she dragged painful air
into her lungs, he stared at her with eyes as cold as shards
of diamonds and said beneath his breath, 'God, what
the hell are you doing to me?'

Stephanie's world had turned upside-down, been
wrenched from its foundations by a kiss, as it had not
been by the preceding nightmarish days. For a lifetime,
for an aeon encompassed by the space between two
heartbeats, she was captured by those eyes, dragged into
a world where winter reigned supreme. This man,
whoever he was, moved and breathed like a human being,

but, in spite of his gentleness and care for her, at his heart was a core of primeval ice.

The prince of ice, she thought, trying to be flippant, an effort spoiled by foreboding.

'Turn over and get to sleep,' he ordered in that quiet, lethal voice.

Silently she turned her back on him and crawled beneath the covers, enveloped by the instant warmth of down. Tense and resistant, she huddled on the edge of the bed. Heat prickled across her skin, suffused every cell in her body. For the first time in her life she felt a tug of desire in her loins, a strange sensation in her breasts as though they were expanding.

Stop it, she adjured her unruly mind fiercely; stop it this minute. But she couldn't, until finally she fell back on a childhood remedy for unpleasant thoughts and strove to block out the images that danced behind her retinas with a concerted attack on the seven times table.

Out of the darkness he said, 'I'm sorry, that shouldn't have happened, and it won't be repeated. You needn't be afraid that I'll jump you again.'

She couldn't answer; touching her tongue to lips that were tender and dry, she wondered why his kiss should have had such an effect on her. Beyond the somewhat inexpert embraces of several boys not much older than she was, she had nothing to judge it by. Oh, she'd had crushes, but her brother's overwhelming masculinity made other men seem pale and ineffectual, and it had been difficult to let down the barriers of her mind and heart to anyone less compelling than Saul.

Also, her very protective brother made sure that she was kept well away from anyone who might view his younger sister as a tempting morsel. Consequently, most of her friends at school were far more experienced than she was.

Although their family had always been rich, and grown even richer under Saul's capable hands, he wasn't a member of the jet set. He despised people who didn't work, and because he was deeply in love with his wife he preferred to spend the time he had to spare with her and their children. Stephanie, too, loved being with the half-sister she had come to know so late in her childhood, and adored being a favourite aunt. Saul, she knew, kept a close eye on her friends, so although she had spent holidays with schoolfriends she had never gone anywhere except with people he had known and trusted.

Which meant, she thought, as she lay rigidly in the bed, that she was pretty naïve. If she'd been more sophisticated she wouldn't now be so overwhelmed by the powerful charisma of the man who lay beside her in the huge bed.

And perhaps she had been conditioned to look for that concentrated authority in a man; growing up with Saul had persuaded her that there could be kindness and love in a man of imperious character.

Exhaustion gripped her in unrelenting claws, but she couldn't sleep. Acutely aware of every tiny movement her rescuer made, of the length of his body next to hers, of the sound of his breathing, the tantalising, seductive heat of his body, her nerves sang like tightened bowstrings.

She didn't even know his name, and here she was sharing a bed with him!

Resentment simmered, encouraged because it blocked out the strange equivocal warmth seeping through her body. She despised men who thought their superior strength gave them the right to dominate.

And she hated the fact that he was able to sleep when she couldn't.

He'd probably shared a bed more times than she could count. Like Saul, who had been unmercifully pursued for as long as she could remember, the man who slept beside her possessed a smouldering sexuality that every woman would recognise. Squelching a mysterious pang, Stephanie lay longing for him to snore. It would demystify him, make him an ordinary man.

Of course he didn't. Eventually her muscles protested vigorously at being locked in stasis; giving in to them, she turned over on to her back, moving inch by careful inch in case she woke him. He didn't stir, but her change of position had brought her closer, and she scorched in the heat from his body. Surely all men weren't as hot as that? He certainly didn't have a fever, so perhaps he lived on a fiercer, more intense plane than other men.

Hastily, she turned back again.

'Stop thrashing about,' he commanded, his voice cool and slightly amused.

'Goodnight,' she muttered through clenched teeth.

Strangely enough, sleep reclaimed her then, but with it returned the dreams. Unable either to banish them or allow them to take her over completely, she fought back, and woke to find herself once more in his arms, that cruel hand clamped over her mouth again to cut off her screams.

At last, when it had happened three times, he said brusquely, 'Right, that's it. No, don't scuttle back to your side of the bed.' His arms tightened around her; one large hand pushed her head into the warm, hard muscles of his shoulder. 'Stay there,' he ordered.

'All right,' she said in the flat tone of exhaustion.

He pulled the duvet over them both. 'Now,' he said, his voice as level and unhurried as ever, 'let's see if we both can get some sleep.'

Her last thought was that he wasn't naked; she could feel some fine material beneath her hand as she cuddled against him, her body and mind immediately responding to his steady heartbeat.

Towards morning she woke, still in his arms, his body heat encompassing her, his scent in her nostrils, a masculine hand lying laxly along her thigh. At some time during the night she had climbed over him, and was now lying half on top, her leg between his, her arm underneath his other shoulder, using him as a mattress.

Overwhelmed by a demand she didn't fully recognise, a need she had never experienced, by the sheer, male power radiating from him even in sleep, she woke with her senses fully alert, her body in high gear. Unknown feelings tingled through her and before she realised where she was she felt his awakening, and the surge of awareness through his heated body, the swift compulsion of arousal that gripped him.

Stephanie might have been innocent but she wasn't stupid; she had read magazines and books, listened to some of her more worldly friends, and she knew that a man could be instantly ready for making love to any woman if she turned him on. She understood what was happening.

What she didn't understand and couldn't fight was her own reaction, the heady, draining weakness that had invaded her while she slept, making it impossible for her to retreat as prudence commanded. Anticipation coiled through her in sweet, seductive promise, drowning out common sense, washing away morals and logic and caution.

She had to get out of this immediately, scramble free and get on to her own side of the bed. But her muscles refused to obey her brain. Something world-shaking was making her heart race, drying her mouth, dampening her skin with an unexpected sheen.

He said harshly, 'Is this what you want?' And the hand that had been across her back found the full curve of her breast, cupping it, measuring its soft weight in slow, sensual appreciation.

Fire invaded her, robbing her of strength. An incredible sensation shot down her spine and into her loins; in answer she gave a tormented twist of her hips, seeking some as yet unknown response.

'How many men have you slept with?' he asked, that raw note in his voice abrading her nerves as savagely as his expert caress. 'You certainly know how to get what you want.'

She would have sobbed with desolation when his touch lifted if he hadn't slid his fingers down her back, exploring with lingering thoroughness the sharp bones of her hip and the amazingly sensitive hollow beneath it. She held her breath, and suddenly, fiercely, he clamped her hips down, pushing the newly awakened, violently sensitive portion of her anatomy against his growing hardness. Stephanie gasped, biting back a moan, unable to control the shudder that ran through her at the wild pressure.

And then she was almost flung across the bed, and he said in a voice that left her with no doubt about his feelings, 'Sorry, princess, I was paid to rescue you, not act as your gigolo.'

Humiliation burned deep into her soul; she had to swallow before she could retort thickly, 'I didn't—I woke up like that, damn you! And it was you who forced yourself into this bed.'

'Clearly a mistake,' he agreed contemptuously. 'But then, I didn't really know what I was dealing with. According to most reports, you're a sweet, innocent little schoolgirl.'

Sunk in frustration and shame, she lay with her eyes clamped tightly shut while he got out of the bed. However, after a moment she asked miserably, 'What are you doing?'

'Making a bed,' he said curtly.

Her lashes flew up. He hadn't put the light on, but the wintry pallor of early dawn was seeping through the heavy curtains, and she could see his outline, and the pile of clothes on the floor.

'No,' she said involuntarily.

'Yes,' he said, lowering himself to it. 'In another five years, perhaps, I might enjoy taking what you've got on offer. In the meantime, however, I'm going to have to say no, thanks. Nothing personal, princess—I'm a professional, and we like things to be nice and tidy.'

Which made her feel even worse.

* * *

When she woke it was morning, and the sun was shining in through the window with a hearty fervour that released something inside Stephanie. For the first time since she had been kidnapped she believed, not merely in her mind but in her heart, that there might be some future for her after all.

And then her eyes fell on the pillow beside her, and she stiffened, remembering. In one involuntary motion she sat up and looked at the floor where he had slept. The clothes were gone.

Heat flooded her skin; bitterly, angrily ashamed, she sank back against the pillow. How on earth had she let down her guard enough to climb all over him while she was asleep? And then, even when she was awake, to lie there and practically invite him to do whatever he wanted? No wonder he had been taken aback, although he needn't have been quite so brutal.

A self-derisory little smile curled her wide mouth. Perhaps he was afraid she'd make a nuisance of herself. If so, he'd certainly made sure his rejection was cruel enough to convince her never to fall into that trap again. If he still insisted on them sharing a bed, from now on, nightmares or not, she'd keep to her own side.

Forcing her mortification beneath the surface of her thoughts, she gazed around a room in the shape of a half-circle, its walls made of wooden panelling, its ceiling plaster. Both walls and furniture had been carefully carved by superb craftsmen to look medieval. Even the armchair was decorated by over-exuberant fretted wooden carving.

Yet wherever she looked she saw the icy scorn in her rescuer's expression as he rejected her.

She had to face it. And although shame still stained her cheeks she thought resentfully that he had had no right to be quite so—so scathing. There was *some* excuse for her behaviour. Surely after an experience like hers it was normal to crave the reassurance of human warmth, the comfort of arms around her, the momentary return to childhood when parents made everything better, even though from the age of four she had known that parents could die, that love was not enough to keep her safe, that the arms and soothing voice of a strong man were only temporary refuges.

Anyway, natural or not, a need for reassurance was a luxury she couldn't afford, especially if it led to situations like that of a few hours ago. Her fingers crept up to touch her trembling lips. For a moment she fancied she could feel his kiss on them. Very firmly, she banished the memory.

She shouldn't blame herself for what had happened in her sleep, but afterwards—well, that was a different story. If she had immediately climbed off him and made it obvious she wasn't trying to seduce him she wouldn't be feeling like this—embarrassed, ashamed, and with a forbidden fire in her blood that had to be outlawed. Instinct warned her that she was asking for heartbreak if she allowed herself to become even slightly dependent on the man who had rescued her.

Stephanie had learned the value of accepting her own emotions, and now she admitted that keeping her heart whole might be a little difficult. He had come to her like a prince on a charger, saving her from a hideous fate. She was entitled to spin a few fairy-stories about him; he was the stuff of fantasy, the dark hero, at once gentle and dangerous, kind and threatening, armoured in power and a fierce, unknowable authority.

But, tantalising though her fantasies might be, she couldn't afford to fall in love with him, for as well as the heart-stopping attributes of his strength there was that cool, impregnable self-sufficiency and a callousness that hurt. He might be only seven years older than she was, but what had happened to him in those years set a barrier between them.

He was a loner, a man who walked by himself. Prince of ice, she thought again.

She gazed around once more, searching for clues to the personality of the man who had brought her here. She found nothing. There was a dressing-table made of sombre, highly polished wood, on which was a tumbler with a collection of wild flowers. Stephanie wondered if the brilliant blue one was a gentian, then dismissed the query. Candace, her sister-in-law, would know; she was the expert on gardens and flowers.

But the little posy made a pleasant spot of colour, and in some odd way reassured her. Turning her head, she surveyed the other side of the room. The bedhead was against the straight wall that divided the room from the bathroom and the landing. The other walls stretched around her, enclosing and comforting, as though they were holding her in a protective embrace.

'It must be a tower room!' she said out loud, delighted, and flung the covers back.

Still stiff and sore, she staggered as renewed pain throbbed through her, but even so she was halfway to the window when she was caught and pulled back, whirled abruptly and held by a cruel grip on her shoulders, to meet the impassive, glittering eyes of her rescuer. Yesterday she had been too dazed to realise just how unusual they were, although she had registered their concentrated compulsion. Now, imprisoned as unequivocally by them as by his hands, she almost gasped. Instead of the warm, brilliantly clear sapphire she was used to seeing in the mirror, this man's eyes were so pale as to give an impression of translucence, with white flecks in the iris that made them look like splintered glass. Such was the intensity of those eyes that Stephanie's struggles stopped immediately. Her own widened, darkness swallowing up the colour; she shivered with some strange inner confusion.

'Don't go near the windows,' he said roughly.

The fragile moment of happiness shattering irrevocably, she nodded. Instantly, he let her go.

It was the most difficult thing she had ever done, but she managed to look fearlessly at him. He had freed her, slept with her, comforted her and finally held her, his strong arms and the solace of his presence banishing the nightmares. Then he had unfeelingly rejected what her innocent body had offered of its own volition.

Those powerful hands held her life and well-being. He could snuff both out as easily as he had pulled her away from the window.

He made her heart falter. Partly it was his amazing eyes, but they were merely the most arresting part of a truly formidable man. At five feet nine she was accustomed to looking many men in the eye, but he towered above her by at least six inches—possibly seven, she thought, gazing up into a face far more impressive than handsome. Slashing bone-structure formed the basis of features that reminded her of an eagle, the fiercely hooked nose and dominant, angular lines of jaw and cheekbones reinforcing an arrogant authority. His straight mouth warned of self-possession and fortitude, although she recognised something ambiguous about that mouth, a hint of sensuality in its sharply cut outline that set female nerves jangling at some hidden, primitive level.

From the top of his blue-black head to the soles of his feet he was all edged, confident masculinity, but it was a masculinity tight-leashed by an almost inhuman will.

'Who are you?' she blurted.

Apparently not in the least affected by her bold survey, he'd waited until she spoke. At her question his lashes drooped, and a smile, mockingly amused, curved his mouth.

'Duke,' he said laconically, and to her astonishment held out his hand.

Most men looked stupid with a hand held out, a hand that was ignored. This one didn't; completely relaxed, he merely waited. Once more Stephanie glimpsed a monumental, hard-headed patience that sent a cold shiver flicking down her spine as she reluctantly accepted his invitation. She had long fingers and a strong grip, but in his clasp her hand seemed small and white and powerless.

'You know who I am,' she said uncertainly.

'We haven't been introduced.'

Later she would wonder whether he had enough intuition to realise that this introduction was a wiping clean of all that had happened previously, and even before entertaining the idea would dismiss it. In spite of his care of her the preceding night he'd been more forceful than sensitive, and his abrupt rejection in the morning hadn't revealed any insight or empathy at all.

At that moment, however, saying her name, asserting an identity, was a reclaiming of something that the calculated inhumanity of her imprisonment had taken from her.

'Stephanie Jerrard,' she said, and her head came up. While they shook hands she asked, 'Just Duke?' and thought how strange it was that she had called him a prince, an ice-prince. He looked more like a prince than a duke, and yet the name suited his careless arrogance.

'That's all you need to know,' he said, an indifferent note in his voice warning her off.

As their hands fell away he ordered curtly, 'The windows look out over the valley, so the only people we have to worry about are ones with binoculars on the far side. Still, remember that if anyone does see you here word may reach the men who kidnapped you.'

At her involuntary shiver he nodded, pale eyes ranging her face. 'And if that happens we could lose not only the small men but those who gave the orders. Then there are your brother's negotiations; while you're thought to be safely stashed he's working from a position of power. If we can fool them into thinking that you're still their pawn, we're going to catch them all, including the ones who've kept their fingers clean.'

'I only saw two men. What makes you think there might be others?' she asked swiftly, striving to hide the sick panic that clutched her for an unnerving moment.

Broad shoulders lifted in a gesture oddly at variance with his poised, controlled persona. 'Rumours,' he said without expression, his eyes searching her face keenly. 'I need to know everything you can remember about the kidnapping.'

'Now?' she asked, realising that she was still in the thick T-shirt she'd worn as a nightgown. From the way it slid down over her shoulders it was one of his.

'Yes. It's important.'

She said, 'I want to go to the bathroom.'

'All right.' For all the world as though he was giving her permission!

When she came out of the quarter circle of bathroom he was waiting between her and the door on to the landing with the controlled watchfulness of a hunter at last sighting his prey.

'Get back into bed,' he said, and, when she hesitated, ordered curtly, 'Hurry up, it's chilly in here and you're still fragile.'

He was right; she was one vast ache, and her legs felt distinctly disinclined to hold her up. Nevertheless, she was getting heartily sick and tired of being ordered around. A glance at that eagle face, however, blocked any overt protest. Wordlessly, she climbed into the bed, covering her long, thin legs with a flick of the duvet. The T-shirt slipped; hastily, colour heating her skin, she hauled the soft material over her smooth bare shoulder.

Which was stupid, for he hadn't noticed. Those cold, pale eyes didn't move from her face.

'I was walking back to the chalet,' she said. 'There was nobody in the street; it was so still, so peaceful. I was looking at the stars and thinking I'd like a telescope, when they just appeared——'

'What were you doing in Switzerland?'

'Surely you know all about this?'

His expression didn't change. 'Just answer the questions, princess,' he said.

She said angrily, 'I was on holiday with friends, the Hastings. I went to school with Libby. They were going to stay for another couple of weeks, but I was leaving the next day to meet Saul at Frankfurt. We were going to fly to Fiji. Candace and the children are at Fala'isi, in the South Pacific, and the easiest way to get there is from Fiji. Anyway, the Hastings were called back to London; their son was in an accident, and was pretty sick, so I stayed on.'

'Why didn't you fly to be with your brother?'

Stephanie muttered defensively, 'Saul was there on business. I thought it would be fun to be free for a night.'

'What were you doing in a street in the village?'

She looked down at the sheet, watching the patterns her fingers made as they pleated it. 'I decided to have dinner in the inn,' she said. 'It's famous for its food, and the maid at the chalet suggested it. The Hastings took their cook with them; I thought the maid was going to cook, but she said she couldn't. It seemed perfectly safe.'

'Tell me about her.'

'The maid?'

He shrugged. 'Someone knew you were on the street.'

Duke was a skilled interrogator. Whenever she shook her head he asked the right questions to get her mind going again, and he was remorseless, prising information she hadn't even known she possessed from her with a combination of astuteness and unsparing, relentless pressure.

By the end of the session Stephanie's head was throbbing, but she had fully described the maid and what had happened to her on that street—and subsequently—with a clarity that astounded her.

Later, she realised that she was still not entirely sure that she trusted him, for somehow she had forgotten to tell him she'd seen the face of one of the kidnappers.

When at last he fell silent, his face impassive except for the slight drawing together of his dark brows, Stephanie yawned, her lashes drifting down.

'I thought they'd just leave me to die there.' She looked down at her wrists. Almost absently she finished, 'I couldn't believe it when one came back with food and water.'

He swore, words that shocked her, then looked at the raw chafing on her skin where she had struggled against the handcuffs. 'Is that why you tried to free yourself, even though you must have known you'd never make it?'

She said quietly, 'Yes. The will to survive is pretty strong. And if you don't try, you don't get anywhere.' Common sense told her that she shouldn't ask the next question, but she had to know. 'How did you find me? It was like a miracle.'

A smile, half cynical, wholly lacking in humour, touched that equivocal mouth. 'Luck,' he said laconically. 'Luck and gossip. But mostly luck. Your guardian angel has been working overtime for you, Stephanie Jerrard. Right, I'll get your breakfast. Today you stay in bed.'

She rebelled at that, but he was right—she was too exhausted even to want to get up. However, just to assert some sort of independence, the moment he was gone she disappeared into the pretty bathroom and turned on the shower. He reappeared as though he'd heard a shot, coming through the door like one of the avengers of old, his face dark and angry.

'What the hell do you think you're doing? I thought I told you,' he said between his teeth, 'that if you shower I stay in the next room?'

Her mouth hanging open, she stammered, 'I—I forgot.'

'Don't ever forget again,' he warned starkly, his voice leaving her in no doubt that he meant what he said. 'All right, go ahead. I'll make the bed.'

It was bliss; she made a ritual of it, from her hair to her toes, and then, even though boneless with fatigue, cleaned her teeth with the new brush and paste she found beside the basin until her gums bled.

But she was acutely conscious of the tall, intimidating man who waited for her next door.

CHAPTER THREE

STEPHANIE emerged wrapped in a towel.

Without speaking, Duke tossed another of his T-shirts to her, this one smelling of fresh air and sunlight.

'Thank you,' she said.

He gave her an unsmiling look and said, 'Stay in bed this time,' as he left the room.

Arrogant bastard, she thought angrily, waiting until he was halfway down the stairs before pulling it over her head. Surely he could have got her a nightgown?

'Here,' he said, appearing silently and far too quickly at the door with a tray which he must have had stashed on the landing. 'Breakfast.'

Oh, lord, had he seen her getting changed? Did she think she was trying to seduce him again? A swift, horrified glance from beneath her lashes revealed nothing but that inscrutable expression she was beginning to know so well.

Anyway, who was she fooling? The mirror in the bathroom wasn't very big, but it had revealed only too cruelly a gaunt face above a scrawny neck and hollowed shoulders, stick arms and blotchy skin. He might have been aroused in the semi-sleep of morning, but no man would want a woman who looked like her.

A forgotten nursery smell rose to her nostrils. 'Bread and milk!' she exclaimed. 'I haven't had that for years!'

The sense of smell worked its eerie magic. Somehow the simple, easy dish brought back an aura of those happy, protected days. Forgetting embarrassment, Stephanie smiled radiantly at him.

'Hop into bed,' he said shortly, and waited until she had obeyed before putting the tray on her lap. His closeness set off unfamiliar piercing sensations in the pit of her stomach.

As though he knew what he was doing to her he straightened and stood back, those glinting eyes cool and dismissive. 'You don't look much older than when you were in the nursery,' he commented. 'How are your wrists after that shower?'

It was another rejection, a reimposing of the boundaries he had set, and although a little kinder than his previous one it hurt. Pride aroused, Stephanie lifted her head in a queenly gesture. 'Much better, thanks,' she replied.

'Let me see.'

Reluctantly, she held out her hands. The steam from the bread and milk curled around the palms, dampening them.

'Turn them over,' he said crisply.

She obeyed, staring intently at the raw patches.

'You must be healthy, princess,' he said. 'There's no sign of infection, but I'll get you some aloe vera gel to help the healing. How about the rest of you?'

Her gaze flew up to meet his. 'I'm all right.'

Aloof eyes searched her face. 'Did they rape you?'

All warmth drained from her skin, leaving it clammy. She snatched her hands back and turned her head away so that he couldn't see her eyes. 'No,' she said harshly.

'I washed you,' he said without any change in his voice. 'I saw the bruises. I've seen marks like that before, and I know what they mean.'

'What sort of life have you *led*, for God's sake?'

He raised his brows. 'Mostly outside the palace walls,' he said indifferently. 'In places where innocent people quite often get hurt through no fault of their own. Places where virgins are raped and children killed before they've had a chance to live. Did they rape you?'

She hated him for not leaving it alone, hated him for making her face what had been done to her. But his stance and the unhurried resolution of his voice told her that she wasn't going to be let off. Normally she'd have died rather than tell anyone, but without too much of a struggle she surrendered to his stronger will.

'No. I was unconscious until just before they put me in the coffin. I woke up when they were taking my clothes off.' Banishing the memory of the jeering comments that had been the first sounds she had heard then, she said in a studied tone, crystal-clear, totally lacking any expression, 'One of them, not the one who brought me the food, wanted to. Rape me, I mean. He grabbed my legs and was forcing them apart when——' She stopped, remembering those horror-filled moments, her sheer, bewildered terror and useless struggling, then went on in a dispassionate voice, 'The other man wouldn't let him. He said it was wasting time; they'd been seen and they had to get out of there.'

Duke didn't say anything, didn't even move, but naked aggression, cold as the point of a sword, radiated from him. There was no doubt about it; the man who had rescued her was more than capable of killing.

'It could have been worse,' she said, trying to break the sudden, heavy tension with objectivity.

'The older one is a professional.' He spoke calmly, that wave of ferocity subdued by a determination so vast that she was frightened all over again. 'The younger one is a common, street-corner thug. Don't worry, they'll pay for what they did.'

'You know who they are?'

'Oh, yes.' It came as a chilling snarl, but when she looked up he seemed almost to be smiling. 'Yes, I know who they are.'

'How?'

'It's my business to know these things.'

'If you knew so much, why did you put me through all that—that interrogation?' she demanded, angry colour smouldering in her cheeks.

'To see whether you knew any more than I did,' he said unhurriedly. 'Eat your breakfast, and then you can sleep again.'

The quick flare of irritation had exhausted her. Hiding a yawn, she asked drowsily, 'Does Saul know that I'm all right?'

'Yes.' His voice was guarded. 'Don't worry about him.'

From beneath lowered lashes Stephanie watched him leave the room. Although her brother was a tall man, well-made, graceful, Duke was something else again, much bigger-boned than Saul, yet in spite of his size he shared the same noiseless ease of movement, an inherent air of great physical competence.

Sighing, she began to eat, but after several spoonfuls her hunger turned abruptly to near-nausea, and she abandoned the bread and milk. He had put a multi-vitamin tablet in a small dish; she used the diluted orange juice to wash it down, before putting the tray on to the bedside table. Then, as swiftly as a striking arrow, she went back to sleep.

For lunch he prepared delicious chicken soup and some toast, but later she suffered severe stomach cramps for an hour or so. Duke had apparently been expecting them and, while she endured the pain with as much fortitude as she could summon, he sat beside the bed and talked to her. They discussed books, the theatre, art, but nothing personal. His incisive mind, that of an intelligent, well-read man, made her feel inadequate and childish, a schoolgirl.

Which was obviously how he thought of her, if the bread and milk was any indication. A schoolgirl with a vigorous sex life.

That night she was sound asleep when he came to bed; at some time she woke and, drugged by the demands her mending body made of her, put out her hand to see whether he was there. Terrifyingly, the instant her fingertips grazed his hot, smooth skin he pinned her wrist to the bed beside his shoulder, his grip clamping the fragile bones in her wrist painfully together, numbing her hand.

'It's only me,' she whispered shakily.

'All right.' His voice was smooth and steady, with no sign of sleep in it. Releasing her, he asked, 'Did you have a nightmare?'

'No. I just wondered whether you were there.'

'I'm here.'

She couldn't discern anything in his voice, but it suddenly occurred to her that he might think she was making a pass at him.

Again.

Cradling her maltreated wrist, she turned her back to him and lay still, listening to his slow, even breathing. Had he been awake? He had responded with the deadly speed of a hungry animal; what experiences had given him the reflexes of a predator, swift, noiseless, lethal?

Experiences gained in that world outside the palace walls, she supposed, where the innocent suffered unjustly.

Eventually she fell into an unconsciousness punctuated by bouts of restlessness when her nerves jerked her back into the dark tower room with the man who was her rescuer yet a threat to her in ways she didn't yet fully understand. Each time she woke, she sensed that he woke with her, or so soon afterwards that he must have slept with every sense alert, honed to a razor-sharpness. But he never spoke, never made any movement, and she soon slid back into sleep.

That day set the pattern for the following one. Docile and lethargic, once more Stephanie spent ages in the shower and ate, her appetite increasing as she regained strength, but this time she insisted on getting up for lunch, and counted it a small victory when Duke agreed.

Of course, he laid down a set of conditions. 'You're not coming downstairs yet; keep well away from the windows, and you go back to bed after you've eaten.'

'What about some clothes?' Those eyes hadn't ever drifted below her face, but she was self-conscious about the length of thin leg that showed beneath the T-shirt.

'There aren't any, princess,' he said.

'There are. I wore jeans and a shirt——'

'I burned them.'

She stared at him. 'Why?' she asked stupidly.

'I don't want any but my clothes in the place. It's safer that way.'

Such concern seemed almost obsessive, and she said so, snapping the words out because an inner tension strung her nerves taut.

His mouth thinned. 'When it comes to my own safety I am obsessive,' he said brusquely. 'You can wear my dressing-gown.'

'No, it doesn't matter.' Ashamed of her shortness, she gave him an uncertain smile.

His expression didn't soften. 'It won't be for too long,' he said as he left the room.

She curled up in the armchair and stared longingly through the window at the alpine scene across the valley meadow and conifers, a small herd of cows, their cowbells clonking sonorously on the breeze, grass of an intense green. Bright flowers studded the grass, and insects would be humming through them, busy, mindless, their tiny lives measured by a season. Behind the summer-lit meadows and the darkness of the fir trees, the eternal mountains reached high into a cloudless sky.

Sniffing, she scrambled from the armchair and raced back to the bed, frantic to hide any trace of the tears that were gathering.

'What's the matter?'

Her head whipped around. Duke was standing in the arched stone doorway, those blazing eyes shrewd and speculative.

She shrugged. 'Nothing.'

He came in and sat down on the side of the bed, his gaze never leaving her face. 'Missing your brother?'

'Yes.'

His voice deepened, became hard to resist. 'And?'

She hesitated before muttering, 'I'm just being stupid. I'm free, I'm in reasonably good physical shape. I wasn't even raped. I should be relieved, and glad to be alive, and looking forward to the rest of my life...'

'But you're not.'

Without looking at him, she said, 'I just feel—grey. Not depressed, not—anything. I keep asking myself what there is for me, why I wanted to stay alive so much. Which is ridiculous.'

'It's only to be expected,' he said. 'You expended an enormous amount of energy keeping yourself together while you were imprisoned, so you're suffering from reaction now. Your body needs time to recover, but so do your mind and your emotions.'

She said dolefully, 'All I can produce is a kind of tepid pleasure at the thought of seeing Saul and Candace again. I feel as though I'm lost in a cold, foggy world where nothing really matters and where the sun is never going to shine again...'

To her shock and despair she found that she was crying, tears coursing down her cheeks in an unmanageable flood while great gulping sobs shook her. Horrified, she turned her face into the pillow.

'Stephanie,' Duke said.

She tried desperately to stop, but his hand on her shoulder was the last straw.

'Don't try to hold back,' he said quietly. 'Crying is the best way of letting it all out. You've endured more than any kid your age should have to cope with, and you've come through it well. This is part of the healing. Let it go—you'll feel like a wet rag afterwards, but much better. Tears are not a sign of weakness; they heal.'

Surely it was uncommon for a man to understand so much? The thought wandered briefly into her mind before being driven out by the black flood of tears. Stephanie hadn't cried for years; she made up for it now.

When her final hiccups had died away she lay quiescent and motionless, Duke's handkerchief in one hand, her other swallowed by the warm clasp of his, and realised with a pang of dismay that she wanted to be in his arms. She thought caustically, Any man would do; you just want some sympathy, and knew she lied.

His voice was dry. 'I don't suppose you'll really rest properly until the men who did this to you are behind bars and you're back with your brother. Even then you might need therapy. You certainly need time. But don't be afraid; from now on I imagine your brother will make sure you're kept completely safe.'

Oddly enough, she felt perfectly safe now, with him. He was the one who insisted on the precautions.

He was silent for a few seconds, moments that hummed with unsaid words, undivulged thoughts and emotions. When he spoke again, it was on another subject. 'Tell me about yourself.'

'What do you want to know?'

'Well, what about your parents? Why is your brother your guardian?'

Somehow it didn't seem strange to tell him things she had never revealed before, not even to her best friend at school. Perhaps it was exhaustion, or the simple human need to communicate.

And perhaps, she thought, just before she embarked on the history of her life, it might be a good idea to tell him just how dangerous Saul could be when his family was hurt.

'I've had four parents, and lost them all. Careless of me, I've always felt. My father was the wild one of the Jerrard family, the one who never fitted in. He wandered out to New Zealand and found my mother. From all accounts he fell instantly in love with her.' Her mouth tucked in at the corners. 'It wasn't hard to do. Saul says she was fey, a beautiful, fragile thing like a bird with a broken wing. For those days, she was very wild. She'd already had another child before my father came on the scene.'

'You don't look like her,' he said. 'You're a Jerrard through and through.'

'I know.' With no trace of that mysterious sensuality that had impressed anyone who met her mother. She paused, looking down at the sheet. 'When I was four my father drowned and not long after that my mother committed suicide. My father's brother and his wife, Saul's parents, took me to England and adopted me. We were all very happy, but it didn't last. I thought they'd been killed in an accident, but a few years ago Saul told me what really happened.'

'Why?'

Trust him to home in on the uncomplimentary part of the story. She admitted, 'I was being stupid about security arrangements.'

'I see.'

There was an edge to his voice that puzzled her, but she said, 'I was at my most brattish then. I think I've grown out of it.'

'What happened to you after they were killed?'

'I missed them unbearably. Saul did his best, but he was extremely busy; when his father died my uncles thought that Saul was too young and untried to handle Jerrard's, and they decided it should be broken up so that each of them would own the part they were most interested in. Saul didn't agree, and there was a battle that turned vicious. I don't know all the ins and outs, but apparently it ended in a lot of bitterness. Saul was kept at full stretch for a couple of years tidying up the mess.'

'So you were left alone at your very expensive boarding-school.'

'If you can be alone with a couple of hundred other girls,' she said tartly. 'I knew he loved me. He was always there when I needed him, and he came to every sports day and prize-giving. Of course, we always spent the holidays together.'

'A nice, secure life. Are you jealous of his wife?'

Lifting her head, Stephanie stared at him with astonishment and anger. His ambiguous mouth was firmly disciplined, all thoughts hidden by the thick, straight fringe of his black lashes.

'I couldn't be jealous of Candace!' she said curtly. 'Apart from anything else, she's my half-sister.'

'Is she now?' he said.

It was impossible to tell whether he had known that before. He had a classic poker face, as unreadable as the sphynx, responses and emotions completely under his control.

'Yes. She was the daughter my mother had before she married my father, the child who was adopted out. Candace doesn't talk about her childhood, but I think it was happy enough until her parents' marriage broke up. Her adoptive father rejected her when his new wife had children, and her mother married a man who didn't want her. After that she lived in foster homes, but she was determined to find her birth family. By the time she was old enough to start our mother was dead, and Candace couldn't find out anything about her father, so when she tracked me down she wanted to establish contact. Luckily for me, she and Saul fell in love, so it all worked out very well.'

'Especially for Candace,' he said smoothly.

She sent him a very level look. 'Do you know her?'

'No,' he said.

'Then don't presume to judge. She and Saul are very happy together.'

His eyes narrowed further, but he said, 'I'm sure they are.'

'Who are you?' she asked abruptly, giving way to the curiosity that burned inside her. 'How did you find me? And don't give me that rubbish about luck and gossip.

I don't believe in luck, and no one gossips about a kidnapping.

'You'd be surprised what people talk about, and even more surprised at how much intelligence-gathering is just sifting gossip.' His mouth compressed as though her question had hidden ramifications. 'That's my job. I listen to gossip, and I find people.'

'Ah, an investigator.' She waited for him to agree but he said nothing, pale eyes watchful in an inscrutable face. After an awkward pause she asked, 'Do you work for Saul?'

'At the moment.' He got up to walk across to the window.

The hand he'd held felt cold, and Stephanie wondered why his touch had seemed to anchor her. Uneasily, she watched beneath lowered lids as he stretched, his wide shoulders and back flexing beneath the thin cotton of his shirt. Mysterious senses stirred, uncurled deep within her, turning her bones to liquid. She realised anew with a jolt of primal foreboding how very big he was, and how understatedly powerful.

Yet he could be gentle, as some really strong men were gentle. However, he wasn't giving anything away; he was treating her like a child, to be comforted and petted and fed and clothed, but not to be told anything.

Macho, masterful men, she decided indignantly, they were all the same; until Candace had come on the scene Saul had been like that. Candace wouldn't accept it from Saul, and because of her influence he had slowly allowed Stephanie a little more autonomy.

After this débâcle, she thought grimly, he was going to want to wrap her in cotton wool again.

'So how *did* you know where I was?' she asked, her voice lifting autocratically. Duke had evaded the question, and she was determined to make him divulge something.

The glowing light outside silhouetted his form in brilliance. Recalling that the Greek god Zeus had come to

one of his lovers in a shower of gold, she wondered
whether this was how the girl had seen him, dark body
blocking out the light, surrounded by a fiery corona of
sunlight.

He didn't answer until several seconds had passed.
Then he moved away from the window and said calmly,
'I was called in because I'm the best at what I do, and
because I'd passed certain rumours on to the men who
work for your brother. Fortunately, when you were taken
they contacted me immediately instead of waiting until
the trail had gone cold. With the information I had, and
what they'd managed to glean, we were able to work out
who had kidnapped you; after that it was merely a matter
of finding out what they'd done with you. Judicious
questioning and tailing got me that. Then I got the keys
and freed you.'

It all sounded so simple—far more simple than it had
been, she was sure. A shiver pulled her skin tight. 'So
you knew where I was from—when?'

'From when he went back to give you food,' he said,
his tone revealing nothing.

It took a moment to sink in. Then she said incredulously, 'You mean you knew I was there—you let me lie
there for a whole day before you came to get me?'

'Yeah,' he drawled, the word incongruous. 'That's
exactly what I did.'

Although Stephanie had the temper that went with
bronze hair and ivory skin, over the years she had learned
that losing it gave others too much control of the situation. This time, however, as she searched the darkly
arrogant face of the man who had rescued her, she could
feel a familiar turbulence seethe through her, fierce and
white-hot and irresistible. Each one of those hours spent
in claustrophobic bondage, in filth and hunger and
terror, would be imprinted on her memory for the rest
of her life.

Her hand shook as she thrust it through the tangle of
her hair, pushing it back from her hot face. Very evenly

she said, 'I presume you had a good reason for leaving me there?'

'Oh, I did, princess, I did indeed.' His voice was hard and flat, without inflexion. 'I had to make sure that the two men—who are still in this area, and presumably were intending to visit you again—were out of the picture before I went anywhere near you.'

It made sense in a coldly practical way. 'And are they out of the picture?'

'They were then. Temporarily.' His mouth curved in a smile totally lacking in humour.

'Then why,' she demanded, 'all the elaborate secrecy? Why did we have to play cops and robbers all the way up the mountainside?'

'Because although I managed to send them off on a wild-goose chase I wasn't completely sure that they'd stay away for as long as I needed to get you out.'

Again his actions made sense, but—what sort of man was he, to leave her to the mercy of that crypt? He hadn't even known that she was all right. She could have died before he came.

Not for the first time in her life, although never before with such intensity, she faced the essential loneliness of humanity, the gulf that divided one person from another. He'd made a cruel decision, yet one fulminating glare at his face told her that he would do exactly the same thing again if he thought it necessary.

Prince of ice...

'How did you get them out of the way?' she asked, conceding defeat of a sort.

She could tell he didn't want to answer, see him choosing the right words. Finally he smiled again, an unpleasant twist of his lips that made her shiver. 'The less you know about it the better.'

She eyed him angrily, but it was obvious he wasn't going to tell her. Still, she tried. 'How much ransom did they ask?'

He shrugged, then sat down in the armchair, his face in shadow, long legs stretched out, watching her with unnervingly half-closed eyes. 'Twenty million pounds.'

Fighting the chill clamminess of her skin, she said quietly, 'Not even Saul could afford that much.'

Duke said, 'He's rumoured to be one of the richest men in the world, but that would be just a negotiating figure. They'd know he'd be desperate to get you back. You represent a lot of money, princess.'

Is that all I represent? she wondered forlornly. Just money? She had endured enough sycophantic behaviour at school to understand that many people valued her solely for the money her brother controlled, but something in her rebelled at being labelled a poor little rich girl. Damn it, she had things to offer the world, and it suddenly seemed important that she discover what they were, and use them. Then Duke wouldn't look at her with that kind of aloof pity, as though he too agreed with the men who had callously reduced her to a matter of pounds and pence.

Anger and pride and fear were ruthlessly subdued. Trying to speak objectively, she asked, 'Do they know I'm gone yet?'

'I don't know. I have to work on the assumption that they do.'

She cast a swift look at the window. They could be out there searching for her again. 'Then why can't I go home? Why do I have to stay here?'

'I told you. Your brother wants it.'

'He's keeping me out of the way, too,' she said with faint bitterness.

Duke's shoulders lifted. 'He's doing what he thinks is best,' he pointed out, a hint of impatience abrading his voice.

'Do you think he's right?'

His eyes met hers. 'It has nothing to do with me.' His voice was indifferent.

If holding her here was Saul's decision it would have been made with her best interests at heart.

Stephanie could understand her brother's reasoning. With her safely out of the way he had a much better chance of conducting his negotiations with the men who had organised her kidnapping. If she reappeared by his side they would simply go to ground, and possibly try again.

Unfortunately logic didn't ease the sore patch in her heart.

Duke got to his feet. 'Try to get some more sleep,' he advised. 'You spent last night tossing and turning.'

But not dreaming, thank God. Suddenly tired, she turned her head away from the golden glowing sunlight beyond the window. Just before unconsciousness claimed her she realised that while she had been imprisoned she hadn't dared sleep in case she didn't wake; now her body was catching up.

Quite late in the afternoon she woke, her bones lax and heavy, her mind floating free, oddly unconcerned, almost tranquil. For a while she lay peacefully gazing at the peaks, remote and icily silver as Duke's eyes, cutting their way into the tender blue of the sky.

When this was all over she would never again take sunlight and freedom for granted.

She got up and showered, then, rebelling at the in-action that had kept her in the tower, decided it was time she explored the rest of the house. But when she tried the handle on the door that led to the stairs she found that it refused to move.

She stood there, looking at the lock, a modern, completely efficient one, impossible to pick even if she knew how, while something like horror beat high and frantically in her throat.

Her shaking hand across her forehead momentarily smoothed out the puckers of fierce thought. She turned away from the door, then spun around and tried it again, rattling it in her frustration. It didn't budge.

Don't be silly, she told herself sternly as she went back to the bedroom. There's no need to make such a drama of a perfectly ordinary thing. Duke has probably gone to the nearest village for food and, not wanting to wake me, has simply made sure I can't go wandering around the place revealing myself to anyone who might be looking.

It was the sort of thing he would do.

She sat on the side of the bed, eyes fixed sightlessly on the scene through the window as the sun went down over the mountain, edging the sharp rim with gold, then fell into darkness. Dusk gathered itself against the steep slopes, thickened, merged into twilight and night.

Being locked in brought with it a temporary return of the terror she had fought so strongly in the crypt. She was still sitting on the bed, hands loosely clasped in her lap, when he appeared in the doorway. No footstep, no tell-tale click of the door warned her. Her heart sped up, the blood beating hectically through her veins, and for a moment she was held frozen by a bewildering confusion of emotions.

'Good girl; you had the sense not to turn a light on,' he said crisply as he strode across to close the curtains. 'I'm sorry I'm late back. I went down to the village and got waylaid.'

He reached past her and switched on the light. In the sudden blossom of radiance his face loomed, darkly intimidating and powerful, the crystalline eyes searching her face, dropping suddenly to the slender lines of her legs against the crimson coverlet, before flicking back up to her face. She could smell something warm and potent on his breath, and every nerve tightened, but it was obvious that whatever he'd been drinking hadn't been enough to affect him. She couldn't, she thought fleetingly, imagine him drunk. His impressive control would forbid such a weakness.

'They're celebrating their thousandth anniversary,' he went on easily, 'and everyone was enjoying themselves in the bar.'

'Do they know you?'

He shook his head. 'No; I only arrived the day before yesterday, after your brother organised the lease of the castle, but they're shouting free drinks to every passer-by. I don't want to cause any comment so I had a couple with them.'

'Why did you lock me in?'

Did he hesitate? No, although his gaze narrowed as he answered, 'Because I didn't want you wandering around where you might be seen.'

Those translucent eyes were hooded until he smiled. She wanted more of that smile, she craved it, and in that craving, she knew, was a danger more extreme than any other.

'And,' he added deliberately, 'to make sure no one found their way up here.'

It was like being dumped into polar water. A shiver worked its way across her skin. 'I don't like being locked up,' she said quietly.

'I can understand that. When I left you were sound asleep, and I intended to be back before you woke.' He wasn't apologising, or even making excuses. He was simply telling her, and somehow the deep, calm voice soothed her illogical fears away.

Nodding, she looked down at her hands, long and thin, somewhat paler than normal. How stupid she'd been, letting panic overcome common sense.

'Why did you try the door?' he asked.

'I wanted to look around,' she said without expression.

'Even though I told you that you are not to wander around the place?'

He was standing too close; he made her skin sensitive and prickly, sent strange little chills along nerve fibres she hadn't even known she possessed.

Feeling stupid and ungrateful, she said, 'I try to remember, but I'm not used to being a prisoner.'

When he spoke again his words were slightly more conciliatory, but his tone wasn't. 'Try harder. The last thing we want is to let anyone see you here.'

She nodded. 'I know. Believe me, I don't want to jeopardise things.' She looked at him directly. 'Are you in contact with Saul?'

'No,' he said instantly. 'He knows where we are, and he knows you're all right, but we decided it would be better to stay silent from now on.' He paused, then, clearly choosing his words, he continued, 'There's a chance—so remote that it's highly unlikely, but we have to take it into consideration—that someone close to him might be passing information to whoever kidnapped you.'

Indignantly, Stephanie said, 'No, I don't believe it.'

'Anything is possible, princess, especially when large amounts of money are involved, but I'll agree it doesn't seem likely.'

She gave a taut smile. 'And you are a cautious man.'

'It's not a fashionable quality, but it's saved my bacon too often for me to ignore it. You look tired. Get into bed and I'll bring dinner.'

'No,' she said quickly. Staying in bed had lowered her guard, setting up a spurious intimacy that gravely weakened her. She needed some distance between them, to put their relationship, such as it was, on a more normal basis. 'I'll help you get dinner,' she said, getting to her feet.

'Do you know how to cook?'

'Well, no,' she admitted.

'Peel potatoes?'

He was getting at her. She shrugged. 'It wasn't covered at school. But I'm tired of being stuck up here like an invalid, and this may well be an excellent chance to learn how to cook from a master.'

'Most bachelors are reasonable cooks,' he said, and her heart gave an odd little skip. He didn't expand on it, merely added, 'Who said hunger is the best sauce? I don't consider myself a master, merely competent, but thank you for the compliment. All right, you can come on down, but you sit at the table and the moment I decide you're tired you come upstairs again without any quibbling.'

She directed a mutinous stare at him.

'Otherwise,' he said, in a voice that told her he wasn't going to budge, 'you stay up here.'

She didn't have the strength at this time to fight him, so she capitulated, promising herself that one day he'd find out she had a will of her own. 'Did you bring me any clothes?' she asked, knowing the answer.

'No. You can wear my dressing-gown.'

'I'll *swim* in it.'

Brows raised, he surveyed the thin length of her body, too well revealed by his T-shirt. The colourless eyes gleamed, and something moved in them, something that sent Stephanie's pulse leaping into her throat.

Immediately he turned away. 'Wait a minute,' he said, striding across to the wardrobe. He opened the door and took out a shirt with long sleeves and tails. 'Here,' he said curtly, tossing it on to the bed. 'See how that goes.'

She almost ran into the bathroom, and for the first time locked the door behind her. The shirt reached halfway down her thighs. Rolling up the sleeves and fastening the buttons, she tried to convince herself that she was less exposed to him than if she'd been wearing shorts.

But there was a vast difference between wearing shorts and walking around with nothing on beneath his shirts, feeling material that had been against his skin caress hers...

A swift glance in the mirror told her that her eyes were glittering, the sapphire darkening to a brilliant cobalt, and her mouth looked soft and swollen and very red.

'Stop it,' she told the woman in the mirror, the woman with the fierce, turbulent expression. But that woman was busy remembering the glint in Duke's eyes as they'd followed a track from her neck to her breasts, full and high, and then down to her legs. She could feel the heat of his scrutiny on her skin now, burning into it, sending more of those messages to her nerves. For a few seconds he had forgotten that he'd been sent by her brother to rescue her, and there had been a virile male challenge in his gaze that had liquefied her bones. And instead of being upset or frightened or offended she had wanted to meet that challenge with one of her own; she had wanted to display herself, to preen in the light of his obvious appreciation, to show him that in spite of everything she was a woman...

She licked dry lips, trying hard to keep her brain cool and practical. Face facts, she told herself. You're scrawny, ill and unattractive; your skin and hair are both showing the results of several days without food and sunlight and freedom. And you're a girl whose only knowledge of the mysteries of men and women comes from hearsay and books.

So she had better just forget that occasionally Duke's masculine self overcame the prudence of his acute intelligence.

'Are you ready?' he asked from the other side of the door.

Jumping, she snatched up a face-flannel, ran the cold tap on to it, and held it for a moment to her heated face.

'I'm coming,' she said, and put it down before, with head held high and pulses skipping, she went through the door.

The castle, she found, wasn't very big. 'A Victorian whim,' Duke told her as they walked down the narrow, winding staircase. 'A crazy English aristocrat decided to build it here so he could botanise whenever he felt like it. Botany was the fashionable and romantic thing to do, and he was romantic to his heart's core. So he found a suitable crag in the Alps and built this place. But that wasn't enough. His wife decided it needed something extra and persuaded him to add a couple of follies among the fir trees.'

Stephanie smiled, imagining upright Victorian gentlemen sporting the usual amount of facial hair, and well-bustled Victorian ladies with ringlets and coy eyelashes and rosebud mouths.

Duke continued, 'It might look like a castle, but really it's a holiday home, a bach.'

'Bach?'

He directed a long look towards her, a look she had met with cool reserve, hoping very much that no sign showed of the forbidden desires he aroused in her. The only thing left to her was her dignity, and she was going to cling to that for all she was worth.

'I suppose four years old is too young to remember that in New Zealand's North Island a holiday home is called a bach. In the South Island they call them cribs.'

'I didn't know that. Are you a New Zealander?'

'No,' he said abruptly. 'But I have connections there. Have you been back?'

'Several times. I love it. So green and wild and fresh, so—isolated and end-of-the-worldish. When we fly into Auckland I'm always surprised to see a modern city spread out below; the land and seascape look as though the place should be something out of Tolkien, a haven.'

'A romantic idea.'

She reacted snappishly to his irony. 'Romantic notions didn't go out with Victorian aristocrats. At eighteen I'm allowed to be starry-eyed. In fact, I think it's almost obligatory.'

'And here was I thinking you were a little cynic,' he said, smiling, yet when she glanced sharply at him he was studying her as though she were a rare insect to be classified and tabled.

Something swift and keen moved in the pit of her stomach, something akin to fear, giving an edge to the response that still roiled through her. Careful, she thought as she went with him through the high hall with its suits of armour and dim battle-flags, through the green baize door that had separated the master from the servants, and into the kitchen. You must be careful.

CHAPTER FOUR

THE kitchen was a huge affair that didn't appear to have been altered much since the day it was built. A vast range of some sort was backed against a stone wall, purring gently to itself as it warmed the shadowy room.

'Right, you can have your first lesson in peeling potatoes,' Duke said.

Stephanie had always been deft, and the knife was finger-nicking sharp; nevertheless, ten minutes later she morosely transferred her gaze from thick peelings to marble-sized potatoes. When she got out of here, she thought, tipping the vegetables into the sink to wash them, one of the first things she'd do was take cooking lessons. This was ridiculous!

'By the time we leave here,' Duke said, turning from the bench in time to catch her dismayed expression, 'you'll be an expert.'

She laughed, hoping he didn't hear the jarring note. 'We're going to be here that long?'

'I assumed you were a fast learner.' Deftly, he continued doing things to steaks.

'I hope so,' she said, pretending to laugh again. 'Otherwise we're going to be bankrupted by constantly buying potatoes.'

'Not to worry, your brother's paying for them.'

'I hope you're buying them discreetly,' she said teasingly. 'It would be dreadful if, after all your care to make sure no one knows I'm here, someone deduced it because you keep buying potatoes.'

He sent her an unsmiling look. 'I brought most of the food with me,' he said. 'And don't worry, I'm being very careful.'

She sighed. 'If only we knew what was going on.'

'I know as little as you do,' he returned calmly, and, apparently not in the least put out by his lack of information, began to slice onions, the knife slashing through the white flesh with swift, sure movements.

Nodding, she thought with a flash of insight that it was an unusual role for him to play, the passive onlooker. Duke—if that was his real name—had all the hallmarks of a leader, not one who watched from the sidelines.

Nevertheless he didn't seem to be fretting at this enforced inactivity. He possessed a disturbing self-assurance, as forceful as it was seamless. In spite of her misgivings she wanted to know more about him, and she was prepared to bet that every woman who met him wanted the same thing. His particular brand of direct, uncompromising masculinity was an unconscious provocation to the opposite sex. She hadn't had all that much to do with men, but she'd seen women react to her brother, so she'd grown up knowing that there were some men who were almost irresistible to the opposite sex.

He looked up, catching her eyes. Hastily, she swished the potatoes in the water, snatching her thoughts away from such a hazardous premise.

Although she withstood the impact of his gaze on her face for as long as she could, pride eventually forced her to meet it. Apparently not at all concerned by the open defiance of her glower, he continued to examine her face in a slow, unwavering scrutiny, and to her embarrassment heat singed her cheekbones. She was accustomed to being looked at, but not like this, as though he was imprinting her face on his memory for all time.

'It's going to be all right,' he said quietly. 'A few more days here, and then you won't need to worry about this lot ever again.'

She shook her head, hesitating before putting her greatest fear into words. 'But there will be others,' she said eventually. 'Oh, not kidnappers, but there's always someone who wants something.'

'That's what happens when you're indecently rich,' he mocked, sardonic humour bracketing the sides of his straight mouth.

She said acidly, 'Actually, I'm not. Saul's got the money. I'm just something that can be used against him.'

'Did your parents leave you destitute?'

Shrugging, she said, 'I don't know. I suppose they left me enough to keep me out of the poorhouse, but they weren't stupid. Saul is the kingpin, the one everyone depends on; naturally he has the power.'

'What do you mean, you don't know?' He sounded sceptical.

She said defensively, 'Well, I don't.'

'Haven't been interested enough to find out, or has it been kept from you?'

'Of course it hasn't been *kept* from me! I just haven't bothered to find out, that's all. Saul——'

'You're eighteen, and you're making no attempt to train yourself to take the reins of your own affairs?' There was a thread of something perilously close to contempt in his voice, although none of it showed in his face. He tossed a lettuce over to her, saying, 'Here, wash this.'

Stephanie thrust it under the tap, shaking it mercilessly. 'I suppose you think I'm stupid.'

'I know you're not stupid. Do you expect your brother to look after you all your life?'

'Of course not!'

'Then what are you doing about it? What subjects were you going to take at university, always assuming you were planning to go there?'

She bit her lip, because although Saul wanted her to get a degree she had been tempted to follow the example of her best friend and attend a finishing school in France. 'Fine Arts,' she retorted, wrenching the lettuce apart. The crisp leaves exploded in her fingers.

'And then a stint of working at Sotheby's, I suppose,' he said curtly, 'while you find some chinless wonder to marry.'

'That's so old-fashioned.' She exaggerated her accent, clipping the words savagely to give emphasis. 'It's a new world out there now. All the chinless wonders have careers in merchant banks. And I certainly don't want to work at Sotheby's.'

'At least it's a job. How are you going to fill in your days? Lunching and going to beauty salons?'

'Don't worry, I'll manage it somehow.'

He was only repeating what Saul had been telling her for the last few years, and in a somewhat milder form, but Saul had her best interests at heart. Duke didn't even know her well enough to know what her interests were.

'You're drowning that lettuce.' He leaned over to turn off the tap. For a second she felt his closeness like the brush of something at once abrasive and potent, as stimulating as the silken texture of fur against her nerves.

Stepping back, she looked around for a bowl to dump the wet lettuce into.

'There's a colander under the sink,' he said. 'A basin with holes in it.'

'I do know what a colander is,' she said stiffly. 'I'm not completely useless.' She found it, took it as far from him as possible, and dropped the lettuce in to drain. Then she said, 'I haven't really thought about what I'll do. Saul wanted me to do a business course of some sort, but it sounds boring.'

'You've left it a bit late to decide, princess,' he said drily, wielding the knife on some tomatoes. 'By your age most people have a reasonable idea of what career they want. Wash that asparagus for me, there's a good girl.'

Anger sparked through her, an anger she kept well hidden because it seemed too strong a reaction to his observation. He had no right to assume that she was an empty-headed idiot with nothing but a good marriage on her mind; she would, she decided, walking across the stone flags to get the asparagus, show him that she was capable of doing whatever she wanted to do.

In spite of Saul's remarks she had always assumed that he would manage her finances, but it really wasn't fair to expect him to do that for the rest of her life.

When I get out of this, she decided, when I get back to real life, I'll ask Saul what he thinks would be the most helpful course for me to take, and this time I'll listen properly to him!

They ate in the kitchen at the huge scrubbed table; for the first time since Duke had hauled her back to life Stephanie enjoyed the tastes and textures of food, finishing the whole plateful. When Duke asked her whether she wanted coffee she shook her head.

'No, I don't drink it, thank you.' A yawn sneaked up from nowhere, and she said, surprised, 'I wonder why I'm so tired.'

'Today is the first day you've been up.'

Well, of course. She rose, saying as steadily as she could, because the thought of him joining her in the big bed was doing odd things to her stomach, 'So it is.' Her gaze fell on the dirty plates. 'Do you mind if I leave you with the dishes?'

'No,' he said gravely, standing.

She blinked. He was so tall, he seemed to fill her vision. Very rapidly she said, 'Goodnight.'

But he came up with her, waiting in the bedroom while she showered and pulled on the T-shirt she wore at night. He had left his dressing-gown on the back of the door; she looked at it for a moment, then left it there. Her back was very stiff as she came into the bedroom.

Not that he noticed; he was sitting in the chair, looking at a book he had brought up that morning because he thought she might be interested in it. She suspected that he'd chosen it because it was a romance. Unfortunately it was one she'd already read.

'Do you want to read for a while?' he asked, when at last she was under the duvet.

'No, not tonight.' Her tone was as distant as his, her expression as controlled.

'Then I'll go down. Don't put the light on.'

Stephanie looked up sharply. 'Did you find something out in the village?' she asked, trying to hide the note of fear in her voice.

He shook his head. 'Not a thing. Let me do the worrying, Stephanie. That's what I'm here for.'

But when he had gone she lay in the darkness, watching stars as big and clear as diamonds on rough velvet, and wondered. Something about the way he had said she wasn't to turn on the light had set alarm bells ringing. He might not be in contact with Saul, but that didn't mean he wasn't able to talk to others. Perhaps he had a scanner and had picked up some shred of information from it. Or had he overheard a remark in the village that had made him uneasy?

Because he was—well, uneasy probably wasn't the right word. He seemed electric, focused, as though all his formidable resources, physical and intelligent, were concentrated on some problem.

She was sure of it, as sure as she was that he wouldn't tell her what that problem was.

Quelling a bolt of incipient panic, she told herself that of course he'd have some sort of security system rigged. A cautious man, he called himself. He'd admitted it was highly unlikely that anyone was watching them, yet he made her stay inside and keep away from the windows just on the off-chance. Even, she thought resentfully, hauling his T-shirt down over her hips, to the extent of keeping her without clothes in case someone went through their laundry!

It was just her bad luck that he was the most compellingly attractive man she had ever met. He had that impressive aura of—authority, although it was more than that. An impregnable, leashed toughness that even his kindness couldn't hide emanated from him and set him apart.

Wincing at the ache in her thighs and calves, she stretched her legs. Stone floors were hard on muscles that hadn't been used for some days. Tomorrow she'd start exercising.

Eventually she drifted into an uncomfortable sleep, waking in the morning with a thick head and heavy eyes to the sound of something being put down on the bedside table. Normally he moved noiselessly, so he must have meant to make the little clink that woke her.

'Bad night?' he asked, straightening up. The orange juice he'd just deposited glowed brilliant in the sunny room. 'You spent quite a lot of it muttering.'

The casual comment flicked an obscure anger. He didn't need to sound so—so untouched, as though sleeping with her meant absolutely nothing to him.

But then, it didn't.

He smelt of fresh air and sunlight and the soft, ever-present fragrance of pines and grass and wild flowers.

Suddenly overcome by a hunger to escape from this silly mock-castle, from the whole dangerous charade, Stephanie said brusquely, 'Sorry,' and sat up, carefully pulling the sheet and duvet with her. 'What's it like out?'

'Glorious.' He stood observing her with the speculative scrutiny she found so unnerving. 'Getting a touch of cabin fever?'

It was maddening, the way he seemed to be able to gauge her attitudes and moods while withholding any hint of his. She drank half the glass of orange juice before answering, 'Yes.'

'Hang on to your composure for a while. I don't know how much longer this will last, but it looks now as though things are going down fast.'

'I thought you weren't in contact with Saul,' she said.

'I'm not, but I am in contact with other people,' he answered promptly, looking amused, as though he could see through her attempts to find out what was going on. 'Cheer up, princess; soon you can go back to your nice, safe cocoon with nice, well-paid minders to keep you out of trouble, and then all of this will gradually fade like the memory of a nightmare. You probably won't ever forget it, but it won't ruin your life.'

The note of irony in his voice hurt damnably, but she retorted crisply, 'I don't intend to let any greedy thugs affect *my* life, thank you.'

His hard mouth compressed into a smile, humourless, almost cynical. 'That's the way,' he said. 'Arrogant to the wire. Are you coming down for breakfast, or shall I bring it up?'

'I'll be down in ten minutes.' With narrowed eyes she watched him leave, hating the way he called her princess, but because she knew he expected her to demur she refused to object. A day would come, she vowed darkly as she flung the bedclothes back, when she'd tell him exactly how she felt about it. And about other things, too.

After her shower she got into his dressing-gown, rolling up the sleeves and tying the cord several times around her thin waist before setting off down the stairs and through the great hall.

Again they ate in the kitchen, one part of which was chiselled out of the side of the mountain; on the other the hill fell away abruptly to reveal a steep-sided valley carved out by glaciers before the ice had retreated twelve thousand years ago. Through the eastern windows the sun streamed in a golden flood, glamorising the workaday room with its magic.

'What did your contact tell you about the situation?' Stephanie asked.

'It seems that your brother has everything under control.'

'Well, of course he has,' she said absently. 'Is he any closer to the men who actually set this kidnapping up?'

He said coolly, 'There's a possibility they may be disaffected members of your family who told the kidnappers to neutralise you. No, listen. Someone, as yet unknown, is mounting an attempt to dislodge your

brother from his position as head of Jerrard's. If he
didn't know where you were, and was afraid that you
were dead, or close to it, he certainly wouldn't be giving
the bid his best attention.'

When the implications of that sank in, she put down
her knife, her appetite departing in a sickening rush.
'That's a foul thing to say! Uncle Stephen wouldn't do
that. Oh, I know he dislikes Saul, but he's family. He
wouldn't use me like that. And neither would Uncle
Edward, or Patrick.'

'It's only a possibility. Even if it's true, they almost
certainly wouldn't have intended to have you abused so
viciously,' Duke said crisply. 'They'd have wanted you
held, but they wouldn't have known what methods the
men they paid would use to do that.'

She shuddered. 'No. I don't believe it.'

'Finish your breakfast.'

She said numbly, 'I can't.'

'Yes, you can. You need to eat, princess.'

When she shook her head, he ordered inflexibly, 'Eat
it.'

Stephanie flashed him a furious look, but the cold
and controlled menace in his eyes made her blink. He
was angry, and it was not because she refused to eat her
breakfast. Uncowed, she nevertheless found herself
picking up the slice of toast and biting into it.

'The rumours may be wrong,' he said, as though the
naked exercise of power had never happened. 'Unfortunately we have to look at every possibility, not just
the ones that appeal most to you.'

She chewed that thought over with her toast. 'My
uncles might have been greedy,' she said eventually, 'and
the battle they fought for Jerrard's took some very nasty
turns, but they aren't criminals! Isn't Saul's money
enough reason for me to be kidnapped?'

'Twenty million excellent reasons.'

She picked up another piece of toast and buttered it.
'My uncles would never consider doing such a thing.

They know Saul. After what happened when my parents died,' she said at last, her voice very steady, *'everyone* knows Saul is not in the habit of being conned. And that he is very protective—ruthlessly so—where his family is concerned.'

He appeared to know what she was talking about— the merciless revenge Saul had inflicted on the men who'd thought they could use his parents in their brutal bid for power. He had hunted down every man, even the ones who had worked in the kitchen of the jungle camp that had seen his parents' last, anguished days.

'I suppose they thought that any man has his weakness.' Duke resumed his substantial breakfast. Of course a man his size would have to get through a fair amount of food just to keep that big body going.

Smiling tightly, Stephanie spread marmalade on to her toast. 'Not Saul.'

He showed his teeth in a smile that lifted the hairs on the back of her neck, but before he had time to reply there was a hearty knock on the back door, followed by a vigorous rattle of the handle.

Duke looked at her with flat, deadly eyes and said, in a chilling monotone so soft that no one more than three feet away would have been able to hear, 'Get into the pantry, and whatever happens don't make any noise.'

She leapt to her feet and raced across the stone flags. Wordlessly, unable to hear anything above the irregular thunder of her pulses, she dragged open the heavy, old-fashioned door of the pantry and dived through, closely followed by Duke with her plate and knife in his hand.

Another rap on the door made her heart leap into overdrive. As Duke called with a subtle change of inflexion, 'All right, I'm coming!' she snatched the utensils, and watched as he disappeared, closing the door softly behind him.

The lock was not the elaborate Victorian extravaganza she expected, but another smoothly turning, heavy modern one. Duke's hand on the other side sent the deadlock home. The snick as it slid into place made Stephanie jump; for a second the panic she had been trying so hard to overcome surged back, tightening her skin, sending her pulse booming in her ears. Moving with the instinctive care of shock, she put the plate and knife down on the bench.

Be logical, she commanded her frantic brain and body. Of course there was no need to have a locking system on her side of the door. This was, after all, a pantry—butter and ham and vegetables didn't try to escape! But trying to jeer herself out of her mindless fear didn't produce the instant calm and clear-headedness she craved. Perhaps the days spent in the crypt had given her claustrophobia, because a horrible turbulence knotted her stomach.

She sat down on a set of steps, waiting for the nausea to recede. In a few minutes the intruder, whoever he was—a goatherd, perhaps—would leave, and Duke would come and let her out.

Relax, she told herself. Look around you, see what's for dinner tonight. *Pull yourself together*!

Her dilated eyes roamed across wooden shelves lining the wall except for where an elderly refrigerator loomed; she sought the homely comfort of the foodstuffs, only to realise with a jolt that the writing on the packets was in a foreign language. German. For some strange reason that was another blow aimed at her equilibrium.

She forced herself to continue her survey. Cupboards with misaligned doors crouched beneath a well-scrubbed wooden bench. High in the northern wall a narrow window provided dim illumination. Even without the bars that gave it the ominous look of a prison cell, it wasn't big enough to crawl out of...

You don't have to crawl out of it, she told herself. But the trapped desperation wouldn't go away. She had to *do* something. Getting to her feet, she crept across to the door and pressed her ear against the edge. Although they had strange ideas about what constituted good taste,

Victorian tradesmen had built well. No matter how hard she strained, she couldn't hear anything more than a low rumble of voices through the door's solid timbers.

Defeated, she sat down again, the churning in her stomach increasing, and suddenly realised that if she hoisted the set of steps on to the bench and climbed on to them she'd be able to look out of the window. It seemed like a lifeline; she couldn't bear to crouch like this in the half-darkness, with the shelves threatening to fall down on her.

It wasn't easy, but she managed to get both the steps up and herself on to the bench without any noise. The window looked on to a kind of courtyard which had once, perhaps, led to the stables. By craning her neck she could just see the back door. She stared at it for a few moments, willing their uninvited and unwelcome guest to come through it. It remained obdurately closed.

Balked, she turned her head to glance along the other side of the wall.

It plunged down the mountainside, meeting up with a band of fir trees, dark and thick and impenetrable. Stephanie was assailed by a feeling of *déjà vu*, as though she knew this place, had climbed that slope in innumerable dreams, had smelt the scented balsam of those whispering sentinels of trees.

On the edge of her vision was a gnarled relic of the glacier moraine, a huge, twisted boulder embedded in firs. At the base of that rock, she knew, was a crevice where—where Duke had hidden her before he'd slid through the forest like a huntsman stalking his prey.

No, she thought, shutting her eyes for a moment. Rocks thrust their way through the earth's thin skin on every mountain in Switzerland. She was imagining the similarity. Her gaze drifted along the edge of the firs to a tiny white circular temple set with columns and a domed roof that nestled most incongruously against the trees.

'Oh, God,' she whispered. 'Oh, God, oh, God...'

The second time Duke had stashed her in their climb up the mountain so that he could go and reconnoitre, she had glimpsed white columns through the trees and thought she was hallucinating.

She hadn't been. The slope, the trees looked so familiar because she had actually been there. Further down, at the base of the mountain, the fir trees would press closely around an outlying stub that had been hollowed and barred to make the crypt.

The castle was only a few hundred yards up the mountainside from her prison.

A noise from the opposite direction whipped her head around. The back door had opened, and a man appeared; the sun struck his peaked cap. Dressed in non-descript clothes—grey trousers and a blue shirt with rolled-up sleeves and open neck—he didn't look like Stephanie's notion of a goatherd. He just looked ordinary, nothing frightening about him at all.

He turned and walked off through the arched tunnel that must lead to the forecourt. Behind him the door clanged shut.

Panic drove through her like a solar flare. It became imperative not to let Duke know she had seen him with the man. The inchoate suspicions she had been trying to subdue, the intuition that warned her she knew next to nothing about Duke, impelled her down. Swiftly she dragged the steps after her. She was sitting on them, chin in hand, when the deadlock began to slide back and a voice, still muffled by the heavy door, said quietly, 'Stephanie?'

She froze, licking suddenly dry lips, unable to speak. Was it Duke, or someone else? There had been no one else at the door—had two men arrived, and was Duke even now a prisoner? If he wasn't, why was he fumbling as he opened the door? Duke never made an unnecessary move; his predator's grace gave his every gesture a fluid elegance.

Without thought, she snatched the heavy wooden rolling-pin from the bench. Adrenalin pumped through her as she positioned herself to one side of the door. Tensely, she waited, panic and indecision swamped by determination. Her knuckles gleamed white on the handle of the rolling-pin; she forced herself to relax, to be ready.

'Stephanie,' the voice said again.

The door began to open. She braced herself. If there had been another man—— Then Duke walked in.

Some animal instinct warned him. Just in time to stop the rolling-pin from crashing on his head, he ducked and swung, catching her wrist in a numbing grip. The heavy wooden pin fell clattering to the floor.

For a moment they stood motionless, Stephanie's eyes imprisoned by his icy glare, her senses in top gear. His anger was a palpable, living entity in the small room, as fierce and savage as the narrowed eyes that held hers so mercilessly.

Then he smiled, and the freezing fury was gone, banished by an exercise of will that shattered her.

'Damn it,' he complained mildly, 'you could have killed me.'

'For a moment I thought—I thought it might be someone else. Why on earth didn't you say it was you?' she demanded, taking refuge in sheer rage.

'I thought you'd recognise my voice.' The mockery in the deep voice sent her blood-pressure rocketing up.

'I didn't. You scared the hell out of me,' she said robustly. 'Don't do it again!'

'No, ma'am.' He wasn't in the least meek; like his use of the word princess, the 'ma'am' emphasised his refusal to be impressed by her arrogance.

Stephanie didn't care. If he wanted to point out the distance between them she was all for it; she was far too aware of him, unbearably conscious of the pulse beating in the bronzed hollow of his throat, overwhelmed by the sheer size of him, which was both intimidating yet oddly comforting, too affected by the focused male sexuality.

The Stockholm syndrome, she thought scornfully, and asked with what she hoped sounded like crisp hauteur, 'Who was that?'

'One of the locals. He was surprised to see someone here, and wanted to make sure it wasn't squatters.'

She asked, 'Do they have squatters in Switzerland?'

'Not that I'm aware of,' he returned.

Something in the way he spoke, some faint intonation, caught her attention. She looked at him keenly, but there was nothing in his eyes, his expression, to reveal what he was thinking. 'So?' she asked on a belligerent note.

'So I'll take a look around. I don't imagine our visitor is anybody to worry about, but he could have been asked to check out the man renting the castle.'

A cold chill settled in her stomach. 'By whom?'

'We don't know that.'

Although, she thought, bristling anew, some of us have our suspicions. But, try as she might, she simply couldn't see either of her uncles, or her cousin, in a conspiracy like this.

'Remember,' he said, watching her from beneath thick lashes, 'this is all supposition. He was probably just a passing villager who doesn't indulge in gossip.'

She took a deep breath, but she had to ask. 'Why didn't you tell me this castle is just above the crypt?'

Those intense eyes settled on the steps, flicked back to her face. 'Because I knew you'd hate it,' he said casually.

She frowned, wondering whether to believe him, knowing that she mustn't appear to be overly concerned. 'But why did we have to come the long way round in the car? We could just have walked up the hill.'

He said drily, 'The trees are well back from the castle. I didn't want to carry you across the grass in full view of anyone who happened to be looking. At this time of the year there are tourists swarming like ants over every mountain in Switzerland, and tourists talk in bars and clubs.'

She nodded, but persisted, 'Surely it's dangerous? So close?'

'No. The men who kidnapped you would expect any rescuer to take you straight back to your brother. They're not likely to look for you a few hundred yards up the mountain.'

After a moment she nodded. It made sense, even though the thought of that hideous room so close by iced her blood.

'I suppose you're going to lock me in the bedroom again while you're out,' she said.

'Not this time,' he said deliberately. 'You can come with me. In the boot of the car, I'm afraid, and it will be profoundly uncomfortable, but you'll cope.'

Of course he knew that the prospect of being shut up again made her sick with a disgusting combination of helplessness and anger, but one glance at his face told her that he wasn't going to change his mind. Swallowing, she said, 'Yes, all right.'

'Go upstairs and strip everything from the bedroom and bathroom that could connect you with the place.'

'Why?'

He smiled, a meaningless movement of his mouth. 'Just in case someone decides to snoop while we're gone.'

'Oh.' So that was why they were leaving the castle. What would have been fear if Duke hadn't been there abraded her nerves.

'Leave the sheets on the bed and my stuff, but put everything you've used into this bag.'

Within a very few minutes she had emptied the room of anything that might be construed as feminine, ruthlessly stuffing her toothbrush and the hairbrush he'd provided into the plastic bag, even putting in the historical romance she'd been rereading in case they—if *they* came looking—thought it was suspiciously feminine.

When he appeared in the doorway she couldn't prevent a start. 'I wish you'd make a noise,' she said irritably. 'It's not normal for anyone to move as quietly as you do.'

'Don't go imagining kidnappers under the bed,' he advised, giving the room a swift survey. 'The man was probably exactly what he said, and I'm being over-cautious.'

Efficiently he went through the room, searching with an expertise that chilled her further. At last he smiled and said laconically, 'You've done a good job.'

'For a novice. You're a professional,' she commented without inflexion.

He looked at her. 'Yes.'

That was all, but she shivered.

'Never mind, princess,' he said quite kindly. 'It shouldn't be too long before you're safely back home.'

'I don't think I'll ever feel safe again,' she said, striving to conceal the forlorn note with a crisp no-nonsense manner.

'You will. From now on you'll be so surrounded by bodyguards you'll probably never be alone again.'

'A horrible fate,' she said gloomily.

Silently they went down to the car. Without comment Stephanie climbed into the cavity of the boot, endeavoured to get comfortable on the mattress, and closed her eyes, striving to empty her face and mind of any emotion.

'Try to sleep,' he advised tersely.

Her eyes flew open. For a moment sheer panic darkened them. And then, as he bent his head, they darkened even more. Strong hands holding her still, he pressed a kiss on her lips.

'Think about that,' he said harshly, and straightened up. The boot lid clanged down.

Stephanie lay immobile as the engine started up. Through the stunned reaches of her brain and body the glittering promise of his kiss surged like a wild, irresistible tide. Without thought, without holding anything back, her soft, untutored mouth had shaped itself to his in a response that still shimmered through her, sweet as run honey, a mindless, helpless obedience to a summons older than time.

It made her giddy with pain, because now he was well aware of the helpless attraction that clouded her judgement. His kiss had been a calculated power play, and her ardent response would have told him that his influence over her was almost limitless.

As the car eased down the steep drive she wondered what was going to happen now.

The ride seemed to go on for ages. Several times the car stopped, and once she heard the sounds of a busy village street, but the lid remained obdurately closed, and she had to stay quiescent, barely daring to breathe. Much to her astonishment, she finally managed to doze.

At last, however, the sound of the engine died, replaced by an intense silence. Once more Stephanie lay breathing shallowly. Was this merely another route stop, or were they back at the castle?

Time dragged by. Tired, uncomfortable and more than ready to call someone to account for it, she tried to dampen down the anger seething through her. She heard nothing until the lock clicked and someone opened the boot. She lay pretending to be asleep; she had already worked out that if it wasn't Duke she'd have a better chance of getting free if they thought her unconscious. However, beneath the thick fringe of her lashes she recognised his harsh-featured face, and sat up, blinking in the semi-gloom.

When she opened her mouth to ask what was going on his hand snapped out and covered it. Her eyes, already dilated, widened even further. He leaned forward and breathed into her ear, 'The place has been bugged. We have to go.'

Panic dragged her thought processes into a whirlwind. She heard her jagged intake of breath and above the hard command of his hand her gaze sought his face, frantically begging for comfort. Instead, the icy command in his eyes warned her to keep silent as he pushed her inexorably back down, deposited his bag behind the curl of her knees, and closed the lid.

Stiff and cramped, Stephanie lay fuming impotently. At first anger won out over fear, but as the car retraced its path down the side of the mountain a cold, empty pit expanded in her stomach. Exactly when it turned into active nausea she didn't know.

But Duke was with her; she clung to his image like a talisman, a charm to keep the enemy at bay. Duke wouldn't let anything happen to her.

The car was moving fast over the excellent Swiss roads. Once they went through a large town; the car slowed, stopped at several lights. She heard the sounds of revving engines, the occasional hiss of brakes, horns, wrinkled her nose at the odour of other cars' exhaust and winced at the abrupt turns of narrow streets. Once or twice the turns were so sharply taken that she was tossed around and grunted painfully as tender bits of her anatomy met the unyielding surround of the boot.

Losing track of time, she became more and more aware of an increasing discomfort that had to be contained, the very real threat of being sick, so that by the time the car stopped she was barely able to think.

The boot lid was raised. Once more they were in the gloom of a garage of some sort, but this one was smaller than the other, much cleaner and tidier, and lit only by a high window.

'OK,' Duke said soothingly, lifting her out as though she were a child. 'We're here, and as far as I can tell we haven't been followed.'

'Where's here?' she croaked.

'A safe house.'

'Safer than the last, I hope.' Goading him was dangerous, but it gave her some illusion of control.

His mouth tightened into a thin line, but when she staggered his arm came out instantly, supporting her with a rock-like strength. 'It will have to be.'

Returning feeling brought a familiar pain to her limbs. Biting her lip, she relaxed and let it wash over her as she asked, 'Did you suspect that the castle might be bugged?'

'If anyone was wanting to know about the people who lived there it seemed the logical thing to do,' he said quietly, 'so I gave them the opportunity.'

The heat from his big body enfolded her, weakening her. She pulled away, trying to unfog her brain from the memory of his kiss. She asked doggedly, 'Who are *they*?'

'We don't know their identities, but we'd be on safe ground assuming they were the ones who organised your kidnapping.'

Stephanie looked at his face, but no expression escaped the absolute control he imposed on his features. The flashfire of panic that had engulfed her for a second ebbed. 'How did they find out I was there?'

He shrugged. 'I don't know. At least we were ready for them. We'll have to be even more careful here.'

'How do you know no one followed us? Surely that's what they'd have done? It's what I'd have done.'

He looked down into her face. She read a tough, unwavering confidence in his honed features. 'Two cars took it in turns,' he said casually. 'I gave them the slip in Lucerne; by the time they backtrack—if they manage to do it—the trail will be stone-cold.' He urged her towards a door.

Stephanie asked sharply, 'Does Saul know we're here?'

'Yes.' His voice was cool and controlled, giving nothing away.

They were in a modern house, small and white and clean, a chalet with geraniums and begonias brilliant in boxes outside windows shielded by net curtains. On the ground floor the rooms ran into one another, so that they stepped from the garage into a colourful, pretty kitchen and dining-room, and thence to a sitting-room with a panelled front door opening directly into it and a spiral staircase in one corner. There was very little furniture in the place, but its very sparseness after the fake antiquities in the castle gave it a charm Stephanie warmed to. Like the castle it was on the side of a mountain, and outside on the alp the grass was starred with flowers, their bright forms emphasised by the setting sun.

Duke had been watching her, noting her quick survey. Once in the neat sitting-room, he said, 'Never mind, princess, it's almost over. You'll be back home soon.'

'You've been saying that right from the start,' she said half angrily, staring at the blank face of the television screen as though she could see her future in it. 'I'm sick of platitudes. Why won't you tell me anything?'

'Because,' he said deliberately, 'if by some remote chance they recapture you, I don't want you to know anything. That way, you can't be forced to spill any beans.'

Almost, she thought hollowly, she'd prefer evasions, even lies, to this brutal bluntness.

'I see,' she said.

'But that's not going to happen,' he said, and for a moment she thought there was sympathy and understanding in his deep voice. 'It's just that I'm a cautious man.'

She was getting heartily sick of that phrase. 'I need a shower,' she said.

'All right.'

'I wasn't asking permission,' she flashed.

Dark brows shot up. Those piercing, crystalline eyes made a leisurely survey of her flushed face. 'No, I can see that,' he observed.

Immediately ashamed, she said reluctantly, 'I'm sorry. I'm a bit—jittery.'

'You're allowed to be.'

The tone of his voice relegated her to the nursery. She could almost see the words 'spoilt, arrogant child' forming in his brain, and felt like bursting into tears and indulging in a proper tantrum, something she had never done even as a child.

CHAPTER FIVE

AS THEY walked up the stairs Stephanie found herself wondering about the difference she discerned in Duke. Outwardly there was none. He appeared the same—invulnerable, guarded, the uncompromising angles and planes of his face proclaiming an unreachable, adamantine man totally in command of himself and the situation.

Yet senses more discriminating and perceptive than sight assured her that he had changed. He was waiting, she thought, for something he knew was going to happen, alert, poised to respond instantaneously and ruthlessly.

The stairs finished in an open landing with two bedrooms opening off it; the one above the sitting-room was a big, dormitory-style affair, separated by a bathroom from another with a double bed.

'In here,' Duke said, opening the door into the smaller room.

She asked, 'What do we do now?'

'Nothing.' His smile was narrow, mirthless. 'Just what we've always done, princess. We leave the work to others.'

'You'd rather be one of those others, wouldn't you?' He wouldn't tell her, but she was trying to keep her mind off her queasiness. Possibly the exhaust that had penetrated the boot in whatever city they'd passed through had affected her; certainly something had made her stomach a battleground.

His brows climbed. 'Don't you think I make a good nursemaid?'

The ironic undertone told her that he hated this inactivity.

94

She said honestly, 'You make a brilliant rescuer and knight-errant. I may never be able to thank you enough.'

One corner of the hard mouth lifted. 'Don't even try,' he advised. 'Think of yourself as part of my career path.'

Stephanie laughed, as he'd meant her to. 'All right, but just the same—you've been very kind, and I am truly grateful. I won't ever forget what you've done for me, and neither will my brother.'

Even as the words left her lips she knew it was the wrong thing to say. Not that his expression changed, but she felt the sudden chill, the instant, unyielding withdrawal.

'Even better for my career path,' he said, that faint hint of another accent very much to the fore in each drawled word.

His New Zealand connections must be close to have given that flavour to his pronunciation. Embarrassment at her *faux pas* sent heat crawling across her cheekbones. She said clumsily, 'I didn't mean it like that, and you know it.'

'Then what did you mean?' he asked, refusing to allow her any face-saving evasion.

She wished she'd shut up. Her blue eyes shifted sideways, then came back to his face. 'All right,' she said crossly, 'I suppose I did. If it's hurt your pride I'm sorry. But I *am* very grateful, and I always will be.'

'Always,' he said with an odd, humourless, enigmatic smile, 'is a very long time, princess. Don't make promises like that.' And the cold, corroding anger she had sensed disappeared. Now totally businesslike, he said crisply, 'All right, you must be exhausted. Have your shower, and then get into bed. Just remember there's only supposed to be me in the house.'

A fundamental element in their relationship had altered. Her unsubtle promise of material rewards hadn't caused the change, although, she thought miserably, it hadn't helped. Except that she hadn't meant the reward to be financial; she barely knew what she had meant, and at the moment she shied away from searching her soul for the answer.

Perhaps his kiss had done the mischief. No; she would always remember the heart-stopping intimacy of it, but she was sure it had meant nothing to him. He had kissed with skill and bone-melting expertise, so there had been plenty of other women in his life. Her mouth tilted wryly, defensively as she told herself that one kiss pressed on an eighteen-year-old wasn't going to tilt his equilibrium.

But the slightly mocking camaraderie had been replaced by a steely inflexibility. Possibly his professional pride was hurt. After all, he had promised to keep her safe, and although he'd kept his promise they'd been driven from the castle.

Unable to respond to the cheerful surroundings, so different from the castle's mock-Gothic splendour, she looked around the bedroom with a heavy heart. This was like a doll's-house, fresh and small and newly painted, although most dolls'-houses had far more elaborate furnishings than this. Here there was only a bed and a shiny cream wardrobe.

The grabbing bitterness in her stomach urged her towards the tiny bathroom. If she was going to be sick she wanted some privacy for it. 'I'll have that shower,' she gabbled.

'A good idea. I'll be back in a few minutes with some food.'

Once she was in the shower the nausea decreased so swiftly that by the time she had dried herself and her hair she was feeling much better. Nevertheless, she obeyed Duke's command and got into the bed, although when he appeared with a tray she said, 'I'm not hungry, Duke.'

'Tension,' he said calmly. 'Eat up, there's a good kid.'

'I'm not a kid!'

His dark brows drew together. 'Then act like a mature adult,' he said coolly, 'and refuel. You went without lunch; you must be hungry.'

Perhaps he was right. It could be lack of food that was making her stomach grumble testily. Sullenly, knowing she was behaving badly yet unable to stop herself, she lifted the knife and fork and ate while Duke stood watching. She felt like a child told that it couldn't leave the table until its plate was clean.

It didn't help matters that he was right; she did feel much better, at least physically, for the food.

'What's your problem?' he asked, startling her.

Seized by a temptation to tell him exactly what her problem was—in order, she realised, that he could convince her she was wrong—she drained the last of the too sweet orange juice and muttered, 'I'm frightened, I suppose. I want this to be over, life to be the way it was before.'

Wide shoulders moved in a slight shrug beneath the fine cotton of his shirt. 'Life will never be the same again,' he said dispassionately. 'You're setting yourself up for a fall if you think it will be. You can never go back. That doesn't mean you can't be happy, because of course you can, but it won't be the same happiness.'

Stephanie darted him a resentful look. The forceful features were completely without sympathy. Not for him any easy, lying platitudes.

'I know,' she said, capitulating. She added with a painful smile, 'I suppose I just want my mummy.'

His answering smile was wryly sympathetic. 'I know the feeling. It will soon pass, and in the meantime you need rest. Try to get some.'

She waited until he had left the room before lying back, but almost immediately knew that whatever was wrong with her stomach was not lack of food.

Ten minutes later she walked quietly out of the bathroom, relieved that he hadn't come up to check on her. Now that her stomach was empty she felt amazingly better, but tired.

Almost immediately exhaustion and emotion overtook her, and she dropped off to sleep, waking much later with a dry mouth and an incipient headache. An automatic glance at her naked wrist made her decide angrily that she was going to demand a watch. It wasn't the first time she'd wanted to know the time, and apart from finding it infuriating she hated being without any of the familiar things that reinforced her identity. However, the room was dark with the shadows of evening, so she had slept for quite a long time. Turning her head, she saw that the other side of the bed was empty, so it couldn't be too late.

At least, she thought after an experimental check on her well-being, the gripe in her stomach had gone. A headache nagged dully behind her brows, making her brain sluggish and thick, and in her mouth there lingered a faint, unpleasant taste, but she felt a lot fitter than she had when she'd gone to sleep.

Yawning, she slid out of the bed, went into the bathroom, and got a glass of water. It ran cool and refreshing down her throat, and she felt much better, good enough to go downstairs. Duke's dressing-gown hung on the back of the door; she shrugged into it, tied it around her waist, rolled up the sleeves and set off.

The house was so still, she almost expected to find the door on to the narrow upper landing locked, but it opened without impediment, swinging back silently. Nevertheless she hesitated, the hairs on the back of her neck lifting.

You're being utterly stupid, she told herself. Go on, go down, right now.

But she lifted her feet slowly, carefully as she walked out on to the landing.

And then she stopped, because voices floated up the spiral stairs. Muted voices, so that she couldn't hear the words, but voices nevertheless. And something in the timbre told her that Duke wasn't simply watching television or listening to the radio, although there was the sound of electronic conversation in the background, conversation in another language.

Over the sound of the Swiss German, someone—not Duke—was talking in English.

Panic thickened her throat, caught her by the nerves and strangled her, so that she stood frozen and witless until some atavistic survival instinct smashed the shackles of horror. If Duke was in danger she was damned well going to do something about it, not die of fright.

Holding her breath, she crept towards the top of the staircase, carefully avoiding the edge so that she couldn't be seen. After strained moments of hearing no distinguishable words, she lowered herself to the floor. Surprisingly, the position seemed to sharpen her hearing.

'Right,' Duke said, his voice imperturbable, and she relaxed, only to tense again when he went on, 'So tell me what's so important that you had to come here. And make it quick. I gave her a knock-out pill to keep her under, but I'm a cautious man and I don't trust them.'

'I came here to tell you that someone followed you.'

'I know,' Duke said impatiently. 'You did.'

'And one of Jerrard's men.'

'Rubbish. I'd have seen him.'

'Perhaps you're not such a good getaway man as you thought.' Satisfaction tinged the other man's tone. 'Because he's here.'

Stephanie knew that voice. It belonged to the younger of the two men who had kidnapped her, the one who had wanted to rape her and found her helpless, shackled resistance funny. For one hideous moment the blood drained from her head. She shook it impatiently. She felt so slow, so stupid...

Duke's voice echoed hollowly in her ears. 'Who is he?'

'Hell, how should *I* know? Calls himself Nicholson. He's Jerrard's man, that I do know. He was one of the ones closing in on the castle. Sounder recognised him— he ran across him couple of years ago.'

Duke cursed.

'Yeah, well, he's here, so you're going to have to kill the girl and get up to the top road as soon as you can.

And don't waste any time about it. Jerrard's lot are going to be here in spades before the night's over.'

Shaking, her heart thundering loudly in her ears, Stephanie closed her eyes. More than anything she wanted to believe that this was a dream, that those terrifying words were simply grim fantasies caused by an overheated imagination, the aftermath of her imprisonment in the locked crypt. She couldn't bear the wait until Duke spoke. Each moment seemed to stretch out, to dance crazily on the edge of eternity, until the sound of his voice, cool and indifferent, crashed against her eardrums.

'Bloody hell,' he said dispassionately.

'I wouldn't mind giving you a hand. The bitch fought like hell when we snatched her,' the other man said nonchalantly. 'She managed to rip Sounder's Balaclava off, and he's not too keen to have her testify in court. Or to have her brother know who he is. He's got a reputation for revenge, has Jerrard.' So matter-of-fact was his tone that Stephanie's doubts oozed away. He laughed. 'He wrapped those dagoes that killed his parents up in tinsel and handed them to the law. Most of them got a firing squad. He'll do the same to us if she's still around to identify anyone. You'll be the first they find. Not too many men of your build around. Anyway, we can do without the publicity.'

He paused, then asked with sly malice, 'Squeamish, Duke.'

'A bit,' Duke admitted without emotion. 'I don't like killing women. However, it will be easy enough to smother her. And what do I do with her body?'

'There's a pit in the garage. Leave the car over it. Looking for her should keep them busy for a couple of days,' he said cheerfully.

Even through her horror, Stephanie noticed the alteration in the newcomer's voice. Now he sounded matey, almost friendly, as though Duke's cold-blooded lack of concern had calmed some suspicion.

'What's she like in the sack? Bit skinny for my liking, but she looked as though she could be quite tasty. I wouldn't have minded a go at her myself—I've never had a rich bitch—but we saw a couple of bloody hikers in the woods when we were carrying her to that weird dungeon. They didn't see us, but he's a bit of an old woman, is Sounder, and he threatened to lock me in with her when I suggested a quick tumble.'

Duke said nothing, and the second man continued in a slightly dampened manner, 'Not that I care. When this is all over there's going to be money like you've never thought of before. We'll be as rich as Jerrard ourselves, and the girls'll be lining up to get into our beds.'

Duke laughed. 'That's worth a bit of grief,' he said easily. 'Right, you'd better get out of here.'

The other man said something so crude that Stephanie quite literally didn't believe her ears, then laughed. 'All right, I'm going.'

Stephanie had thought she was so shocked that nothing could have added to her terror. She discovered now that she was wrong. Something inhuman in Duke's tone when he'd spoken of killing her, at once casual and merciless, screwed her fear up a further, unbearable notch.

Soft sounds of movement coming towards her brought her heart into her mouth. Oh, God, were they coming up the stairs? The sound of a door opening made her sag with relief. No, they were going out the front—why didn't they go through the garage so she could make a break for it through the front door?

Not daring to breathe, she inched forward, peered over the edge. Duke stood in the doorway.

Go *on*, she thought, willing him to move out. Please, God, let him go out, so I can——

He said something and stepped back in, closing the door. Stephanie shrank back as he turned, but he didn't look up. Instead, he went across to the television and turned the sound up. He sat down in a chair, his back to the staircase.

She eased away from the edge and crawled back into the bedroom, her mind clamped into impotent anguish by the sudden, appalling truth. It was too much to have her latent suspicions flushed so brazenly into the open. She had to get out of here, and it looked as though the only way she could do it was through the window.

Holding her breath, she made her way across the room, testing the casement with cautious fingers. It was now dark, and she could see nothing but the faint glow of light from the downstairs windows on the grass. Desperately she heaved on the window-frame, but she couldn't force it past a certain distance, and there was no way she could climb through the narrow gap. She was a prisoner, had always been a prisoner.

A hideous thought struck her. Had it been *Duke* who set up the whole situation? Had he arranged the brutal kidnapping, the will-sapping time spent in the claustrophobic darkness, to establish a docile hostage he didn't need to watch nearly so closely?

Somehow she had to get out of this neat little prison. What was she going to *do*?

In books hostages seemed to find ways out of their predicaments with astonishing inventiveness, but her mind was totally blank. Not only that, she had fallen so rapidly into some sort of emotional dependency on Duke that in spite of the evidence of her ears she was still trying to find some logical reason for his words.

She had told him things about herself that she'd never divulged before, had slept in his arms with the trust and faith of a baby. Wincing, she thought she'd been utterly pathetic, her need for security conspiring against the cooler dictates of her brain.

Because her suspicions had been roused early. Stupidly, she'd let him disarm them. And now he was going to kill her. If she got out of this she was never ever going to let her hormones guide her behaviour again. At least she had one thing on her side; her bout of nausea had stopped the knock-out pill before it was able to plunge her into deep unconsciousness.

It must have been in the orange juice, she thought, tasting again the sweet sickliness.

Her heart pumped like bullets in her chest, forcing adrenalin through her bloodstream as she stepped hastily back. She stood motionless, drinking in the sweet night air, cudgelling her brain for help.

Prince of ice had been right, but prince of lies was even more appropriate. It explained things that had kept nagging at the back of her mind: his refusal to take her home to Saul, the fact that she had no clothes and had to wear his T-shirts or go naked, the insistence on secrecy...

And the keys. Of course he'd been able to get the keys to open the crypt, and the box, and the handcuffs.

Her hand stole up to her throat, covering the rattling pulse there as though she could calm it down by touch.

Oh, God, she had been such a fool! Oh, God, oh, God, oh, God...

Her thoughts jangled endlessly around inside her skull while panic caught her in its sticky clutches.

Think, she told herself. For God's sake, think! Forget that he's been kind, ignore the fact that he's rescued you from hell, looked after you—Duke is the enemy.

And in spite of his pragmatic distaste for it, he was going to kill her. Stupefied by the mixture of panic and shame that surfaced so quickly in her mind, she pressed her lips together to hold back a scream and began to search the room silently for something to defend herself with.

So he turns you on, she told herself, using scorn and contempt to defeat the terror. That's all right; you're not the first woman to be excited by a murderer. At least you've got a chance...

Hastily she scanned the wardrobe, glancing over her shoulder from time to time in case he was coming up the stairs with those noiseless steps.

Nothing in the wardrobe. Moving swiftly, noiselessly, she crouched to look under the bed.

People could do the most atrocious things for money, or for power, or for their beliefs.

Girls at school had pretended to be her friends because she was rich, some of them weaving so seamless a fabric of deceit that she had been entirely taken in; women had pretended to love her brother, eyeing his assets with greedy glances as they'd cooed at her, spoken lying words of adoration to him.

Nothing under the bed. Hurriedly, she tiptoed into the bathroom. By now her eyes were accustomed enough to the dark to be able to see quite well, but even so the only thing that in any way approximated to a weapon was her toothbrush, and that was a pitiful weapon against Duke.

She stood with her hand against her mouth, keeping back a primitive cry of outrage and pain.

Nothing else, not even a hair brush, or a heavy book.

Duke must have set her up in the pantry to see whether she would actually defend herself. Once he knew she would, he'd made sure the cupboard was bare. Well, the toothbrush was better than nothing. If she managed to thrust it into his eye...

The prospect made her feel sick, but she clung to the image, trying to psych herself into the right frame of mind.

She crept back to the staircase, but he was still watching television. Once more in the room, she searched yet again for something to hit him with, but there was nothing she could use. The wardrobe had no drawers she could pull out. Her fingers clenched on the toothbrush.

Fear kicked hard in the pit of her stomach. Each moment that went by brought her closer to her death, and she couldn't do anything about it.

She was crouching by the window trying to make out the mechanism that kept it closed when she saw the lights

below go out. Whatever reprieve she'd had was over.
Well, she thought defiantly as she stood up and raced
across to the bathroom, she was damned if she was going
to make it easy for him. The only hope she had was that
he'd admitted to being squeamish. She was awake, not
lost in drugged sleep; it wasn't going to be as easy as a
pillow over her face while she slept.

Just possibly, he wouldn't be able to do it.

While she had been wrestling with the window an idea
had popped into her brain, an idea she'd examined with
avid urgency. If she could lure Duke into making love...
Both men and women were at their most vulnerable then.
There were ways to disable a man for long enough to
give her a fighting chance.

He appeared in the doorway, a darker thickening of
the darkness, coalescing out of the night like some demon
lover. She knew then. The danger she was in was real
and clear; she could sense his tension across the room,
the subtle change of his body chemistry. Her hair stood
up all over her skin, pulled tight by thousands of min-
uscule muscles left over from primeval times, and the
quick fix of fear-induced hormone cleared her brain
miraculously. Until then she had been operating on mixed
signals, unable to believe that he really meant her harm;
now she knew, and her mind and body joined forces.

'What's the matter?' he asked harshly, coming into
the room.

The drug. He'd expected her to be sleepy and dazed.
'Something woke me,' she said, yawning, making her
voice slow and stupid. 'I had a drink of water. I was so
thirsty.'

She couldn't see him, but she could feel him relax.

'Sorry, I should have turned the television down,' he
said smoothly, coming across to her. 'Hop back into bed.'

For a moment she wavered, then said drowsily, 'My
legs won't carry me.'

He hesitated before catching her up in his strong arms. How could he be so evil when he held her so sweetly, so tenderly?

'Why have you got your toothbrush clutched in your hand?' he asked, sounding amused. Or trying to sound amused, she thought shrewdly.

'My mouth tasted nasty,' she said, as though that explained it. Afraid that he might realise why she had it, she murmured his name in as sultry a voice as she could manage. As she felt his breath lift his chest she turned with a fluidity of motion she had never experienced before and, driven by instincts that had lain waiting for this moment, kissed the hollow in his throat where his pulse beat heavily.

'Stephanie?'

For the first time ever she had succeeded in surprising him. She had to hold that element of surprise. 'Dear Duke. You're so good to me...'

With something like hope she felt the involuntary reaction that scorched through him, a response that had evaded the reins of his will. *Yes*, she thought, dazed by her success. This was the way to do it. First the seduction, and then the swift, crippling knee to the groin...

She followed that swift, tentative kiss with others across the neck of his shirt, until he dropped her into the bed, saying grimly, 'Stop this, Stephanie.'

The toothbrush went under the pillow. Making herself sound bewildered, she pulled him down. 'Why, what's the matter?'

Although he hadn't been expecting it and she might have caught him off-balance, she suspected that he came down on to the bed because he wanted to, and for a moment her resolve faltered.

She set her jaw. She was going to use woman's oldest weapon, the persuasive lure of her sexuality, to get out of this deadly trap, and then, she thought as she ran her hand up his arm and over the taut muscle of one broad shoulder, she was never going to trust another man again.

Making that initial caress was shamefully easy because, although her brain understood that she was in dire danger from this man, his dynamic masculinity clouded her resolution. Common sense whispered despairingly, but the last flickering warning of her conscious mind was close to being wiped out by the blatant electioneering of her own body.

Although she almost yielded to the heated tide of passion that rolled over her, and her breath shuddered in her lungs as she pressed her body against the powerful length of his, she knew what she was doing, and why. Like all whores, she thought wearily, she had to make sure he got his money's worth while she kept possession of her wits. It was like being split between her brain and her body.

Detachment didn't come without effort. One Stephanie kept guard while the other drowned in sensation, no longer resisting the feral need that clawed and pierced. Mute anger drove her to bite him, setting sharp white teeth to the ridge of his collarbone, then licking delicately along the mark. He tasted of salt, and musk, and the evocative flavour of male, primitive and wild.

'Stop that,' he said, but a deep, slow sensuality in his voice told her that she had won.

'Make me,' she retorted, and lowered her head to find the hard little point of his nipple. His chest lifted and for the first time in her life she heard the excited thunder of a man's heart.

He groaned something, the noise echoing in her ear, and when she moved sinuously against him he finally surrendered, an impatient hand beneath her chin lifting her face so that he could kiss her. His mouth was rapacious, hungry, as he made himself master of hers, returning fire with fire.

Body and mind duelled in a fierce, silent battle; her mind won, but barely, and then only because it occurred to her that he might use this moment to kill her.

So her shiver as his mouth took hers again in a kiss beyond desire was only partly caused by passion. Somehow, she thought confusedly, the keen edge of danger intensified everything, forced her responses into unnatural and all-consuming intensity.

And perhaps, although she didn't understand how, a naïve corner of her heart still trusted that he wasn't the callous professional criminal he had seemed to be, but the man who had cared for her and comforted her and held her warm in his arms to keep the nightmares at bay.

When he kissed her throat and ran a shaking hand down her shoulder and over her breasts, it was not entirely fear and outrage that made her shiver.

'I was afraid of this,' he said in a gritted voice that told her how savagely he was struggling for control. 'Stephanie, you're too sleepy to know what you're doing.'

'I've wanted this since that first night.' Her slurred tones held nothing but complete conviction.

'I know,' he said, his voice rough and intense, 'but we can't, not now.'

'Why?'

She held her breath, but instead of answering her fears he said, 'Because you don't really know what you're doing. Go back to sleep, my little love, and if you still feel the same way tomorrow morning we'll do something about it.'

His fingers tightened deliciously on her breast, as though he was reluctant to leave her. She arched against him, gave an involuntary wiggle of her hips, and felt the sudden tension in his big body, the quick, indrawn breath.

'No,' she said huskily. 'Now, Duke, now,' and she wriggled against him again, feeling the hard ridge that told her how aroused he was.

His mouth crushed hers, forcing it open, exploring the sweet depths as he responded to her provocation with a strong thrust of his narrow hips.

Sensation shot through her, violent and uncontrollable, like a flashfire. At that moment she wanted nothing more than to take him so deep inside her that he would no more think of killing her than he would of killing himself.

Lifting his head, he kissed the length of her throat, his mouth a heated brand against the smoothness of her skin. Exulting, Stephanie traced down the tense muscles of his back, pulling him into her, cradling him in the bowl of her hips—and felt the keys in his hip pocket. And although the fire and urgency in her blood didn't fade, the red tide receded from her brain and she knew that this was her chance. She slid her hand into his pocket, kissed the side of his throat and said, 'These are going to be uncomfortable in a minute,' and took the keys out.

His head came up, but when she dropped them on to the floor he kissed her again, this time on the sensitive hollow beneath her ear. Swallowing, because she could feel her control slipping away from her down silken paths of physical pleasure, she sent her hand past his lean hip, and onwards.

Remembering what a friend had told her about teasing a man, she stilled her fingers before deliberately stroking across the straining flesh. She had read books; she had listened to more experienced girls discuss the male psyche; she just hoped that everyone was right when they said that men were at the mercy of their hormones.

His body clenched and his arms clamped her against him, but at the moment of her triumph he reimposed his will. She felt the methodical relaxation of his muscles, the implacable energy with which he fought his battle with the desire that had seemed to have him so completely in thrall. He rolled over on to his back and said gutturally, 'No.'

Fear propelled her across him in an abandoned sprawl, spread her out on top of him; fear drove her kiss. She sank into complete carnal enjoyment of the tastes and flavours of his mouth, relishing the primitive power of his hunger beating through him to her, carrying her off with its consuming intensity.

And then, when it was almost too late, she took her opportunity. It took a supreme effort of will, but it was with all her strength that her knee came up, catching him in the one vulnerable part of his anatomy, and as he jerked and grunted with the ferocious pain she remembered something she had seen on television once and hit him across the throat with the edge of her hand. He slumped, and she flew off the bed, scooping the knot of keys from the floor.

He lay so still that she had to spend a precious second feeling for his breath; in spite of everything, her heart jumped at the rise and fall of his chest. Driven now by an imperative need to survive, she ran from the room and down the stairs, praying that the first key would open the door.

To her complete astonishment it did, which was lucky because she could hear Duke at the head of the stair, his voice thick and distorted as he called her name. God, how difficult was it to knock him out cold? He had to be made of iron. Panic and a queer sort of shame shook her hands as she pushed the door open and slipped through. She pulled hard on it, but her heart thudded high in her throat as she realised it hadn't locked.

He was far too close, moving with his usual lethal speed, showing no sign of the body-blow she had given him as he burst through the doorway. Even as she ran Stephanie knew she'd muffed her chance of escape, but she forced her legs to cover the ground, bare feet stinging on the road, her breath clattering noisily in her chest.

Suddenly, out of the darkness a flat, vicious crack seared her eardrums and at the same instant something whined past. Pain knocked her sideways, flung her off the road and into the black shelter of the firs. More pain rocketed through her shoulder and the side of her head where she'd been catapulted into an overhanging branch, but her cry was muffled by the heavy weight of Duke's body and the hard imperative of his hand across her mouth. She thought he had shot her, but in those moments crushed beneath him she realised that he had saved her from whoever was shooting.

A soft, ghostly whisper from down the hill froze her into terrified stupor. 'Stephanie!'

Instinctively she flinched, but Duke forced her face further into the dry leaf litter on the ground. She felt the movements of his chest as he fought to control his breathing. Desperately she tried to pull his hand from her mouth, but when his other hand came around and gripped her throat in a menacing signal she stopped struggling.

For long moments they lay there. Stephanie could smell sweat mingled with the scent of her own fear, feel Duke's alertness, as keen as that of a hunted animal.

And then Duke got to his feet and pushed her sprawling against the trunk of a fir. Stars swung and catapulted around her head. Her quickly extinguished yelp cut through the cool night air. Cowering, a hand pressed against her cheek, she opened her eyes enough to see two men facing each other, one crouched in the classical unarmed combat position, the other, Duke by his size, motionless a few feet away.

What happened next was imprinted in her mind along with the scent of the fir trees on the crisp mountain air. A blur of motion knocked the first man to the ground. He didn't have a hope, she thought confusedly. One moment Duke had been still as a great predator, lean and cat-like in the darkness, and the next he was speed and savagery and brutal efficiency.

Terrified, she began to crawl down the slope. Another shot sang past her; this time there was no mistake. Duke was trying to shoot her. She huddled along the ground, the coppery taste of blood and fear in her mouth, her face pressed once more into the fragrant leaf litter.

The man on the ground lay without moving. Fighting nausea, Stephanie tried to ascertain whether Duke had murdered him in front of her. The whine of another bullet too close by made her jump again. She closed her eyes in terror. After long moments she opened them again. Duke was standing with his back to her, his head moving slowly as he looked between the trees. And then he was gone, melting into the darkness as silently as a shadow, leaving her as noiselessly as a wounded beast seeking sanctuary. Leaving her to die?

A slight sound dragged her head around. Someone was coming through the fir trees, moving quietly but with speed. Panic kicked deep inside her; she tried not to breathe, tried to still the reverberating tattoo of her heartbeat.

And then the man coming through the wood said her name, and it was Saul. She breathed his name. Instantly Saul raced towards her, catching her as she stumbled to her feet, holding her tight in the warm sanctuary of his arms. But almost immediately he demanded, speaking close to her ear, 'Where is he? The man who was with you?'

'I don't know.' He pulled her behind the inadequate shelter of a fir trunk, shielding her with his body as she whispered, 'He's got a gun.'

'Was he shooting at you?'

She swallowed. 'Yes.'

Saul swore savagely beneath his breath, then asked, 'Are you all right?'

'Yes, none of the bullets hit me, but there's a man on the ground.' Who chose that moment to moan, thereby relieving her immensely. She had been grappling with the knowledge that she had let Duke kill him without lifting a hand to help; now she knew he was alive she relaxed a little, only to tense again when two other men appeared, both with blackened faces, both carrying what to her horrified eyes seemed to be rifles.

'It's Halliday,' one of the new arrivals said, dropping on to his knees beside the man on the ground. 'He doesn't seem to have been too damaged. No broken bones.'

'All right, pick him up. We'd better get out of here before someone comes up from the village to see what's going on. I'd rather not try to explain to the Swiss police what this is all about.' Saul kissed her cheek. 'Come on, darling, not much longer.'

She hesitated. Duke might still be within a few feet of them, waiting for an opportunity to disarm the two able-bodied men and snatch both Saul and her.

Only he wasn't. Something impalpable, something sharp and significant, had gone from the atmosphere.

'Come on,' Saul said again. 'We'll head for the helicopter. Quietly.'

He was wonderfully kind to her, and he stayed kind on the trip across the darkened continent to England; he was kind to her when he made her talk the whole thing through in the days that followed. Candace was kind, everyone was kind; even the police and the men who seemed to have no identity but asked the most penetrating questions were kind in an absent way.

'I feel such a fool,' she said miserably to Candace several days afterwards, when the flow of people who wanted to ask her questions seemed to have dried up. 'Just because he said he knew Saul I trusted him. He said I had the same eyes, and that I looked like the Jerrards.'

Candace took her hand and squeezed it hard. 'You had a very lucky escape,' she said with a shiver. 'He sounds terrifyingly clever.'

'I should have known. I did wonder. When he said that the uncles might be behind it, I refused to believe that.'

'I should jolly well think so! Your uncles would have had a fit if they'd known what happened to you. It was clever of him to use them, though. He must have known a lot about us.'

'Not necessarily,' Stephanie said bitterly. 'I told him about the battle for Jerrard's. He used it against me when it was convenient.' She turned to her brother. 'Saul, I have to know—was Andrew Hastings deliberately rammed in his car so his parents would hurry back to England?'

Saul looked grim. 'It looks like it. The maid was definitely in someone's pay; she doesn't know whose. All she could tell us what that a nice gentleman—a tall gentleman—gave her a couple of hundred pounds to tell him what you were doing, and to suggest you eat at the restaurant that night. He fed her a nice line about a secret lover arranging a surprise. She's not very bright.'

Stephanie put her hands over her eyes. 'I'll never forgive myself,' she said in a muffled voice.

'Darling, you can't take the sins of others on your shoulders.' Candace gave her a hug. 'It's not your fault.'

'If it's anyone's fault,' Saul said, 'it's mine for not looking after you better.'

'It's not yours either,' Candace said robustly. 'Both of you suffer from that well-known Jerrard syndrome, an over-developed sense of responsibility. Stop indulging it right now.'

Stephanie smiled. 'I still feel responsible for Halliday,' she said. 'How is he?'

Her brother got to his feet. 'He's recovering. He didn't take much damage—a chop to the neck that could have killed him. Either it was judged to a nicety, or misjudged.'

The same chop she had used to try and disable Duke. No, she wouldn't think of Duke...

Everyone continued being wonderfully kind to her in the weeks and months that followed, when no one found any trace of the kidnappers, or ever discovered what had happened to the man who called himself Duke.

The prince of lies...

Everyone told her she would get over it, and, of course, she did. It took her a while, but eventually she managed to overcome her residual fear, the pain that had ripped her life into shreds, and the shame that niggled away beneath her other emotions.

However, she never forgot. Occasionally she woke in the night to find herself crying, weeping vainly for something she had never had, for a man who had never existed, for a love that was merely a cruel illusion.

CHAPTER SIX

'SAUL?' Stephanie's voice was amused and astonished.

Her brother lifted his head. Blazing eyes the rare, clear colour of a sapphire took in the letter in her hand. 'What is it?'

'It's from a man who wants to name a rose after me. He says it's exactly the same colour as my hair. How does——' she consulted the expertly typed letter again '—Adam Cowdray know what colour my hair is?'

Saul's eyes sharpened. 'Adam Cowdray?' he said softly, and flicked a glance at his heavily pregnant wife, who was slowly consuming a piece of toast with an absent, inward expression. 'Dear heart, have you heard of a rose-breeder called Adam Cowdray?' he asked.

Candace, in the seven years since she had married Saul, had transformed the gardens of the various Jerrard residences around the world into recognised showpieces. The glorious tropical vista that spread around them now was a tribute to her skill. The English accent she had picked up from her husband and sister softened and deepened by the underlying New Zealand drawl, she answered, 'Of course I've heard of him. Met him, too. The firm's a New Zealand institution, but it's known worldwide. His father produced some wonderful flowers. Maniopoto was one of his, and First Dawn, and rumours have it that the son has inherited his eye and his skill at breeding. Cowdray roses usually do better in milder climates, although his Hinemoa was a real hit at Chelsea a couple of years ago.' Mischief curled her mouth. 'So was the man. Even my unsusceptible heart went pitter-pat, while Lavinia Potts-Neville almost dropped at his feet. One of those magnificent males who *don't* look as though they've just stepped out of *Gentlemen's Quarterly*!'

Saul's brows shot up. 'Did you like him?'

'Oh, yes. He was very pleasant, and didn't freeze me off as abruptly as he did all the others. Although that was probably because he's a New Zealander too. We Kiwis stick together.'

'It could also be that you're very beautiful,' Saul said, the hint of steel in his tone sending Stephanie's brows upwards in turn. It still surprised her that he could show jealousy, even though he knew that his wife was as besotted with him as he was with her.

'Only in your eyes,' Candace said amiably, but something in her tone, in her eyes made Stephanie feel an intruder.

She should, she thought as she put the letter down and picked up a mango, be accustomed to it by now. Although she had her own apartment in London, she spent a lot of time with her brother and his wife and family in the house in the Home Counties that had been the Jerrards' base for centuries. And when Candace had decided that she would like this baby to be born in Fala'isi, the idyllic island in the South Pacific where they holidayed at least once a year, Stephanie had offered to come too, so that as the last months passed Candace would have company. Although Saul stayed close to his wife at all times, in his position some travel was essential.

'*Not* over the breakfast-table,' she said crisply now. 'Behave yourselves, both of you. You're mature people, not adolescents in the throes of your first love-affair!'

Unabashed, they traded a small private smile before Saul transferred his gaze to her. 'Do you want a rose named after you?'

Stephanie's red-bronze head tilted. 'It would be a lovely way to be remembered,' she said doubtfully. 'He says that it's a seedling hybrid tea with a scent like no other rose he's ever smelt. Which could mean it's vile, of course.'

Candace put down her piece of toast. 'Don't be so cynical,' she commanded. 'I can cope with it in your brother, but I'm damned if I'm going to listen to it from you.'

Sometimes Candace's transparent honesty and open, delighted appreciation of life grated painfully, and before Stephanie could stop herself she said on a lightly mocking note, 'Goes with the territory, darling. Too much money, too much power—bad for the character, you know. You were lucky, growing up in your foster homes. At least you never had anyone butter you up because your brother was one of the richest men in the world.'

'That's enough,' Saul said, the smooth note in his deep voice an unnecessary warning.

'Don't take any notice of me,' Stephanie said immediately and penitently. 'I'm a pig, and I got out of bed on the wrong side this morning.'

After a narrow glance Saul went back to his newspaper while Candace observed with a trace of acid, 'I wish you'd both stop treating me as though I'm some delicate little butterfly carrying her illusions around like a banner. I'll have you know that I was looking after myself more than capably by the time I was eighteen. Furthermore, pregnancy does not turn your brain to whipped cream and your feelings to slush!'

Saul's hard face softened fractionally as he looked at her. 'Neither Stephanie nor I think you're stupid and over-emotional,' he said.

'Never,' Stephanie agreed promptly, more than a little guilty at precipitating this. Candace had sailed through her first two pregnancies but this one, five years after the second, was being more of a trial. 'You're bright, you're tough, you run our lives with flair and charm and love, you can intimidate strong men if you want to, and your family adores you. As well, you have the crustiest gardeners on every estate eating out of your pretty little hand, even when you decide to change shrub borders that have been in place for a couple of hundred years. What more do you want, you greedy wench?'

Candace said solemnly, 'Respect.'

'Respect?' Saul sighed. 'Dear God, woman, you're insatiable. You really will have to take some advice about setting your sights too high, you know.'

And that, thought Stephanie, listening to her sister's delighted gurgle of laughter, was what the matter with her was. No one could live with Candace and Saul and not realise how hopelessly, utterly in love the two of them were. In their world, as Stephanie knew well, such love was a rare thing.

In the very newspaper that Saul had put down were discreet headlines detailing the messy break-up of yet another marriage among the rich and famous. Stephanie remembered a woman who had been three years ahead of her at school, a brilliant student and then a radiant bride. She had envied Imogen her fairy-tale marriage yet apparently it had been hollow almost from the day after the huge society wedding.

Love, the kind she wanted, the only kind she would settle for, didn't seem to last in their hothouse circle. Except for Saul and Candace. Even for them there had been tense moments; there were always rumours, and several women in the gutter press had insinuated that they had slept with Saul. Not recently, however; for himself Saul didn't care, but he did for Candace, and the resultant court cases had been prompt, savage, and successful.

Wondering forlornly whether she was going to drift through the rest of her life trying to find the same sort of love, Stephanie looked back at her letter. 'I rather like the idea of having a rose named after me,' she said contemplatively. 'When I wander round the garden at home and listen to Peter talking about Madame Georges Bruant—"she's looking lovely this year; always a good doer, is Madame, although a bit coarse, mind you, for real good looks"—well, I don't know anything about the real Madame Bruant, but her name lingers on and gives me enormous pleasure. Yes, I'll tell him he can do it. Of course, I want to see the rose first.' She glanced up at the address. 'Oh, he lives close to Auckland,' she said. 'I can fly down and do some shopping, see the rose, and come back the next day. Do you want anything from Auckland, Candace?'

Her sister's gaze travelled across a lawn green and lush as they could only be in the tropics, over a bank of trees that positively vibrated with life and fecundity, and on to a lagoon glowing with the colours of a black opal. Greens and blues so deep and intense that they hurt the eyes contrasted with areas of milky opalescence, the gleam of scarlet and crimson saved for the evening when the brief tropical sunset drenched everything in saturated colour. Two children played beneath the shade of a mango tree, chattering in the local Maori language to each other. Holidays at Fala'isi had given both Angharad and Matthew a good working knowledge of the island tongue, a knowledge now being honed by their temporary attendance at the school down the road.

'No,' Candace said simply, transferring her eyes back to the austerely splendid structure of her husband's face. 'Not a single thing.'

A truly happy woman. Sometimes Stephanie found herself wondering if that transparent happiness was merely a cover for less attractive emotions, if beneath it there lurked dislike and growing irritation and the taking-for-granted boredom she had seen so often in other faces.

No, if she started suspecting Candace and Saul she might as well give up and try to lose herself in drugs as others of her privileged set had done, risking everything for the deceitful promise of chemicals.

So she wouldn't worry about them, and she wouldn't look at every marriage as though it might be rotten at the core and ready to break; she'd stop being cynical.

In the meantime there was this business of a rose...

'You'd better give me his address,' Saul said, folding his paper and rising. 'I'll get someone to check it out.'

Wordlessly Stephanie handed over the letter. She knew the rules, none better. Adam Cowdray and his background would be pried into, examined by experts in their murky field, and if anything in the least suspicious turned up there would be no meeting.

Some hours later, still wet from a swim, she paused on her way back to the house beside the only rose that seemed to grow on the island, a small, raspberry-flowered scrambler, and gently touched the warm of the petals.

A flower-breeder, she thought. What a blissful, calm, tranquil career. To spend your life in a garden... She lifted the rose to her face, and inhaled the faint, delicate, unmistakable perfume.

'You're looking pensive,' Candace commented from her lounger in the thick shade of the mango tree. She was embroidering tiny yellow rosebuds on a tiny cream dress. 'Are you getting bored?'

Stephanie sighed elaborately. They had been over this before. 'No, I could never get bored on Fala'isi, and yes, I like being here with you, and with faxes and telephones I can conduct all my business just as well as if I were in London. It should be better, because here we're twelve hours ahead of London, but Saul says that's a fallacy!' She settled the thin twig back into the bush. 'I was just deciding what a rose-grower would be like,' she explained. 'Earthy, I think, yet not too much, because roses are rich and intense.'

Candace moved her bulky figure into a more comfortable position, her dark grey gaze steady and a little speculative. 'Ruthless,' she offered, and when Stephanie looked startled, 'I believe that for every seedling that's worth growing on you have to throw out hundreds, possibly thousands. And he'd need to be patient, too, as well as dextrous.'

'Dextrous?'

'Someone has to fertilise the blossoms,' she explained. 'You can't just hope for a stray bee to do the job, you know. Intelligent, too, to understand the genetics. And you will never know how much I've enjoyed your company here these last few months.'

'Well, it's a terrible sacrifice to give up the scintillating weather of a London autumn for the dreariness of a South Sea island, but virtue is its own reward, they say. No more about it, all right? He'd need to be practical.' Stephanie wandered across to the other lounger and lowered herself into it. 'A good businessman.'

'Reliable, because of the records he'd have to keep, with a dash of the visionary thrown in. And tough.'

Stephanie yawned. 'Tough? Come on now, all that would happen to him would be a few scratches from roses reluctant to give up their pollen for the greater good of rosekind.'

'Don't forget those almost-winners he'd have to discard. Anyway, I've met him, and if ever a man is tough Adam Cowdray is that man. I wonder whether he could be tender too?' Candace pondered this thought, then laughed softly. 'All in all an intriguing character. I'll be interested to see what you think of him.'

'I don't know that I really want to go, but I'm not having the man put out an inferior product in my name.'

'Sometimes,' her sister observed, 'you remind me very much of your brother.'

'He almost brought me up so I suppose some of his attitudes have rubbed off on me.'

'Most of them, I'd say.' Her sister's voice was dry. 'But he did a good job. Still waiting, Steph?'

Before she could stop the small, betraying movement Stephanie turned her head away so that her sister's eyes couldn't see beyond the fall of her hair and the curve of her cheek.

'No,' she said lightly. 'Another thing Saul taught me was never to hanker after lost causes.'

'When you arrived on our doorstep that night I could have killed the man who had done that to you, but— you were only eighteen, love, barely more than a child. No one blamed you for falling for him. He sounded an immensely charismatic man, and he'd cared for you.'

'He was a criminal.' The ugly, uncompromising word hung in the balmy air. Levelly she resumed, 'He tried to kill me.'

'Did he? I've often wondered.'

'I felt the bullets whistle past,' Stephanie said.

'Yes, but have you ever wondered why, if he was that close, he didn't hit you?'

Of course she had, and sometimes she had even allowed herself to hope that he had deliberately missed her. But only a few months ago she had forced herself to face the truth. For the last five years she had been in love with a figment of her imagination, and it was time she stopped it, gave up the lingering miasma of the past.

'Perhaps,' Candace finished, 'he was trying to save you.'

Stephanie smiled obliquely. 'Oh, over the years I've come up with a whole variety of reasons for him to be helping the men who kidnapped me, but none of them fits. He was in it for the money and I was expendable. He did try to kill me. He didn't manage it because I was running like hell, and it was dark. And handguns are not particularly accurate.'

If he'd been caught and put on trial she'd have seen him for what he was, instead of harbouring pathetic hopes that he was some sort of Scarlet Pimpernel figure playing a dangerous double game. It would have been over, and she'd have been able to get on with her life. Instead he'd disappeared as irrevocably as the men who had kidnapped her. Nothing had ever been heard of them again.

Candace persisted, 'Yet he took you out of that horrible crypt. Why did he do that?'

'I think I was only left there to calm me down and make me trust him. They couldn't kill me because obviously Saul needed to know that I was still alive.' It hurt to say it, to remember how naïvely gullible she'd been. 'He knew that if he was kind to me I wouldn't believe that he was one of them.'

Candace frowned. 'Logically it makes sense, but I don't believe you would have been so easily fooled. I've always felt that you have a really good understanding of character. If you fell in love with him——'

'It's called the Stockholm syndrome,' Stephanie interrupted. 'And it's a protective mechanism. Hostages identify with their abductors because it seems the only road to survival.'

'I know.' But Candace persevered, 'All the same, I think there must have been some good in him or you wouldn't have fallen so hard. Oh, women do love criminals, but most of them know damned well they're fools. And you've never been quite convinced, have you?'

She saw too much. For five years Stephanie had tried to persuade herself that Duke was evil, and for five years her emotions had warred with logic.

'Oh, yes, I'm sure. Don't forget poor Halliday. Duke almost killed him.'

'He knocked him out.'

Stephanie said brusquely, 'It was just sheer good luck he wasn't killed. If the blow had been a little harder— it's usually fatal, that chop to the throat.'

'Funny about that,' Candace said. 'Halliday disappeared shortly after that, did you know?'

'No. What's funny about it?'

'Well, he just vanished,' Candace said vaguely. 'And hasn't it ever occurred to you that Duke couldn't manage to hit you when he fired at you, and he didn't kill Halliday, yet everything you've said about him makes him sound like a man who doesn't make mistakes?'

'On the contrary, he made several,' Stephanie said angrily.

'Do you think that he could kill anyone in cold blood?'

Stephanie bit her lip. 'Oh, yes,' she said with remote composure. 'I heard him discuss it, and believe me, he was not philosophically opposed to the taking of life. Of course, he didn't much like killing women, but he was going to make himself smother me. I just wish I could get rid of him,' she cried passionately. 'He made a total and complete fool of me, but however hard I try I can't get him out of my head! Not even by——'

'Not even by falling in love with someone else?'

Stephanie grimaced. 'Not even by falling in love with someone else. Because I did love Philip.' As always when speaking of the man she had planned to marry, her voice took on a defensive note. 'Only...'

Candace supplied the answer she couldn't. 'Only you couldn't go to bed with him. And you could with Duke.'

'I didn't go to bed with Duke. I quite deliberately set out to seduce him so that I could betray him.'

Candace said quietly, 'You did what you had to do to survive. Don't you think it's time to stop punishing yourself because you enjoyed seducing him and wanted to make love properly? You were very young, and very inexperienced...'

'Perhaps I should have slept with him.' Stephanie had never spoken to Candace with such frankness before. In a way, it was desperation, because Duke was still embedded in her life like grit in tar, so deeply established in some rebellious corner of her heart that she didn't seem to be able to free herself from the sinister clutches of her obsession. She said moodily, 'If I had, I might have got him out of my system.'

'Perhaps. You're not ever going to know, and that's what you have to accept. Sometimes in life things don't get resolved. The whole experience was horrifying, and you've come out of it remarkably well, because you were very vulnerable,' Candace said astutely, adding with a shiver, 'Saul wanted to kill him. I was very glad he disappeared so completely. I didn't mind him being dead, but I did not want Saul to go to prison for doing it.'

Stephanie shivered a little. Her brother had some extremely uncivilised responses. 'Let's hope he's moderated his attitudes by the time Angharad grows up.'

'I think it was because he felt so powerless. He's not accustomed to not being able to do anything. As for Angharad, I've no doubt she'll make him see sense,' Candace said placidly.

Both women grinned, for Saul's daughter was as strong-willed as he.

'What's it like living with someone as tough as Saul?'

'You should know, you've lived with him almost all your life.' But Candace smiled, and her voice altered as it always did when she spoke or thought of her husband. 'It's not easy, but then, I didn't expect it to be. He doesn't find it easy to live with me, either. Loving someone is difficult; it gives you strength, but it weakens you too. You've delivered a hostage to fortune. I don't think I'm neurotic but occasionally I wonder what my life would be like if fortune behaved cruelly. Because I know there will never be another love for me like that. Saul is an impossible act to follow.'

Oh, yes, an impossible act.

Yet once Stephanie had been sure she'd discovered a man who measured up to Saul, a man who had come to her in the midst of pain and terror and humiliation and saved her, faced down her demons and fought through hell to rescue her.

Childish sentimentality, she thought now, five years later. At the impressionable age of eighteen, when it was still possible to believe in heroes and princes on white chargers, she had been in dire peril. Duke had rescued her, so she had endowed him with all the noble qualities she wanted in a mate. Instead, he had betrayed her.

The smile that curled her full mouth was more than a little ironic. And she had fooled him.

Candace's voice interrupted her unprofitable thoughts. 'But you can't live like that, worrying about the future. All you can do is take each day as it comes and extract the utmost from it. When are you going to Auckland?'

'Tomorrow. I'll stay a couple of nights—there's a suffrage exhibition I'd like to see while I'm there.'

'Will you call anyone? Guy and Mike Lorimer will be at home; Mike's like me, not travelling at the moment. Their baby's due three weeks after this monster here.'

'I'll see them, of course, but I don't want to socialise.' She stretched out languidly and closed her eyes. 'I don't want to spend too much time there—I'm enjoying this too much.'

The biggest Polynesian city in the world, Auckland sprawled across the isthmus between its two harbours, so intricately interwoven with the sea that even in a plane it was impossible to separate one harbour from the other.

Stephanie shivered slightly as she walked the short distance to the car that waited for her. It was the middle month of spring, but although it was fine the temperature was considerably lower than the balmy airs of Fala'isi. Still, she liked Auckland, even with a nippy little easterly wind blowing off the Pacific Ocean.

Once settled at the hotel she rang the number from the letterhead on Adam Cowdray's letter. A feminine voice answered, middle-aged, brisk, efficient.

No, she couldn't speak to Mr Cowdray, he was busy, but if she'd like to leave a message ...

'Please tell him that Stephanie Jerrard called,' Stephanie said, and left her number. 'I'm going out now, but I'll be back around four.'

'I'll make sure he gets the message,' the secretary said, a hint of frost in her tones.

Probably thinks I'm chasing him, Stephanie thought wryly as she hung up. Ah, well, if he's half as good-looking and charismatic as Candace says, I just might, too!

Saul's security man rang just as she got in from the exhibition. 'Adam Cowdray seems as clean as a picked bone, but we haven't run a full check on him yet. I suggest you take young Robinson with you when you see him,' he said.

It wasn't a command, but Stephanie knew that she had no chance of getting away without the bodyguard's presence. 'OK,' she said amiably.

She had just put the telephone down when it rang again. It was the secretary, still frosty-voiced, who said, 'Mr Cowdray will meet you at the nursery at ten tomorrow morning. It's at Te Atatu.' After giving an address which Stephanie wrote down, she added, 'Please try not to be late. Mr Cowdray is very busy.'

'I,' Stephanie said pleasantly, 'am always punctual. I'm relying on you to make sure that Mr Cowdray is too. Goodbye.'

And she hung up, rather basely enjoying the startled gasp her comment had caused.

She spent the evening quietly with the Lorimers, coming home early because, like Candace, Mike was finding the last stages of her pregnancy tiring.

As she got her key from the desk she thought wearily that she didn't begrudge her friends and relatives their happiness; she merely found it a bitter irony that she couldn't forget the man who strode like a colossus through her past.

The next day was fine and summery, the air softening with the departure of the wind. Stephanie ran down to the car and, smiling, gave the address to the large man behind the wheel.

'How's your wife and the new baby?' she asked, and spent the drive along the north-western motorway catching up. She had known Brett Robinson for several years, and liked him very much, so she listened to his bashful rendition of the delights of his baby with interest. After three sons he was a doting father to the little girl.

The rose nursery was set behind high conifer hedges down a side-road surrounded by vineyards. A discreet sign announced that it was the Cowdray Rose Nursery. Equally discreet white-painted gates were firmly closed.

'I'll open them,' Stephanie said.

'I'll do it.' Brett Robinson was already halfway out, and for the first time she remembered that he was only half-chauffeur. The rest was bodyguard.

Sighing, she settled down in her seat.

Inside, a white-painted office was set in rose gardens, brilliant with the season's flowers. Some distance away behind another, lower hedge was a house, double-storeyed and sprawling beneath an orange tiled roof. A huge jacaranda tree to one side was budding up, the intense violet tips of the branches hinting at the joyous bounty to come.

It was very still, with no sign of anyone about.

'I'll come with you,' Brett said, looking around keenly.

Stephanie was a little uneasy herself. There seemed to be an unusual waiting quality to the warm silence, a feeling that something was happening, or about to happen. Not, she thought wearily, that that was anything to go by; she had felt perfectly safe walking down the silent street in Switzerland a few seconds before the kidnappers had struck.

Still, she was glad of Brett's large presence beside her as she walked up to the office and opened the door. No one was inside, no frosty-voiced female, no rose-growing hunk.

Brett called out, but no one answered.

'Perhaps I got the time wrong,' Stephanie suggested, knowing very well she hadn't.

Brett said briskly, 'I'll see if I can rustle someone up at the house.'

They were halfway along the path to the house when a woman came around the back hedge and strode towards them. The frosty female, Stephanie decided.

Sure enough, in arctic tones the newcomer said, 'Miss Jerrard?'

'Yes.'

'I'm sorry, but Mr Cowdray has been called away on an emergency.' There was not so much frost as fluster in her voice when she went on, 'He asked if it would be all right to make another appointment for tomorrow.'

'Yes, of course.'

Two minutes later Stephanie was back in the car, wondering what sort of emergency a rose-breeder had. A bee pollinating the wrong flower?

Brett left her at the hotel door, and she had coffee in the elegant coffee-room, watched the people who frequented it with interested eyes, and then went up to her room, deciding to fill in the extra hours with a visit to her favourite spot in Auckland—the Aquarium along the Waterfront Drive. She had just opened the door when a hand fell on her shoulder; she was pushed unceremoniously into the room, and even before she turned she knew who was standing behind her.

His dark face was eagle-featured, strong and uncompromising, from the glittering crystals of his eyes, pale, icy as slivers of quartz, to the scar that ran up the right side of his face from the arrogant jaw to a point just under his eye.

A complex, bewildering mixture of emotions—fear and a wild, singing, unrepentant joy—ran through her, followed fast by anger and the sickening panic she remembered so well.

'Hello, Stephanie,' he said calmly, closing the door behind them both. 'You should always look along the corridor before you open your hotel door.'

The room was very quiet, its restrained opulence in infinite counterpoint to the undiluted masculinity of the man who stood before her. Although she knew she should be yelling at the top of her lungs, pressing the security button, doing anything rather than standing there as though she'd been frozen, she couldn't move.

'D-Duke?' she stammered at last.

'I'm Adam Cowdray,' he said.

'But...'

His smile was sardonic. 'You didn't really think that
I'd been christened Duke, did you?'

'What are you doing here?' she asked; eyes stretched
so wide that they were painful in her white face.

Duke—Adam—Cowdray's glance was searching. 'I
applaud your caution, but I refuse to talk to you with
a bodyguard in attendance,' he said.

'You were there,' she whispered. 'At the nursery.'

'Yes.'

She had known. She had recognised his presence—
that peculiar, waiting stillness, the feeling of impending
doom. Fighting off the suffocating intensity of the emotions churning through her, she asked with a bitter smile,
'Have you come to kidnap me again?'

'I didn't kidnap you last time,' he said curtly. 'If you
remember, I rescued you.'

'You were going to kill me. I heard you that last night.
"I gave her a knock-out pill to keep her under... it will
be easy enough to smother her",' she mimicked bitterly.

'How did you manage to wake up so fast? I expected
to have to throw a couple of gallons of cold water over
you, then make you drink gallons of black coffee before
I got you in a fit state to run for your life.'

'I was sick,' she told him. 'Either a bug or exhaust
fumes when we were going through the city. And don't
change the subject. You shot at me. Twice.'

'And missed you, twice. Don't try to pretend you're
a fool, princess.' The taut mouth closed like a trap on
the words. 'If I'd wanted to kill you you'd be dead. You
didn't believe it then and you don't believe it now. Look
at you—you're not scared, you're bloody furious!'

He was right, damn him.

'You lied to me and betrayed me. You told me you
were working for Saul, but he'd never heard of you,
didn't even know that I was all right.'

'I got you back to him,' he returned blandly. 'He may not have known that I was working for him, but I was.'

Rage, bushfire-fierce, all-consuming, rose like bile within her. She reined it in, because if she gave way to it now she'd try to kill him. And that, she knew, was impossible.

'I got myself back,' she snapped.

'Come off it, Stephanie. Do you honestly think I didn't know what you'd planned? As soon as I came up the stairs and saw you there I was almost certain you must have overheard what we were saying. The toothbrush was a pretty good indication too, as was your amusing imitation of a woman who wanted nothing more than sex, quick and hot and heavy. I knew for certain when you flicked the keys from my pocket. Actually, I was quite proud of you. You kept your head and used the only weapon you had, and you chose exactly the right moment to do it.' He smiled at her astonished, affronted face. 'Which, princess, was why your knee in my groin didn't have quite the expected effect. I knew the exact moment you gathered yourself to do it and managed to take avoiding action.'

'If you knew, why did you let me go on making a fool of myself?'

His eyes were colourless beneath his black lashes, as unreadable as his expression. 'It was as good a way as any I could think of to get you out of there and still keep my credibility with the rest of them,' he said coolly. 'It worked, too. Just. We agreed that you must have overheard the conversation I had with Benny, and of course none of them blamed me for accepting your offer of sex, especially as I thought I had plenty of time. They even considered I'd done quite well to get myself off the bed so quickly after you'd kneed me. Pity I hadn't managed to kill you, but, as we decided afterwards, it wasn't absolutely necessary. Actually, it was Sounder's idea. He hadn't bothered to clear it with the bosses.'

Dragging her eyes free of his mesmeric gaze, Stephanie shook her head. 'So you're not a murderer,' she said coolly. 'Big deal.' She swallowed to ease a rasping dryness in her throat. 'What do you want now? Another go at twenty million pounds?'

'Don't be a fool, Stephanie. I want you to listen to me.'

She gave him a scathing look and took another small step backwards. 'I have to. I can't throw you out.'

He showed perfect teeth in a smile as humourless and callous as granite, walked over to the telephone table and picked up the inconspicuous electronic device she would have had around her neck if Brett hadn't been with her that morning.

Duke's—Adam's—long, tanned fingers looked capable and strong as he held it out to her. 'Use it,' he said. 'Or ring through to the switchboard here. The hotel will send someone up if you really want to get rid of me.'

She looked at the device, then slowly raised her eyes to his. Beneath his thick lashes they blazed, light refracted in ice. He was smiling, but there was no humour in it. She knew her face reflected her tormented uncertainty, because he said softly, 'Your decision, princess.'

'You don't know what you're asking,' she said bleakly.

'I'm asking you to listen, that's all. I realise it's a hell of a step for you to take, especially as you've spent the last five years thinking of me as a criminal of the worst sort.'

Don't, common sense shrieked. You trusted him once before, and look what happened; you fell in love, and you have never got over it.

She looked up, into eyes colder and more distant than polar seas. He wasn't going to help her; he'd made no promises, given her no excuses.

'All right,' she said in a muted voice, thinking, you fool, oh, you fool!

Nothing altered in the scarred warrior's face. 'Sit down,' he said. 'Can I get you a drink?'

'No!'

But she sat down, collapsing with more speed than grace on to the sofa. He sat down too, looking oddly at home in the muted luxury of the room, dominating it effortlessly.

Now that she had taken the plunge she didn't want to hear what he had to say; telling herself that she needed time to collect her thoughts, she asked, 'What are you doing growing roses in Auckland?'

'It's the family business,' Duke—Adam—said.

She nodded. 'Candace said it was an old firm.'

Without inflexion he told her, 'My grandfather set it up as a hobby at first, then, when he became obsessed with it, as a business. My father followed him.'

Feeling as though she had walked into *Alice in Wonderland*, Stephanie looked around the quiet room, similar to a hundred other hotel rooms she'd been in, attractive, soothing, impersonal, but not so impersonal as the man who sat opposite her.

'Have you come to tell me that you agree to my naming a rose after you?' he asked, apparently, like her, in no hurry.

'I want to see it first,' she said, fighting to overcome the odd, frightened hysteria that threatened to clog her throat.

'Naturally. I thought I could donate the profits to some sort of charity. One of your choosing, of course.'

She realised anew how very intimidating he could be. There was something overwhelming about him, an un-compromising aura of force and authority found in few men. Saul had it; and that, she thought, trying to be objective, had to be one of the reasons she had fallen so hard for Duke.

Because although he didn't have Saul's money, or the sort of power Saul could call on, Duke—Adam—had the same effortless, unfaltering impact. Dazed and traumatised though she had been when she had first met him, she had recognised that controlled strength and responded helplessly to it.

'Yes, I'd like that,' she said. 'The Save the Children Foundation. If it's going to make lots, why don't we divide it up and send some to the Fred Hollowes Fund? The Third World could do with some more factories making optical lenses.'

The sun through the window beat on to his head, coaxing a blue sheen from his hair, gilding his olive skin. The aquiline nose and square chin were separate statements of ruthlessness. He looked older—all of his thirty years.

Dangerous, criminal, a man with no softness, yet something blind and passionate stirred and stretched inside her.

'So tell me,' she said crisply, before that weakness could conquer her better judgement, 'what you were doing in Switzerland five years ago.'

He leaned back in his chair and looked at her from beneath his lashes. 'I was trying to infiltrate a criminal gang that was organising the stealing of nuclear weapons from Russia in order to smuggle them at exorbitant profit to organisations and countries I won't name.'

It was nothing like she had expected. Fighting her instinctive need to believe, she said acidly, 'And where did I fit into that?'

'You,' he said deliberately, 'were the cash cow. They needed money to pay their contacts in Russia, and Saul Jerrard was an obvious target. When I finally got an entry into the group they'd just kidnapped you. I managed to convince them that you were better out of that crypt and in my care.' His smile was cold and predatory. 'Looked at from their point of view, it was a good move. If anyone managed to track you down, I'd be the fall guy.'

'So the man who came to see you at the castle was one of them.'

'Yes. Your brother wasn't in any great hurry to pay over the ransom, probably believing that if he did it could sign your death warrant. His security division had done some damned fine work and got too close, and as things weren't nearly ready for the ransom drop we had to move out of the castle before he could rescue you.'

'How did you know they were closing in?' she asked swiftly. 'I can't imagine they were exactly obvious.'

'Someone allowed himself to be heard asking questions in the village.'

'Who?' she demanded.

'Halliday.' His smile was pure irony. 'Didn't you guess? I thought you might; your brother certainly did, which was why Halliday suddenly disappeared. He was my contact in your brother's organisation.'

'Halliday was a criminal?' She shook her head. 'But you tried to kill him.'

'I tried very hard not to kill him,' he returned laconically. 'I hit him hard enough to look good and take the pressure off him. And no, neither Halliday nor I was a criminal.'

She swallowed. 'Who were you both working for?'

'I can't tell you that, but it was a British-based undercover organisation. Barely official. We did the real dirty work.'

She said thinly, 'Does Saul know this?'

'Saul knows that Halliday was as clean as any of us. I doubt if my name ever appeared in the consultations he had with some of my bosses when the five million pounds he did finally pay over was refunded.' He smiled grimly. 'I believe he scorched their ears and told them in no uncertain terms that if any of his family was made use of again like that he'd see that heads rolled. And as he has the power to do it they were suitably chastened.'

Stephanie said, 'Go on. Saul's money was necessary to the gang, and it was necessary for you to let them get it. So they moved us on to the chalet. I don't suppose the castle had been bugged.'

'No. That was another convenient lie.'

'I was a complete idiot,' she said stonily.

He shrugged. 'Why shouldn't you believe me? We went to a lot of trouble to make my story hang together. And the fact that I'd rescued you made it quite easy for you to trust me.'

She showed her teeth. 'Not entirely.'

'No.' He smiled. 'You might have been a little naïve, but you weren't stupid.'

She glowered at him, but the forceful countenance revealed nothing. Losing her composure wasn't going to get her anywhere; she took a deep breath. 'All right, go on.'

'I thought you might have got over that arrogance,' he said mildly, not attempting to hide the diamond glitter in his eyes. 'Too much to expect, I suppose. Anyway, then Sounder sprang his little surprise; he decided that I should kill you.'

She said, 'Wasn't that intended right from the start?'

'It was always on the cards, of course, but they had a pretty good idea of the sort of hornets' nest they'd bring about their ears if they did. No, that was Sounder's little scheme. You'd seen his face—which, incidentally, was something you didn't tell me—but, more than that, he was suspicious of me.'

'I didn't tell you,' she said, 'because I wasn't entirely taken in by your lies. I was pretty sure that you were telling me the truth, but I had some confused idea that if you weren't and I did tell you I could well be signing my death warrant. I wasn't thinking too clearly at the time. Anyway, what good would it have done?'

'I could have made some contingency plans,' he said caustically, 'instead of having the whole thing dumped in my lap at the last moment. As it happens, your seeing his face was only an excuse; they wanted a hold over me and murdering you would have given them the best. So they sent Benny in to tell me to do it, and taped the conversation so they'd be able to use it against me.'

'How do you know all this?'

'I found out,' he said. 'That's what I was good at—collecting information.'

He was taking the past and turning it on his head, and she wanted—oh, how she wanted—to trust him. But it wasn't going to be so easy. 'Would you have killed me?'

'You know the answer to that. I had the chance,' he said without hesitation or expression. 'I was prepared to do almost anything else, because infiltrating this group was important; if those nuclear weapons got through, a lot of innocent people would have died. However, I drew the line at killing anyone to get there.'

She bit her lip. 'How were you planning to get out of it?'

'I didn't dare break cover; too much was riding on my staying in the group.'

'And you didn't trust me to keep quiet.'

He said crisply, 'You were going to be interrogated by experts, and we did not want anyone to know what we were doing in case word found its way back to the group, some of whom had ties with the murky world we all worked in. I contacted Halliday and we decided to engineer a rescue. He was going to come in with guns blazing, shoot me in the arm and gallantly rescue you. Not particularly brilliant, but it could have worked. Then you made your charming attempt at seduction, and that was an even better idea.'

'Why?'

He showed his teeth in a formidable smile. 'Because you initiated it, and you'd be interrogated by men who would understand just how tempting an offer like that would be to an unprincipled cad.' His tone was subtly mocking as he said the last three words.

'I see.'

'Unfortunately,' he went on, 'we hadn't planned on Benny keeping close watch. He let off a couple of shots at you as you hared off down the road, so I had to get you out of his way and make it seem as though I was trying to shoot you in the woods. They didn't really care whether you were dead or not, as long as they had the tape of me saying I'd kill you. Amusing, because the last thing I intended to do was let them toss me out. Anyway, it all worked out well enough. They decided the five million pounds they'd collected in England the night you got away would have to do, and my cover was still unblown.'

'So I played completely into your hands.'

'You did, princess.'

She could have bridled at the hated nickname, but she was too humiliated to make the effort. She said, 'What happened after that?'

'I can't tell you, but the men who tried to smuggle out the bombs and missiles are now either dead or so far behind bars, they aren't coming out again.'

'So what you're saying is that there's no way anyone can find out whether what you've told me is the truth or not,' she said slowly.

His lashes drooped further. 'Unless you want to visit several gaols in the less salubrious parts of the world, that's about it,' he said indifferently.

Did she believe him? Taken all in all, she thought she did. He might have been lying, but unless he had killed the real Adam Cowdray he was almost certainly who he said he was.

That didn't, of course, mean that he wasn't a criminal. At the very least he had used her callously. But his story reconciled the two sides of his character, the perverse dichotomy that had so bewildered her: the man who had cared for her and the one who had casually talked about killing her.

Perhaps Candace had been right.

And perhaps not.

Because what decision she came to didn't really alter anything. While she had been falling in love he had seen her as a commodity, a pawn to be sacrificed for the greatest advantage. Possibly he'd had the welfare of the world at heart, but he certainly hadn't cared about hers. She had been a means to an end, discarded with no thought when her usefulness was over.

'Why have you contacted me now?' she asked at last.

Something evanescent and dangerous gleamed in those unusual eyes. 'Perhaps I wanted to see how you'd turned out,' he said smoothly.

'I'm not much different,' she returned every bit as smoothly. 'A few years older, that's all, and probably more than a little bit wiser. A person's basic character doesn't change much.'

His brows lifted. 'So you're still the pretty innocent of five years ago.'

She said drily, 'I don't know that innocence is a part of one's character. Of course I'm not so guileless—I spent four of those years at university.'

'Doing what?'

'A business management degree,' she said, refusing to look at him. 'But that's not particularly interesting. Why have you told me all this now?'

'Because it's time you knew the truth. The men who kidnapped you are both dead.'

She stared at him in horror. 'Did you kill them?' And she knew even before his mouth twisted that he wasn't going to answer.

But he did.

CHAPTER SEVEN

'No.' Duke looked directly at her, pupils dark as midnight, ice-rimmed. 'They died in a shoot-out. However, I was instrumental in making sure they ended up like rats in a cage. I set the trap, and I baited it, and I'm not in the least sorry they decided to shoot it out rather than surrender.'

A weight Stephanie didn't even know she'd been carrying rolled free. She hadn't realised how much difference it would make. 'I shouldn't be pleased they're dead,' she said quietly, 'but—I used to dream that they came back for me. Thank you for telling me.'

'They were no loss to humanity, believe me. They'd have killed you without a qualm if it had suited them to.' That cold smile narrowed. 'You were a victim in someone else's war. I thought you needed to know that they were no longer a threat.' His hooded eyes were unreadable, the strong, harsh lines of his face closed against her.

A small, bittersweet smile tilted the corners of her mouth but she said nothing. What else had she expected? That he had contacted her because he had been wildly, obsessively, passionately in love with her for the last five years? Grow up, Stephanie. That's not how the world works.

He went on, 'No one can recompense you for what you endured, but I can name a rose after you. It's no restitution of what we took from you, but it's the best I can do.'

'I see,' she said slowly. 'When can I see it?'

'May I use your telephone?'

She nodded, and watched him get to his feet and walk across to the table. It was difficult to reconcile the man she had known five years ago with this man, seemingly content to breed flowers.

Oh, physically he hadn't changed much; he still moved with the swift, noiseless grace that she had seen so often in the tangle of her dreams. Although he was young enough for his blue-black hair to show no strand of grey, the lines that bracketed his mouth were a little more deeply engraved. The scar hadn't aged him; it merely emphasised the edged, dangerous look that had kept her so off-balance five years before. And the potent, blazing aura of sexuality was just as elemental as before.

He didn't look at her as he rang Reception and ordered the roses he'd left there to be brought up, yet Stephanie felt him in every cell of her body, an itch in her blood she had never been able to soothe.

As he put the receiver down she got to her feet, unable to cope with a silence filled by the aching poignancy of her memories. 'Excuse me,' she said, 'I'll be back in a minute,' and fled into her bedroom. In the bathroom she washed her face and let the cool water play over her wrists until she heard the doorbell.

'I'll get it,' Duke said.

From the bedroom door she watched as he went across to the door, noting that he opened it with caution although he didn't check the peephole. Something pulled at her heart.

It was, however, the bellboy with a vase of flowers, a great mass of red-bronze petals with a perfume that floated like incense across the room.

Stephanie made a sound of appreciation.

'See if you like the scent,' Duke—Adam—said, putting them down on the coffee-table.

Obediently she bent to smell the blooms. Rich but not heavy, an intriguing blend of true rose with a faint hint of something else—the citrus tang of freesias?

'How could I not?' she murmured, lost in an evocative haze.

She sniffed again, and a lean hand reached out, twisted a bloom free and held it against her hair. 'Yes, I thought I had it right,' he said.

She kept her lashes lowered. 'They're lovely,' she said simply.

'Not quite the common thing,' he replied, an ironic note shaping his voice as he handed her the rose.

Stephanie looked up sharply, her eyes lingering compulsively on the scar that marred the arrogant angle of his cheek. 'What happened?' she heard her voice say, stroking the rose petals because her fingers longed to trace the jagged line.

'I had a difference of opinion with a sword,' he said laconically.

Something painful broke, shattered into tiny shards deep inside her.

Dragging her eyes away from his face, she focused on the flower that glowed in her hand, saying with a note of light amusement, 'Thank you for this; it was a nice thought. Creative, too. I rather fancy the idea of having a rose named after me, but if it's exposure you want Candace would be the better bet. She's already being written about as a great innovator.'

'I might ask her one day,' he said, his voice telling her nothing. 'But this one is yours.'

She smiled, smelled the rose again, and said, 'I'd be honoured to sponsor it. Thank you, Duke.'

'Then you had better sign a release,' he said. 'And my name is Adam.'

'Who gave you the nickname?' she asked.

Impatience edged his tone. 'It was just somebody's idea of a joke.'

She gave him a swift sideways look. He might think it a joke, but she didn't; she understood why that unknown person had thought Duke suited him. He carried himself with an air of unconscious self-confidence, a natural aristocrat, looking down from his great height

at lesser beings. Arrogant, yes, profoundly irritating
certainly, but those characteristics were inborn.

'If you can give me the release, I'll get a lawyer to
check it out,' she said, 'and post it to you.'

'I have it here,' he said, taking a paper from his pocket.
'Get him to do it today and you can give it to me tonight. I'll take you out to dinner.'

Anger sparked inside her; yes, arrogance was definitely the word.

'I'm sorry,' she said calmly, 'but that's not possible.'

'How about if I *ask* you to dinner?' Adam said
shrewdly.

She knew she shouldn't—she still didn't know whether
she really believed him. And yet if she went out to dinner
with him she'd be proving that he no longer affected her.

'That's different,' she returned.

'I'll pick you up at seven-thirty.'

It was still an order, but she said slowly, 'All right.'

The minute the door closed behind him she rang
London and asked for the man who ran Saul's security.
Yawning, because it was the middle of the night there,
he answered. After a heartfelt apology, she spoke to him
for five minutes, and hung up. Five hours later he rang
back.

'What do you think I am, a miracle-worker?' he
grumbled, but he'd enjoyed the hunt; she could tell by
the tone of his voice. 'These are dangerous waters I've
been fishing in. I'll have a few words to say to young
Dave. What he got for you was the nicely sanitised
version of Adam Cowdray's life in the British Army,
and the idiot didn't think to dig any deeper.'

Stephanie realised that her knuckles were turning
white. 'Was he in the army?'

'Oh, yes. SAS. I had to call in a few old favours, and
apply quite a lot of pressure, and even then they weren't
very forthcoming, but a couple of years after he'd done
his training he was picked to go into a very covert agency.'

Stephanie dragged in a painful breath. The army had turned him into a warrior, case-hardened him, made him a killing machine.

Apparently unaware of her response, the man in London said, 'I couldn't find out what he'd been doing but he's clean. He resigned four years ago, did a couple of private jobs——'

'What?'

'Oh, the usual. Legal but expensive jobs involving the possibility of violence. You can earn a lot in a short time if you're clever and not particularly concerned about dying.' While she thought this over he asked, 'Did he say what agency he worked for?'

'No. Not a word.'

He gave a grunt of approval. 'Staunch, but then, that's the man. He's been out of circulation here for about six years.'

Two years during undercover, and then the last four years spent breeding roses. Yes, it hung together. 'So I can trust him.'

'I'd trust him with my life,' he said carefully, 'and my wallet, but if I were a woman—well, I don't know. According to my envious informant, at one time he used to have to swat women off him. He had a reputation for being cold-blooded but that didn't seem to worry the females who went after him.'

After another apology for having kept him up half the night, Stephanie put the receiver down with something like relief.

For the past five years she had been unable to trust her own heart when it came to men; she had erred so badly in judging Duke that she had chosen his very antithesis in Philip. And when that hadn't worked out she hadn't dared try again. But the inner promptings of her heart had been right; oh, he had used her, and no doubt she meant nothing to him beyond a woman he had treated badly, but at least he wasn't the criminal she'd thought him to be. She didn't have to despise herself any longer.

Was that why he had contacted her again?

No. He was a hard man. He probably had no idea what he had done to her five years ago.

She wouldn't fall into the trap of endowing him with qualities he didn't have, just to comfort her romantic soul. But now she knew he hadn't lied to her there was no reason why she shouldn't enjoy the evening out with him, and try to lay the ghosts of the past.

She'd packed nothing but a very plain dress, and she didn't know just how much money he could afford to spend. She had no idea whether breeding roses was profitable or not, although presumably he had bankrolled himself by the private jobs he had undertaken, those legal but dangerous positions where it helped not to worry about the possibility of death. The thought of them made her feel sick.

So she wore her plain dress, a silk shirtwaister in her favourite shades of autumn, and deliberately left her hair in its usual curly unset style, wearing only the pearl studs Saul had given her for her twentieth birthday. The fabulous teardrops, faintly gleaming with a pale gold sheen that harmonised so well against her ivory skin, were treasures from Fala'isi's warm lagoon.

Wondering what differences Adam saw, she gazed at her reflection. In Switzerland she had been thin, her skin sallow and rough and patchy with fear and confinement, her hair lank and unkempt in spite of the constant washing she had indulged in. Now her skin glowed with the creamy matt finish that photographed so well, and her eyes were a glittering, audacious blue. Colour crackled through her hair; she turned her head in a consciously preening gesture, then made a derisory face at herself.

She was an idiot.

Ready ten minutes early, she sat down in her room and gazed blindly out over Auckland's waterfront, hands linked tensely in her lap. It was starting all over again; she could feel that hopeless, mindless hunger curling through her veins now.

Remember, he's no prince on a white charger, she told herself impatiently.

All right, so he lied to you, the small, unregenerately hopeful part of her brain argued. He had to. And he's made contact now. That must mean something.

It could mean he's cashing in on the name, she thought cynically. Although that didn't really make sense. Gardeners wouldn't buy a substandard rose simply because it carried the magical Jerrard name—he had to know that many of them wouldn't know who the Jerrards were, and couldn't care less.

She tried to dam the rising tide of excitement and anticipation because it made her far too vulnerable. She wasn't the girl of eighteen who had fallen in love with her rescuer; she was five years older, a mature woman who had been engaged, who had taken a degree in business management, who ran her own affairs.

Yet she had a lot in common with that naïve girl. To begin with, she was still a virgin, with a virgin's instinctive fear of the intensity of her emotions. Going out for the evening with the only man who was able to make her feel like this was the most dangerous thing she'd done in the past five years. The fact that Adam's power over her was solely physical, something to do with genes and conditioning, didn't make it any easier to deal with.

When the telephone rang she jumped, only lifting it after the fourth summons. 'Ah, Ms Jerrard, you are there,' the receptionist said pleasantly. 'I'll tell Mr Cowdray that he can come up.'

'No, I'll come down.'

Dressed in the starkness of dinner-jacket and white shirt, Adam dominated the large, marble-lined, fountain-murmuring foyer.

Those clothes, Stephanie thought warily as she paused a moment outside the lift doors, had been tailored especially for that long, heavily muscled body, their elegant, spare sophistication somehow emphasising the unconcealed toughness of the man who wore them. Adam Cowdray was more than a little uncivilised, his steel-reinforced core too close to the surface to be hidden. Once a warrior, it seemed, always a warrior.

The autocratic, high-held head turned, and she felt the full effect of his eyes, their cutting intensity still probing for weaknesses.

Conscious of the covert glances of others, Stephanie pinned a smooth, cool smile to her lips and moved out to greet him. Her breath caught in her lungs; lord, but he was big! He overwhelmed her, made her knees tremble and her belly clench in a primitive, feverish response.

She held out her hand, keeping it steady by an effort of will. Of course she expected him to shake it; she was astonished and not a little confused when he raised it and kissed her knuckles.

'Heavens!' she said, irritated by the slight but definite recoil that must have given her away. 'No one does that now, Du—Adam, unless it's middle-aged European aristocrats saluting the hands of elderly dowagers!'

'I make my own rules,' he said, something untamed glinting in the depths of his eyes.

Oh, yes, he made his own rules. And if people got hurt, that was their bad luck.

He'd left his car underneath the hotel portico; to Stephanie's surprise, the doorman greeted him by name as he opened the door for her.

Still, why should she be surprised? He stood out; his very size made him easily recognisable. Wondering how he had managed to be a good secret agent when he was such a commanding, authoritative figure, she settled back into the car and looked out at the pleasant Auckland street, angling her jaw purposefully. Five years ago he'd held all the cards in his spare, graceful hands; this time she would maintain her autonomy and reclaim her self-respect.

He took her to a restaurant that was small, secluded and family-run, where he was also greeted by name. As they sat with the menu, she said, 'Tell me how an intrepid agent turned into a rose-breeder.'

'My father was dying,' he said, his voice aloof, his eyes never leaving hers. 'I knew that more than anything he wanted me to keep on with the roses, and I knew that he wouldn't say a word about it.'

'Did he approve of your life rescuing maidens and slaying dragons?'

'Most of the dragons were sleazy criminals or wild-eyed fanatics, and many of the maidens not much better,' he said ironically. 'It was a sordid business at best, and although my father wouldn't have dreamed of asking me to give it up he certainly didn't approve.' His mouth twisted. 'The regular army was fine; covert operations were unprincipled and shady. Better be a soldier and die honestly than a spy and end up too crooked to know whether you had any principles left. He wasn't far wrong, either.'

'What made you do it?'

A coldly amused light glimmered in the depths of his eyes. 'Ideals, mainly. I thought I could make some sort of difference to the world, redress a balance that seemed to be tilting in the direction of evil. I was young and I thought I could make a difference.'

'You did make a difference. You saved my life,' she said. 'I haven't thanked you for that. It may not be worth much in the global view of things, but it's important to me.'

'It became important to me too.' He smiled at her startled glance. 'So important that after you were safe I decided I'd see how you were getting on when you were twenty-one and all grown up.'

It was like a thunderclap. Her eyes flew to his face, met a shimmering, enigmatic gaze. Well, two could play at this game, dangerous though it might be.

'What stopped you?' she asked, head high, her smile aching on her mouth.

'Common sense.' He spoke caustically, not sparing himself. 'I soon realised that although I thought I knew you well I'd been fooling myself. There is a basic and unalterable difference between the life I lead and yours.'

The pulse beat fast in her throat, but she managed to control her voice enough to say calmly, 'Poor little rich girl?'

'Exactly. I saw a photograph of you on the cover of *Tatler*, dressed in fifty million dollars' worth of blue diamonds. They were the same colour as your eyes, and you wore them with complete negligence, as though they were costume jewellery. Any ideas I might have had about meeting you again were just cobwebs tacked together by wishful thinking. So I did what any sensible man does. I cut down the cobwebs and got on with real life.

She remembered that photograph. She hadn't wanted to do it, but it had been a sort of celebration after months in therapy working through fear and bitterness and rage as well as the ever-present pain of betrayal. Posing for the photographer had been a defiant gesture to fate and everything that conspired against her.

At that time it had seemed that the men who had kidnapped her would never be brought to justice. It was an enormous relief to learn that thanks to Adam and men like him—unnamed soldiers who fought their dirty war in the dark shadows at the edge of humanity—justice of some sort had been done.

'Don't tell me you waited with palpitating eagerness for me to come back,' he said harshly. 'I'll bet you did your best to forget.'

'I very carefully avoided thinking about it,' she agreed. Except for him. She had never been free of him. 'Tell me what being an agent was like.'

'So you've decided to believe me?'

'I got someone to check,' she said.

His smile was a nice blend of cynicism and assessment. 'Of course. And what did they find out?'

She told him. A frown gathered between his black brows. 'You've got good sources,' he said slowly.

'Yes. It won't go any further, Adam.'

Broad shoulders moved in a slight shrug. 'It doesn't really matter. It's over now. Most of it was dirty, far from romantic, and secret. You tell me about your life.'

Although his voice was neutral she discerned the faint note of scorn beneath the words, and felt like hitting him across his autocratic face. 'What would you like to know?' she asked sweetly.

His smile was cruel. 'How about your lovers?' he suggested with ice-cold malice. 'Tell me about the man you were engaged to. What happened?'

'That is none of your business.' The memory of her engagement still had the power to hurt her, especially when she was confronted by the cause of the whole fiasco.

'Didn't he measure up to your brother?'

'I don't know any man who measures up to Saul.'

He looked across the room to their waiter who immediately, as though that swift glance had been a summons, came over. 'We're ready,' Adam said.

When the food and wine had been ordered, and the little ceremony of the tasting gone through, the waiter poured them each a glass of excellent New Zealand Sauvignon Blanc and disappeared.

Adam looked at her. 'It doesn't augur well for your prospects if you can't find a man who measures up to Saul, does it?'

'I don't want to marry my brother,' she said, and sipped the cool, flowery liquid with gratitude. 'Or even a man like him.'

'Sensible woman.' A couple passed by, both smiling at Adam—the woman, Stephanie noted sourly, with definite coquetry.

'Friends of yours?' she asked, her eyes on the consciously seductive sway of slim hips in pleated chiffon as the woman undulated away from them.

'Acquaintances,' he said dismissively.

So the elegant, provocative invitation was wasted. Stephanie looked down at her hands, furious at the pang of jealousy that was only now subsiding. 'I believe New Zealand is in the throes of an election,' she said. 'What are the issues?'

Accepting the change of subject with a mocking glance, he told her what the issues were, concisely and, as far as she could judge, fairly. Over the years Stephanie had developed an interest in politics, so she was able to keep her end up. That subject lasted until the first course arrived, delicious Bluff oysters for him, kingfish in a subtly flavoured orange sauce for her.

'Now,' he said, after the waiter had poured more wine, 'what other neutral subject can we talk about?'

'The roses,' she suggested. 'I imagine you don't just breed on a whim, that you have some sort of plan. What exactly are you trying to do?'

'I'm trying to produce a good healthy bush which will grow and flower well in our humid, warm, temperate climate, with scent and form and a strong constitution,' he said evenly.

'So how do you go about doing that?'

He was fascinating, and obviously enjoyed his work, but Stephanie couldn't help wondering whether it filled his life. And if it didn't, what did? It was difficult to imagine a man who had walked on the edge for years settling down to breed roses with no hankering for the adrenalin and danger that had once been his constant companions.

'And do you miss your other career?' she asked a little daringly.

'Not in the least.' He scanned her face. 'Have I gone down in your estimation?' he asked. 'Does the prospect of danger excite you, Stephanie?'

She looked directly at him. 'Far from it,' she said, 'but it's been my experience, limited though it is, that people who are attracted to jobs where danger is a constant companion need that fix.'

'Those people,' he said implacably, 'die. And they take others with them. Adrenalin junkies don't last long—they forget that ninety per cent of any successful job is the preparation. No, I don't miss the excitement or the prospect of being stabbed in the back.' In his voice there was a sardonic weariness that she understood rather than heard.

'Who tried to kill you with a sword?' she asked abruptly.

'A Colombian drug baron. He was one of the customers for the nuclear weapons from Russia. He thought that as he was descended from Spanish *conquistadore* a sword was a more polished, not to say refined way of dispatching a nuisance than the guns and explosives his hired killers used.'

The muscles in her stomach clenched. 'What happened?'

'Fortunately I took fencing at school,' he said, and she knew that that was all she was going to hear.

An innocuous remark hovered on the tip of her tongue, but he forestalled it. 'What are you planning to do? Or do you have no plans?'

She looked at him coolly. 'I've taken over responsibility for my affairs,' she said.

'What affairs?'

Beneath the autumn-coloured silk her shoulders moved a fraction. 'Oh, there's a family trust, and stuff like that,' she said vaguely. 'At the moment I'm finding my way through the ramifications; then I'll see how I go as a manager.'

'It sounds a good life,' he said. 'You'll be able to attend charity balls to take your mind off the boredom of business matters.'

'I don't like them much,' she said. 'I intend to help with the real work of several charities.'

'Thereby salving your conscience?' he asked.

She smiled deliberately at him, letting her eyes wander down his angular face to linger on the straight, hard mouth with its surprisingly sensual bottom lip. 'Surely you're not going to allow me a conscience?' she said lightly. 'After all, I'm a spoilt rich kid, remember?'

He took the gibe with a slight backward jerk of his head that threw the slashing line of his jaw and chin into prominence. 'Am I being unbearable?' he asked, his voice dark and mocking, underpinning the words with a subtle intimacy that sent a swift prickle through her skin.

'No more so than you ever were,' she retorted.

He was watching her with hooded eyes, his face not softened by the smile that curved his mouth. Deep in the pit of her stomach a quick, involuntary shiver of awareness, that primal, intense response that only Adam seemed to evoke, stirred into life; she felt it progress to the base of her spine, and then diffuse through her, potent as old brandy.

She asked abruptly, 'Where did you go after you got out of Switzerland?'

'I can't tell you.' No emotion in his voice, not then, and not when he added, 'There's a lot of my life I can't talk about.'

'I see,' she said, picking up her fork.

'Did you consult a counsellor?'

She nodded. 'She was very good, and it did help. I had nightmares for a few months——' there was no need for him to know that she still got them occasionally '—but apart from that I've been fine.'

'The resilience of youth.'

His gently teasing voice surprised her into a smile. For a moment they were caught in a small bubble of awareness, eyes locked together as the restaurant and

the other diners faded into a dimness. Then he made a
comment about the food, and the bubble was broken.

They ate the rest of their meal with outwardly easy
conversation, discussing books, a film made in New
Zealand that had won several prestigious awards, the
reason that modern roses were so prone to disease—it
came in with genes from the yellow Persian rose—and
whether tourism was going to be the salvation of the
Pacific basin, and, if so, how it should be organised.

Adam made her think; he looked at things from a
different angle, a slightly mordant, more practical point
of view, and behind everything he said was a penetrating
intelligence that had her reaching further than she ever
had before.

Talking to him was exhilarating, like being on a roller-
coaster with no fixed destination, and when eventually
they'd drunk their coffee and it was time to go she saw
with a feeling of astonishment that they were almost the
last people in the restaurant.

In the car back to the hotel she said, 'That was a super
evening, thank you very much.'

'You sound like a little girl,' he said. 'A very English
little girl.'

'You sound English too. How is that?'

'My father met my mother in England and stayed on.
Although we moved out to New Zealand when I was five
they sent me back to school when I was eleven, so I
never really lost the accent.'

'I see.' She looked across at the arrogant profile
harshly outlined against the lights of the street outside,
and said, 'I'll bet you got teased when you moved out
to New Zealand.'

'Not after the first time,' he said. 'I was a young
tough.'

Yes, she could imagine that. Would he have sons who
were as tough as he'd been? She tried to resist, but an
image of a much younger Adam slid into her brain, and
she felt her heart clutch, deliquesce . . .

'Did you go to university?' she asked brightly to banish it.

His mouth tilted. 'No, straight into the army. I was determined to prove that having a rose-breeder for a father didn't weaken my masculinity.'

Surely—no, he had to be joking. She said solemnly, 'It must have been a great cross for you to bear.'

His mouth curved further but he said with equal seriousness, 'By the time I'd fought my way through the lower forms people were getting tired of calling me petal and blossom.'

That surprised her into a gurgle of laughter. 'Really?'

'They didn't try it after the first time. I was handy with my fists. And my size helped. I was always a lump of a boy.'

'I doubt whether you were ever lumpish in your life,' she said. Big, certainly, but it was impossible to imagine him moving with anything other than the easy masculine grace that was so much a part of his immediate impact.

'I was always six or seven inches taller than any other boy in the class.'

'It's all right for a boy,' she said, and immediately wished she hadn't.

'Were you teased?'

She nodded. 'Girls aren't allowed to clobber each other, and I wasn't quick-witted enough to defend myself with my tongue. Still, I got over it. By the time I was fifteen I was rather glad I towered over everyone.'

The car turned into the hotel forecourt. The door was opened with a flourish. Stephanie got out and Adam came around and took her elbow, his long, lean fingers resting lightly but with determination against silk warmed by her skin. She thought that tomorrow she'd have five little dots burned into her flesh.

'You don't need——' she began.

'I'll see you in,' he said calmly.

They were almost at the desk when someone said from behind, 'Miss Jerrard?'

Stephanie stiffened but didn't turn. She felt Adam's shockingly swift movement as he positioned himself between her and the intruder.

'Miss Jerrard,' the voice repeated, turning itself into Brett's distinctive tone.

'What do you want?' Adam's voice was deep and cold and forbidding as he turned to survey the interloper.

'I've got a message for Miss Jerrard.'

Stephanie said, 'What is it, Brett?'

'Your brother wants you to ring him immediately. He said it's important.'

'Thank you,' Stephanie said tonelessly, holding out her hand for the key. Candace, she thought, and without looking at either man set rapidly off towards the bank of lifts, her heels clicking on the marble floor. But when she reached the lift she stared at it for a moment, trying to remember what floor she was on.

A long arm reached out and stabbed the button. 'I'll come up with you,' Adam said without emphasis.

'Mr Jerrard wanted me to stay with her.' Brett wasn't objecting to Adam's presence, merely making it clear that he didn't intend to go.

In spite of the pressure in her chest Stephanie understood the younger man's attitude; Adam was not a man you tried to block.

Up in her room she put the call through to Fala'isi and stood with her head turned away, knuckles white as she gripped the receiver. Asa, their housekeeper answered.

'I'm sorry,' she said, 'but he's not here, Stephanie. Your sister isn't well, so he took her to the hospital. He's just rung to say that she's all right, but they're keeping her in tonight and he'll stay there. He'll ring you first thing tomorrow morning.'

Stephanie leaned against the wall, relief washing over her in great waves. 'She's not likely to lose the baby, is she?'

'It doesn't sound like it, so don't you go worrying about her, now. She's all right, and the baby is fine. I think she just got a bit hot, that's all. We've had a heat wave here for the last two days, and it's been raining all the time.'

'All right, I'll expect to hear from Saul in the morning. I'm coming home tomorrow anyway. Goodnight, Asa.'

She put the receiver down and turned to the two men, but it was Brett she addressed. 'Everything's all right,' she said. 'My sister's suffering a bit from heat exhaustion and had to go to hospital, but she's fine.'

'I'm glad to hear that,' he said, then looked at Adam, tall and somewhat possessive beside her.

Adam's smile had something tigerish and challenging about it. 'I'll stay for a while,' he said.

The other man's face was a study in indecision. He looked swiftly at Stephanie. 'Is that——'

'I'll take care of her,' Adam said smoothly, and to Stephanie's astonishment Brett's obvious worry began to dissipate, overwhelmed by the calm authority of the man beside her.

'All right,' he said, yielding to Adam's stronger will. 'Stephanie, I'll book you seats on the first Air New Zealand plane up in the morning.'

'Thank you very much. I'm sorry you had to break up your evening . . .'

'No problem,' he said. 'Well, goodnight, then.'

She saw him to the door, then turned, saying indignantly, 'What on earth did you think you were doing? You embarrassed the poor man——'

Adam put out a hand and drew her close against him, holding her, refusing to let her go. 'I've waited five long years for this,' he said quietly, and bent his head and kissed her.

'I wanted to do this the first time I saw you,' he said an aeon later, and kissed her again. 'You were terrified yet so valiant, with your thin wrists rubbed raw where you'd tried to free yourself.'

His mouth hovered over hers, so that she felt each word as well as heard it. 'And when you set your jaw and staggered up the mountainside with me, refusing to give in, then I knew I was in deep, deep trouble.'

'How could you?' she whispered, enchanted, yet unable to give up her suspicions so easily. 'You didn't show any signs—you slept beside me each night and never touched me once——'

His arms contracted tightly around her. 'I didn't do much sleeping, believe me,' he said grimly, 'and I was only able to keep to my side of the bed by reminding myself that you'd had a hell of a time, and only a sadist would force any sort of advance on to you.'

'You were very scathing that first morning when I—when we——'

'When I woke up and found you sprawled out over me in innocent abandon.' He laughed beneath his breath and tilted her chin so that he could see into her eyes.

His own were not soft—they could never be soft, she thought confusedly—but they gleamed with a certain rueful amusement, more gentle than ironic. 'You were utterly scathing!'

'I had to be cruel, otherwise I'd have taken you then and there, and God knows, I knew you weren't ready for it.'

'You told me I was a tart!'

'I wanted to frighten and offend you. I was getting far too interested in a girl I had to keep at a distance.'

'You needn't have been so brutal.'

'It was a measure of how much you affected me. You put me through hell,' he said roughly. 'Those long legs beneath my shirts, the way you snuggled up to me each night, the innocent open awareness I could see blossoming in you—I've never had such a difficult damned assignment. But I had to keep my hands off you because there was no room in my life for you then. I had a job to do.'

Although it was not particularly flattering to be second to a mission, she respected him for his determination and resolution. And now, with that equivocal, sensuous undertone roughened and lazy in her ears, she understood so much more than she had before.

'And do you have a job to do now?' she asked demurely.

'No,' he said, and his mouth came down on hers, and this time there was nothing tender about his kiss; he stamped possession on her, took his fill of her eager mouth, and she faced his strength and demand and met it and matched it.

It had been coming ever since he'd lifted her out of the makeshift coffin. The arid years of waiting and separation had served to whet the edge of the need and the hunger, making the traditional preliminaries unnecessary.

Stephanie didn't try to stop him when his fingers undid the silk at her breast. Indeed, she was busy freeing the studs on his shirt, her body aching with desire, her mind clouded by passion too long frustrated. Nevertheless, when his fingers touched her skin she shuddered, reacting with a swift abandon.

For a moment his big body clenched. He said hoarsely, 'You scare me.'

'Why?'

'I want you so much I'm afraid I'll hurt you.'

'You couldn't hurt me,' she said, because a great and glorious certainty wrapped her in its embrace. At long last it was, she thought, gazing into his narrowed, glittering eyes, the right time, the right place... Only to wonder almost immediately whether her confidence had been a little premature. She had never seen him naked, his body in the pride of his masculinity.

'We'll fit together perfectly,' he said, touching the full curves of her breasts with knowing fingers, seeming to relish the contrast between the pale, soft mounds and his lean hand, ivory skin and olive, light and dark, female and male in potent, age-old polarisation.

Her head fell back over his arm as he lowered his mouth and took the proud nipple into his mouth. Stephanie lay voluptuously exposed, her hands on the broad expanse of his chest, feeling the speeding thunder of his heart beneath her palms, the rhythm of his life.

Sensation ran like jagged arrows of ecstasy, like electric impulses connecting nerves and heart, joining skin and the deepening heat at the pit of her stomach, tightening every sinew and cell. Only once before had she experienced such delicious tension; she stretched, racked by delight, a conspirator in her own torment.

He was like a god, she thought, lifting heavy eyelids so that she could see him, glory in the steel muscles, the sleek, damp skin that caught across the sensitised tips of her questing fingers. As he made himself master of her responses, found his pleasure in the lush abundance of her body, she conquered the shyness that had been so long a part of her and fed her own desire with judicious exploration of all that made him a man.

He kissed her voraciously, hungrily, yet tempering his strength so that, although his hands trembled with the force of his passion and his mouth was hard and hot and almost angry, he didn't hurt her.

She was just as fierce, freeing the shackles of repressed longing, holding nothing back. She didn't fool herself that this was love; there had been nothing of love in his face, in his hands, in the predator's drive of his body.

'Adam,' she said thickly. 'Adam, please...'

'What do you want?'

'You. I want you.'

He laughed, the guttural, triumphant laugh of a lover, and kissed the shallow dimple of her navel. 'How?' he asked. 'How do you want me? Have you dreamed about this, princess, and woken shaking and starving and empty, untold times, until the craving became part of you, insatiable, gnawing at the roots of your heart? Is that how it is with you?'

A shiver gathered deep inside her, began to move through cells and nerves in ever-widening circles.

'Yes,' she whispered, 'that's exactly how it is.'

His hand moved down, down, found the slick centre of her heat, and she convulsed, crying out as her body bucked in his hands. Waves of sensation gripped her inexorably, tossed her higher and higher, beyond thought and reaction, so helplessly was she flung beyond anything she had ever experienced before.

And then it faded, and she clutched him.

'What's the matter?' he asked.

'You haven't—you didn't...'

His laugh was closer to a growl. 'No, not yet, my lovely.'

In the time that followed she learned of the myriad ways that a man could pleasure a woman; she learned that Adam could keep his self-control almost indefinitely, until eventually she grabbed him by the shoulders and demanded that he give her what she most wanted, reinforcing her command with a swift, forceful movement against the coiled strength of his loins that brought another of those soft laughs from him.

But the last laugh was on her. Fearlessly she looked up at a face drained of everything but the need to curb his desire; lips drawn back, the warm lamplight honing the planes and angles of his face into a mask of almost demonic intensity, he was exultant, primal man.

One powerful thrust took him home, stretched her so far that at first she thought she'd cry out with pain. Yet almost immediately the pressure eased. Eyes locked on the crystalline fire of his, she gasped. She saw comprehension and anger flare deep in the colourless depths, but when she pushed experimentally both emotions were replaced by the flickering of a heat that seared her.

It was a journey unlike any other. Almost instantly they set up a rhythm of giving and taking so intermingled that there was no difference, until at last, weakened by pleasure, she sobbed something, and was hurled back into that place where time ended and only sensation existed in its purest, almost unbearable form.

This time it was even better; his beloved weight added an unknown quality to the experience, and as she lay imprisoned by the fiery sweetness he joined her, his body arching in raw compulsion, his head thrown back as he too reached that place.

How sad, she thought as she lay beneath him, sweat-streaked bodies still joined, that there would be no child. He had made sure of that.

His chest fell and rose, until he turned on to his side and gathered her against him. In a deep, sensual, slow voice he asked, 'Why didn't you tell me it was the first time for you?'

A yawn cracked Stephanie's face. 'Does it matter?' she mumbled, trying to fight off waves of exhaustion.

'No.' He kissed her forehead. 'We'll talk about it in the morning. Go to sleep now.'

CHAPTER EIGHT

SOMETHING was buzzing in her ear, some lost bee, dive-bombing——

'Stephanie! Wake up, princess, someone's calling you on the phone. Stephanie! Come on, wake up and answer the bloody thing before I do!'

Duke's voice. No, Adam. Not Duke.

Slowly, with enormous reluctance, she reached out a hand and groped for the telephone, wondering at the feeling of boneless contentment that flooded her. 'Hello?' she muttered.

'I'm sorry to wake you, Stephanie, but it's Asa here, and I think you should get back here as soon as you can.'

'Asa?' Then she remembered. 'Asa, what's happened?'

'It's your sister. She's not well. Saul rang me ten minutes ago from the hospital and said you were to come back.'

'Has she lost the baby?'

'I don't know.'

Asa the unflappable, Asa whose serene Polynesian presence had always represented calmness and dignity, was crying. Stephanie sat bolt upright in the bed, clutching the receiver. The light flicked on.

She stared at Adam's unshaven countenance with blind appeal. 'What about Candace?' There was a short silence. Stephanie's heart contracted tightly in her chest. 'For God's sake, Asa, how is Candace?'

At last Asa said, 'She's not good, Stephanie.'

'Oh, God,' she whispered.

The receiver was taken from her hand. As he slid his other arm around her shoulders and held her close Adam

164

said crisply, 'I'm a friend of Stephanie's. Tell me exactly what is going on.'

It didn't seem strange to lean against his reassuring strength. Frantically trying to empty her mind of everything but calmness, Stephanie waited until he had finished listening, then asked abruptly, 'Where's Saul's Learjet?'

Something moved in his eyes, but he relayed the question. 'On it's way to China,' he said. 'No, it's all right. I'll get her up as soon as possible, probably within four hours.' He hung up.

'How?' Stephanie croaked.

He was already dialling another number. 'I know a man who runs a charter service out of Auckland,' he said. His warm hand held hers. 'His Learjet will take you there in less than three hours from take-off. I'll get him to land at Whenuapai—that's the Air Force field ten minutes from my nursery.'

'Can he do that?'

'I'll ask the commander as a favour.'

She said huskily, 'It's very kind of you, but I can't impose——'

'Don't be an idiot. Ring the maid and get her to pack.'

Shivering, she said, 'I'll pack. It will give me something to do. Oh, here, you'd better give him my credit-card number.'

He didn't look at the card she hauled out of her purse, so she put it down beside the telephone. Five minutes later when she came out of the bathroom it was still in the same place. As she pulled on jeans and T-shirt, then began to stuff the rest of her clothes and toiletries into her bag, she heard his voice, calm and cool and confident. He didn't sound as though he was asking a favour. It was difficult, she thought wearily, to imagine Adam asking favours of anyone.

A couple of minutes later he put the receiver down and said, 'It will be ready when we are. I'll pick up some clothes and a passport on the way.'

She said, 'I can't let you come with me.'

'Don't be an idiot,' he said. He got up, as beautiful and powerful, as potently evocative as a bronzed statue of some antique time when only the most perfect athletes were chosen to represent gods, and began to dress.

She should protest, but the thought of three hours by herself in the Learjet, sick with fear, kept her silent. Sitting down, she pulled on a pair of shoes. 'I'll ring Brett,' she said.

On the way out along the motorway she muttered, 'I'm afraid, Adam.'

He glanced her way. 'It's almost certain to be a false alarm. Doting husbands are notoriously easily upset.'

'Not Saul.'

'In that case you'll have to face whatever happens. But people rarely die out of the blue like that, Stephanie.'

'I know,' she whispered. 'But there are always exceptions.'

His hand dropped over her restless ones, squeezed hard, and resumed its place on the wheel. He didn't say anything, but his silent understanding eased a little of her fear and foreboding.

Dawn saw them a hundred miles out from Fala'isi, flying over a sea that began as the colour of a dove's breast, the purest, softest grey, then changed, as the glowing hues of the sunrise faded in the east, to a brilliant, saturated emerald. Ahead on the horizon was the cloud that clung to the island's mountainous core, the cloud that had drawn the ancient Polynesian navigators across the endless expanse of the Pacific. Usually Stephanie's heart lifted when she saw it white in the sapphire sky; this morning she felt only dread.

'All right?'

Adam's voice in her ears dragged her from her thoughts. She nodded and gave him a bleak smile. 'Yes, thank you.'

The Learjet arrowed north with all the verve and speed of a humming-bird. Since they'd left the Air Force base Adam had insisted she talk to him; whenever she had fallen into frightened silence he had revived the conversation, his confident voice helping to ward off the dreadful images of Candace ill and dying.

She had learned that it took seven years from breeding a rose to marketing it, so none of the roses coming out under his name was yet of his breeding. However, he had several coming on with which he planned to win both the All-American Award and the European Championship.

'My father won that, the Golden Rose of the Hague, twice,' he'd said.

Stephanie had looked at him. 'So you plan to win three times?'

'I believe in building on what's already been done. We have a good name, and it's going to be even more highly regarded by the time I die.'

She'd said, 'How do you choose roses to breed from?'

'It's all a matter of eye.'

'Candace said it would be genetics.' Her mouth had tightened suddenly. 'She said you'd have to be ruthless.'

'Why?'

'Oh, because you must plant so many seeds, then cull most of them.'

'I suppose ruthlessness comes into it.' He'd sounded amused. 'Out of fifty thousand or so seedlings I might end up with twenty roses, and out of those I might choose only one to patent.'

'I didn't know you could patent plants.'

'New Zealand has plant breeders' rights that last for twenty years. Until they were legislated for plant-breeding was a hobby; nobody could actually earn a living from it.'

Desperate to keep her mind off what was waiting for them, she had asked, 'How do you prove that your rose is a good one?' and listened while he told her of the

budding sticks sent overseas to rose trial grounds where
they were grown and evaluated, of the tightly interwoven old boys' network that was the world of roses,
of triumphs and failures, of the different ambitions rose-
breeders had for their seedlings. Some wanted elegantly
stemmed beauties for cutting, some bred for long-
flowering bushes for the garden, some searched obsessively for rare and unusual shades of colour.

She said now, with a twisted smile. 'Thank you.'

'Why?'

'For—oh, for being kind. You always seem to be rescuing me.'

'Hardly.' His voice was dry, as though she had hit a
nerve. 'This doesn't constitute a rescue. A helping hand,
possibly.'

'Are you sure there isn't anyone who's going to miss
you?'

'If you mean someone with claims on me, then no,'
he said bluntly. 'Don't worry, princess.'

'I used to hate it when you called me that.'

His smile was mocking. 'I didn't intend you to like
it.'

'So why did you do it?'

'To remind myself of the distance between us. And
the lies.'

The pilot's voice came through the speakers. 'OK,
strap yourselves in; we're landing in ten minutes.'

Although there was nobody there to meet them, it was
obvious that everyone on the island knew why Stephanie
had come back. They were waved through Customs with
a speed and efficiency tempered by warm, unspoken
sympathy that had her groping futilely for her
handkerchief.

'Here,' Adam said from beside her, and thrust an im-
maculate one into her hand.

She was glad of his presence. To her he was invincible, so that nothing bad could happen if he was beside
her. Stupid, and wrong, clutching at straws, but it was

a small comfort, one she clung to, because no one had told her that Candace was better. Knowing how swiftly news ran through the island community, she understood that this must mean her sister was still in danger. Anguish and dread twisted her heart.

Outside she blinked in the brilliant sunlight, temporarily stunned by its heat and the humidity.

'Is that your car?' Adam said calmly, indicating a large, dusty vehicle just drawing up beneath a magnificent raintree.

'Yes.'

He nodded and set off towards it. Obediently Stephanie followed him, recognising the man who was coming towards them, his handsome brown face set in lines of gravity and concern. It was Apiolu, who acted as chauffeur for Saul in between fishing forays.

'Morning, Stephanie,' he said, grabbing the bags from the porter.

She introduced the two men, then asked urgently, 'How is she?'

The islander's pleasant, blunt features tightened. 'Not too good,' he said briefly. 'Saul wants you at the hospital straight away.'

Colour drained from her face. She put out a shaking hand, which was caught by Adam as he hustled her inside the car, saying curtly, 'Take deep breaths, in through your nose, and exhale through your mouth. Fainting isn't going to help you or your brother or sister.'

He was an unfeeling bastard, but she did as he said, and the icy nausea faded, to be replaced by something perilously close to terror. She said aloud, as she had been saying silently ever since the call, 'Women don't die in childbirth any longer, not in the western world. Candace is strong. And the hospital is an excellent one. Grant endowed it.'

'Who's Grant?'

'A cousin. A distant cousin. Grant Chapman. He's the paramount chief of the island.'

'How did that happen?'

He persuaded her to talk about her family's connection to the island, about the original buccaneering Chapman who had landed on the island at a time when most of its inhabitants had been killed by assorted exploiters and the diseases they brought, and who, to his shock, had been recognised as the saviour promised by prophecy. Forced to marry the paramount chief's only child, he had reluctantly grown into the role assigned to him, and the direct descendant of that union, Grant Chapman, was now paramount chief in his turn.

'I didn't realise a chiefdom could pass through the female line,' Adam said.

Stephanie knew what he was doing, but she was grateful nevertheless. While she was telling him about these colourful ancestors she wasn't worrying quite so futilely about Candace.

'She had immense prestige and power,' she told him. 'It was understood from her birth that she would do great things. And the Polynesians are a pragmatic people. Family is of vital importance, more so than the individual. If the chief's son wasn't strong enough to hold the tribe together, someone else of the same lineage who did have the necessary qualities would be chosen.'

'What about the original Chapman?'

'He gained authority from his ruthlessness when it came to fighting off the assorted blackbirders and pearl pirates and sandalwood-cutters, and the marriage gave him the necessary tribal *mana*, especially when his wife produced three sons.'

'He sounds fairly intimidating.'

'I think they both were. For the last five years I've thought he probably bore a startling resemblance to you.' She looked at him, and said with a quivering smile, 'Some of the stories about his wife would make your hair curl. Their marriage wasn't a romantic South Sea idyll; it was quite literally a fight for life.'

The car drew up outside the hospital. Stephanie's voice wavered; she swallowed, and for a moment her hand was covered and held in a solid, comforting grip.

'Is your sister a fighter?' Adam asked.

She lifted wet eyes to his. 'Oh, yes.'

'That's the most important thing,' he said. 'Because they were fighters I've seen people recover from wounds that should have killed them several times over.'

They were met at the door by a deputation comprising the matron and the medical superintendant. In a voice that barely trembled, Stephanie asked, 'How is she?'

Candace had, it appeared, been gravely ill, but was now on the mend.

Clinging to Adam's hand, Stephanie looked from one grave face to the other and said, 'Can I see her?'

The medical superintendant traded a glance with the matron. 'She wants to see you, but she's still very sick. Can you just let her know that you're here, and then come away?'

'Yes, of course.'

Adam's grip was warm and strong. Stephanie introduced him as they all went across the highly polished floor and into the lift; the hospital was built of wood on a hill overlooking the town and the sea, and, although only two storeys high, was as modern and up-to-date as any in the Pacific.

Candace was in the small critical care unit; the matron took Stephanie in. As she opened the door she leaned closer and murmured, 'She's going to be all right.'

But fear chilled Stephanie's swift relief as she took in the still, unresponsive figure in the bed, and the tall form of her brother, his arrogant face lean and haggard, holding his wife's hand as he bent over her and spoke, low, insistent words meant only for her ears.

Saul looked up. Accurately judging her emotions, he said softly, 'She's going to make it, Steph.'

'Oh, thank God,' Stephanie breathed, taking her sister's other hand in hers. 'I thought I might get here too late . . .'

'For few minutes I thought that too.' Saul touched his wife's cheek. Unconscious though she was, a smile curved her mouth. As though he couldn't help himself, he bent his head and kissed her.

Stephanie asked, 'What was the matter?'

'Toxaemia. It can happen in pregnancy, and apparently her doctor in London told her to watch for it. She didn't want to upset me, so she didn't say anything, but she gave Losa Penia her medical notes, and as she's been going to him each week he knew exactly what it was and how to deal with it.'

'And it's not going to come back?'

'It doesn't go away. She'll have to stay under observation until the baby's born.'

'Another month. Is the baby all right?'

'Yes, thank God. And I won't be going away from now on. Candace is far more important to me than anything else in my life, infinitely more important than Jerrard's.'

'I know,' Stephanie said serenely. 'So does she.'

'I hope so.' He lifted his eyes from his wife's calm, pale face. 'How did you get here so quickly?'

Stephanie made a small grimace. 'Hired a Learjet. We came up in that.'

'We?'

She said quietly, 'Nobody you know, although you know of him. He's Adam Cowdray. He also happens to be the man who rescued me from that crypt five years ago.'

Candace moaned something as Saul's fingers crushed hers. 'Sorry, my darling,' he said, holding them to his mouth. He kissed their pale limpness before turning to Stephanie and saying through thin lips, 'That man is a criminal.'

'As it happens, he isn't.' She held up her hand to stem the words she could see forming on his tongue. 'I'm not a complete idiot, Saul. I got London to run a check on him. Apparently he was working for some organisation in England, very hush-hush——'

'Stephanie, he's spun you a nice tale——'

'Saul, *listen* to me——'

'Stop it, you two, and let me be ill in some degree of peace,' Candace muttered drowsily.

Face transfigured, Saul slid to his knees by the side of the bed. 'Darling,' he said in a voice Stephanie had never heard before. 'Oh, God, darling, don't you ever do that to me——'

Stephanie got up and left them, her throat thick with unexpressed emotions, her eyes bright. She had no right to be there; it seemed voyeuristic to eavesdrop on her brother's nakedly innermost emotions.

Before she got out of the ward she despised herself for wondering whether any man would ever look at her like that, with his heart in his eyes, stripped of everything but his love. Not Adam, she thought, swallowing hard. Never Adam. In spite of the incandescence of their lovemaking he hadn't said anything about loving her, anything at all except that she was beautiful, that he had wanted her for so long...

He had delivered the heaven he'd promised her, but love didn't enter into the equation at all.

'Stephanie?' He touched her arm.

She stared up into eyes that held all the world in their watchful, blue-white depths, and said, 'She's going to be all right. She told us to stop fighting and let her be ill in peace.' Her voice trembled and tears ached behind her lashes.

His hands caught her arms, held her upright with a bruising grip. 'You need something to eat and a cup of good strong coffee—and I don't care whether you still don't like it, that's what you're going to have. Sit down and I'll be back in five minutes.'

Somehow he procured a croissant, hot and buttery, a sliced papaw chilled to just the right degree with passion-fruit pulp lending its tang, and coffee whose fragrance lifted her heart immediately.

'Didn't you get any for yourself?' she asked.

He said dismissively, 'I'm not hungry. Eat up.'

She had eaten the food and was halfway through the cup of coffee when Saul emerged. 'How is she?' she asked urgently.

After one comprehensive glance at the man beside her Saul looked at her. No emotion gleamed in the blue eyes; nothing was revealed in his expression. 'She wants to see you,' he said.

Stephanie's gaze flicked from one strong-boned, implacable face to the other. Although Saul was tall and well-built, Adam was a couple of inches taller and his shoulders were wider, but both men took up the same amount of psychic space. Arrogant as lions, they snatched her breath away. Or they would have, if the antagonism neither was making any attempt to hide hadn't crackled so ominously about them.

'All right,' she said crossly. 'Play your stupid masculine games. But I warn you——'

'Stephanie,' Adam interrupted quite gently, 'go and see your sister.'

With what came very close to a flounce she walked away and left them there.

Candace lay with her eyes closed and her skin still too pale, but she opened them as Stephanie came in and said, 'What was the rose like?'

'Who cares about the wretched rose? How dare you do this and scare the hell out of everyone?'

Her half-sister grinned. 'Sorry, I'm sure! Saul just panicked. I'm going to be perfectly all right in a few days. I was worried about the baby, but Losa assures me it's fine, so all's well.'

Stephanie bent and kissed her, saying fiercely, 'Don't do it again! You terrified everyone. I've never seen Saul look like that, never.'

Candace's lashes drifted down. 'That's the problem with loving someone,' she said dreamily. 'It's those hostages to fortune. But there's no other way, really...'

Stephanie looked around wildly for the nurse, who came forward and soothed, 'She's just gone off to sleep. That's what she needs now, sleep and rest.'

'Thank you.' For a few moments Stephanie stood looking down at her sister's peaceful face before turning away.

She didn't know what she expected to see outside the ward. Blood on the floor, possibly; she certainly didn't think she'd see the two most important men in her life conducting what one glance told her was an outwardly reasonable conversation. Both men were experts in controlling their body language, so she couldn't work out how amicable their conversation was, but as she approached both looked up.

And suddenly she laughed, because both dark faces were stamped with an identical expression of watchful reserve. They were, she thought, two of a kind, the men in her life.

Saul fell silent and she could feel the tension sizzle out to meet her. The fans in the ceiling lazily swished air already heated by the rapidly rising sun, and everywhere was the smell of the tropics—frangipani and coconut oil, salt from the ever-present sea, and the tangy, elemental scent of fecundity.

'Have you had fun?' she asked, acid-sweet, looking from one non-committal set of features to the other.

'It's been interesting,' Saul said guardedly. 'Why don't you two go home? I'll stay here for the rest of the day, but there's no reason for you to.'

Stephanie looked at Adam, the man she loved with all her heart, and said steadily, 'Are you going back with the Learjet?'

'It's already gone.' His hard mouth relaxed fractionally. 'Your brother has asked me to stay on.'

She wouldn't look at Saul. She wouldn't! Keeping her eyes fixed on Adam's face, she said in her best social tone, 'Well, that's fine. Shall we go?'

He didn't like her cool relegation of him to guest status; a savage flare of emotion lit the crystalline depths of his eyes, was immediately controlled. Good, she thought angrily. He liked to play things really cool—two could do that. Perhaps he'd realise what it was like to be the one shut out.

So she persisted with her best hostess behaviour all the way to the house, pointing out the local sights, carefully avoiding Adam's eyes, and all the time his anger, disciplined yet as threatening as a bushfire flickering beyond distant hills, beat against her.

Asa was waiting. As Stephanie knew she would, she gave Adam a swift glance, lifted her brows, then showed him to the guest room next to Stephanie's.

'Where are you?' he asked as Stephanie prepared to go out.

'Next door,' she told him colourlessly.

This time it was his brows that shot up. 'A trusting soul, isn't she?' he asked, looking at the door Asa had left by.

Stephanie's mouth twitched. 'I think she'd just about given up on me,' she said cynically, and only her heart knew that she waited breathlessly for some sign, some indication, however tiny, that he cared more for her than just as a willing sexual partner.

He gave her a long, considering look. 'I don't intend to sleep with you in your brother's house,' he said.

Stephanie knew her smile was stiff and meaningless. 'How touchingly conventional,' she said.

His smile had no trace of humour in it; it was a warning and a promise at once, although he ignored the open provocation of her comment. 'But I am not here as your brother's guest,' he said quietly. 'I'm here because of you, and if you don't realise it yet perhaps this will help fix it in your mind.'

The kiss was almost brutal, as though he was staking a claim. Certainly the hands that slid the length of her body, moulding her against him with explicit promise, were not tender. He was aroused, as aroused as she was by the time his head lifted. Breathing hard, he said, 'You'd better get some sleep. You only had an hour or so last night.'

She didn't feel tired, but neither did she feel up to coping with Adam in his present mood. Refusing to acknowledge the heat that flamed across her skin or the passionate hunger summoned by his touch, she said, 'I'll do that. Asa will get you some breakfast if you want any, and then perhaps you should rest too.'

First, of course, she went to see the children. Safe with Peri—nursemaid, good friend and never-ending source of tales—they were curious but not alarmed by their parents' absence. Stephanie spent some time with them, at first explaining why Candace wouldn't be home that day, and then promising to take them to see their mother when the doctor said they could. Finally tiredness drove her to her bedroom.

She didn't expect to sleep, but she did, heavy eyelids almost immediately blocking her view of the huge timbers that supported the thatched roof of pandanus fronds. Saul's beach house was built in the same style as the fales of the island chiefs, and like them it was magnificently cool without the need for air-conditioning.

She woke to an evening perfumed with dusk, the brief, heart-stopping moment of hesitation between the open, brash beauty of the tropical day and the mystery and glamour of night. A look at the bedside clock had her sitting up, horrified, to ring the hospital.

Candace was fine, getting better by the minute, she was told.

Humming a little tune, she climbed from the bed and drifted towards her bathroom. By the time she had

washed her hair, brushed it dry and wound herself in
one of the cotton pareus she kept in her drawer, the all-
purpose island outfit that looked so good with her long
legs, the velvet Pacific night had completely enveloped
the island. Absently aware of the gentle rustling of the
palm fronds, she went out on to the terrace and walked
swiftly past Adam's empty room, pausing at the smooth,
twigless branches of a heavily scented frangipani to pick
a cream and gold flower and tuck it behind her ear.

There had been no wind for weeks, so the ocean-
circling waves that could sometimes smash down on the
reef were barely audible. Wooed by the ravishing spell
of the South Seas, she stood for a moment looking down
over the thickly forested bank to the beach below, a
proper Robinson Crusoe beach where the sand was white,
coarsely crushed coral, and the coconut palms leaned on
elegant grey stems towards the lagoon.

She loved Fala'isi, but the quickening in her body had
nothing to do with her pleasure at being there. Adam
waited for her, and during her sleep she had made the
decision not to worry about the future. She would take
everything he had to offer, and when the time came to
say goodbye she would do that with grace and style, and
then, perhaps, freed from this heated desire that had
bedevilled her for years, she would be able to get on with
her life.

She heard their voices before she saw them. They were
sitting in chairs out on the terrace, and just before she
saw the blur of their light shirts the clear, bell-like song
of the tikau bird floated through the soft air. Of course
she had heard it before—although a denizen of the high
peaks, it occasionally came down to the coast—but a
local legend said that if you heard the exquisite roulade
in the company of the one you loved it meant that your
love was reciprocated.

Although Stephanie didn't believe every old legend
she'd been told, that didn't stop her heart from speeding

up at the sweet, seductive call. Perhaps, just this once, it might be true?

Stopping, she looked through the scented darkness towards the terrace where the men sat. She wanted to see Adam, but not with Saul watching, not when she had to be polite and fence with words against a background of tension that cut into her heart. Turning away, she walked down the steep path to the beach.

She didn't hear him coming behind her; she didn't know anyone was there until he put his hand on her shoulder just as she reached the sand.

Stephanie reacted instantly. She lashed out, but he was ready for the flat-handed blow, and before the lethal edge could catch his throat he'd countered it. She was good, but he was better, and within seconds she was held so completely that she couldn't move.

'I'll bloody talk to whoever taught you to do that,' he said through gritted teeth. 'One of these days you're going to kill someone.'

'No. It's all right, I'm sorry,' she panted. 'You took me by surprise, that's all. You can let me go now.'

'Put her down,' Saul said from just up the hill, a note in the command that would have made any other man drop her.

Instead Adam said curtly, 'Get out of here. This is between Stephanie and me.'

'Stephanie?'

Adam said grimly, 'It's all right, I won't let her hurt me. You're going to have to stop this habit she seems to have developed of trying to kill anyone who comes up behind her.'

'I did not try to kill you,' she said furiously, because the conversation was slipping away from her. 'Damn you, if I'd tried to kill you I'd have made a much better fist of it. I've learnt a hell of a lot since I was kidnapped.'

Unbelievably, Saul laughed. 'She's right, you know. You'd better be aware of what you're getting into.'

He was talking to them both, but mainly to Adam, who let her go, and asked interestedly, 'Has she learned to cook?'

'Why don't you ask her?' And to Stephanie's horror her brother turned away.

She opened her mouth to call him and Adam said quietly, 'Go with him now and you'll have made your choice forever.'

The moon had come out, huge and round and full, a lovers' moon, the moon the South Pacific had made her own, the moon of trade winds and spice breezes and the tikau bird. In its kindly light Adam looked cold and forbidding, the harsh features of his face set in obdurate granite.

He said quite calmly, the mask of control once more firmly in place, 'I'd have thought your teacher would have made sure you didn't go off half cocked like that.'

'You gave me a fright and I lashed out.' She hesitated, then said, 'Yes, well, he'd have my head if he saw what I did. I am sorry.'

She had never reacted with such lack of control before, and it was Adam who had tilted her off-balance, rubbed her nerves raw and stripped away her self-possession. Defensively, she attacked. 'You were angry before you touched me. Why?'

He looked at her for a moment, then turned so swiftly that she flinched and chopped his hand down on to the solid trunk of the closest coconut palm. It must have hurt, but he didn't flinch. 'Why are you pushing me away? You wanted me to go back on the Learjet, you spent the trip back from the hospital setting me at a distance, and you deliberately turned away when you saw me with Saul tonight.'

The first hectic charge of adrenalin was fading now and she was feeling exhausted and depressed, all energy drained from her. 'I'm not—I didn't——' She stopped, searching for words.

'It won't work,' he said harshly. 'I won't let you pull away, not now.'

A shimmering hope began to grow in her heart. She turned away and leaned back against the bole of the nearest palm, looking out over the lagoon. Moonlight had blocked out many of the stars and those that were left were robbed of much of their glory, but a silver snood cast on the surface of the sea gleamed like the pathway to glory, glittering across the sand, edging the fronds of the palms with silver.

Resolutely Stephanie kept her eyes on the silhouette of one of the tiny islands that the sea and the sand had thrown up on the edge of the barrier reef. Feeling her way, she said, 'I don't know what you want, Adam.'

'I want you.' He spoke slowly, in a flat, emotionless tone. He hesitated, before finishing, 'I would have told you this morning, only—it seemed crass, when you were so worried about your sister.'

'Told me what? That you want me? Last night rather proved that.'

Exasperated, he bit out, 'That I love you, of course.'

Equally shortly, she retorted, 'There's no *of course* about it!'

'Oh, for God's sake!' Before she had time to work out what he was doing he turned her and swept her into his arms. His mouth came down on hers in a kiss that burnt through the barriers she had set up, the painfully maintained defenses.

At last he lifted his mouth and said in a voice that had been stripped of everything but raw need, 'I *wanted* you right from the start. How I kept my hands off you I'll never know, but you were only eighteen, a virgin, sheltered and loved and protected, and I was seven cynical, hard years older, and I couldn't remember when there hadn't been women for the taking. I was doing a job that had to be done, a dangerous job where both our lives depended on my not putting a foot wrong. But whenever I looked at you I forgot about the job and

wanted to get you out of there. Too much was at stake.
I couldn't have done my job properly. I almost certainly
put the whole scheme in danger because I wanted to
protect you, not use you. And I had to use you. That
was the beginning of the end for me.'

'The beginning of what end?'

Her eyes were snared by the splintered ice of his. His
mouth tightened. 'That was when I realised I'd had
enough of killing, of darkness and deceit and men with
minds like calculators. You were the catalyst; I ter-
rorised you and humiliated you, gave you traumas that
might last a lifetime, lied to you——'

He laughed, and there was something straight from
hell in the sound. 'That's what I was trained for, princess.
To lie so well that no one would be able to catch me out
in the truth. I'm very good at it. I've lied to men who
were born lying, and got away with it.'

'Don't,' she said, understanding at last. 'Adam—
don't.'

'I could promise that I'll never lie to you again,' he
said in a level monotone, 'but that might be the biggest
lie of all. I built a life on lies, Stephanie. I thought I
could leave it behind me, but the past reaches its filthy
hand out over the future, and I know now that I can't
expect you to trust me. I've caused you enough grief,
betrayed you in ways you don't even comprehend. When
I sent you down the mountain into your brother's arms
that night in Switzerland I had every intention of coming
back for you; it wasn't until I came home to New Zealand
and sanity that I realised what I'd done to you. And
then I knew it was impossible.'

'You could have given me the choice,' she snapped.

'Oh, I knew I could have you,' he said coolly. 'But
although making love to you is like finding paradise, I
want more than that from you. I want your trust, and
I know I can never have it. You showed that when you
turned on me just now.'

He spoke calmly, without self-pity, with complete conviction.

Stephanie tried to sort out her emotions, and realised that he meant it; he wasn't going to persuade her, or try to coax her into either love or marriage. He honestly believed that he had put himself beyond the pale.

However, he wasn't going to let her go; that gave her hope.

She didn't dare look at him. This was something that had to be done without falling prey to the smouldering sexuality that flamed between them.

Her hands clenched by her sides. And then, quite suddenly, it was easy. All she really had to ask herself was whether she loved him, not the hero who had saved her from the crypt, not the man who caught every woman's eye, not the man whose potent male charisma wove a dark spell about her, but Duke, the man who had lived a life of lies and still wondered whether he was caught in their lingering webs.

'Of course I trust you,' she said.

'Just like that?'

She turned her face away from the silver glory, the perilous enchantment of the moon, and looked into the shuttered face of the man she loved. 'Yes, because I love you,' she said casually.

There was silence, and then he said dangerously, 'You little bitch,' and reached for her and caught her in his arms, holding her so close that she gasped. 'Are you a direct descendant of that island chieftainess and the buccaneer?' he asked.

'Yes.'

'I see.' His mouth hovered over hers. 'I can see I'm going to have my work cut out for me. Kiss me.'

Oddly shy, she looked into the blazing fire of his eyes. Then she reached up and pulled his head down and kissed him, her mouth demanding and eager, until he took over and they lost themselves in the world of passion and love reciprocated.

A long time later he lifted his head and surveyed her face with such complete male satisfaction that she laughed.

'We have to talk,' he said, leaning back against a convenient palm tree before taking her more gently in his arms and resting his cheek on her head. 'Don't wriggle. When you do that I can't concentrate.'

'What do we need to talk about now?'

'Your money,' he said, a note of irony hardening his voice.

'Oh, Adam, for heaven's sake, don't tell me you've got old-fashioned ideas about marrying money. Although actually the old-fashioned idea was that it was perfectly all right to marry money.'

'When both understood that after the necessary children were born it was fine to find love outside the marriage,' he said harshly. 'I'm not so damned accommodating, princess.'

'Neither am I,' she retorted smartly.

He gave her a small shake. 'Listen, will you?'

But he didn't speak immediately. Stephanie rested her head against his neck and smiled secretly at the rapid throbbing of his pulse.

He said reflectively, 'It's not so much the money, I suppose, it's the life.'

'Don't give me that rubbish about the difference in our situations.'

His smile was hard and narrow and mirthless. 'Because you're a modern woman and I'm a modern man? That's nonsense and you know it. You've grown up with money beyond most people's dreams—you're so accustomed to it that you don't even think of it—but if it was taken away you'd miss it.'

'You think I'm incredibly shallow,' she said, hiding her concern with delicate scorn.

'I think you're being deliberately obtuse,' he said sharply. 'Shallowness has nothing to do with it. Think, Stephanie.'

'It works very well for Saul and Candace,' she said stubbornly, hardly knowing what he was implying. Did he mean marriage?

'Nobody had to give up anything in that relationship.' His voice was impatient.

'You're a total chauvinist,' she retorted. 'Candace had to give up her anonymity, and believe me, she found that difficult. Anyway, where is all this talk of giving things up leading to?'

He put her to one side and looked out over the lagoon, his profile angled with a fierce beauty against the seductive silver and black nocturne of the night. He said evenly, 'I love you. I don't care what you do with your money, but if you marry me your life will be very different from the life you lead now. You've called me arrogant a couple of times, but you have your own brand of high-handedness, and the two of us are going to be dynamite together. It isn't going to be easy, princess.'

'Let's do a deal,' she said demurely. 'I'll stop calling you arrogant if you stop calling me princess.'

He laughed. 'No. That's how I think of you, as a princess.' His voice altered, the deep note of sensuality slowing his clipped intonation into a drawl. '*My* princess.'

She said, 'You can call me that for the rest of our lives, then.'

Much later that night Saul warned, 'Do you know what you're getting into? He's a hard man, and a possessive one.'

'I know. Adam's already told me that.' She added on an acerbic note, 'I'm not stupid, you know. I can see the pitfalls; what neither of you seem to realise is that life without him is flat and tasteless. I'd rather be shouting at him than living in perfect peace by myself.'

He laughed. 'I suppose you don't have that hair for nothing. Well, if you want it you have my blessing.'

'Do you like him?'

He shrugged. 'Would it matter if I didn't?'

'It would matter, but it's not going to make any difference.'

'As it happens, I do.'

He hadn't expected to, she knew, and in some ways it was surprising that they had got past the suspicion so quickly; they were too much alike to enjoy a simple camaraderie.

'Just as well,' she said peacefully. 'He likes you too.'

He laughed wryly. 'Well, he will when he realises that he has all of your heart.' He looked at his watch and got to his feet. 'I'd better be off; I'm going to sleep at the hospital. Candace made me come home so that I could deal with your Adam, and if I know her she's lying in her bed dying quietly of curiosity. You've got yourself quite a man there, little sister. But then, he's got enough woman to keep him busy for the rest of his life.'

About twenty minutes later Stephanie walked out of the wide door of her room, along the terrace and into the open door of the room next door.

'I said,' Adam's voice came through the darkness with a note of humour in it, 'that I wasn't going to make love to you under your brother's roof.'

She laughed and moved across the floor to the big bed. 'That's all right. I'd be the last person to try to make you change your mind. You just lie there and think of England while I make love to you.'

She slid beneath the sheet and leaned over him, kissing the straight line of his mouth. 'I love you,' she said softly.

As she had expected, he was naked. 'I can see that I'm going to have a hell of a time with you,' he said against her lips. 'Do you think that kissing you back is included in making love?'

'No, of course not.'

And in laughter and gentleness, in moments of sublime savagery and others of heart-shaking tenderness, they formed a pattern for their life together, a life without lies.

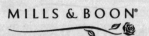

MILLS & BOON®

Next Month's Romance Titles

♡

Each month you can choose from a wide variety of romance novels from Mills & Boon®. Below are the new titles to look out for next month from the Presents™ and Enchanted™ series.

Presents™

PACIFIC HEAT	Anne Mather
THE BRIDAL BED	Helen Bianchin
THE YULETIDE CHILD	Charlotte Lamb
MISTLETOE MISTRESS	Helen Brooks
A CHRISTMAS SEDUCTION	Amanda Browning
THE THIRTY-DAY SEDUCTION	Kay Thorpe
FIANCÉE BY MISTAKE	Kate Walker
A NICE GIRL LIKE YOU	Alexandra Sellers

Enchanted™

FIANCÉ FOR CHRISTMAS	Catherine George
THE HUSBAND PROJECT	Leigh Michaels
COMING HOME FOR CHRISTMAS	Laura Martin
THE BACHELOR AND THE BABIES	Heather MacAllister
THE NUTCRACKER PRINCE	Rebecca Winters
FATHER BY MARRIAGE	Suzanne Carey
THE BILLIONAIRE'S BABY CHASE	Valerie Parv
ROMANTICS ANONYMOUS	Lauryn Chandler

On sale from 4th December 1998   H1 9811

CHRISTMAS

Affairs

MORE THAN JUST KISSES UNDER THE MISTLETOE...

Enjoy three sparkling seasonal romances by your
favourite authors from

MILLS & BOON®
Presents™

HELEN BIANCHIN
For Anique, the season of goodwill has become...
The Seduction Season

SANDRA MARTON
Can Santa weave a spot of Christmas magic for Nick
and Holly in... *A Miracle on Christmas Eve?*

SHARON KENDRICK
Will Aleck and Clemmie have a... *Yuletide Reunion?*

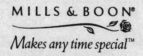

MILLS & BOON®

Makes any time special™

Available from 6th November 1998

Your Special Christmas Gift

Three romance novels from Mills & Boon® to
unwind with at your leisure—
and a luxurious Le Jardin bath gelée to pamper
you and gently wash your cares away.

for just £5.99

Featuring
Carole Mortimer—Married by Christmas
Betty Neels—A Winter Love Story
Jo Leigh—One Wicked Night

MILLS & BOON®

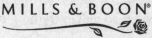

Makes your Christmas time special

Available from 23rd October 1998

SHANNON OCORK

SECRETS OF THE TITANIC

**The voyage of the century
—where secrets, love and destiny collide.**

They were the richest of the rich, Rhode Island's
elite, their glittering jewels and polished manners
hiding tarnished secrets on a voyage that would
change their lives forever.

They had it all and everything to lose.

"Miss OCork is a natural writer and storyteller."
—New York Times Book Review

MIRA®

1-55166-401-1
Available from October 1998 in paperback

HEATHER GRAHAM POZZESSERE

Never Sleep with Strangers

Jon Stuart watched his wife plummet to her death.
Although cleared of any involvement, he endured
years of suspicion. But it was no accident, and he's
now determined to prove it was murder. The prime
suspects are gathered together, and the scene is
set for past and present to collide.

"An incredible story teller!"

—Los Angeles Daily News

MIRA®

1-55166-445-3
AVAILABLE IN PAPERBACK
FROM NOVEMBER, 1998

RACHEL
LEE

C A U G H T

Someone is stalking and killing women, someone with
a warped obsession. And with loving devotion the
stalker has chosen Kate Devane as his next victim.
What he hasn't realised is that Kate is not alone. She
has a lover. A lover she has never met.

*Rachel Lee takes readers on a "sensational journey
into Tami Hoag/Karen Robards territory."*

–Publishers Weekly

1-55166-298-1
**AVAILABLE IN PAPERBACK
FROM NOVEMBER, 1998**

MILLS & BOON®

Makes
any time
special

Enjoy a romantic novel from
Mills & Boon®

Presents™ *Enchanted*™ *Temptation*®

Historical Romance™ *Medical Romance*™